2014 Winner of the Paris Book Festival Awards
Best eBook, five languages, all categories

2014 Winner Gold #1 Global Ebook Awards
Best Multicultural Fiction

Praise for

THE GIRL FROM FRANCE

'Laurent Boulanger is a gifted writer with an acute understanding of individuals and the choices they make or have forced upon them. His writing in The Girl From France is cool, clear and unfettered by hyperbole. He brings a refreshing honesty to everything he describes, be it young Clotilde disconnected from her home, or the landscape of a country whose shape she doesn't yet understand.

Boulanger is a talent worth watching.'

Venero Armanno
*Queensland Premier's Literary Award Winner
for Best Fiction*

LAURENT BOULANGER was born in Strasbourg, France in 1966. He migrated to Australia at the age of thirteen without any English. After working a multitude of dead-end jobs, he returned to study and earned a Bachelor of Arts in Writing from Deakin University and subsequently a Master of Arts in Writing and a Ph.D. in Writing from Swinburne University. His crime novel *Better Dead Than Never* was shortlisted for the 2007 CWAA's Best First Crime Novel and won the 2014 Bronze eLit Award for Best Multicultural Fiction. *The Girl From France,* his first literary novel, won the 2014 Paris Book Festival Awards for Best eBook, five languages, all categories, and the 2014 Winner Gold #1Global Ebook Awards Best Multicultural Fiction. It was originally published by the Rock View Press (Melbourne, Australia).

THE GIRL FROM FRANCE

THE GIRL FROM FRANCE

Laurent Boulanger

Lighthouse

FOR ALAIN & PHILIPPE,
who remember it all too well

&

CAROLYN,
for her unfaltering faith

The author wishes to acknowledge the invaluable assistance of the following people in the realisation of this novel: Carolyn Beasley, Josie Arnold, Kitty Vigo, Jacqueline Ross and Dan Stainsby. Special thanks to Venero Armanno for taking the time and effort to read a manuscript from an unknown.

THE GIRL FROM FRANCE

CHAPTER ONE

One Sunday afternoon my father and I hovered over the white, water-column heater in the living room, the only place in the two-bedroom apartment which trapped the heat. My back was resting against the hot, galvanised pipe connecting the ceramic block to the water supply. The heat from the pipe would inevitably go through my blue dress and leave a red, vertical mark along my spine and down to the small of my back, like it had every time I attempted to fight the bone-chilled air that occupied the other rooms of our home. I liked the way my skin felt after I removed myself from the pipe—warm and soft ridges branding the doughy texture of my unblemished flesh like a line in the dirt drawn by a single finger.

My father was sitting on a chair made from dried straw and wood and held together by an assortment of strings that varied in thickness and length. The surface smelt strongly of varnish, even though it had been in the house for as long as I could remember and had never been restored by my father or by visitors who had commented how it might be time to get a new chair—to let go of the past, as they liked to put it. But the past is often the only comfort we have, and that chair was my father's sanctuary—a place where the world didn't demand anything from him, and from where he made no demand in return.

From the double-glazed window, Strasbourg looked like a postcard—chestnut trees and beeches had lost their leaves; bony branches reached out towards the heavens like sinners, hoping ardently for the warmth and mercy of the sun. Rooftops of the

1

medieval vernacular buildings—as common in Alsace as on the other flank of the Rhine—were painted virgin white by the hand of God. We could barely hear the rumbling of cars, whose owners had foolishly decided to take for a drive in spite of the fifty centimetres of unrepentant snow covering every road from here to the German border and beyond.

Winter in the North-East of France can be deadly for those who have only experienced the sapping heat of summer from down South—the earth is frozen, blanketed by powdery snow, and bathed in a light so bright and pure, it scorches the pupils if one stares at it for too long.

Every year the old and the homeless are found frozen in the streets or in their beds. *La Mairie de Strasbourg*—the city council —takes preventative measures to avoid blame for the deaths, firstly by inundating *Les Dernières Nouvelles D'Alsace* with press releases demanding of its citizens to fulfil their civic duties by keeping an eye out for the frail and the old, and secondly by opening churches and local halls to the homeless whenever the temperature drops below -10° Celsius. But winter deaths in the region are as inevitable as road accidents.

I was eleven years old and feared for my father. I longed for spring and summer to come, for winter was as cruel to his health as a wolf's fangs tearing through the warm flesh and beating heart of a wandering deer.

'Winter is man's punishment for losing his faith,' my father said, 'for not believing in eternal life, for thinking himself ruler of the world and his destiny. And when all goes wrong, he will blame God Almighty, never himself.'

I moved from the heater and kneeled next to his chair. My small hand searched for the comfort of his. His fingers were long and thin and unspoiled, like those of an artist who has never endured a labourer's hard day's work. My eyes scrutinised his bony face and tried to comprehend how a man who had once been so strong, a man who had led the flock into the righteous path of true believers could have been forsaken by the one whom he had devoted his entire life. Where was the God he had blindly followed like Gauls followed the moon three millenniums ago and believed it to be their saviour? Was the God he believed in another shooting star to be adulated from a distance by enduring myths of ancestors' tales?

2

His blank stare was aimed at the street below. Sometimes he sat there for hours, speechless and lost in reverie, as if nothing or no one mattered any longer. He smelled of piped tobacco and *eau de vie*—a wild-berry-fermented brandy, typical of the region of Alsace, whose fruits were harvested in the wilderness of the Black Forest.

I loved my father more dearly than he could have ever imagined.

'Why don't you go and see the doctor?' I asked.

'A man can't cure what God has cursed,' he said.

'You haven't been punished, Papa. Sometimes things happen for no reason. You used to tell me so yourself. You used to tell everyone God moves in mysterious ways.'

He didn't reply. Instead he squeezed my hand to let me know he was listening but had no answers to offer.

Now and then he did go to hospital for treatment, but only when he ran out of medication, or when he was so short of breath he could hardly stand on his own two feet. But the medication he'd been prescribed was as good to him as drinking *piquette*—cheap, bitter wine favoured by those who cared more for quantity than quality—since he never bothered taking the drugs in spite of my protesting that faith in God could only do so much.

In one corner of the lounge room stood a small Christmas tree decorated with red, blue, yellow and silver balls, plastic angels, and assorted lights flashing at two second intervals. Hand-stretched, white cotton wool had been used effectively to mimic snow slung over the branches. At the crest of the tree was the Star of Bethlehem crafted from silver foil and thin wiring. My father had helped me attach it even though I had insisted on doing it myself.

For the first time that Christmas my father chose not to bother with the hand-painted, clay figurines that normally sought shelter underneath the branches of the pine tree like people seek shelter from the pouring rain. That year there'd be no Joseph, Mary, baby Jesus, Wise Men, shepherds, camels or lambs. A light faded in my father's heart—a flame that had gradually diminished and failed to cast off the darkness around us like it had done for so many years when the world seemed like a mad and hazardous place to inhabit.

I was conceived out of wedlock for my father was a Catholic priest. Even though he had once been in love with my mother, he had to renounce her for the keeping of his faith. She had vanished to some far-away country after they'd made love, and she asked him to choose between the life of a married man and that of a servant of God. She had left me behind soon after birth, and there was nothing I remembered of her. I was my father's sin and the result of my mother's impetuousness.

To the world outside, I was an orphan whom my father had taken into his home, sheltered from a life of foster homes and corporal punishment, injustice and inadequate education, uncertainty and scarcity of paternal love. Faced with the adversity of being a single parent and a Catholic priest, he had done his best to raise me in a world which none of us fully understood.

Money was meagre, but I was well looked after. My father had always put himself last when it came to food, clothing and childhood necessities so that I wouldn't feel inferior and unworthy to my eyes and those of other children. France in the late twentieth century was still very class-oriented and materialistic, and the prejudices of adults were naturally passed on to their children like rivers flowing to the sea. Unknowingly, I too became a practitioner of class division and its intolerance for Arabs, Protestants and illiterate factory workers. I couldn't help feeling slightly smug whenever my father bought me new clothes or the latest toy-of-the-day. As a child, I had already noticed that those with the most friends were often those with the most possessions. My father said that consumerism was the religion of the devil, and everyone had fallen under its spell. People were so busy with their daily tasks that they hadn't even noticed that evil was rampant and was ruling the earth.

'What was she like?' I asked, knowing my mother was constantly on my father's mind now that death hovered over our home like the snow-filled clouds above the city. He had never showed me pictures of my mother because he said he had never kept any after she vanished from our lives. To look at her face would have been unbearably excruciating, so he felt it better to get rid of all photographs, erase from his vision what she had looked like so many years ago, and let his faith strengthen his stance.

'Beautiful,' he said and filled his pipe with tobacco, 'tall, blonde, free like a wild horse who had no idea of her limitations, of how small and cruel the world can be.'

My hair was dark, and it was obvious to me I would never grow to be tall and beautiful the way my father described my mother. I was my father's daughter without a doubt—but there was little in me that resembled the portrait of my mother my father painted.

He refused to tell me her name, and when I asked him why, he just said 'because', the way parents brush off children's questions without explanation because grown-ups unjustifiably believe that the truth hurts more than lies.

He inhaled from his pipe and squinted.

It pained me to see him smoke when he couldn't even breathe properly. He said smoking the pipe was not as bad as smoking cigarettes. I wanted to believe him, but his coughing told me otherwise.

'Why did you leave her?' I asked.

I had asked him the same question a million times before. I needed to know what he had seen in God that he hadn't seen in her; why he'd spent the past eleven years lingering over the loss of her love; why he never tried to track her down once he realised he loved her too much to continue living without her; why he had deprived me of a mother when it would have been easier to step down from his pedestal than to keep his head high in the clouds. I needed to know why, but I didn't blame him, for I had yet to experience the kind of love he had experienced from my mother, and the one he had endured from God. Faith in my father was all that I had left.

'She left me,' he said.

'You didn't want her.'

'I wanted her. She didn't want God.'

There was no answer to that.

'Love is the cruellest of all,' he added. 'It knows no mercy. It can take the strongest people and bring them to their knees. Don't listen to what they tell you. Love is not kind. Love is a traitor.'

At Christmas I received a boxed set of writing paper, a silver Mont Blanc fountain pen and a hand-made, leather-bound diary.

'So that you can record your thoughts and your perceptions of the world,' my father said when he saw me handling the diary like an older sister holds her newborn baby brother for the first time. 'People change. You'll see one day when you'll be a woman, and you'll wonder what it was like to be a young girl. Childhood shapes us into the people we become. Now you are malleable as clay to the outside elements, but one day you'll be as set as stone.'

Fascinated, I sat cross-legged near the Christmas tree—its multicoloured lights flashing like fireworks at a carnival—and held on to my diary as if it were made from eggshells. My fingers ran through an old map of the world etched on the brown leather jacket. It smelled like a new pair of shoes. I flicked through the thick, sand-colour pages, thinking it a shame to cover them with my own words.

'It's too nice,' I said sheepishly. 'I don't know if I can write in it without making a mistake. It would be ruined.'

My father looked down from his chair and smiled. 'Don't wait for your prose to be flawless, or you'll be waiting forever. Nothing in life is so pure and perfect that you have to wait until death for it to be used.'

I recorded my first entry in the diary that same night.

After Christmas festive I returned to *L'Ecole De Monseigneur*, a Catholic, mixed-gender school, where my father taught religious studies whenever he was robust enough.

Much to my despair, the splendour of the stone-built, mid-17th century building—with its Ionic columns rising the full length of two storeys, its triangular pediments over the doors and windows, and its Dutch-designed steep roof—did nothing to cheer me up.

I should have been in my last year of elementary school, but after completing a series of mathematical and grammatical tests the previous year, it had been decided—by those who knew better than my father and myself—that my ability lay a year ahead of the current one. I protested profusely at changing school before it was time for me to do so, not so much because I had lost faith in my ability to succeed academically, but because I had spent the last five elementary school years with other children who had become the brothers and sisters I longed to have—Camille, Anne, Thierry, Françoise and Sandrine were as much part of my life as the five fingers on my right hand. I begged my father to let me stay at the lower level, but he insisted it wasn't up to him.

'If God has blessed you with the gift of intellect,' he said, 'you must grab this gift with both hands and be thankful that the Almighty has chosen you as one of the selected few who will influence the world with their minds rather than their hands.'

'But why does God punish me by taking my friends away?' I

protested.

'God does not punish. He gives you choices, and if you're wise enough, you'll make the right choices.'

'How do I have choices when everyone tells me what to do?'

'We have to obey the Will of God. Nothing else matters.'

Winter and its coldness disappeared like a deadly plague that had occupied Europe for a good part of three months and miraculously vanished with the help of a magic vaccine. The nights became shorter and the days longer, and people began walking their dogs again without wearing gloves and scarves and coats rolled up to their ears.

Spring replaced winter, flowers and new leaves blossomed everywhere, pigeons gathered on rooftops, and my father's health improved as it always did during that same period every year.

Old people dressed in their favourite cardigans sat on park benches and soaked up the warmth of the sun instead of staying home staring at four walls, listening to talk radio or watching endless hours of American television programs dubbed in French.

Bicycles were brought up from dark cellars, and children and adults rode them again after three months of hibernation. Rain and sun created phenomenal rainbows at sunset over the Cathedral, which was surrounded by cafés where my father and I often strolled in the evening amongst the English and German tourists, who too were mesmerised by the enormous Gothic 12th century construction and its 142m spire.

The earth smelled of hope and possibility, like the first rain after a seven-year drought.

School was monotonous, and I made no friends to speak of. There were no classes on Wednesdays, much to my relief. Wednesdays were reserved for teachers' class preparations, detentions and corrections. I used them to do the little homework I could be bothered with and to practice my recorder.

Music was compulsory, as was French, English, mathematics, religion, science, history and physical education. I wasn't particularly fond of music, but our teacher, Monsieur Auteuil, was a perfectionist, and I had no choice but to take the learning of the instrument seriously. Playing the recorder with one note out of place meant a Wednesday-morning detention. In front of the class, we took random turns playing the piece we had practised diligently the previous night in fear of being the next person who'd be called up for an impromptu performance. Sometimes I wasn't called up for weeks—sometimes two or three weeks in row. There was no rhythm or reason to Monsieur Auteuil's cruel and sadistic selection process.

Whenever my turn came to play in front of the class, the prescribed repertoire of Bach's chorales I had mastered the day before was ruined by the sweat on my fingertips, which made it impossible for me to accurately block the holes of my wooden recorder and perform to Monsieur Auteuil's satisfaction. My anxiety prevented my mind being relaxed enough in order for me to play with confidence. My failure at performing the pieces perfectly resulted in Monsieur Auteuil's face reddening as if he'd choked on a handful of pins, and me ending up with a detention slip for the following Wednesday. There was no exception to the punishment, unless your nose was dripping with mucus, or you carried with you a doctor's certificate detailing why you couldn't play the recorder in front of an audience.

Other subjects bored me, so I chose to sit right at the back of the class, hiding from everyone, but gaining the privilege of a full view of the entire room. Rather than paying attention to my classes, I spent my time reading Marcel Pagnol's *La Gloire de Mon Père*, *Le Chateau de ma Mère*, *Le Temps des Secrets* and *Le Temps des Amours*—autobiographical accounts with a novel-like-quality I studied over and over again, imagining myself living in Provence, away from the greyness of Strasbourg and its pale-skinned inhabitants who fed on cold meats, sauerkraut and white wine. I saw no future ahead of me, for not only was I too young to plan years ahead, but also because my father had been so ill the past winter. We both knew he wouldn't make it through another winter. Yet, the dread of leaving me alone in the ruthless hands of fate scared my father even more than it scared me. He didn't say it as such, but the sicker he became, the more he fussed over every aspect of my life, like a poet fusses over every word of every stanza.

Reading Marcel Pagnol's novels was my escape from the everyday monotony of my existence. Anything was better than sitting in an English-language class, repeating senselessly how to order a coffee and a piece of cake from an imaginary cafeteria in London, a place which I had no intention of visiting neither in the near future, nor at any other time in my life.

But I knew that all the solitary activities I involved myself in and the crushing loneliness that choked me even in the middle of a crowd were because I missed my friends from elementary school.

One night, my father and I were sitting at the kitchen table, dining on a tarte flambée and a green salad tossed in red vinegar and lemon juice. The cream and onions aroma had taken over the apartment. The smell of good food had a way of making me feel secure and comfortable, liked being rugged up in a blanket at night time when a blizzard was ferociously beating against the window pane of my bedroom.

'I've spoken to Miss Tennant,' my father said. He sipped from his glass of Pinot Blanc the way he smoked his pipe. 'She's informed me that you're making no effort whatsoever in her class. What is happening, Clotilde? Don't you want to pass English?'

'I've got no interest.'

'Well, it's not a matter of interest—it's part of your education. A good education is the total understanding of man and not an emphasis on one fragment of his life.'

I had heard him use those same words two weeks prior during a Sunday sermon, and I knew he'd taken it from a book by Krishnamurti that had been travelling from his bedside table to the lounge room, and that I sometimes found forgotten on the kitchen bench, next to the microwave, like a leftover from the previous night that nobody had bothered cleaning up. Krishnamurti was a privately, English-educated, Indian philosopher, whom many of my father's Catholic friends disapproved of. Some would have said that Krishnamurti's beliefs had been the genesis of my father's erosion of his Christian faith. I had not formed an opinion either way because Krishnamurti's readings were complex and harder for me to appreciate than stories from the Bible. I had made several attempts at studying the book, which in a nutshell told me that to grow wise, I should enjoy gardening as much as study. At my age, unsurprisingly, I felt that Krishnamurti contributed little to my wisdom or intellect in any way, which is not to say there was no value in his teachings. At the age of forty-five, it was undoubtedly easier to accept and find enjoyment in the mundane because with age comes patience, and patience was something I had yet to acquire in my young life. My father—the most patient person I knew—had obviously found something within the white pages of

9

the slim hard-cover volume reprinted some three years prior. He was well read for a Catholic priest, and not just in the affairs of religion. His study at home contained hundreds of leather-bound volumes on the subjects of philosophy, science and world politics. Amongst his collection were also novels, including the entire works of Marcel Proust, of which he had been an avid reader since his years of intellectual awakening that seemed to have begun immediately after the successful completion of his baccalaureate, if his memory served him well.

I often borrowed from my father's collection, but found Proust's novels too long-winding for my understanding and enjoyment. With the passing of time, and my inevitable thirst to understand the human condition, I knew one day I would eventually get to read them, and if blessed with enough time, maybe even to finish them.

'What do I need English for?' I asked, sipping my white wine, which my father had diluted with Evian water. 'I mean, it's not like I'm going to go and live in England or America.'

'Because you never know where life will take you,' he said. 'I never thought I was going to spend the rest of my life in Strasbourg, and here I am.'

My father was born in Reims, in the Champagne province. He'd only moved North because of his ministerial obligation. A post had been made available to him through the Catholic Church, and at the time, he'd been young and inexperienced, and not in a position to refuse. He fervently believed in his calling and was willing to travel to the other side of the world if the Vatican had requested him to do so. He was twenty-three and had his whole life ahead of him.

'I hate English, Papa, I don't understand it. It makes no sense to me. Everything is backwards. Why do they place adjectives in front of nouns?'

He lowered his head, played with his fork and salad, looked up and said, 'Well, dearest, I, too, wish life was designed around my needs. Unfortunately, it's not the case, and the earlier you come to accept this fact, the easier you'll make it on yourself.'

'I want to grow up. I want to be an adult so that people stop on telling me what to do. Everyone tells me I can do whatever I please, but it's a lie.'

He locked his eyes with mine for a full minute. I never realised how sad he looked, as if someone had extracted all the joy from his life like a dog in a cage that knew his final hour was about to come. The skin on his face was soft tissue weathered by time, and his lips an arched doorway to a world that fascinated and scared me all at once. The blue of his eyes was almost translucent. A mist of vapour veiled his irises like morning dew blankets a whole village standing next to a swamp. His once-charcoal-black hair had turned salt-and-pepper in just one year. Permanent creases had formed above his cheekbones and across his forehead. His complexion was fine china, as one would have expected from someone who'd suffered from pulmonary infection and constant bouts of asthma for the majority of his adult life. He looked tired beyond his forty-five years, like a junkie who'd lived fast and recklessly during his youth, and whose body was now rebelling against all those years of carelessness and self-mutilation.

'I'm doing my best to give you what you want, Clotilde,' he finally said. 'I'm sorry if my best is not good enough.'

I placed my tiny hand on top of his and swallowed my pride the way an alcoholic fills another glass, knowing too well it will make him feel worst in the end.

'I'm sorry,' I said. 'I didn't mean to be selfish. I know you've always been good to me—it's not like I haven't noticed.'

He smiled gently and placed his other hand on top of mine.

'If the Lord forgives you, then I forgive you.'

He smiled, and I smiled in return as if life was nothing more than a mimicking game.

We finished dinner with two crème brûlées drowned in caramel so rich and dark, it would have been a sin in anyone's eyes.

On weekends I managed to see Camille, Anne, Thierry, Françoise and Sandrine, but as time went by, I found myself having less in common with them. They still went to the same school, saw the same people and were interested in the same games, books and television shows. I was an outcast, and it was my fault that I'd been forced to skip a year, that I was supposedly an intellectual freak when in fact I never felt so stupid in my life. My whole existence was a gush of wind blowing between cars on a congested freeway.

I told my father about Marcel Pagnol, and he said we could go for a holiday to Provence in the coming summer as soon as I finished my school year, and only if I scored well in my exams At

11

night I dreamed of fields of lavender, endless days of sunshine, and of losing myself in the same mountains Pagnol had lost himself as a child. I dreamed of a life where my father could run with me along the shore of the ocean—and in my dreams, he breathed the air and sprinted like a wild animal, free of his illness.

In the mornings, I wrote everything in my diary and held it close to my heart and prayed to God for my father to get better.

In early June, just before the long holidays of my first secondary school year, I came home to a street filled with two ambulances and a crowd of noisy neighbours. I felt pain in my chest—strong hands choking my heart like a killer chokes his victim to the last breath—and knew immediately the ambulances were there for no other reason than my father.

My father had been doing well with summer only a couple of weeks away. His doctor even told him the way his health was improving, there'd be a good chance he wouldn't experience bouts of asthma throughout the coming winter, as long as he took his medication diligently and remained indoors during extremely cold days. My faith was not on par with his doctor, for I had seen my father's condition the previous winter, and none of the symptoms had indicated any improvement over the previous years—only the deterioration of a body that refused to heal itself.

Still, in spite of my less-than-enthusiastic outlook on life since I'd begun attending *L'Ecole De Monseigneur*, I had not expected his health to turn for the worse so early in the year, especially when the second half of spring had been uncommonly warm, and rain had been infrequent. His asthma had always been a by-product of cold weather and humidity.

The early hours of the morning were the most difficult when a cold wind from the Antarctic North swept across the entire continent. I could hear him cough from my bedroom, even though he was sleeping at the other end of the hall, three rooms and a bathroom separating us. His cough sounded as if his lungs were being torn apart by a giant shredder. Many times I had rushed to his room only to find him hunched over like a wounded animal, the victim of a hit-and-run accident. His whole body was covered in torrid perspiration as he desperately tried to ingest air into his lungs. I would tap him on the back to no avail and was finally forced to drag him to the bathroom, fill the bathtub with hot water, and toss him in there like sailors unload a dead body into the sea. It was a rather difficult and almost-impossible task, given that I was only a young girl, and he was a grown man. The warmth of the bath eventually helped to ease the cough and to facilitate his breathing, but this was only a temporary relief, and at some stage during the day, I would book a house call with his doctor. My father, of course, didn't want to see his doctor, but by the time I had announced that I'd made the call, the doctor was already ringing the doorbell of our apartment, and my father had no choice but to welcome the doctor's visit.

But such catastrophic events only occurred in the core of winter, so surprisingly enough, on that particular June day filled with sunshine and hope, where the risk of an asthma attack was minimal, something had gone drastically wrong. Maybe winter cold wasn't the sole perpetrator of the disease that was slowly but surely killing him, and some invisible house-grown killer dust had finally achieved its deed by chewing up his lungs like white ants chew up the wooden stumps of a weatherboard home.

Panicking, I pushed my way through the crowd to the front door of the foyer of our apartment, where a paramedic was blocking the way to curious on-lookers. I tried to get past him, but he grabbed my arm.

'I'm sorry, but you can't go inside the building,' he ordered.

I pulled my arm back, 'I'm his daughter.' My eyes filled with tears. 'You've got to let me in.'

He stared at me for a few seconds. 'All right, but don't get in their way.'

I climbed two steps at the time, my lungs burning as I gulped air in small bursts, depriving my body of the oxygen it needed to function adequately. By the time I reached the fourth floor, my legs were rubber, and I had to rest against the wall adjacent to the front door of our apartment to catch my breath. I had no idea what I was going to find once I entered our home. Was my father already dead? Would it be too late for the paramedics to save his life?

As I stumbled to the front door, thousands of questions ran through my mind. What would happen to me if he'd left me, if he'd decided that he could no longer hold on to life? Where would I go? Who would love me if he were gone? I had no immediate family that I was aware of, and no money to support myself. Was my uncertain fate *God's Will* as well?

I pushed the heavy, wooden front door of the apartment, ashamed that I was only thinking about my welfare at a time when my father was hanging on to his last breath.

He was lying on the kitchen floor, two paramedics by his side, one with his mouth over my father's, the other pushing the palm of his hand on his chest at regular intervals. I stood frozen, unable to say a word, painfully aware that this might be the last time I'd ever see my father again.

The paramedic who breathed in and out of my father's mouth placed two fingers on my father's neck and said, 'All right, I'm getting a pulse. Let's take him downstairs.'

I followed them down the hallway and the four flights of stairs. The building was old and had been designed and erected at a time when there was no such thing as elevators. The paramedics struggled with the stretcher around each corner, where the stairs joined another floor of apartments. At every new flight of stairs, I feared they were going to drop him.

Hot tears streamed down my face like candle wax. We finally reached the street. Onlookers blocked the entrance to the apartment. I recognised a few of my neighbours—the son of the butcher, a fat kid who gorged himself on sweets every time I saw him; a young couple who lived a floor under us; a single mother with two kids and a Doberman whom I'd met a few times in the park around the corner from our apartment; and the owner of the newsagent and tobacco shop at the end of our street where I bought tobacco pouches to fill my father's pipe.

With the help of the paramedic who'd been waiting by the door, the two paramedics who were carrying my father on the stretcher managed to get to the ambulance. I followed them. A sea of voices was coming at me like bullets from a machine gun.

'Is he dead?'

'I don't know.'

'Sweet Jesus, have mercy on the man's soul.'

'Isn't that the priest who teaches at *L'Ecole De Monseigneur*?'

'Poor child, what's going to happen to her now?'

'They'll probably take her away.'

'*Mon Dieu, ce n'est pas possible!*'

'I heard she has no family.'

'They'll probably send her to an orphanage.'

The ambulance sirens cut through the crowd and its pointless mantra.

The crowd surrounded me, but I'd never felt so alone in my life. All I could see was the ambulance vanish down the end of the street and race to the *Hôpital Civil*, where my mother had given me life just over a decade ago.

As the sun partly blinded my sight, I knew that—now matter what God's plans were—from that moment on my father and I would always be together.

I shared my mother's blood but wore my father's heart.

My father stayed in hospital for more than a week, so they sent me to an orphanage because nobody had the time or the place to take care of a troubled young girl who was drowning in self-pity. Until he gets better, they said.

I was Little Virgin Mary because my father was a Catholic priest. Everybody knew now he was my real father. Somebody told the world, but I didn't tell my father. I had no idea of the identity of that somebody, and how he found out I was my father's daughter. The first I heard about it was at the orphanage when I caught a snatch of conversation from two girls queuing for some food at the canteen. They kept staring at me, and one of them said to the other, 'Why do they keep calling her Virgin Mary?'

'Her father's the priest at *L'Ecole De Monseigneur*... well, was. He's now in convalescence at the hospital. Immaculate conception, wouldn't you say? She came out of thin air. She's got no mother.'

I wanted to tell them it wasn't true—my mother existed somewhere in a foreign country, my father had been in love once, and I wasn't an apparition but made of flesh and bone like they were. But instead I looked down at my feet and pretended I hadn't heard a word.

I stopped reading Marcel Pagnol, forgot about Provence, and began reading Marcel Proust. I rebelled. I did my homework and sat at the front of the classroom. I was never sent to Wednesday morning detention again. I played the recorder in front of the whole classroom, note for note in perfect pitch, not a drop of sweat on my fingertips.

CHAPTER TWO

City public hospitals are all the same. They are crowded with the sick, the wounded, the weary, doctors, nurses, specialists, cleaners, visitors and flower sellers. They smell of commercial detergent and chemicals, and nobody ever smiles unless they feel like they have an obligation to cheer someone else up. They are maze-like, and it's easy to lose oneself right at the end of the west wing when one is supposed to be at the end of the east wing, or to go up and down for a half hour just to find a toilet accessible to visitors, not just patients and hospital staff.

I'd been in and out of hospitals whenever my father's health deteriorated, but I had never attended a hospital on such a regular basis. My father usually came back home on the same day after being checked and administered the right cocktail of medication, like a victim of an epileptic fit who needed to get on with life.

Hospitals scared me. They are like churches, where some-one else decides the fate of other people's lives; where the sins from the past come to haunt you; where you find yourself repenting and praying to a God you have ignored for the majority of your life. In hospitals, the doctors are the gods, and the nurses are the angels.

Sometimes, while sitting in the waiting room of the critical care unit and flicking through a magazine or losing myself in Proust's *A La Recherche Des Temps Perdus*, my concentration was snapped by someone's cry of pain and despair. The shriek of another person's suffering cleaved the core of my soul like a hand to the throat. I was suddenly reminded that nothing lasts forever, and life doesn't always end in the peaceful quietness of the night in the comfort of one's home amongst the familiarity of objects accumulated over a lifetime.

16

During my first month at the orphanage, I visited my father every Tuesday. The people at the orphanage wouldn't allow more visits, no matter how sick my father got. There were rules and regulations written in stone over a century ago, and nobody was willing to bend them, even if the sky suddenly fell to the earth and swallowed us all. I could beg and put on a sorry face; I could have bribed the entire establishment had I had the means to do so; but it would have made no difference whatsoever. The rules were the Ten Commandments of the orphanage, and the only ones who lived outside those rules were those who had escaped to a better world.

My father's left lung collapsed without warning a sunny June afternoon, and our lives radically changed. The doctor in charge of my father's convalescence at the hospital told me the technical term for a collapsed lung was *tension pneumothorax*, but I could refer to it as *tension pneumo*. Doctor talk, he confided to me as if he were my big brother. I liked him. He was in his late-twenties and good looking—different from other doctors who sported grey hair and bulging stomachs like overfed turkeys ready for the annual festive season slaughter. I was a child, but he spoke to me as if I were an adult. He never bothered to change his intonation or vocabulary to bridge our age difference or tried to patronise me with his encyclopaedic medical knowledge. He shared complex diagnosis and prognosis like loved ones give you a cuddle after you've run into a door left ajar.

We were sitting in his office at the hospital when he explained what had happened to my father. He used the help of a colour chart pinned to the back wall, right behind his chair. The chart showed a full-frontal cross-section of the respiratory system, including the larynx, trachea, bronchi, diaphragm and lungs. Next to it was a chart of the heart in blue and red sections, showing the pathway of blood travelling from body tissues to the right atrium and to the right ventricle. I had seen similar charts pinned to the walls of the science classroom back at school and remembered the difficulty I had in memorising all the strange names someone had assigned a long time ago to every organ and function of the body.

The doctor's name was Alfred Herrmann, and his family originated from Germany. He'd been born in Strasbourg in the very same hospital he was now working for. He insisted I call him by his first name, which felt strange because at school we were forced to address the teachers by their surnames. Even the teachers

17

addressed us by our surnames. I wasn't Clotilde, but Mademoiselle Benoît.

With his plastic biro, Dr. Herrmann pointed to the left lung on the colour chart—the one coloured blue—and said, 'See this large blood vessel?' He indicated a large artery attached to the top end of the heart.

I nodded.

'For some reason, it has burst and caused the lung to collapse in the process. As a result, your father's heart doesn't pump enough blood, and thus is incapable of delivering the required amount of oxygen to the vital tissues and organs. Your father will remain in critical care for the next few days, but we'll look after him as best as we can.'

'Is he going to live?'

'He's stable and he's being constantly monitored. His heart is still weak from the trauma, so it's important that he rests.'

'When can he go home?'

'I can't say at this stage, but I'm going to be honest with you, Clotilde, you're looking at least at another two to three months in hospital, and that is if his condition improves gradually without any complications.'

I sighed. How was I going to cope for so long at the orphanage by only seeing my father once a week? I missed him like a plant misses the healing rays of the sun.

Dr. Herrmann took me to the hospital canteen and bought me a lunch of salad and Swiss cheese and a chocolate mousse. I told him they didn't feed us well at the orphanage, and the food tasted horrible. I told him people were making fun of me, called me Virgin Mary, and I was scared and I wished I didn't have to be there. I wanted him to know he had to hurry and make my father healthy again.

'I'm doing the best I can,' Dr. Herrmann said, 'but life is cruel sometimes. We're not always the ones who decide on people's fate.'

I locked my eyes with his and said, 'It's God's Will, I know.'

He didn't reply, but his face expressed surprise at my answer.

He reached for my hand and squeezed it.

I let tears roll down my face. 'I'm so tired of everything, I want

18

a normal life again.'

'You're a brave little girl,' he finally said, 'maybe I can do something about getting you out of the orphanage. I have a friend who knows a friend who's a caseworker with the department of social security. A few phone calls, and we might be able to find you a placement with a nice family.' He smiled as if he'd just revealed the meaning of life. 'How does that sound?'

'It sounds fine,' I said because he was being nice, and I hated the idea of upsetting him.

But his offer wasn't agreeable.

I didn't want a placement with a nice family. I wanted my father back, and I wanted to go home.

I shared a room with another girl, Martine, thirteen years old, long greasy dark hair down her back and a china-white complexion. Her green eyes peered out from two small slits, which looked as if they'd been cut into her flesh with a scalpel. She wore the same pair of jeans every day, jeans so tight she could hardly move, and a white, cropped cotton top, and no bra. Her little *nichons* were clearly visible through the tee-shirt. I had no breasts to speak of, so at times I was envious, and at others I thought she was cheap. She spoke to me even though I didn't respond, because the last thing I needed were people trying to be my friend. Most of the time I was moody and thought about nothing but my father.

I stole a packet of shaving blades from the nurse's room and tucked it on the inside cover of my pillow. I wrote everything I thought and felt in my diary. If I beat the odds and somehow managed to live to be older, I would remember what it was like to be the girl the world had rejected like a dog forced to fend for itself in a world that no longer had the heart to care for those who needed it the most.

I recorded my innermost desires.

If my father died, I wanted to die on the same day. They would bury us together in the same grave, shamefully hidden at the back of the cemetery amongst tall weeds, a site nobody visited, where the homeless, bastards and criminals were concealed from the public.

When it was known I was my father's daughter, the Catholic Church stripped him of his ministry like a judge strips a convicted criminal of his dignity. I was the burden of his shame, and I would follow him to the grave.

'Martine!' I yelled.

Martine—who was sleeping next to me in a single bunk—
grunted in reply. She'd been at the orphanage on-and-off for six
years now. Her parents were junkies, and she'd been made a ward
of the state. Every time social security found her a placement in a
home, it didn't last. It was hard for her to get on with anyone,
including myself. I didn't like her, but on that particular night,
there was nobody else I could turn to.

I jumped from my bed. 'Martine, I think I'm dying!'

She stumbled from her metal-frame bed and flicked on the light
from her side table. 'What? What have you done?'

I looked down my legs—dark blood painted my thighs and my
nightgown like random brush strokes from the doubtful hands of a
painter's apprentice—and remembered the shaving blades hidden
inside the cover of my pillowcase.

'I think I cut myself.' I pulled my nightgown up to my thighs.
Where did the blood come from?

Martine's eyes met mine and I read cruelty in them.

'You're menstruating, *espèce de petite conne*,' she said with a
smirk.

'You're a woman now,' my father said. The skin on his face
appeared gaunter than during my previous visits, almost
translucent, and the bags under his eyes were so heavy, they might
as well have been drawn with a charcoal pen.

His room at the hospital was small, but at least he didn't have
to share it with anyone. A large crucifix hung above his bed. A
plastic tube was coming from under the white sheets, as well as
wiring attached to an EKG monitor. All this machinery scared me.
Even though I knew nothing about medical procedures, I was
certain that if someone still had to rely on a lot of equipment to
stay alive, it meant he couldn't be doing all that well.

I sat on a white plastic chair next to his bed, my small hands
grasping at my knees. He no longer smelled of pipe tobacco, but of
freshly washed sheets and disinfectant. His hair was dull and
combed to one side like a schoolboy whose mother had just
cleaned him up before he had to go out into the big, dangerous

world. He looked helpless—a lamb caught in a hunter's trap. This was not the father I knew and the memory of him I wanted to take back to the orphanage with me.

'There are many things I should have told you about what happens when a man and woman get together,' he said. 'It should have been your mother's job, and I didn't know how to go about it.'

'It's all right,' I said, 'Martine has told me everything.'

The expression on his face eased as if someone had just announced he would be able to go home that same afternoon. I realised he must have been counting the days backwards as to when it would have been appropriate for me to know about human reproduction, but Martine had fortuitously saved him from the burden.

I explained how Martine was my room mate, how her parents could no longer take care of her, and other family members didn't want the burden of bringing up a child who wasn't their own. I told him there had been a court case where her mother tried to retain custody of her child, but a government social worker convinced the judge she was an unfit mother who was still a junkie, and Martine was better off without her. I told him Martine had been raped at the age of twelve by a twenty-five-year-old man whom she'd became too friendly with. I told him how she wished people would understand what she'd been going through and stopped treating her as if she had a mental disorder. If they just realised she was a victim of fate. She refused to talk to psychologists or psychiatrists because she was too proud, and doing so would have been an admission there was something wrong with her.

My father listened attentively without interrupting.

'Is she a good friend?' he asked when I had nothing more to say.

'She's here and I'm there.'

There was a pause, which felt like eternity. I could see the effort it took him just to breathe, and it made me sick to my stomach. I wished I were the one lying on his bed with him sitting next to me, comforting me and telling me how I was going to pull through. I didn't know what to say to him to make him feel better. He'd always been the parent, and now it was my turn. He didn't say how guilty he felt that he'd become an affliction in my life, but the pain was clearly visible in his eyes, like that of a man who'd stopped believing in angels.

When I left the hospital I cried all the way to the orphanage.

Martine and I inevitably became close friends. I turned twelve, and she made me drink two full glasses of white wine to celebrate my rite of passage to womanhood. My father usually diluted the wine with water before giving it to me at lunch or dinner. I had never drunk wine undiluted before, and the alcohol went straight to my brain. It was liquid fire blended with fruit juice. Firecrackers exploded in my head.

I shared my first cigarette with Martine and coughed through its entire length. With my second cigarette, I stopped inhaling completely, but held the smoke in my mouth for a few seconds before releasing it in the confinement of our bedroom.

We were not allowed to smoke or drink at the orphanage, but Martine had never been caught.

'If you get caught, deny everything, there's nothing they can do.' Her fishnet stockings had a hole in them, and she wore her mascara generously like Brigitte Bardot did in the sixties.

'But lying is a sin,' I protested.

'So?'

'So, you shouldn't lie.'

'If it gets me out of trouble, I lie. It's easy, nobody can tell the difference anyway. No wonder they call you Virgin Mary. Haven't you ever done anything wrong in your life?'

She kept the cigarettes and the wine locked in a large, green metal trunk under her bed. She was really clever, assertive and proud, and her defiant attitude excited me.

That night when we ate dinner at the canteen, I threw up all over the table and was sent to the infirmary. My throwing-up had a domino effect, and three other kids vomited straight after seeing me emptying my stomach contents onto my plate of mash potatoes, green peas and low-grade minced meat.

'Have you been drinking?' the nurse asked, her pointy nose too close to my breath. She was young and seemed to be of no serious threat. She was almost smiling when she asked me the question.

'No,' I lied.

'Who gave you the wine?'

'I haven't been drinking.' A headache was thundering on both my temples, and I just wanted to lie down and die.

My first white lie.

Maybe they'd put me in hospital in the same room as my father's, and we'd share the same EKG monitor—two heartbeats pulsing into the one machine. Maybe they'd think my left lung was collapsing, that I was suffering from some kind of hereditary illness passed on from fathers to daughters, and then they'd realise we were meant to be one forever, and it would be pointless to separate us because fate would inevitably bring us back together.

'I'll let it go for the time being,' the nurse said. 'I'll put it down as indigestion, but if you come back here drunk again, I'll have to report you.'

She gave me a tablet and sent me to my room.

Martine was right.

Lying was easy.

That same night Martine told me more about boys.

'They're only after one thing,' she said, both of us lying on my narrow, single bunk in the dark, sharing a cigarette. A lamp post outside lit the room brightly enough for us to see. The glow of the cigarette was the most visible thing, and every time one of us took a drag, the smoker's face became clear.

'What?' I took a puff, coughed and passed it on to her. I felt grown-up because I did what grow-ups told me I couldn't do.

'Your body.'

She said that as if it was a bad thing, but I wasn't so sure myself. At school I began to notice boys, but I never wondered if my curiosity was a bad thing or not. I knew their thinking differed from our thinking, and I was intrigued by my own body, so maybe it wasn't so strange at all. I could understand why they'd be interested in Martine's body because I was too. I wanted to look like her—to have more curves without trying, to walk with my butt wiggling, to project an air of confidence, to as if I knew what life was all about. I wanted that badly. I didn't want to be a girl any more. I wanted to be a woman, and I wanted boys to look at me the way they looked at her.

She told me how her father forced her to have sex with him when she was nine years old, and at first I didn't believe her. She had already told me about how she was raped at the age of twelve,

23

so how much worse could her life have been?

'He used to come at around midnight,' Martine said and lit another cigarette, 'when mum was asleep, her brain simmering in Valium and alcohol. The bastard crept into my room like a killer in the night. I never got to sleep before then because I knew he would be coming. He made it sound like there was nothing wrong with what we did. I didn't know at the time because I never told anyone. It just felt bad, that's all. I didn't like doing what he made me do, but he was my father, and at school they kept telling us we had to obey our parents. I thought other girls' fathers did the same to them—I thought that was what fathers did.'

I couldn't even imagine my father doing what he did to her. It wasn't even something that had crossed my mind because I had never imagined people could be horrible enough to do things to their own children.

I blew smoke into the air.

'But why?' I asked.

'Because he wanted to,' she said and took another drag.

'But why? What about your mother?'

'It wasn't the same. He liked them tight.'

'Oh,' I nodded, pretending I understood what she'd just told me.

I thought about my father at hospital. Dr. Herrmann told me he was getting better. Herrmann also told me he'd rung up a friend, the one who knew a caseworker, and they would find me a family soon. But now I was getting used to being with Martine. She was older than me, and she knew more than I did, and she told me things about life my father never told me. It was like having a big sister.

'You want more wine?' she asked.

'Don't think so, I'm still feeling sick.'

'Ah, come on, don't be a baby.'

She poured me another glass, a cigarette butt hanging from one corner of her mouth, and we fell asleep drunk in each other's arms.

On my next visit to the hospital, I wore tight jeans and a white-cropped cotton top. When I climbed the steps to the foyer, I noticed people were looking at me more than they usually did, especially men. It didn't matter whether they were older or younger, doctors, janitors or patients, they all looked at me the same way—I was a slice of chocolate cake and they hadn't eaten for a month. I loved the attention I was getting.

I kept my chin up and walked straight across the polished floor. I didn't need to stop at reception because I knew where my father's room was. I had been visiting on a weekly basis for three months now. It was my thirteenth visit, and the visiting felt as if it would never end. At times I wondered what my life would be like if he died. Probably not much different from now except I would visit him once a week at the cemetery instead of the hospital. I felt a lump in my throat.

Inside the elevator, I checked my reflection in the mirror. Martine had helped me with the make-up. I'd never worn make-up before and still had to get used to the idea. My lips were painted with blood and my cheeks rosy like those of an alcoholic. I had Brigitte Bardot's eyes—eyelashes twice as long and thick as they were that morning. Martine said I looked sensual. I checked *sensual* in the dictionary and it read *tending to arouse the bodily appetites, esp. the sexual appetite.* That was exactly what I had been aiming at. My father said I was a woman now, and he was right. I was going to make him proud.

'What on earth has got into you?' my father screamed when he saw me walk in the room. How could he scream so loud with his lung condition? The beeping on the EKG quickened like I had seen on TV when someone's gets a heart attack. He hunched himself over on the bed.

I stood there as if someone had just grabbed me by the throat and held me against the back wall of the room and was about to shred me to pieces.

'Is it this Martine girl?' he said.

I had never seen him so angry before, thundering words at me like bullets from a gun when all I knew from him was kindness and patience. For a split second I thought about Martine's father, and how maybe there was a dark side to every man I didn't know about —even my father.

'But, Papa—'

'Look at yourself, Clotilde, you look like a slut!'

I wanted to tell him that was exactly how I wanted to look like, and who was he to tell me off since he wasn't even looking after

25

me any more. I wanted to tell him none of this would have happened if he'd never let my mother leave us, and if he'd married her. I wanted to tell him he'd ruined all our lives by not marrying my mother, and I missed her even if I didn't remember ever being with her. Fat tears rolled down my cheeks.

'I'm sorry,' I said.

'What were you thinking, Clotilde?'

'You said I was a woman now.'

He rolled his eyes to the ceiling and forced a smile. He seemed upset by my crying.

'Come here,' he said.

I walked hesitantly towards the bed and thought about what Martine's father did to her.

He made me sit on the bed next to him. His hand reached for mine, but I couldn't take it. He wiped the tears from my face with his bony fingers and covered them in dark mascara, like black ink stains on an illustrator's skin.

'You're burning steps,' he said matter-of-factly. He pulled a tissue from a box on his side-table, wet it with his saliva and began to remove the make-up from my face. 'Don't rush through the stages of your life. This girl you're with, Martine, she's not the same as you. She been around the block a few times. Who knows what she's been up to.'

'But she's nice to me, she's the only one who gives a shit.'

'I'm not saying she's not a nice person, but look at the influence she has on you—even your language, listen to yourself talking.'

He pointed gently with his right hand to the crucifix above his bed to make me aware God was in the room with us.

He added, 'You're not my little Clotilde any more, are you?'

'I'm sorry, Papa, I'm only trying to do my best.'

'I know you are, and I'm sorry things have turned out the way they have.'

'I just want to go home.'

'Soon.'

I wanted to believe him with all my heart, but he looked sicker than he ever had. The veins on his temples and neck were snakes crawling out of his skin. Dr. Herrmann told me in two to three months my father would be ready to come back home. Three months had passed. Nothing had changed for the better.

26

'I want you to be careful out there,' my father continued. 'People are going to take advantage of you if you're not careful.'

I had nothing to be taken advantage of—no money, no home, no belongings. What could possibly be gained from taking advantage of me?

I stayed seated on the bed a little while longer, but neither of us said a word. Sadness weighted his eyes, and I couldn't help feeling I'd let him down. I wished I could just go back a few steps and be the little Clotilde he wanted me to be. I wished I'd never met Martine and her so-called 'wise ways'. But I somehow realised it was hard to step back into darkness once you've seen the light. The world wasn't made of lollipops and pink fairy floss, but of fathers and sluts, vanishing mothers and people who mysteriously took advantage of you.

I was on a full pack of cigarettes a week when I heard the news. Dr. Herrmann said my father had put on a hell of a fight until the last minute. His right lung collapsed from doing too much work. There was nothing they could have done.

Back in July, Dr. Herrmann told me my father was going to make it. A little white lie. And I believed him. I was learning fast.

Late September is the beginning of autumn in France and the start of the school year. Everything around me was dying. Deciduous trees were losing their leaves and birds migrated down South for a long summer. But people couldn't escape. They stayed in their own private hell, like sinners chained to their penitence.

My private hell was to exist in front of my father's grave for what felt like infinity, my knees digging in the dirt, my eyes burned by the flood of tears I had cried. The grave was at the back of the cemetery, hidden behind a mature black poplar, a massive tree with large lumps of rough bark on its trunk and heavy branches curved downwards, wanting desperately to plunge into the dirt and lay beside my father.

I pressed the palm of my hand against the cold, white tombstone, then traced with my index finger the chiselled, gold epitaph—*Jean Philippe Benoît, né le 3 juin 1952, décédé le 4 septembre 1998*. When I closed my eyes, I felt his warm breath blow at the small of my neck. The effects were shivering spasms, my body doted in goose bumps, blood rushing to my head like someone who'd run a million miles.

I visited him two or three times a day at the cemetery, half conscious of where I was and what was going on. Even when it rained, I came and let the merciless clouds cry all over me to wash away my sadness like dirty sheets left out on the line in the hope nature would right the wrongs of our existence.

At times, I lay over the tombstone for hours. I knew he wouldn't come back, it was over, but I wouldn't accept it. I could still hear the melody of his voice sailing in the wind through time and space and advising me to not give up and to hold my head high during difficult times.

I withdrew from the world around me. I didn't want to meet or talk to psychologists or psychiatrists or social workers, or believers who kept telling me I was going through a phase called grief, and one day the thundering grey clouds would leave my path, and the blinding love of God would refill my cup with hope, strength and understanding, and I would become the strong person I once was.

For the next two months, my world became a blur of white wine, cigarettes, tears and hours lying on my bed, staring at the ceiling, images of my father constantly drifting in and out of my mind's eyes. My body was weightless and severed from my mind. My existence became surreal, dreams and reality blending into one. At times it felt as if my father was still alive and waiting for me back home in the comfort of his straw chair, and I would soon wake up from my purgatory existence.

Mornings were the hardest when the sun cut across the darkness of my room and landed on my face and made me realise who I was and what had happened. But when the pain become too strong to endure, I reached under the bed for a bottle of white wine and drowned my sorrow like people drown newborn kittens they can't afford to feed.

I refused to go to school, and, given the passing of my father, no one forced me to. At least they were patient, but I knew it wouldn't last forever. My placement with a 'nice' family had been postponed. I wasn't presentable enough, the caseworker told me when she came to visit. They knew I was getting alcohol from somewhere, but they didn't know where, and frankly neither did I. It just seemed to be there all the time. It must have been Martine who kept refilling my stash because she felt sorry for me. I was turning into an alcoholic even though I was still a child. In the five months since I left home, I had lost my innocence and was disturbingly aware I would never get it back.

Dr. Herrmann came to see me on the weekends, but we had little to say to one another. He eventually gave up on me when I asked him if I could move into his home. I was too young, he said, and people would start talking. What did he care what people said? Wasn't my life more important? He said people might think he was taking advantage of me. That word again—*advantage*.

Martine had also given up on me. She'd tried to talk some sense into me during the first two weeks, but afterwards she left me alone.

One night she packed her things like someone going on a long holiday.

'I'm going down South,' she said and transferred all her precious belongings from the metal trunk under the bed to a backpack she bought with allowance money she had saved up. 'I've been writing to this guy in Toulouse and he's got his own apartment. I'm in love with him. I'm going to live there.'

She showed me a picture. He had dark, curly hair and blue eyes. I didn't find him handsome whatsoever, but I knew attraction was subjective, so I didn't comment. I just gave the picture back and said, 'he's nice', without meaning it.

She'd just turned fourteen and was in love with someone she'd never met. I wished I had been in love and someone had been in love with me. I wished I could have gotten out of this place and found a home and curled up in someone's arms and felt like I belonged somewhere. But I was the girl nobody wanted. I was the 'nobody-gives-a-shit-about-you' girl.

Martine left me two bottles of white wine, a packet of cigarettes, clothes she had outgrown, and the metal trunk. I was lying on my bed when she left. She bent over and kissed me on the forehead

She said, 'You'll get over it—we all do eventually.'

I didn't believe her. My father had never been a drug addict, so how would she know? My father had never had sex with me. My father was a good man who'd been cursed with a bad life. Couldn't she understand that?

I stopped writing in my diary—my life had become blank, and there was nothing to report or forecast.

The night Martine left, I removed the shaving blades from the cover of my pillow. I didn't know what I was doing. It was dark and my eyes were welled with tears. I cut my forefinger while pulling the first blade out of the plastic packaging. It didn't hurt. I placed my finger in my mouth and sucked the blood. It tasted good, like the first ray of sunrise.

I'd never seen people slash their wrists before, and I'd never read anything about it, so I cut across my left wrist. Had I cut along the main artery instead, I would have bled to death in a crimson pool, my soul united with my father's. They would have found me in the morning, the little Virgin Mary, the 'nobody-gives-a-shit-about-you' girl, the slut, the 'little-Clotilde-bad-people-are-going-to-take-advantage-of'.

I dreamed of white wine turning red. The crucifix above my father's hospital bed bleeding where the hands and feet of Jesus had been nailed. My face covered in bright red lipstick. People throwing stones at me while I walked my way to school. People taking *advantage* of me.

I dreamed of being alone and everyone leaving. I dreamed of screams no one could hear. I dreamed of my father's face distorted with pain as he tries hard to breathe the suffocating air around. I dreamed of his pipe and smelled his *eau de vie*, of the way my small hand felt in his, of the way he sometimes laughed when I made a joke. I dreamed of a black crow. I dreamed of Provence and Marcel Pagnol as a child. I dreamed of Marcel Proust and Jesus Christ. I dreamed of sunsets over the Cathedral of Strasbourg, of English and German tourists with cameras.

I dreamed blood.

Lots of blood.

CHAPTER THREE

My caseworker was a woman in her mid-thirties who had been in the job for over a decade. She cared about children, she told me, and as a result decided to become a welfare officer. Her name was Louise. I could call her by her first name. Martine told me before she left how caseworkers told us to call them by their first names because it was supposed to make us feel at ease. It was another trick grown-ups played on us in order to trust them. Apparently I had to get used to people telling me to trust them, as if their one and only concern was my welfare.

'Fact is they're getting paid to be nice to us,' Martine had explained over wine and cigarettes in the confinement of our room, two weeks before my father's death, 'and not because they give a shit. It just makes them feel good someone else is worse off than they are, that they can go home at night and realise how lucky they are to have a family and a reason to carry on.'

Martine was cynical, but she had travelled the twisted road of dealing with government welfare officials and psychiatrists for most of her life. She'd been cheated, lied to and sexually abused. I could understand why she didn't trust grown-ups. If I'd been in her position, maybe I would have started bumping them off one by one.

'There's a war out there,' she explained and sipped wine from an empty *Moutarde De Dijon* glass. 'It's invisible to most people, but you just look around and see how many rules are designed to piss off adolescents, and you'll understand what I mean. People forget we're going to become adults one day, and we won't forget all the shit we've been handed down. Doomsday will come, believe me.'

I listened to her attentively and inhaled the smoke from my

cigarette. My father had never mentioned the 'war' to me, and I suddenly realised how sheltered I'd been from the ugliness of the world. Martine's understanding of life impressed me. She didn't even realise she already spoke like an adult—an adult trapped in a child's body.

Louise and I were sitting in the canteen at the orphanage, indifferent to our body space, like a mother and a daughter from a conventional family who could sit so close to one another and not feel overwhelmed by the presence of the other person. She bought me a chocolate éclair glistening in fresh custard and sugar glaze, and a mocha coffee that smelled like the deep jungles of Africa.

Her blonde hair was down to her shoulders, styled in last decade's fashion, while everyone else's was cropped or grown long to the small of their backs. Her face was round and filled out and reminded me of a baby whose nutritional demands were met on a daily basis. Her green eyes scrutinised me the way people scrutinise the label of a can of food they've just pulled from a supermarket shelf. She wore a long cream-colour coat over her skirt and white blouse. She smelled of efficiency and compassion, and that's what scared me the most.

My file, held by a large, red rubber band, sat unopened on the table in front of her. It was thick, and I wondered why could be so important about me that needed to be written on so many pages of paper and fastened into a manilla folder. I felt like a criminal about to be charged for a crime she didn't commit.

Louise wore a gold wedding band on the third finger of her left hand. Her fingers were long and fleshy, her nails carefully manicured. They were the hands of someone who'd been shuffling papers all her life; someone who'd undoubtedly had a dishwasher installed at home, the expensive brand from Germany; someone who had a cleaner coming in once a week to vacuum and put the dishes away; someone who only stopped at petrol stations with full service.

'Married?' I asked and took a bite from my chocolate éclair. The vanilla custard spread on my tongue like church bells on Sunday.

Louise rolled the wedding band with her right index and thumb —a trophy she won after years of hardship and celibacy since gold signified eternal life.

'Two years now,' she said.

'Is it nice to be married?'

'Yes, it is.'

It was the first time I'd conversed with anyone for two-and-a-half months. The only communication I'd had was with Martine —hand-written letters filled with pain and laboured into clumsy, mistake-ridden sentences. I wrote to her, and she wrote back to me for a little while until the differences in our lives were too great to pretend we still had something in common.

Martine was happy with her twenty-five-year-old boyfriend. He'd been married previously and had a daughter who lived at her mother's place. I wondered if his wife knew her ex-husband shared his life with a fourteen-year-old girl and made her his lover. At the same time, I realised how lucky Martine was to be living with a man who loved her for her womanhood. After reading her letters, I would have traded places without hesitation. Suddenly, she stopped writing to me. I had no idea what happened to her after that. She must have got tired of me complaining about my existence and my contrived little world.

Louise grabbed my hand across the table and turned it over gently. She passed the palm of her other hand over my wrist, as gently as if she were caressing a sheet of silk, which she was about to spend a month's salary on. Her fingers were cotton wool. I shivered. No one had touched me so tenderly since my father.

'You can hardly see the scars now,' she said.

The morning after I slit my wrists, I was taken urgently to hospital, disinfected, stitched-up and questioned. Doctors treated me as if I were inflicted with a contagious disease and feared they were going to catch it. I stayed at the paediatric unit of the hospital for two days and was subjected to harassment by various psycho-specialists wanting to know why I had decided to end my life when it couldn't have been more obvious. Did they actually think I wanted to bleed to death because I enjoyed it? Hadn't they read my case history? Hadn't they been informed my father had recently passed away? Did one really need to be a doctor to figure these things out?

Dr. Herrmann came to visit. He apologised profusely for not having taken me under his wing—if only he'd known how bad I felt, he would have done something before my life took on such a dramatic turn. I refused to speak to him and kept my eyes glued to the wall in front of my bed.

Clearly upset by my detrimental state, Dr. Herrmann threw his hands up in the air like a traffic-control officer caught in the middle of a busy intersection. But for all I cared, he could have drowned in his remorse. He'd never reached out when I sought his help, and by now I had bottled up too much anger to give a damn about the world around me. Both my wrists were heavily bandaged, and I noticed he couldn't take his eyes off them. When he left the room, I could have sworn he was about to cry, and it brought me some bitter satisfaction. I had never felt unadulterated anger before, and, as much as I took the experience to heart, it kind of frightened me. I'd never pictured myself as someone who could actually enjoy the pain of another person. But pain has a rippling effect, like a waves crashing to the shore.

'You've healed quickly,' Louise continued, the softness of her hand still resting on my fading scares.

And then I remembered what Martine told me about adults, and caseworkers in particular. I wasn't going to buy into Louise's maternal approach. You get too close to people, and then they cut you down at the knees. Everyone leaves you in the end anyway, so there was no point getting too attached. This woman wasn't my mother, or my father, or someone who would always be there for me when I'd become too difficult to handle.

I pulled my hand back.

'You can hardly tell I'm a damaged product,' I said. 'Maybe you'll be able to pass me off as something new.'

The harshness of my comment surprised both of us.

I sipped from my coffee and avoided eye contact.

Louise forced a sympathetic smile. 'I'm only trying to help you, Clotilde, there's no need to take *that* attitude.'

'And *what* attitude is that?'

'The tone of voice you're using with me. I understand you're angry. If I'd lost my father, I'd be angry too.'

Well, you haven't, I thought. I shrugged and emptied my cup of coffee. Everybody knew how I felt somehow, even though I had yet to figure it out myself.

Louise pulled off the red elastic attached to the file she had in front of her. 'I think I've found you the perfect family.'

I kept my eyes on my empty cup to avoid getting caught in the emotional trap of believing she actually cared about me.

34

'They're good people,' she continued and browsed through the pages of the manilla folder, 'and they're *wealthy*.'

'I don't need a family,' I said, clipping my words. 'I've already got one.'

'The orphanage is not a family—it's a temporary shelter. You need a father and a mother.'

I pulled my head up and locked my eyes with hers. 'My father's dead, all right—and I've still got a mother, so I don't need another one.'

She glared suspiciously. 'Well according to my records, you no longer have a mother. Your birth parents died in a car accident after you were born, and your step-father—the one you call your father—adopted you soon after.'

'That's a lie.'

'I'm sorry?'

I told Louise everything about my father being a Catholic priest who had produced a child out of wedlock, and how his would-be bride vanished into foreign territories when he refused to marry her.

'Where is she?' she asked.

'I've got no idea.'

My explanation was so detailed, I could read from the expression on her face she knew I told the truth. I told her everyone at the orphanage knew who my father was, so I was surprised she didn't know, and if she didn't believe me, all she had to do was ask around.

'No one said anything to me. It's not even on file.' She scribbled on the top sheet of her manilla folder. 'Okay then, it's a matter of tracking down your mother and seeing if she'd like to take you home. If she doesn't, then we'll find you a foster family.'

The thought of meeting my mother had crossed my mind, but I never took it seriously. If she hadn't tried to make contact with me for the past twelve years, what made Louise think she would want to see me now? I hadn't figured out if I was prepared to live with my mother, but it seemed any place was better than being stuck at an orphanage. Or handed over to a strange family until they tired of me and passed me over to another family, the way people traded their old set of wheels when it no longer served their needs.

At night, I suffered from insomnia. I tried to imagine what my mother looked like from the descriptions my father gave me.

'Beautiful, tall, blonde, free like a wild horse who'd had no idea of her limitations, of how small and cruel the world could be.'

I didn't even know her name. My father passed away without telling me. Would she be the same now? And what country did she move to? My father never told me because he claimed he didn't know himself. When he blankly refused to marry her, she wanted nothing to do with him ever again. My father had told me the story many times over the years, and every time there was a void in his eyes, where one could read despair and regret, and most likely guilt for my motherless existence.

I sat on my bed and lit a cigarette and puzzled on how painful it must be to have let go of the person you loved the most in the world, only to realise years later you made a mistake. How excruciating it must have felt to concede there was no way to remedy your decision. But why didn't he try to hunt her down if he missed her so much? Had he loved God so much that he refused to act on his feelings for my mother for so many years? Did he really believe God didn't want him to be happy? He never told me exactly why he hadn't bothered tracking her down, but there must have been a reason—maybe that was what really killed him in the end.

I feared walking the same path. I couldn't take the chance of never finding out if she was the missing link in my life.

If my mother was still alive, I had to see her.

I failed my first year at secondary school and had to start all over again. I had attended no classes since September and was two months behind on my school work It would have been impossible to catch up, even if I had attended remedial classes or been offered private tutoring. School work no longer interested me and I stubbornly refused to return to study. Still, attending school was compulsory until the age of sixteen, and it would be another three years before I would be allowed to leave and pave my own way through life. It was hard to conceive how just over a year ago I had been a child prodigy.

It was almost mid-December. Frost covered Strasbourg like a giant ice blanket and forced residents to spend most of their time inside in the company of family or friends, or for those unfortunate enough, by themselves. The streets were empty throughout the day, and only the occasional car, fitted with chains, appeared in the snow-filled landscape like a stray dog trying to find its way home.

If I could convince everyone I was still too devastated over my father's death, I wouldn't have to go back to school until the following year. And it wasn't as if I had to fake my grief in the first place—only to make it more obvious to those around me. The Christmas holidays were almost upon us, so all I had to do was to persuade my caseworker it was not really worthwhile sending me back to school for a couple of weeks. Why not wait until the holidays were over and make a fresh start?

We were both sitting on my bunk—me sucking obsessively on a cigarette, as if I were on death row and would never get the chance to smoke again, and Louise looking through my file and refreshing her memory on my case history. She no longer wore her long coat, skirt and white blouse, but a pair of jeans and a blue cashmere jumper. She didn't look like a caseworker but like someone's aunty or cousin who came to visit at the orphanage. She even looked tired, pencil-drawn circles around her eyes, an indication insomnia was as regular in her life as in mine.

'So what do you think?' I asked. 'Do I really have to go back to school for two more weeks? You know it's going to be a waste of time.'

'Let me talk to the principal.'

It was so cold in the room I smoked my cigarette faster, believing it would raise my body temperature.

'You shouldn't be smoking at your age,' she said and flicked through my case-file in the hope she would find some secret map that would lead me back to my mother. 'It's bad for you, and you'll never be able to stop.'

'I don't want to stop.' I purposely blew the smoke in her face.

She ignored me.

Then I noticed the gold wedding band on her finger was missing.

'Didn't work out, did it?' I asked.

She looked up from her file and stared at me for a few seconds, her brow creasing.

I glanced at her hand and back at her.

Her eyes lit up like candles.

'No,' she said, 'it didn't, it was a mistake.'

'You were happy a month ago.'

'I didn't know.'

I blew more smoke at her face. 'Was it he or you?'

'Look, Clotilde, I'm not here to discuss my relationship. It's none of your business, *d'accord?* And put that *merde de cigarette* away!'

I ignored her request and continued to smoke.

Now I began to really understand what Martine's pet-hate for caseworkers was all about. First Louise treated me as if I were her own child, told me she was on my side, how I could trust her like I trusted my best friend. But when I became too much of a friend, and I asked too many questions, all of a sudden, I was only an orphan who was sticking her nose into what was clearly none of her business.

'I'm sorry,' I said, 'I didn't mean to upset you.'

She didn't reply immediately.

'Okay, look,' she finally said, 'I'm having problems tracking this mother of yours. Are you sure you've been telling me the truth?'

I threw her darts with my eyes.

'Fine,' she said, 'I believe you. But all I've got is a first name given to me by the hospital. For some reason, her surname was written down as that of your father. The hospital staff must have thought your parents were married. And I've got an approximate date of when she would have left the country. This is going to take forever. I've already been in touch with twenty embassies, and they're combing their records from July to September 1986, which is when your mother would have left. Correct?'

'You know my mother's name?'

She looked at me, surprised. 'Yeah, like I said I got it from the hospital. You don't know it?'

'No.'

She told me my mother's name.

'So let me double-check this,' she continued. 'Your mother left straight after you were born?'

'My father said she left right after she gave birth to me, so yes, it would have been just after July '86.'

'Anything else you can tell me which could be helpful. He never mentioned the country she was going to?'

'No.'

'Did she speak a foreign language?'

'Don't know.'

'Did your father want you to learn another language?'

'English—he said I should learn it because I never knew where life would take me.'

The expression on Louise's face changed from one of despair to one of hope. 'Well, that narrows it down. How many English-speaking countries can there be in the world?'

'It doesn't mean anything.' I squashed my cigarette in the ashtray by the side-table.

'Of course it does. Can't you see? He knew he was going to die one day, and that you might decide to go back to live with your mother. That's why he wanted you to learn English.'

'Surely he would have left more details if that were the case.'

'Maybe he didn't know where she'd gone to.'

'If he didn't know where she'd gone, how did he know it would be an English-speaking country?'

'Her background maybe—with a first name like hers.'

I was clueless as to whether Louise was right or wrong, and, frankly, I didn't care. I just wanted her out of my room so I could light up another cigarette.

My mother's first name was Rhonda.

I spent Christmas by myself in my room with a packet of cigarettes and a bottle of wine. The bottle of wine only had half a life. I emptied the rest in the sink of the communal bathroom, after which I stood under the hot shower for an hour, steaming water reddening my skin and causing it to soften like a sponge. I closed my eyes and listened to the water crash against the tiles and fill my ears like a mantra. My skin smelled of house-grade soap and cigarette smoke. I had no idea if there was anyone else at the orphanage, but it felt as if I was the last person left on the planet.

At night I feared when I would get up the next morning, there'd be no one left in the world, and I would be walking the earth endlessly in search of another soul, only to find myself over and over again.

Outside it was freezing, and the whole of Alsace was covered in a blanket of snow. Pipes were bursting, and homeless people who'd given up trying to find shelter died in the streets, like many others who froze to death the previous year. Maybe I was fortunate and I didn't realise it.

After the shower, I lay on my bed. Sadness settled in like autumn leaves on pavement, but there were no tears left in me—only a sense of despair with a glimpse of hope.

I flicked through an atlas on loan from the orphanage library. How many countries in the world were there where English was spoken? I came across an alphabetical listing of places where English was the first language spoken—Anguilla, Antigua, Australia, Bahamas, Barbados, Belize, Canada, Dominica, Grenada, Guyana, Ireland, Jamaica, Montserra, New Zealand, St Christopher, St Vincent, South Africa, Trinidad, Tobago, UK, USA, Zimbabwe. Apparently there were other British territories the atlas didn't bother listing. I never realised the usage of the English tongue was so widespread.

I pictured my mother lying on a vast, empty, white beach stretching as far as the eye could see, her skin the colour of coffee-and-milk and smelling of coconut oil, her blonde hair bleached by the sun and seawater. I pictured a tall, slender woman, the type I'd seen in magazines on news stands I daydreamed of Barbados and the Bahamas, even though I'd never been there.

I closed the atlas, kneeled on my bed and prayed for God Almighty to make my mother want me. I promised I would stop smoking and drinking. I promised I would be a good girl again, I would be nice to people, I wouldn't feel bitterness towards anyone, not even Dr. Herrmann. I promised so many things, it would have taken an entire exercise book to list them all—promises I knew I would be incapable of keeping. I held my hands so tightly together, the joints of my fingers hurt, and my overgrown nails dug into my soft, white flesh like a knife cutting through a loaf of bread.

I just didn't want to be alone any more.

CHAPTER FOUR

Four weeks went by before I heard from Louise again.

The worst of winter had come and gone, but the temperature still reached below zero at night and covered every morning the entire city in a layer of frost. Car engines had to be warmed up ten minutes before their owners could drive to work. Radiators without anti-freeze filled with ice and there was nothing to do but wait for the ice to turn back into water. Public transport was more popular during winter but somewhat less reliable because of the hazardous condition of the roads—snow, ice, road accidents. People took time off work for a variety of reasons—mostly from flu and symptoms associated with the cold weather—or stayed behind at work because the boss was paying for heating, and winter power bills were more frightening than post-Christmas credit card statements.

I had been back at school for nearly two weeks, but my mind didn't adapt well to the routine of classroom lessons and domineering teachers. All I could think about was to escape the miserable and delusional world that made my life more unbearable to endure. The cold cut through my winter coat, red scarf, gloves and beanie, and burned my skin until tears welled from my eyes from the bitter pain. I dreamed of hot weather and sunburns, of a world where winter didn't exist, of people who didn't look as grey as the clouds hanging above their heads.

School work was relatively easy, but it was the other kids I had to get used to again. Everyone around me seemed so childish—all they thought about were games and pranks. I wasn't interested in joining groups or getting too close to a particular person. Closeness frightened me because I knew once I depended on friends, losing them would leave me as weak as a sparrow in the

41

dead of winter.

I had spent so much time by myself in the confinement of my room at the orphanage, I hadn't even realised I'd become a new person—a person who had acquired an aberrant taste for solitary activities. I liked reading, or sitting by the window of my room and watching the snow-filled landscape for hours, wasting time because it was all I knew how to do without choking on the crushing feeling the world was expecting something from me, something I would never be able to give.

Repeating the first year of secondary school meant other students I attended elementary school with were now in my grade. There were eight first-year classes at school, and as a result not everyone I knew ended up in the same class as mine—only Sandrine and Thierry. We had lost touch with one another in the past year, the way people often do when they move to a new place and have nothing left in common with old neighbours, other than memories of easier and less overwhelming times.

I borrowed glossy picture books from the school library on America, Canada and some of the English-speaking islands. America seemed like a beautiful country with endless possibilities, but I'd heard it was a violent place, where people carried guns in their glove box and shot each other in the face at traffic lights whenever they felt frustrated at the world around them. I pictured all the angry kids at school carrying guns and shooting one another every time something went wrong. Half the students in my class would have been dead before Easter if they'd been allowed to carry handguns.

Initially I'd liked the idea of living in Canada, where residents spoke French and English. But moving to a place colder than the North-East of France terrified me. Apparently it was a fact that the city of Montreal spent nearly fifty million dollars a year on snow removal, and to my young eyes it seemed absurd when I realised snow was just frozen water, and people were dying of thirst somewhere in Africa.

At night, I pressed my face against the windowpane of my room and let the cold sizzle against my skin just to remind me this was the real world and I was alive and there was no turning back time.

Louise picked me up unannounced at school. Her blonde hair wasn't real blonde—a centimetre of dark roots was now showing

—and her face had aged five years in just three weeks. There were crow's feet attached to her eyes like rusted nails to the hands of Christ, and her make-up needed touching up, especially the cherry lipstick, which seemed to have been carelessly smudged rather than applied by a caring hand.

As soon as I saw her, I prayed to God to never let me fall in love if that was what love did to people—first my father and now Louise.

Louise drove a white Peugeot 505 with headrests and a working heater. I liked the smell of her new car. It reminded me of the smell of new pencil cases, which my father used to buy me every time a new school year begun. He'd filled them with new Bic pens, a new eraser, a red or blue plastic sharpener, a grey-lead, and twelve colour pencils. New school stationary made me excited about going back to school the way grown-ups are excited about three-day weekends.

I tossed my bags in the back and sat in the front with Louise. The black, leather seats squeaked under my weight, as if I'd just sat on a bag filled with kittens.

We drove towards the city centre along Avenue Jean Jaurès, past the city council offices and toward La Place de L'Etoile.

Louise asked me about school, and how I was getting along with the other students. I told her school was okay now, but it was only because I was repeating from the previous year that everything seemed easy. I said I had little to do with the other students—they were still into games and toys I'd given up since my father died, and I was more into books and literature. His death seemed to have cursed me with a precocious existence, which others might have foolishly confused as a sign of wisdom instead of one of despair.

'I've started reading Proust again,' I said.

Louise nearly ran through a red light and knocked over a pedestrian, who swore at her as she pressed heavily on the brakes, forcing the tyres to scream and leave a thick, black line of rubber trailing.

She looked at me suspiciously. 'Do you understand his writing?'

'Yes.'

'Really? I've never read him. Someone told me once his work is too depressing. Life is tormenting enough as it is without having to delve into other people's misery.'

'He believes suffering builds character.'

'Good for him.'

I noticed her wedding band was still missing from her finger, but I knew better than to inquire.

Louise parked the car, and we walked down to the Cathedral since the centre of Strasbourg was off-limits to vehicles. Car exhaust fumes were corrosive to the medieval buildings and the Cathedral, forcing the city council to monitor traffic flow in affected areas.

We sat at a café just opposite the Cathedral, where Louise ordered two hot chocolates. We could have sat on the terrace, but January in France is the middle of winter and extremely cold. Unless one is desperate for an unspoiled view of the Cathedral, the inside of a café was the only place to be.

'So,' I said impatiently, 'you didn't just pick me up from school to buy me a hot chocolate, did you?'

She smiled and removed my file from her briefcase.

'I've got good news for you.' She pulled the red elastic band from the manilla folder.

'What?'

'I've found your mother.'

I frowned.

'Aren't you happy?'

I added a third sugar cube to my hot chocolate and stirred the contents with a silver teaspoon resting on the saucer next to my cup.

'Yes, I think I am,' I said.

She smiled. 'You'll never guess where she's living.'

'America?'

'No.'

'England?'

'No.'

'Not Canada, I hope.'

'Australia.'

'Where?'

'*En Australie.*'

I added another two sugar cubes to my hot chocolate.

Before we left, I asked her if she had any other information about my mother. I was curious, but she said she wasn't the one who tracked my mother down as such, so there was nothing she could add. I would have to find out by myself as I went along, like a blind person thrown in the middle of peak hour traffic.

I went to the municipal library and looked up anything I could find about this mysterious country. Australia was a British colony discovered by someone named James Cook in 1788, although some experts claimed it was actually the French who got there first, and others claim it was the Dutch some two-hundred years earlier. It was arguably the largest island in the world with a surface area fourteen times that of France and only one-fifth of its population. People sat in the sun all day, went to work on horseback and kept kangaroos and koalas as pets.

Australians were blond with blue eyes, and there were jobs everywhere, but no one really wanted to work. People didn't shoot each other with guns at traffic lights, and French was learned at school.

The following day, I asked my science teacher if he knew anything about Australia.

'L'Australie?' he said, 'Why do you want to go there for? It's an iceberg. You'll freeze to death.'

He must have thought Australia was Antarctica, but I didn't want to argue with him, or he would have given me a bad grade at the end of the semester.

Most people I spoke to had no idea what country I was talking about. Others thought Australia was a large desert inhabited by cowboys living on cattle ranches.

I went to the school library to search for books on Australia, but there was nothing there. Instead I looked up references in encyclopaedias Many of the entries focused on the political and historical facts and provided me with little up-to-date information as to what I should be expecting. I tore a coloured map of Australia from one of the encyclopaedias and threw it in my school bag. When I got home, I stuck the map above my bed-head with clear tape, this way all I had to do was roll my eyes every time I wanted to fantasise about the horse-head-shaped island.

At night I went to sleep with Proust's *Les Plaisirs et Les Jours*, and later on dreamed of endless beaches with kangaroos and blue-eyed cowboys and tall, blonde women—my mother the leader amongst them.

As the weeks went past, it become difficult to concentrate on my school work, still I tried to be particularly diligent with my English classes. But my effort proved to be futile and frustrating. I just couldn't get those *th*-sounds right, and they all ended up sounding like *s*-sounds and *z*-sounds. *The* became *ze*, and *that* became *zat*. I finally admitted to myself I had no talent for learning new languages, and then I thought since Australians learned French at school I might be able to get by communicating in my mother tongue.

Louise called me two weeks later at the orphanage. I answered the call from the grey service phone down the hall when a younger girl two rooms down from mine came to fetch me.

Thick ice encrusted the outside of the window next to the phone. My breath exhaled from my lungs in steamy clouds, and there was a tingling pain in my ears and fingers from the cold. I was wrapped up in a brown blanket from my bed like a homeless person waiting for those more fortunate than myself to take pity on my predicament and spare whatever change they carried in their pockets. But unlike a homeless, it wasn't loose change I was after, but a surplus of love, the kind everyone took for granted when they were bathing in it and only realised it was missing when they carelessly discarded it like yesterday's trash.

I suffered from bouts of insomnia since I'd last seen Louise. My anticipation of moving Australia had now turned into fear of the unknown and the apprehension that maybe my mother would not want me after all. I dreaded the thought I might have to spend more time at the orphanage, or I would be forced to live with some strange family who had missed out on the first twelve years of my life and would have no idea of how to handle me.

'We got in touch with your mother,' Louise said at the other end of the line, 'and we've explained your situation to her.'

I twisted the telephone cord several times. 'And?'

'She said she expected your father would eventually die.'

There was a pause.

'And?' This was like Chinese water torture.

'She had already made an agreement with your father when you were born in case something happened to him—she would take

46

care of you.'

I felt my heart racing. 'So why didn't my father organise this when he was sick in hospital?

'Maybe he didn't think he was going to die.'

'Does she still want to take care of me?'

'Clotilde, you're going to Australia to stay with your mother.'

The blanket fell from around my body.

'Clotilde?'

The date of my departure had been set for July, two days prior to my birthday, which meant the day after I'd land in Melbourne, I would turn thirteen. No one ever gave me a whole country for my birthday. I felt like a princess who'd just inherited the largest kingdom in the world.

When I told the other students at school I was definitely going to Australia, they pretended they didn't care. But I could tell by the glint in their eyes they were jealous. We all dreamed of America when we watched westerns on television. Australia wasn't America, but it was close enough. As long as I could ride my horse to school and turn crispy brown in summer, I'd be happy.

But most of all, I was excited, and a little scared, of getting to meet the mother I remembered nothing about. Louise had been incapable of telling me a little more about my mother than what she had already told me. She wasn't the one who had spoken to my mother on the phone, she insisted, and even if she had, apparently the conversation had been of a short duration and formal in context.

Rhonda.

Even her name sounded like a name borne by a warrior princess.

I dreamed of my mother strolling amongst muscle-bound naked men, flowers in her hair, merging into the sea like the strong river her name carried. I dreamed of my dark hair turning fiercely blonde, the colour of the sun in wintertime. In my dreams I smelled the ocean of a far-away world, where a happy, nomadic race lived a carefree existence amongst an exotic wildlife delineated by the hand of God.

CHAPTER FIVE

A week after Easter I met David.

I'd seen David before in the concrete-and-steel courtyard of our school, reading by himself instead of joining groups of boys who were either playing soccer using rubbish bins as goal posts, or hanging around and shouting provocative comments every time girls walked past.

I distantly admired the strong, silent types, the bookworms, those who had no need to draw attention to themselves by being loud and obnoxious. The mysterious mind is more fascinating than the extrovert one—it doesn't need to hide behind a mask of performance to seek acceptance amongst its peers.

I could tell by the way David looked that he must have been in form three or four—dark hair curled up at the back of his shirt, neatly-trimmed side-burns, and an indifference to the mismatch colours of his clothes. His eyes were as blue and translucent as the chlorinated water of our local swimming pool. There was sadness in them, which reminded me of my father's eyes. He had a brown mole the size of a five-centimes piece on his right cheek, which made him even more fascinating. He wore gold-rimmed glasses and ash corduroys, from which he kept picking invisible fragments of lint while reading his book.

I walked past him a few times and hoped he would notice me, but he was too self-absorbed in his reading to give me even two seconds of attention. And of course, the more he ignored me, the more determined I became to get to know him.

One night I stood naked in front of the mirror of the communal showers at the orphanage and wondered what a boy of his age would see in me. Would he find me attractive? The thought of being attractive to someone of the opposite sex had only occurred to me when Martine introduced me to make-up. I styled my hair in a variety of ways and tried to imitate the hairstyles of women I'd seen in magazines. Self-consciously, I puzzled over the size of my breasts. Martine told me boys were all after the same thing. If the 'same thing' was the size of my breasts, then I'd lost the battle even before I started. If love was a game, then I had yet to learn the rules.

Since I began secondary school, I'd been wearing jeans, but now that I was trying to get David to notice me, I began wearing dresses.

It was spring—flowers hanging from balconies, blossoming in trees, adorning shop windows and offices, worn on hats and braided in hairstyles—so my wearing of summer dresses wasn't so out-of-season, even though some days were still chilly when I left for school. I avoided wearing make-up altogether after the drastic backlash from my father when I visited him at the hospital. David seemed conservative—someone who went around looking like a slut probably would have repulsed him the way loud boys repulsed me.

My conversion from jeans to dresses did get me the unwarranted attention of other boys in my class, which I diligently ignored. In my eyes David was a man—mature, sophisticated and intellectual, while boys my age were nothing more than drooling puppies. I was naturally more attracted to intelligence than Marilyn Manson, body piercing and blatant flirtatious behaviour.

My father had taught me well. Delving into Proust's novels seemed to have filled me with an understanding of human behaviour, but no amount of reading enriched me with the practical skills that dealt with matters of the heart. I was cursed with the same fate that awaited those who had yet to fall in love for the first time, children in many cases—untamed hearts giving themselves unconditionally to those whose promises of love seemed more real and more attainable than the dreams of the world we lived in.

Not being able to get David's attention kept me awake at odd hours of the night. I tossed and turned and concocted cunning ways to get to meet him 'by accident'. I thought of tripping over myself while walking past him, or dropping an entire pile of books, which I carried from the library, or asking for the direction of one room or another. But the more ideas entered my feverish imagination, the more they seemed laboured and transparent. By the time daylight filtered through the yellow drapes of my bedroom, I realised no matter what plan I would choose to execute, I would only end up looking like a fool.

I thought about my mother in Australia and tried to convince myself I should avoid a meaningful friendship with David because in three months time I would have to decide between him and her. I'd only recently prayed to God to never let me fall in love, and yet I couldn't disregard a fiery desire to get David to know me. Was this love? If it was, then God hadn't really answered my prayer. God chose to torment my soul instead, the way he had tormented that of my father.

When school was over for the day, kids hung around the high, steel front gate to chat or to wait for their parents. Mopeds, Vespas and motorcycles under 50cc were parked just outside the school grounds, their owners, mostly boys in oversized tee-shirts and baggy trousers, smoking cigarettes to look cool and waiting to pick up their girlfriends or for a chance to flirt with some fresh innocent faces.

I hated the crowd so much I stayed behind at the school library for another fifteen minutes or so before making my way home. It was also a good time to return the books I'd borrowed and to amass more books I would never find the time to read.

One Thursday in September I'd just come back from the library with a copy Proust's *Pastiche et Mélange,* where Proust willingly attempts imitating the works of writers he worships. I checked the time on my cheap watch and decided to get back to the orphanage —too many books and not enough time. I wanted to know more about the world, about people, about ideas, about cultures, about art, about myself.

I passed the high steel gate of the school, my backpack hanging from one shoulder, and removed a packet of cigarettes from one of its side pockets.

Most of the crowd had now vanished, and only a few students remained behind because their parents were late picking them up, or because they had nothing to look forward to by going home early. I wondered what it would be like to have a mother picking me up from school, to have a caring person welcoming me at home with a cooked meal, to know that no matter how difficult the day had been, she would have enough love in her heart to appease my thirst for adulation—a love unconditional and plentiful like the rays of the sun on a hot summer day.

I removed the silver foil from the packet of cigarettes, pulled out a Gitane and cornered myself against the concrete wall separating the school yard from the street to stop the wind from extinguishing the flame from my lighter. I inhaled the strong cigarette. The smoke ripped through my lungs like fists against flesh and made me cough.

The sun cut shyly between grey clouds and bathed my world in a dull light, as if someone had forgotten to turn off the lamp on a side-table just before falling asleep. The air was crisp and smelled like freshly washed strawberries, but not cold enough for me to bother with wearing a jumper. I stood alone in a blue cotton dress that sat on my thighs—a willing victim of the current fashion trends in spite of my willingness to exert my independence.

The nicotine travelled quickly through my nervous system and settled effectively but temporarily the anxieties I carried with me throughout my school day. Cigarettes provided me with a sense of independence, and since I was forbidden to smoke them, the vice seemed even more satisfying. I wanted to be an adult more than anything in the world—I would smoke and drink and eat, and indulge in anything I desired without having to listen to the voices of authority. People kept telling me cigarettes were bad and I would become addicted. But I was young and I didn't care—if I did become addicted, at least something in life would permanently become a part of me.

I'd just taken my third drag when someone appeared beside me without warning.

'Shouldn't be smoking at your age,' he said. 'Mind if I have one?'

It was David. For a moment I though it might have been one of my teachers patrolling the area to catch nicotine-addicted teenagers in the act and later on delight in reporting them to the school principal as if they were career criminals who were responsible for everything that was wrong with this world.

The teachers on yard duties sometimes reminded me of the undercover cops I saw in American films as they silently monitored the school yard and beyond, knitted fingers behind their backs, blending in with the crowd, visiting boys and girls toilets and entering cubicles without warning to catch daring juveniles. Some kids were known to spend every Wednesday in detention because they had smoked one cigarette—just for claiming their right to slow self-destruction. The price of independence was costly, but some acts were worth getting in trouble for no matter how harsh the repercussion.

'*Merde*, you scared the hell out of me,' I said and felt heat on my face. I fumbled with my cigarette and nearly dropped it to the ground.

'Sorry, I didn't mean to,' he said.

Today, he wore green corduroys and a *Tintin-et-Milou*-printed tee-shirt. His dark hair seemed longer up-close than from a distance. The mole on his cheek was slightly hairy, but his complexion was flawless, a rarity in the young world of my existence. Fortunately, I was also one of the lucky ones who had escaped the acne invasion, but at my age, everything was still possible. Dormant microscopic pus volcanoes were waiting to erupt under the germinal cells of my face, where they would eventually turn my nose, forehead and cheeks into a battle-zone. The many secret joys of puberty were yet to unfold.

My heart was thundering, but I tried to remain calm and in control of my lecherous emotions. I had prayed for this day for weeks, and it suddenly caught me off-guard like the jaws of a hunter's trap crushing through the bones of a helpless hare.

I sucked obsessively on my cigarette and said, 'Here, have this one.'

He took it and I lit up another one for myself.

There was an awkward silence for the next fifteen seconds, as we absorbed the significance of this shared moment.

'I've seen you in the school yard,' he said. His voice was dripping honey. 'You're that girl who keeps walking around by yourself with a ton of books under her arms.'

And all along I thought he never noticed me.

'Yes, I've seen you too, you're the reader.'

He took a drag from his cigarette, inhaled the smoke fully and exhaled it through his nose. He didn't even twitch. 'You should have come up and talked to me instead of just walking past.'

'What do you mean?'

'Every day during recess, you walk past and try to catch my eye.'

The heat on my face had gone up by a couple of notches. I took three drags in succession and flicked the hardly-consumed cigarette to the ground. I stepped on the butt, my eyes cast downwards.

He went on, 'And by the way, you do look good in a dress, I did notice that too.'

He wasn't as shy as I first made him out to be. Maybe it was a good thing—I wasn't sure now that he was so close to me.

'I'm David.'

'Clotilde.'

We shook hands—his grip firm, mine flimsy.

'My parents seem to have forgotten I exist,' he said. 'They usually pick me up straight after school. I'll have to walk instead. Would you like to walk me home?'

'Yes,' I said without the slightest hesitation. I had no idea where he lived, and whether it was in the same direction as the orphanage, but I didn't care. After weeks of fretful anticipation, he could have lived right on the other side of the Rhine—a good hour's walk from where we were standing—and I would still have followed him like a puppy on a leash.

His spine was slightly curved—scoliosis, he would later on inform me—as if he was carrying the world and all its misfortunes on his shoulders. The frown on his face gave him substance and depth because happy people are never as interesting as those crippled by anxieties.

'Where do you live?' he asked.

'Down the other side, near the *aérodrome*.'

He asked me about my family, and I lied. I told him my father was a doctor and my mother an optometrist. I told him I had an older brother who was studying law at university. He was impressed—I could tell by the way his eyes turned into marbles.

'My parents are factory workers,' he said with what seemed to be all honesty. 'They don't see the value of books. They've never had an education. They want me to complete my CAP so I can get a trade. I want to study at the *Lycée* and obtain my *baccalauréat*. They are supportive, but they also think I'm trying to be someone I can never be—they say I am rejecting their values, that I think I'm better than they are. But it's not true. I just want to do something with my life.'

'What are you going to study?'

'I want to become a *Professeur de Littérature*.'

Now I wanted to tell him I lied, I didn't have any parents to go home to, and I knew what it was like when everyone had lost faith in you, and in return you have lost faith in the world. I wanted to tell him my parents had also forgotten about me—permanently. My father was dead and I had no idea whether my mother ever loved me. I wanted to tell him I was the last person in the world—a child forgotten in the darkness of the last hour of the coldest day of winter.

But now we had found one another like two survivors of a plane crash. He was fifteen and I was twelve, and we could still shape our destiny any way we dreamt. We would walk side-by-side through the puzzle of life. We were young. There was still hope, even if the rest of the world had stopped believing in us.

I wanted to tell him my views of life, but they were so confused and messed up I didn't how to begin, so I kept to myself.

When we got to his place—a fourth-floor apartment on Avenue Aristide Briand in a post-war construction designed to pack people together like laboratory mice—we stopped at the entrance of the foyer and faced one another.

'Want to come in?' he asked. 'I can make coffee and jam sandwiches. In spite of what I've said, my parents are pretty cool—they'll like you.'

'No, it's getting late, my folks are going to worry.'

The words had come out too fast. I swallowed my tongue like a modest warrior swallows her pride.

I had fantasised for weeks for David to invite me to his place, where we would cuddle and he would give me my first kiss, the one I would remember for the rest of my life because the first one will always and forever be the first one.

'Okay, then,' he said, 'I'll see you at school tomorrow.'

'Sure.'

'And don't be a stranger.'

We stood near the front door of the foyer like two dogs a little afraid of one another. He locked his eyes with mine, and I thought he was going to kiss me. Instead he removed a set of keys from the pocket of his jeans and inserted the longest one into the lock of the door. He turned the key and pushed the door opened.

'*Au revoir,*' he said.

The door shut in my face like a punch.

I pulled another cigarette from my bag and lit it with hands trembling like autumn leaves struggling to hang on to a summer forever gone.

That night I hardly slept. I sat on my bed and let the tip of my cigarette glow in the darkness of the room. David's face flashed in front of my eyes like falling stars. I wanted to know him the way people know the sun is going to rise the next day. I'd never kissed a boy, but in my mind's eyes, I knew he should have been my first kiss.

When morning came, I was so tired I arrived half an hour late for school and was in a trance-like state almost through the entire class of religious study. Monsieur Silvain, our teacher ignored me, partly because he knew my father well, and partly because he didn't care to inflict discipline on anyone attending his classes. Religious studies was the only subject that was not run as a military regime. We were even allowed to bring lollies and consume them while he was lecturing. No one argued with anyone. Religious study was like a big family on Christmas Eve, where everyone successfully pretended to be happy.

I sat at the back of the class and focused my attention at a large, Roman numeral clock that hung behind the teacher's desk. The seconds felt like minutes, and the minutes like hours. I watched the big needle of the seconds going around and around for what seemed to be infinity. The minute hand crawled so slowly around the circumference of the clock, at times it felt as if it were running backwards. How cruel it felt to be forced to sit in a room with other people my age and be subjected to endless boredom.

Voices around me were muffled like in a dream. I wanted to close my eyes and be taken away to another world. I daydreamed about David and Australia, the two of us riding virgin beaches set against the bluest ocean. I smelled the salt in the air and grabbed a fistful of white sand.

I must have fallen asleep because the last half hour of class whisked past me like a gentle summer wind. The school bell jolted me from my slumber and forced to gather my thoughts. Other students around me were packing their school belongings into their bags whilst chatting amongst themselves, looking forward to the next half hour of recess. I hadn't taken any notes during the entire class and hastily copied the homework instructions written on the blackboard into my school diary.

Just as I was about to leave the class, Monsieur Silvain called me, 'Mademoiselle Benoît?'

I turned around and feared he was about to caution me for dosing off in class. 'Yes?'

'My condolences about your father.'

David was sitting in his usual spot, a book in his hand, and looked as if he had full control of his life and his environment. Today, he hadn't bothered with the gold-rimmed spectacles , which gave him an air of wisdom and authority beyond his school years. Maybe he didn't really need them after all, and only wore them to project an image of intellect. The effect certainly made an impression on me.

I held Proust's *Pastiche et Mélange* tightly against my chest and let my anxiety eat me up like raw fruit. David didn't see me approach the stairs where he was sitting..

'*Salut, le lecteur,*' I said.

He looked up and smiled. 'I was hoping you would come.'

I sat next to him in a nonchalant manner, as if I'd known him all my life. I pretended to be completely comfortable with our second meeting, but my nerves and emotions collided with one another like two speeding vehicles coming head-to-head on a busy highway. I couldn't believe how nervous I was. I thought that after thinking about David all night, I would be casual about meeting him again. But instead I felt as if we had never met.

A group of boys sitting near the bike shed noticed us. They chatted and giggled amongst themselves. One of them yelled, '*Les amoureux!*' The lovers. I wished.

'Don't worry about them,' David said, 'they talk but they're pretty harmless. They're just kids.'

'I know,' I said as if I were not a kid myself.

I showed him the book I was reading, and he seemed surprised.

'It's rare for someone of your age to be reading Proust,' he said. 'I only began reading him last year.'

He was reading Proust.

I was reading Proust.

Destiny.

I stood up. 'I'm dying for a cigarette. Do you think we could go for a walk instead of hanging around here?'

We had half an hour for recess, and students were expected to remain in the school yard, but many hung around the front gates of the school. The teachers choose to close an eye because it was probably easier than getting into arguments on a daily basis.

He grabbed his books. 'Okay, let's go for a walk.'

Ten minutes from school, there was a park where people walked their dogs or strolled around by themselves to unwind from the morning's work. I was hungry, but David mentioned nothing about food, so I kept my hunger to myself like a shameful sin.

When we arrived at the park, the greenery around us smelled like bees and honey, thick and sweet with love and hope for the world. Birds hidden in beeches were singing the simple joy of existence. Nature seemed so uncomplicated and yet so perfect.

David liked French and literature best, which did not really surprise me since he had already told me he wanted to become a professor of literature.

I told him I liked English. Not totally true, but I didn't want to tell him because of my hidden agenda of moving to Australia, I'd forced myself to better my English. If he'd knew I had to leave the country in three months time, maybe he wouldn't bother with me.

We sat under a beech, our backs against the trunk. The air was mild and the sky almost clear. Two old women in long coats walked past us and whispered as if they were revealing some life-long secrets hidden during all those years in a concealed closet they kept under lock at the back of their minds.

'I love spring,' David said and took a deep breath. 'Everything is so alive.'

'Me too.' I paused and added, 'Spring is the season for lovers.'

He just smiled and I felt heat on my face.

I wanted to make hold his hand but I was too scared he would laugh at me. What if he just wanted to be friends? What if I'd read everything wrong? What if everything I felt was not what he felt?

Come on, do something.

My head was resting comfortably against his shoulder, so I took a chance and placed my hand in his. He offered no resistance whatsoever. It felt like the most natural thing in the world. Neither of us said a word as the rays of the sun caressed us with its warmth like a parent blankets a child from the cold.

For two weeks David and I were seen everywhere together. We spent recess sitting on the stone steps near the cafeteria and read our books or talked about our classes. Other girls at school called him my boyfriend even though we had never done anything more than just hang around together. I told them he was just a friend. But deep down, I knew he was more than just a friend. He was the only boy I could really talk to without feeling as if my world would fall apart.

One night, alone in my room, I was trying to figure out how I was going to admit I had lied to him about my parents. The following day I told myself this was the day when the truth had to come out, but by the time I arrived at school I was too afraid he would feel shattered by my betrayal and leave me. If I had started our friendship with a lie, how many more lies would I be willing to tell just to keep him by my side?

Fear of rejection was seeded deep inside me, and all the courage in the world would have not sufficed to persuade me the truth would set me free. I hadn't been close to anyone since the death of my father, and it was only now I realised I'd spent a rather lonely existence for almost a year. I'd gotten used to David too quickly. He was now part of my every day life, like the air I breathed and the food I consumed. He provided me with the emotional stability I'd been searching for since my father had left me. He was a huge emotional layer sheltering me from the outside elements and the uncertainty of life.

I thought about the mother I had yet to meet. How would I find the strength to leave David for the unknown? Just as I hadn't told him about my parents, I hadn't told him about Australia. Was that a lie too? Ideally, I would have taken him with me to this mysterious country, but I knew this was an impossible fantasy. He had his life and his dreams to follow, and we would be seen as too young for anyone to take us seriously.

I turned off the light by my side table and let the darkness of the night drown my dreams.

One afternoon, right after school, David invited me to his apartment. His parents had gone out for the evening, so we were left by ourselves to do as we pleased. David and his parents were the only ones living in the apartment. It was a spacious dwelling—four bedrooms, a lounge room, a living room and an entertainment room, all smelling of cinnamon and home-baked bread. I was surprised by how much space three people could occupy, and I could easily picture myself as one of the family. I was also astonished at how different the place looked inside compared to what I had been expecting. I'd imagined a cramped lifestyle because the grey, stoned building reflected that from the outside. David explained how the apartment used to be rented to someone important, so the rich owners had added an additional room from the apartment next door by changing doors on the walls. This meant David's neighbour had two rooms less than he did.

'How can your parents afford something so big?' I asked. 'I thought they were factory workers?'

'This is housing commission. My father works in Germany, so when the deutschmarks are converted to francs at the end of the month, his salary is twice that of what a factory worker makes in France.'

'But this apartment is so huge. Why don't they move to a smaller place?'

'My sisters have left home,' David explained, 'but my parents like to keep their bedrooms the way they are for whenever they decide to come and visit. They can always stay the night, or if they chose to come back home one day and stay forever, my parents would let them. It was hard on my mother when my sisters left. You know, after having them around for twenty odd years, them vanishing suddenly left an empty gap in our lives.'

I thought it would be nice to have parents who let you come back home, no matter what. David was lucky to have that kind of security in his life.

David's sisters were twins, five years older than him, and both married—from one sugar daddy to another, but I wouldn't realise until years later.

David showed me around the apartment. Each room had a different type of wallpaper. The lounge room was chocolate brown swirls, the dining room bright orange, the hallway green, and the kitchen yellow. A ping-pong table occupied the entertainment room. The furniture in the lounge room was solid wood and good quality. There were wood-carved African figures on the bookshelves, and not a single book in sight. An expensive-looking hi-fi system sat behind a smoked glass partition in the wall unit.

'Where are you parents now?' I asked.

'They're visiting a friend of my mother who's in hospital. She's had a nervous break-down.'

Just the word *hospital* made me feel sick. An image of my father on his deathbed came to mind. I pushed it away like bad food and focused on my surroundings.

David showed me his bedroom. There was a single bed, a small white desk with a red chair and matching lamp, bookshelves filled with books, comics, Star Wars figurines and Matchbox cars. Sweetness hung in the air, like roasted chestnuts.

There was a poster of Heath Ledger with long hair and a denim shirt. The actor had just made it big with *Knight's Tale*. His real-live lover was also an Australian—a gorgeous blonde with blue eyes. I wondered if that's how my mother looked. Her name was Noami Watts, and I had seen pictures of her on the cover of various magazines. She looked so pretty, it made me envious.

David did an interpretation of Britney Spears. He cranked the volume up on his portable CD player and swung his pelvis to the hit single *I'm Not a Girl, Not Yet a Woman*. He sang to the lyrics, but he didn't know English, so he just made up sounds, which sounded like English. He made me laugh so much I thought my bladder was going to burst. Tears rolled down my face like big pearls of joy.

We sat on the bed and tried to figure out what the lyrics in the songs meant. We played the record over and over. It was hard to understand. The English on the record was different from the one we learned at school. David said it was because Britney sang in American English, and at school we were taught British English. It all sounded like mumbo jumbo to me.

And then, without warning, he pushed my hair back and kissed me on the forehead. I had hoped something like that would happen, but it still took me by surprise.

He kissed me down the side of my face and moved closer to my mouth. I tried to catch his eye, but he had them closed. I was facing the wall in front of me. His kisses came close to the corner of my mouth. I knew what I wanted, and I knew it would be easy to get it. I turned my face towards him and held myself still in spite of feeling as if my heart had just exploded. My lips were on fire as he pushed himself towards me. His hands rubbed on the sides of my arms as he kissed me. I felt light-headed at the realisation this was *the* first kiss I had longed for—the one I would remember years later, the one I would keep stored like a photograph at the back of my mind.

His fingers were brushing my tiny breasts while our lips were still touching.

I pulled back gently.

'Don't.'

He ignored me and placed the palm of his hand on my chest, this time with more determination. He squeezed with his fingers and breathed into my neck. He was hurting me.

I was about to protest again but he pressed his lips against mine. The second kiss was as good as the first, maybe even better. I wanted more, but fear gripped me like someone twisting my arm to break it off.

I pushed him gently. 'No, David, I need more time.'

'Come on,' he said. 'We both want this, there's no need to be shy here.'

'I don't want this, David. Why don't we just continue to kiss? That was nice.'

He glared back at me.

'What are you afraid of? I'm not going to hurt you.'

My heart was drilling through my chest. 'You're hurting me.'

And then he rushed out of the room and left me alone on the bed like rubbish one leaves behind.

I thought she was just a friend when I first saw her. David and she were standing by the high steel gate in front of the school, and I had finished early for the day. Our mathematics teacher was sick, and there was no replacement teacher available. We were told we could leave. It was only an hour before school would end, so I was going to wait for David and walk him home.

The sky was cloudless as far as the eye could see, and the temperature in the mid-twenties.

I'd been walking on clouds for days now, since that first kiss in his bedroom. We made up after he stormed out of the room. He said it was all right, and he understood if I had objected about going all the way, I was only twelve, anyway, so he didn't want to pressure me into anything I would regret later on.

Life was good again, and I had decided maybe I didn't want to leave for Australia after all. Even though I wasn't really paying attention to what was going on in class, I didn't mind being there, knowing David was there too, and I would see him during recess. I thought about him all the time, carved his name with my Bic pen on the wooden tables at school, kept staring at the passport photo he gave me so I wouldn't forget what he looked like. His existence told me there might be a place for me in this world after all.

Summer was just around the corner, and we were looking forward to spending more time together. We talked about taking the train down to Provence for the holidays. David had family in Nice and Toulon, and he also had access to a holiday home in Spain, a property bought by several of his relatives as an investment and a way of indulging in a holiday without having to pay for expensive summer rentals. I'd never been to Spain, or anywhere for that matter, and was looking forward to it—just David and me, covered in coconut oil, soaking up the Mediterranean sun, eating Italian ice-cream, strolling hand-in-hand, getting drunk until we couldn't stop laughing.

David was the only person in my life I needed right now, and the only person who made any sense out of all the madness around me.

I crossed the concrete yard and walked towards David and the girl.

The two of them were smoking. She was a blonde with long legs and pointy breasts. From the distance I could see the bright red lipstick and the rouge on her cheeks. Her denim skirt was so short, if she bent down to pick up anything, everyone would have seen the colour of her knickers. I'd never seen her at school before. Maybe she was one of his sisters who'd come to visit—wishful thinking.

But as I got closer, I realised the girl was too young to have been one of his sisters. David's sisters were married, and they wouldn't have dressed in such a provocative manner, parading the streets as if they were selling their bodies and souls. Deep inside I knew what was going on, but I automatically switched on to denial mode.

They didn't see me approaching them.

I was about to call David's name when they kissed. I froze and stared at them. My heart missed a beat.

But he loves me, doesn't he?

Something inside me ruptured as if I'd just swallowed a grenade. All the Proust reading in the world couldn't help me now.

I dropped my bag to the ground and ran back inside the school building, tears streaming down my face.

The following week, I refused to go to school. I wouldn't talk to anyone or explain myself. I stayed at the orphanage alone and began drinking and smoking heavily again.

At times, especially when darkness had fallen over the city, alone in my room, my head filled with the buzzing of alcohol, I could smell the smoke from my father's pipe. I knew he was in the room with me. I noticed him standing next to the window. He just looked down at me, the way he used to from his chair, his eyes filled with pain and pity all at once, his long, bony fingers flicking back a strand of hair, which had fallen, out of place. I wanted to talk to him, but no words came out of my mouth.

And then I dreamed, or at least I thought I did—we were back in the old house, and it was Christmas, and he just stood there and smiled at me. But he was no longer coughing. He just smoked his pipe and filled the air with a bitter-sweet aroma and seemed contented with himself.

And then he lectured me about one thing or another, but I couldn't hear. His voice was trailing off like the sound of a locomotive disappearing down a train track and into the darkness of the woods. I reached for him, but my arms were too short. My fingers were centimetres from his face. I stretched and stretched but couldn't reach.

As he continued to smile and look at me, his eyes were no longer his. They were David's.

And his smile was David's too.

Then his face.

I woke up trembling like dog waiting to be put down.

Someone at school had told Louise I'd been away. She came to see me at the orphanage. No one else did. I'd never told David I lived at the orphanage, so if he ever tried to find me, he would have had to ask around. The only people who really knew where I was were the schoolteachers. I doubted he was going to ask them where I lived. Yet, every day, I was hoping he would walk through the door of my room, beg for forgiveness and cover my face with warm and tender kisses.

I was sitting on the edge my bed, chain-smoking, a pile of Proust's overdue library books by my side. I'd stopped reading the day David cheated on me. People made me so depressed, I didn't even want to read about them. Everybody's lives seemed agonisingly complicated and caged with emotions and lust they had no control over. I didn't want to feel any more. I didn't want to love or hate or need anyone or anything. I wanted to tear my chest open, pull my heart out and throw it against the grey wall facing me. It was nothing more than a traitor's heart.

Empty bottles of wine were lined up against the wall opposite my bed, like soldiers waiting for an inspection. Green ones, brown ones, clear ones, maroon ones. I managed to get the wine from a homeless drunk who slept in the park, not far from the local supermarket. I gave him some of money from my monthly allowance, and he bought two bottles—one for himself and one for me. The wine ended up costing me twice as much, but it was better than not having any at all. I was under-age and could never have purchased it myself.

Louise was sitting next to me on the bed. Her skin smelled of house-grade soap and facial cream. The business attire had gone. It had disappeared the day her husband stole her love from her and never returned it. She wore denims and a tee-shirt like the rest of the world. Her shoulder-length chestnut hair—the blond was gone because she never bothered retouching it—was styled into a ponytail with the help of a common, bone-colour elastic band.

From my bedroom window, I glimpsed the blue sky and heard traffic outside. The days were getting longer and the nights shorter. The world was moving on but I had stopped living. I didn't even know what Louise was doing because I forced myself not to look at her. When she first walked in the room, she didn't say a word but just took her place next to me, her presence oddly comfortable, even though I had no desire to see or to talk to anyone.

She massaged gently the back of my neck with three fingers. I let her do it. No one had touched me for a week, and in spite of my verbal denial I missed human contact—David and I had been so physically close.

'So, what's going on?' she finally asked, her hand still at the back of my neck.

I didn't reply.

'They'll be others, you know.'

I locked my eyes with hers. I read pain in them. At least we had something in common.

'You can't trust them,' she went on, 'one minute they tell you they love you, and the next they're gone. You can't trust any of them.'

I didn't want to believe her. David couldn't have loved that girl. It was me he loved. I knew it from the way he kissed me, the way he looked at me, the conversations we had, the moments we shared together. He would realise he'd made a mistake, and he would come back to me. I was sure of that. I would make him go down on his knees and beg, and he would be forgiven.

I turned my attention back to the window.

She removed her hand from behind my neck. 'You're going to have to let go. You can't let them ruin your life.'

'It's not *them*, it's *him*,' I said.

'You'll be leaving for Australia soon—let it go. School is nearly over. You don't want to repeat another year.'

I didn't care. They could have kept me in secondary school for the rest of my life. I didn't want to grow up any more I didn't want to become accustomed to pain and tell myself everything was going to be all right.

'You're too young to be in love,' she said. 'Give it a few weeks and you'll see things are not as bad as they seem.'

How could people drown in emotional sewerage, gulp mouthfuls of anguish and tell themselves they were living? Her husband stopped loving her, and that was more than a few weeks ago. I hadn't seen her looking any happier. On the surface maybe, but I sensed her pain in every limb in her body. She could deny it all she wanted, but I knew the hurt was caged inside her forever, and she knew it too.

I glared into her eyes for a few seconds. The irises were small and grey. The colour had washed away with the life that was once there.

I lit another cigarette.

'Give me one,' Louise said matter-of-factly.

I passed her mine and lit another for myself.

'Do you still see him?' I asked and turned to face her.

She took a deep a drag from her Gitane and blew a perfect ring. She knitted her brow. 'We tried again, but it didn't work out.'

'How so?'

'It just wasn't the same. Once the trust is gone, you can't get it back.'

I nodded and went on with my smoking.

My room was drowned in a haze. The sunlight from outside filtered itself through the smoke and bathed the air in a surreal atmosphere, as if we were standing at the gates of hell waiting for our fate to take place.

I took her hand in mine and said, 'Do you want a glass of wine?'

We drank the whole bottle.

CHAPTER SIX

Summer came around faster than I had anticipated. The air was maple syrup thick and smelled like freshly-made salad. I was a squirrel who had been hibernating during the winter months and suddenly sneaked out of my hiding place to spend more time outdoors and to gather energy from the white, healing rays of the sun.

Once more I became accustomed to my solitary existence and feared intimacy. I had painfully learned it was the rejection of another human being that was the hardest to bear—not so much the loss.

Louise had arranged my passport and other travel documents because I was too young and incapable of doing it myself. After much deliberation about what to do about David, and further lecturing from Louise, I was resigned to migrating to Australia. I never wanted to go back to school or to see David again because I was still too hurt and too much in love. My mind loathed him for his betrayal, but my heart was blind to it all.

I avoided visiting places where David and I had hung around together because if we'd suddenly met, I feared I would be too weak to reject him. What could you say to someone in whom you had vested your trust and opened your heart, only to watch it bleed as if it'd been torn straight out your chest? What had I done to him to deserve this punishment? Perhaps I should have made love to him that afternoon in his room, and then he would have never cheated on me and looked for love in another girl. Maybe it was me who had failed him by holding back when he wanted the whole of me, not just a relationship which had barely passed the stage of what most people would have described as an intimate friendship.

In my room, Louise filled out yellow immigration forms with my personal details, including who my parents were and the reason why I wanted to leave for Australia. She ticked a box with a black felt pen, confirming my English was competent, even though I couldn't utter a single sentence without tripping over myself.

'Aren't they going to notice?' I asked.

'It's just formalities, it doesn't really matter.'

'What if they want to conduct an interview?'

'I'll do all the talking.'

'Can you speak English?'

'No.'

The summer sun filled the room so brightly, it felt as if we were in a place we'd never been before. I'd never noticed how high the ceiling was or the whiteness of the walls. In artificial lighting my room was a dull grey, like a prison cell designed to promote boredom and an increasingly desperate desire for repentance and freedom.

Louise went on to explain how the forms were standard immigration documents, and how it made no difference what we wrote in them because my only parent was in Australia, and I had every right to be with her regardless of how incompetent I was in English.

My mother had been forewarned of my arrival by phone. This was followed by an official letter sent by certified mail from the welfare division of the Department of Social Security, a section of the *Mairie de Strasbourg*. If she was indeed my mother and no mistakes had been committed in identifying her, I would be granted Australian citizenship without any unnecessary delays. Being born on French soil, I would also retain my French nationality until the day I died. The perks of having dual nationality meant as long as I was in the possession of an Australian passport and a French passport, I'd be able to travel forth and back for the rest of my life without having to fill in forms or explain myself to anyone. Louise clarified these details, which really meant nothing to me at the time.

Midweek Louise and I took an overnight train to Paris to visit the Australian Embassy. The immigration officer who interviewed me had a strong English accent. It was Australian, Louise told me, but I couldn't tell the difference. Much to Louise's and my relief, the interview was conducted entirely in French. My English was never put to the test, saving Louise the embarrassment of explaining why some of the answers on the official immigration application form had been deliberately falsified, specifically those relating to my English proficiency.

Regretfully, our stay in Paris was of short duration, not long enough to even visit the Eiffel Tower. This was a work trip for Louise, not a holiday, so I was told several times when I persisted on spelling out how silly it was to come all the way to Paris without indulging in some sightseeing. I begged her to let me visit the Centre Pompidou, the famous Bois de Boulogne and the Louvre, but my request fell upon death ears. Angry with Louise, I didn't utter a single word all the way back to Strasbourg, and sulked like the child I was and dreaded to be. Not having had the chance to visit Paris made me feel a stranger in my own country.

I hated the way everyone seemed to be rushing from one place to another, as if duty was always so important that living life had to be placed on a back burner. We existed in a world where experiences no longer mattered, where every action had to be justified by reasoning, productivity and end-results. I was young but I could already see the madness of it all.

Halfway between Paris and Strasbourg I wanted to jump off the train and spend an hour breathing the night air and gazing at the stars, the way my ancestors would have taken the time to do thousands of years ago when man and nature were still one.

Night time was the hardest. I lay in bed and tried to drink myself to sleep to no avail. All the alcohol did was intensify the string-pulling sensation of my despair and grated my nerves raw until they bled like open wounds. Sleep was replaced by drowsiness, and then, without any warning, the first ray of the sun seeped through the curtains and bathed my room in shades of amber and yellow, like photographic filters capturing the portentous essence of light. The sun on my face was an angel's wing flapping gently against the cold, outer layer of my skin, a reminder the outside world was as real as the despair I found when questioning too long and too hard the esoteric value of my existence.

As the days followed the nights, I chain-smoked to give myself a sense of control over some aspect of my life.

Like the wine, I was too young to buy cigarettes, so I hand-wrote a note from a fictitious father authorising his daughter to buy him a packet of cigarettes. I placed the note in a yellow, sealed envelope with the correct change and handed it over to the tobacco shop owner, a man in his early fifties with salt-and-pepper hair who reminded me of the singer Serge Gainsbourg. Like Gainsbourg, the tobacco shop owner looked permanently drunk and had a cigarette hanging from the corner of his mouth. His blue shirt was open halfway down his chest, revealing a serious amount of white body hair, and his complexion was raw hamburger.

I liked the way the shop smelled of ink and paper, tobacco and cheap aftershave. I liked the colourful row of lighters displayed in a smoked glass cabinet underneath the counter—the paraphernalia associated with smoking was as addictive as smoking itself.

The first time I tried to buy cigarettes from him, he grilled me.

'Your father wrote that note, did he?' He eyed me as if I were a professional forger, all while waving the note up in the air like a little tricolour, national flag—blue, white, red—the type used to cheer cyclists in Le Tour de France. But I did my best at looking as innocent as a choir girl on Sunday morning, my eyes cast down to the smoked glass cabinet, and then up at him, mimicking the expression of a cocker spaniel who had been deprived of food for an entire week. I even felt heat on my face, but that might have been more from the position I had found myself in rather than my attempt at acting innocently. I was still an apprentice in the art of lying, but I knew with practice I would eventually become as confident and as arrogant as Martine.

'Yes, he wrote it,' I said.

Silence cut through the air like a giant circular saw.

He took a drag from his cigarette, his blood-shot eyes smiling at me as if he'd figured out my little scam. I thought he was going to scream, jump over the counter and pin me to the floor until the police arrived and took me away and threw me in a two-by-three cell for the next fifteen years of my life. Juvenile delinquent sentenced for obtaining cigarettes by deception—front banner of *Les Dernières Nouvelles D'Alsace*, the daily paper of the province.

Then without warning, Gainsbourg turned his back on me and snatched a blue packet of Gitane from the dispenser. He slammed the packet on the counter as if he'd just squashed a mosquito about to draw blood.

'If you get me in trouble,' he said, 'it's going to cost you more

70

than the price of cigarettes.' There was spit at the corner of his mouth.

I nodded and maintained my innocent look as if his threat was of no consequence to my deed. It was common practice amongst busy parents to purchase cigarettes through their kids with a note of authorisation. Still, the shopkeeper could never be certain as to the genuineness of the hand-written document.

After this first incident, cigarettes were easy; Gainsbourg never questioned the contents of my envelope. In fact, he had already pulled the packet of Gitane from the dispenser behind him as soon as I had walked in the shop. In less than ten seconds, I was back in the street, much to his contentment and my relief.

I smoked first thing in the morning. I smoked after breakfast. I smoked after lunch. I smoked at three o'clock. I smoked under the Cathedral. I smoked by the Rhine. I smoked outside the local supermarket. I smoked in the park.

I smoked.

Weeks went by, and Strasbourgeois migrated south for the holidays. I was doomed to stay in my birth town in spite of having looked forward to spending the summer in Provence with David. I occupied my days strolling through the centre of Strasbourg, visiting the Cathedral Notre Dame, walking along the banks of the Rhine, spending my afternoons at the Musée de L'Œuvre Notre-Dame, the Château des Rohan, the Musée Historique, or enjoying the Park de L'Orangerie with its shaded paths, flowerbeds, children's playgrounds and its famous swan-dotted lake.

The city was scarce of people, other than German tourists and retirees, who made the most of the few months of sun that bathed the region of Alsace.

From the sixty-six-metre-high platform of the fragile-looking Gothic Cathedral—which took the effort of climbing a 330-step spiral staircase—I revelled to an unspoiled stork's-eye view of Strasbourg and its adjoining suburbs. I never realised how vast Strasbourg was. The high-rise buildings were on the edge of the town and clearly visible. The city was a contradiction of architecture—half-timbered medieval houses and the newly-build concrete-and-steel Palais de L'Europe, home of the European Parliament—and seemed to be confused as to which century it

71

belonged.

Spending the long days of summer by myself, I still thought a lot about David, and, in spite of his infidelity, I missed him awfully. Many a time I wished we were a couple again, walking hand-in-hand in the park, debating and reading literature, drinking hot chocolate by the cathedral, listening to CDs in his room. I was about to turn thirteen, but already I felt emotionally drained from all I had experienced.

My despair came in waves and gradually peaked towards the end of the week, when I was mostly drunk for a good part of the Saturday and Sunday. The anticipation of leaving for Australia and seeing my mother kept me from slashing my wrists once more.

I wanted to die but I longed for happiness too much to dare.

One sunny Friday afternoon, Louise took me shopping with my father's money—a substantial amount according to a variety of sources, including gossip running around the school yard from fellow students whose source of information was gossip spread by their own parents. For a town with just over 300,000 people, everyone seemed to know everybody else's business.

We were at Bata, a popular footwear chain store, looking for a pair of shoes when I questioned Louise on the matter.

'You must know how much money my father has left me?' I said and tried on a pair of Roman-styled sandals.

'I can't be certain—it's confidential, even if you're only a minor, your privacy is protected.'

'So you have no idea?'

'I heard it was somewhere in the six figures.'

I stood up and walked around with the sandals. I stepped forth and back like a duckling tackling its first awkward steps.

'How do they feel?' Louise asked.

'Hurts a bit at the ankles.'

'Let's try the next size up.'

I sat on the chair again and removed the sandals.

'So, if my father had so much money, why did we live in a cramped apartment?'

'Maybe he was saving it.'

'For what?'

'For you when you're older.'

'Well, I'm older now. Can't I have it?'

'His will states you can't touch it before you turn eighteen. He's left a generous allowance for your everyday expenses.'

We gave up with the sandals and went to a shop next door where they sold bags of all sizes and shapes.

'Who's got the money then?' I asked.

'Your mother will manage your finances until you're old enough to take care of yourself.'

I slid on a blue-and-red backpack and looked at myself in the full- length mirror to observe how it hung on my bony frame.

Louise checked the price tag. 'This one looks good.'

I could get virtually any item I wanted because it wasn't Louise who was paying for it, but myself.

At a department store, I choose summer clothes in spite of Louise's warning it was winter in Australia. As if I had a choice in the matter. Finding winter clothes in the midst of a French summer was like seeking a jug of water in the middle of a sand storm.

'I'm going to miss you,' she said as we returned to her car, our arms filled with paper bags from various boutiques and speciality shops, and my back aching from having done too much walking.

I didn't reply. I wanted to believe her, but I didn't. She was being paid to be with me. It wasn't a conscious decision, and if she'd had the choice and didn't have to make a living like everybody else, she'd probably have chosen never to meet me. I was draining her of her positive energy, or whatever was left of it. Her look was solemn, no matter how hard she tried to paint it with the colours of summer. Her smile was forced like that of a street-performing clown on a miserable rainy day.

Louise was attractive in her own way, but sadness had etched away the prettiness from her face, the way it did on children who grew up abused by their parents. I knew I must have looked just as drained as her because we shared the same tortured spirit. To be unloved and then loved, and then unloved again was the cruellest game people inflicted on one another.

'You can always come and visit,' I said.

She merged the car into traffic, not bothering to use her indicator. 'I couldn't afford it. I'm barely making a living as it is.'

'You don't give a shit—you're just like everyone else. I'm just your bread and butter.'

'Don't be so cynical. I'll write to you, I promise.'

That same night, I wrote in my diary. It had been a year since I had bothered with an entry, and when I looked at the last page I had written, the writing seemed childish and messy, even though I had applied myself at the time. Creating letters with a fountain pen was difficult—the pressure applied to the head of the pen had to be exact, or too much ink blotted out from the cartridge and stained the page.

I carefully wrote Louise's name at the bottom of a virgin, white page and sketched her face above it. I used a new blue Pelican cartridge, which I had inserted in my Mont Blanc fountain pen the previous day. It was an unpretentious line portrait, but I did manage to capture accurately the hurt in her eyes; irises half-concealed by the weight of her eyelids, crows feet prematurely etched where there was once nothing but skin as smooth as cream. The ink smelled like vinegar and sugar but reminded me of chalk and wooden school benches.

I drank straw-like flavoured wine and stared into her eyes. The more I drank, the more the eyes came to life and blinked at me—tears welled up like an overflowing river, excruciating pain jabbing at the back of my skull as if an invisible hand was forcing a knitting needle through its centre.

Two pairs of eyes cried in unison, sharing a flood of superfluous memories, which chained us to an unbearable existence of solitude and self-defeating temperament.

Fat tears smudged the drawing. Blue ink covered my fingertips as I caressed her face the way my father had often caressed mine in times of sadness and confusion.

I emptied my glass of white wine.

Maybe I would miss her after all.

CHAPTER SEVEN

The flight to Australia took just over twenty-four hours. I felt every single one of them. Frankfurt to Melbourne via Los Angeles, Auckland and Sydney.

Sleeping was virtually impossible because every time we crossed a different time zone, we were woken up and fed plastic-tasting food served on small, white, plastic-looking trays. I ate dinner at three in the morning, breakfast at ten at night and lunch at six in the evening. In all, six meals had been served—two breakfasts, two lunches and two dinners. We ate half-sized sausages with small packets of sweet tomato sauce with Heinz written on them, mini spuds with herbs and corncobs swimming in a buttery cream. We ate cardboard-tasting cereals for breakfast and drank coffee. We ate water crackers and New-Zealand cheeses with French names for lunch and drank soft drinks from small aluminium cans. I wanted wine but I was too young so the stewardess wouldn't allow it.

I was sitting between an old woman and a businessman with thinning hair, his cranium polished like an eggshell. The businessman slept for most of the flight, his face pressed against the glass of the window as if it were a pillow. The old woman read the glossy in-flight magazine from cover to cover. The businessman didn't finish his wine so I finished it without him noticing. The wine tasted warm like oak, and I realised I missed drinking even though it had been less than twenty-four hours since my last glass of wine. What had begun as just-for-the-time-being type of drinking had increasingly evolved into part of my daily nutritional requirement.

All my belongings fitted into the blue-and-red backpack Louise bought with my money. Three dresses, two pairs of jeans and tee-shirts, seven changes of underwear, seven pairs of socks, two pairs of stockings, two cheap toothbrushes, toothpaste, make-up and toiletries, two Proust novels in French, a photo of my father and my diary. I nearly took a photo of David with me, but at the last minute I removed it from my bag and tossed it in the waste basket next to my bed at the orphanage.

The businessman next to me snored. I realised how lost I was in the world—a kitten drowning in a bathtub of despair. If I disappeared, no one would ever notice. I had never met my mother, so it wouldn't be like she'd feel the difference. Those who might have missed me had already vanished from my life—Louise, Martine and my father. And maybe even David, who had managed somehow to tangle himself in my heart's web in spite of my willingness to try to forget him.

The businessman was blocking the view. I wished I'd been sitting on the window side so as to have a better glimpse of the outside world at a high altitude—stars in the darkness of the night hanging like Chinese lanterns lighting up the world; clouds disguised as gigantic cotton wool pillows for the gods to rest their weary minds; tiny cities thousands of metres below where people gathered together at dinner tables or in front of a television set and pretended to be alive.

I felt sick at every take off and whenever I finished eating. I wanted to throw up but the food sat in my stomach like a hot iron. I wanted to throw up over the businessman. I wanted to throw up over the old woman and her magazine. I wanted them to notice me. I felt as insignificant as the seat I was sitting on.

We stopped in Los Angeles and Auckland. Day and night dissolved into one like milk and coffee. I had lost complete sense of time and space. My watch read three in the afternoon, but outside the Los Angeles airport lounge darkness filled the air as if the ink from my fountain pen had leaked into the stratosphere.

Halfway through the flight, I was bored, so I read a laminated information card detailing the technical aspects of the plane I was travelling on. The Boeing 747 was measured in pounds and feet and inches. A chart listed the various altitudes the Boeing was flying at during the progressive stages of our voyage. I had no idea how far up we were in the air. I'd been brought up on the metric system, and the English and Americans hadn't caught up yet. The drawings on the card showed smiling passengers, even when the plane crashed and went down into the vast, hungry mouth of the ocean. I wished I could look that happy in the face of death.

I placed the information card back into the slot provided in the seat in front of me.

For fifteen minutes I locked myself in the cubicle and smoked my Gitane cigarettes. The cubicle was a metre by a half metre, so I sat on the toilet bowl, the lid down. I wondered what happened to the human waste. Did they store it somewhere in the plane, or did it come straight out of a pipe between the undercarriages? What were the odds of walking the dog and being showered by someone's shit falling from the sky?

I sucked on my cigarette, closed my eyes and prayed for the plane to crash.

CHAPTER EIGHT

My mother was shorter than my father had described her. Maybe she'd lost some height over the years, or my father's memory had her confused with another woman he met earlier in his life. I didn't really believe the latter because my father had never showed any indication that he was even mildly interested in women, other than my mother, and that certainly was true during the period of time after she vanished from his life until the day he died. If he did maintain a covert interest in women, he must have gone to great length to hide it. Or it must have been at a time when I was too young to really know what was going on around me.

There were still many secrets between my parents my father had deliberately chosen to hold back from me. And then there were those questions, which I asked myself but never shared with him. Why didn't he just go back to my mother if he loved her so much? Why had he loved God more than her when she gave me life? How could he have let me grow-up without a mother, knowing he could have provided me with one if he'd stopped being so self-absorbed in his calling? I reasoned that the choices he made in life had been grounded on the strong faith of his conviction, and all I could do was trust in the path he chose to follow and believe if there had been a better way to deal with the situation he had found himself in, he would have chosen it.

I wondered whether I really wanted my mother to unveil the secrets she and my father had kept sealed for so long. Love seemed too complicated to bother with—I'd learned that much already, and now I wished I hadn't.

My mother was blonde, but not natural blonde—dark roots were showing and soon she'll be due for a re-touch. I was slightly disappointed because my father had gone to great length to elaborate on the blondness and texture of her hair, the way people tell you with genuine but inflated enthusiasm about the newborn in their lives.

Her complexion was speckled with freckles, and she wore little make-up other than pale blue eye shadow and red lipstick. She had a button nose and tulip lips and a high-pitched voice. Her arms were bony, and I imagined them snapping as easily as matchsticks if she ever got into a fight with someone. She wore jeans and an undersized, marine blue cardigan that emphasised the size of her breasts, as if she had to prove to the world than she was still attractive after time and youth had gone past her like a week-long packaged holiday in a remote island in the Pacific.

She picked me up from the airport with a man called Michael —a name I couldn't even pronounce properly, my tongue travelling back and forth between my palate and the back of my throat like cold spinach forced-fed to a five-year old. I didn't ask who he was, but they were making the type of body language I had seen with couples—a tilt of the head, a swing of a hand, a blink of an eye, finger-brushing each other's arms. Still, I felt there was little affection between them other than for the purpose of communication. They were almost acting like brother and sister, the way I had seen kids at school behaving with their own siblings.

She hugged me, but it was kind of formal and restrained, and lasted less than five seconds. I didn't mind because, after sitting in a plane for twenty-four hours, I stank like a fish left out to thaw for too long, self-conscious to the point of wondering if she was going to notice and make a comment. And to make matters worse, she smelled good—peaches and strawberries laced in fresh cream and honey like a baby after being washed and powdered.

We left the airport in a large, yellow car the size of two Peugeots. The inside of the car smelled of cigarette smoke, grease and sweat. Ii was like waiting at a mechanic's workshop for an oil change and a forty-six-point safety check. I wanted to unwind the back window just a little in spite of the cold weather but felt too shy to bother. I had anticipated Australia to be tropical all year round, and the chillness had taken me by surprise.

As a couple, Michael and my mother seemed almost mismatched. She carried herself with pride and laboured elegance; he was tanned with black hair curling down to his neck, worker's arms and scarred fat fingers, a naked woman tattooed on his forearm. I couldn't study the tattoo properly since I was sitting at the back of the car, but I had detected bare breasts and a long pair of legs traced in black ink on his bronzed skin.

I wondered how my mother had gone from nearly marrying a priest to living with someone who tattooed himself with a picture of a naked woman. It didn't feel right. Maybe it wasn't her partner after all. Maybe he was just a neighbour who'd decided to go with her to pick me up from the airport. Maybe he was a lover who only stayed at her place now and then. I didn't want to ask. I would find out in time.

Every vehicle around us was larger than life. I felt as if I'd just entered a Hollywood movie, roads the width of a French freeway, flat landscapes with a generous horizon like the edge of a foolscap paper.

My mother spoke French with an English accent. Michael could only speak English. She had to translate everything we said. She played translation ping-pong between Michael and me.

Michael's eyes met mine in the rear-vision mirror—eyes green and translucent with the kind of sadness I had noticed in too many people in the last two years of my life. He didn't hold my stare long enough to mean anything, but still I felt inappropriately uncomfortable, as if he had just undressed me with his look and was savouring luscious images he had constructed in the comfort and privacy of his own mind.

The sky was blanketed in white clouds, and I could smell rain in the distance. I was wearing a white, summer dress and felt the cold cutting through my skin like sheets of ice sharpened on a giant grindstone. Everything around me was big, as if I were standing in a room where someone had removed half the furniture. The grass and the leaves were pale yellow and brown, lacking the intensity of European greenery—the light so bright and pure, it hurt the inept eye.

We drove past weatherboard factories, which looked more like giant sheds than buildings with their corrugated iron roofs in sun-fading reds and greens, and car parks large enough to lodge a fleet load of buses or trucks.

Before we reached the city, clusters of houses began to appear in what would be later be known to me as the 'suburbs'. Green, yellow, pink, white, blue, brick veneer, weatherboard, rendered, cement, wood, old, new, single and double storeys, single and double garages, carports, fenced, unfenced, short or long grass. My face was glued to the window like that of a child looking through the front display of a confectionery shop, just contemplating rather than being judgemental My breath formed a perfect circle on the cold glass like the rim of a coffee cup.

As we got closer to the city, Michael explained, via my mother, how all those houses stuck one next to each other were called terraces and were products of early Victorian architecture. Wire fences and small yards with square wood-framed windows and ornamental-design, iron balconies fronted the terraces. The houses looked tiny and made me think of railway workers' cottages I had seen in a book about England. Michael said what they lost in width, they made it up in length. I had no idea what he was talking about.

Michael was driving, one hand on the steering wheel, the other holding on to the top section of the door, his elbow sticking outside in the shape of a right-angle triangle like a taxi driver waiting patiently for a fare. The cold wind whisked into the back of the car from the opening of his window and made me feel even colder than I already was. I pictured myself as a lone penguin standing on an iceberg in the middle of Antarctica, my frozen heart longing for the warmth and comfort of a home.

'So, you learned English at school?' my mother asked. She looked at me through the reflection of the vanity mirror as if eye contact would determine the genuineness of my reply.

'A little,' I said and felt guilty I hadn't bothered making the effort, even though I had had three months to get ready to answer the most basic questions a new migrant could have been expected to be asked.

Michael said something in English to my mother I didn't understand, and, then she removed a package from under her seat and passed it on to me between the headrests.

She said, 'For your birthday, a gift from Michael.'

The unwrapped gift was still in the large, white, plastic shopping bag where it had been purchased. I pulled it out of the bag. It was a game of Monopoly *in English*. What was I going to do? Play Monopoly by myself?

I was twelve, and I would turn thirteen the following day. Louise must have said something to my mother, or my mother had remembered my birthday in spite of not having sent me a single birthday card for the past twelve years. Tears welled up in my eyes. I didn't really like playing Monopoly, but I felt gratified nonetheless—someone whom I'd never met had gone to the trouble of buying me a present.

And then I wondered why the gift had been from Michael, and not from Michael and my mother.

The house was made of wood and painted green; a dirty, broken white picket fence; buffalo grass; a faded-green corrugated iron roof; small windows with rusted hinges; overgrown trees and bushes; a brick-paved walkway leading to a run-down veranda barely supporting the overhanging roof; a metal letterbox with the flap missing. Number 1 George Street. It was the only house in a street filled with factories and looked as if it been built over a century ago, and no one had ever bothered to maintain it. It reminded me of an invalid pensioner forgotten by society, left to fend for herself in spite of her incapacity and lack of enthusiasm for the few remaining years of her life. I was slightly disappointed with my new home—from the outside this was the ugliest house I had seen of all those I'd observed from the back seat of Michael's car since we'd left the airport. Why did I always have to end up being the odd one out?

'There's a bus depot right at the end of the street,' my mother said, as if it was something of significance. Maybe she thought it would remedy the fact the house they lived in was worse than a hole dug in the ground, and somehow I was supposed to jump up and down with excitement at her revelation. Jeez, I waited all my life to live next to a bus depot!

We stepped out of the car, me clutching my plastic bag with the Monopoly game, and Michael circling to the back to get the rest of my belongings. The air was so clean, I could smell the bushes in the front yard—minty eucalyptus and moist bark with a hint of liquorice and honey wax.

When we went inside the house, the hall was plunged in darkness like a prison cell with no window, no electricity and mildew-smelling wallpaper. There was light at the end of the passage, but not enough to figure out the colours of the walls or the carpet. They might as well have painted everything black, it wouldn't have made the slightest difference.

'Come on, what are you standing here for?' my mother said,

hands on her hips like a matron, 'follow me.' I obeyed, my Monopoly game tightly held against my chest like a friend who'd protect me from evil lurking in unforeseeable, dark corners of my new home.

Past the hallway, the windows were small, not letting enough natural light through, so every time we entered a new room, my mother had to switch the light on.

My bedroom was at the far end, past the kitchen and near the back door, which opened up to a large courtyard with overgrown grass and a toilet the size of a walk-in wardrobe attached to the back porch. The porch was falling apart, every plank rotten and cracking with every step I took. I feared if one snapped, I would fall straight through and end up in the burning fires of hell.

Still, I counted my blessings by acknowledging the house was spacious, much bigger than my father's or David's apartment. I told myself I was fortunate to have a bedroom all for myself, even though the wallpaper was frog green, and the room was half-used as a storage facility—cardboard boxes lined up against the back wall, piled up to the ceiling like food boxes in a pantry.

My mother announced it was 9.30 a.m., and I would have to adjust my watch accordingly. It was Saturday, and she and Michael would take me to school first thing on Monday morning. I panicked at the thought of having to go to school without being capable of uttering one proper sentence in English. What were they going to do with me? Make me sit at the back of the class like a retard so I could watch the circus of students and try to figure out what the lesson was about by reading the teacher's body language?

For the next twenty minutes, I unpacked my backpack in *my* bedroom. I carefully unfolded the jeans, tee-shirts and undergarments I had taken with me all the way from France on the green bedspread of the metal-framed, single bunk bed pushed against the wall at the far right corner of the room. My clothes still smelled nicely of washing powder but most were too wrinkled from being in the bag for me to wear immediately.

Once the backpack was empty, I looked around the room with the critical eye of a holidaymaker who'd just rented a hotel room at an exorbitant price and wanted to assure herself it was worth every cent. Someone's idea of interior decorating had been to match every item in the room with the frog green colour of the wallpaper, including the bed-side table lamp, the curtains, the carpet and the protective paper placed inside the bottom drawers of the wardrobe. It was like standing in the middle of a backyard—and if you added a fern in each corner of the room, it would have been like standing in the middle of the Amazon Forest.

I shelved my Proust novels by my side-table after clearing the layer of dust with my hand and pushing it to the floor. As much as the rest of the house looked reasonably clean, its occupants had neglected my room for as long as they possibly could.

I tried to make the room homey with whatever items I had bought over from France, but the green wallpaper was making me dizzy, and I ended up sitting on the edge of the bed for a couple of minutes just to catch my breath and take the time to realise where I was and who I was and how I got into this house.

My mother was drinking coffee from a brown ceramic mug. Michael was playing an acoustic guitar with a grey plectrum, his right hand swigging over the strings with the graciousness of a violin player. Sheet music lay like a deck of card in a game of black jack all over a red Formica table with galvanised legs. The chairs matched the table, making me think of a mother duck and its ducklings. Pale light the colour of dirty water peered through the orange drapes of the kitchen window.

'Sit,' my mother ordered. 'It's time to talk about the rules.'

It felt as if I'd gone from one orphanage to another, and I could already tell this wasn't going to be the paradise found I had pictured at the back of my mind.

I sat facing her and avoided eye contact because I felt intimidated by her authoritarian attitude and the tone of her voice.

The mother of my dreams turns out to be a bully.

Firstly, she confirmed Michael was living with us, but, no, they were not married. And, yes, they did have children, two in fact, but they were away for the day and would be back tomorrow morning. One boy and one girl, both older than me. The boy was sixteen and the girl fifteen. The children were from Michael's first marriage.

'What about the rules?' I asked daringly.

Michael strummed *Spells like Teen Spirit* on his acoustic guitar but refrained from singing.

My mother said something nasty to him in English, which I

didn't understand. He stopped playing. He placed the guitar against the edge of the table and rolled himself a cigarette from a packet of tobacco with the word 'Drum' written on it. I'd never smoked roll-your-own. I wanted to ask him for one, but I knew better. He didn't seem to mind how my mother had just yelled at him in front of me, the new kid on the block, the latest addition to the family, the least of his worries. Instead he smiled tenderly, accepting his fate with graciousness, like someone who'd driven through thunder and hail many times before, bracing himself and taking it blow-by-blow.

'Ah, yes, the rules,' my mother said, as she'd truly forgotten why she ordered me to sit at the table with the tone of a drill sergeant. 'Everyone shares the chores in this house. The last person who uses the shower cleans it every night. You get to dry the dishes for a whole week, you wash them for a whole week, then it's your brother's and sister's turn.' She paused and added, 'Any questions?'

'No.'

'Good, then we'll get on just fine.'

I hadn't even met the rest of the family yet, and they were already my brother and sister. I was still trying to get used to the idea I had a mother—and a stepfather. Instant family. Just empty the sachet into a cup and add water.

She went on, 'On Saturday mornings, we clean the whole house. Today is an exception because we had to pick you up from the airport and we're too tired. One weekend you'll get to vacuum, the following weekend you'll dust. On odd days you'll help with pulling the weeds out. Do your homework and don't cause any trouble.'

'Am I suppose to be writing this down?' I asked.

She frowned, the way a person does when they're talking to you and you haven't noticed the bogey hanging from your nose, but she has and is too scared to mention it.

'Don't be stupid,' she said. 'I'll remind you enough times—by the end of the month you'll have all the rules engraved in your skull.'

My eyes met hers, but all I saw was emptiness—it was like peering into a dark cave and waiting for a grizzly bear to shred you to bits.

I shifted on my chair and suddenly I had this urge to run to the toilet and pee even though my bladder wasn't full.

This had to be a mistake.

Someone had switched me at birth.

During the first night, I could hardly sleep, my biological clock badly messed up, like a mechanical doll whose batteries had gone flat. The mattress was too soft and the pillow smelled bitter-sweet, as if a cat had been sleeping on it for a good decade and no one had ever bothered changing the casing. Even though it was dark in my room, I could feel the green all around me, sliding down the walls and on my bedspread like mucus from some invisible creature suffering an eternal phlegm disease.

All night I heard strange noises in the house, like someone pacing up and down the hallway, stopping in front of my bedroom door, changing his mind and tracing back his steps.

'The wood is breathing,' my mother would explain to me the next morning when I'd asked her if we had mice in the house.

And then I heard sounds coming from the backyard—leaves moving, wood crackling under someone's weight, small creatures wailing at the moon and tap-dancing on the corrugated iron roof right above my head. Something or someone was on the back porch, and I was certain it wasn't my imagination because I was so fully awake—my heart beat like a kettledrum at a military march.

Halfway through the night, in spite of me getting used to the softness of the mattress and the mantra sound of the 'wood breathing', I had to pass water. The toilet was outside—I knew because I had used it during the day, right after my mother had finished explaining the 'rules' to me.

The toilet had crooked hinges and a broken lock and an off-yellow, china bowl so low, my knees were virtually touching my ears when I sat on it—I could smell the warmth of my urine as it trickled down the darkness and sang a tune like the slow flow from a tap left running during the night.

Someone had painted the inside and the outside of the cubicle green, attempting to match the colour of the house, probably the same person who had so brilliantly managed to turn my bedroom into a nursery. Still, something wasn't quite right. It was like looking at one of those cars whose owner had attempted to repaint with touch-up spray cans in the same colour as the original—the cheap brand bought at a large department store, but the end result never quite corresponded.

86

The night was chilly—goose bumps crawled up my skin, and I could feel a cold sweat at the back of my neck as if someone was panting behind me like an animal.

While peeing I glanced around, partly out of curiosity, partly in fear of what night creature was going to jump on me and devour my tender flesh like the big bad wolf wanted to do with the Red Riding Hood.

Moths fought one another to get to the light bulb, only to burn their wings, sending smoke and a smell of burning hair into the air. They cast giant shadows in the small cubicle and created movement around me. The walls had turned to drapes blown by the wind.

Right above the wooden door, past the door frame, a black, furry spider the size of my hand with legs as fat as my fingers was watching me. I froze. My eyes focused on the enormous creature. I tried to empty my bladder as fast as I could, but panic set in and slowed down my bodily functions.

Even though I still had plenty more liquid to pass, I pushed myself forward and pulled the bottom of my pyjamas up, warm liquid running down my leg. I didn't want to hang on to life desperately, but dying in a toilet from a spider bite on my butt wasn't the most glamorous way to leave the world.

When I returned to bed, I sank under the sheets and bedspread and drifted into semi-consciousness from tiredness and fear—it was like a hangover, but I hadn't drank a drop of alcohol.

The rattling in front of my bedroom door was still going on—footsteps going forth and back like a pendulum with a volume control and someone constantly playing with it. I dreamed of a giant black spider entering my room from under the door, crawling up the end of my bed while I screamed to no avail, its fat legs caressing my cheeks, its big mouth opening wide, ready to swallow me whole.

Big moth shadows flickered around the room—cordless kites without direction, hitting themselves against the walls, frying their wings against the hot bulb of the side-table lamp I had left on from fear of the dark. I smelled the smoke of my father's pipe and Louise's house-grade soap and facial cream. I had no idea where I was or how I got there. I was tripping badly, and I wondered if it was from not having had a drink or a smoke for a while.

Or maybe I was just going crazy.

I bathed in this weird perception—my surroundings weren't real, my life to date had been nothing more than a figment of my imagination, and soon I would wake up and be six years old again.

My soul was separating itself from my body, the way it did when I got totally wasted on white wine. God was slicing me in two with a giant sword—the type used by Japanese samurai—and cut into the tender flesh of my youth as easily as if I'd been a musk melon

And then there was a steady thumping at the back of my skull jack-hammering away through every section of my cranium until I finally gave in and forced myself to sleep through a wrenching migraine.

Sunday morning.

I was first to get out of bed in spite of being the one who probably managed the least amount of sleep. I made myself instant coffee from a tin can with a rusted lid and sat at the kitchen table. I stirred the contents of my mug and hoped to rid the malaise resulting from my night of trepidation. Powdered coffee tasted weak and watery compared to the rich percolated coffee I had been accustomed to drinking in France—it was like switching from wine to water. After a mouthful of the pulp-paper-tasting brew, I added heaped desert spoons of sugar until it tasted like caramel. Eagerly, I drank half the contents of my mug to keep myself warm within the chilly confinement of the kitchen. It didn't work—all I achieved was to burn my palate, and I could have sworn a blister the size of a small mushroom was growing up there within seconds of me swallowing the hot liquid.

I wanted to go to the bathroom to pass water, but I feared the giant spider still resided there, waiting for me like a psychopath, and would delight in scaring the living daylight out of me before injecting poison into my veins like a shot of low-grade heroin. I'd ask Michael to get rid of the spider as soon as he waked up—men always seemed to know what to do when it came to large insects or barking dogs or madman storming into your room at three o'clock in the morning. Normally I would have considered getting rid of it myself to prove women were also capable of killing insects, but I'd never seen such a large spider in my life, and after the nightmares I suffered the previous night, I felt too perturbed to play hero. I resigned myself to squashing ants another day as retaliation.

Outside, the sky was pencil-grey, and it looked as if were about to rain at any moment. The previous day the heavens had suffered from the same condition but they held back lashing tons of water into the world. On my way from the airport my mother had explained how Melbourne winters were erratic, just like men—pouring one day, grey for a week, sunny the next, no pattern or predictably defined. She spoke in French so Michael wouldn't know what we were talking about, and also because I wouldn't have understood a word if she'd told me in English. I was curious about what experiences she'd had with men to make such comment, but refrained from asking her. There would be a right time and a right place for the mother-daughter conversation I'd been longing for.

The closest I'd ever got to having a serious talk about men was with Martine, and even then, looking back now, it was more a lecture than a discussion. Martine had already concluded all men were pigs, and yet she had decided to move down south and spend her life with one of them. Maybe her judgement of men wasn't definitive—it would be up to me to make up my mind in due time. The only boy I'd dated was David, and we'd never had the chance to know each other well. I was a clueless virgin and held no strong opinions on men yet—my heart was an empty vessel ready to be filled with more emotions, more love and more hurt.

The white circular clock above the fridge told me it was 7:45. My coffee cup was half empty and lukewarm. I could have re-heated what was left in it, but I was too lazy to bother and the burning in my palate felt like I'd been chewing on a handful of pins.

I flicked through the music partitions Michael had left lying on the kitchen table from the previous day—books with songs from Nirvana, Matchbox 20, Counting Crows, Cold Chisel, Crowded House, Ben Lee, Goo Goo Dolls, Sheryl Crow, Tracy Chapman and the Datsuns. Because I had studied the recorder at school, I knew what the black ants crawling all over the pages meant, even though I wasn't fluent at reading music.

Michael's acoustic guitar was resting against the edge of the kitchen table like somebody's rifle in a western movie. I grabbed it gently by the neck, rested it on my knees and plucked the strings one at the time, letting them vibrate into notes. I tried to press the metal strings against the fretboard with my left hand, but they dug into my fingertips like blunt razor blades—not cutting, but hurtful enough to make me want to cry. I couldn't even make one note sound good. I didn't know how to associate the notes on the staves to those on the fretboard of the guitar. I knew about chords, and the little boxes above the staves were supposed to tell me how to play them. There was C and G7, F and Em, and instructions, such as 'Capo on 3rd' and 'play moderately'. I was used to DO, RE, MI, FA, SOL, LA, SI, DO, but there were no such notes in English books. English notes were designated by the letters of the alphabet.

When I grew tired of trying to make notes sound right, I sniffed the fretboard in all its length, starting from the nut down to the sound-hole. I closed my eyes and shut out all my other senses and concentrated only on the smell coming from the neck of the guitar. Michael's cigarettes and sweat filled my nostrils then my lungs like a lingering, musky aftershave. I opened my eyes and I ran my hands alongside the smooth, varnished, wooden body of the guitar. *A guitar is a sculpture, a work of art.* I touched the silver tuning heads—chilly like a bottle of wine brought in from the darkness of a cold cellar—but refrained from turning them in case I made the guitar go out of tune.

I thought it would be neat to be able to play any songs I liked on the guitar. It would be better than playing the recorder—you could sing playing the guitar but not playing the recorder. I would be able to compose my own songs, express my pain freely like generations of musicians had done before me. Maybe I'd ask Michael to teach me how to play when I'd got to know him a little better.

I placed the guitar back against the metallic edge of the table, just the way I found it, and drank the rest my lukewarm coffee in total silence, with only the ticking of the clock above the fridge to remind me of the passing of time.

I thought about Louise back in France and wondered if she was going to write to me like she'd promised she would. Now that I was far away, she could just ignore me and pretend I never existed. She could toss me aside the way I tossed David out of my life without explanation. Maybe I had been right when I told her than I was only the bread and butter in her life. I hated to admit it, but sitting by myself, in this strange house, on the other side of the world, in the midst of a sullen, grey Sunday morning, I realised I missed her far more than I had anticipated. I'd been a lone rose lost in the dead of winter, and she'd been my devoted gardener, diligent in her calling, never giving up on me even when I already had, putting up with my obnoxious temperament at times when she could have just walked away or passed me on to someone else, selflessly devoted to finding me a place I could call home. Expecting anything more from her now felt avaricious, like a child who had been given too much attention and developed a delusion of grandeur.

And then I realised how my life was a series of incidents initiated by other people, and maybe I didn't have a life after all, but belonged to whomever world I fitted into—a commodity and a burden to be passed around until I was both old and mature enough to become my own possession.

I searched through the cupboards for wine, but found none—only white vinegar, canned food, peas, baby carrots, breakfast cereals, pasta, spices and sliced bread in clear plastic bags. I'd heard about alcohol withdrawal symptoms, and I feared soon I would become a victim. Maybe I was one already and I hadn't noticed.

I sat back at the kitchen table and stared at my white, doughy hands, waiting for them to shake uncontrollably like red autumn leaves. Two minutes went by, and my hands remained as quiescent as two bread rolls. Still, I knew it would be only a matter of time before they would gain a life of their own if I continued to starve myself from the alcohol my mind and body mercilessly craved for.

Weary of remaining motionless, I shifted on my chair and unintentionally knocked Michael's guitar to the floor. It crashed like thunder against the grey ceramic tiles, the vibration from the six strings echoing within the confinement of the kitchen and undoubtedly throughout the rest of the house. I cringed and feared someone would wake up because my carelessness. I waited a full minute, but no one came to the kitchen.

Still trembling from the loudness of the guitar crashing, I picked up the instrument by the neck and examined it for damage. It seemed to be in the same condition as before the fall—no new dents or scratches. Maybe I had forced it out of tune, but it was impossible for me to tell. I placed the instrument back against the edge of the table and prayed silently that no irreversible damage had been done.

I tried to roll one of Michael's cigarettes but ended up making a mess. I couldn't get the tobacco to stay inside the cylinder of white paper, so I used so much saliva, the cigarette ended up looking like a thawed fish finger. Defeated, I washed it unrepentantly down the sink.

Today was my birthday; I was thirteen, and out of nowhere I'd been given a whole family—brother, sister, mother, stepfather. Maybe there was even a pet somewhere and I hadn't noticed it yet.

I felt light-headed and wondered if all this was real, or if I would suddenly wake up and find myself back at the orphanage in Strasbourg.

I rinsed my empty coffee mug in hot water and returned to my room.

Suddenly hot tears cascaded down my face as if someone had turned on a tap. I lay on my bed, unable to shake off an engulfing and convulsing sense of despair, which held me tightly at the throat like a large pair of hands, its fingers digging into the soft, pale flesh of my neck as if it were moist clay.

I gasped for air and hugged my pillow tightly against my chest the way my father used to hug me.

'This is John and Melissa,' my mother said. She played with the sleeve of a blue bathrobe falling apart at the seams. She looked older in the morning light, before she had time for a shower or to fix her hair, her eyes heavy from lack of sleep, no doubt from anxiety eating her up.

She took tentative steps towards the kitchen table where I was sitting. The sun coming from the small window above the sink caressed the back of my neck. My new siblings trailed behind her without saying a word. They were half concealed in the shadow of the hall, shyness engulfing them as if they were about to meet someone of great importance.

Like a security guard, my mother stepped aside from the doorway leading to the hall to let them through.

John and Melissa stepped forth.

My mother observed us from a distance without saying a word.

My new brother and sister were checking me out. He was good-looking with a mouth full of straight teeth, a strong chin, thick chestnut hair and blue eyes. His shoulders were broad and his skin flawless. He looked like a model from a magazine where only beautiful people adorned its pages.

She was taller than me, blonde hair down to her back and a

long, straight nose. I wouldn't have noticed her if she'd walked past me, but on close inspection, she was prettier than I'd first realised. The upper half of her face looked a lot like Michael's, especially the sad eyes and the arch of her brow. She was thin all over, forcing me to be self-conscious about the thickness of my legs and the ever-expanding width of my buttocks. She looked more woman than girl, but then she was three years older than me.

It didn't take long for everyone to understand the rules of the game. They couldn't speak French and I couldn't speak English, and everything said would have to be passed back and forth through my mother. She was the only bilingual person in the family, and thus would be in control of monitoring all conversations. It was going to be a hell of a way to develop healthy relationships.

My mother told them my name was Clotilde, but neither one of them could pronounce it properly.

I called them 'Jaune' and 'Meliza'.

I told my mother about the spider in French, and she told John in English.

John rushed to the toilet and soon after we heard flushing. Within thirty seconds of the flushing he was back triumphant, St George who slay the dragon.

It was dead now, he told my mother in English, and I shouldn't have any more nightmares. She translated what he said to me. I told my mother to thank him, and how I thought what he did was really admirable. He smiled back at me, his heroic, blue eyes filled with light.

We spent the rest of the morning around the kitchen table and swapped stories and coffee making, my mother doing all the translating as if she was being paid for her services. I couldn't ask John or Melissa anything personal since every word I said had to pass my mother, which meant our conversations were sanitised to the point in which I began losing interest.

They both attended Dandenong High School, which was supposedly the best government school in the area. John said I had to wear a uniform, and Melissa brought one from her room to show me. There was a dress with blue lines running into squares, a blue jumper, and if I wanted to, I could wear blue trousers.

John said the boys' uniforms were grey, but he didn't bother showing his to me. He said he had to wear a tie and he hated it, especially in summer when the temperature sometimes soared above thirty degrees. I said I knew what it was like to wear a tie in summer because my *father* wore one and I use to fold the knot for him.

On Sunday afternoon John and Melissa watched television, even though the sun was out high in a cloudless sky, turning a winter's day into spring. I refused to watch television, not only because I couldn't understand a word, but also because I'd never been interested in watching the stupid thing in the first place. It felt like a mindless and unproductive way to spend a Sunday afternoon, but I didn't want to tell them so—I used to spend my Sunday afternoons drunk in bed, and they might have considered my choice of pastime much more mindless and unproductive.

My mother did three loads of washing—one white and two darks—while I sat at the kitchen table with Michael because there was nothing else to do.

Michael tried to communicate with me, but I didn't understand what he was saying, so he talked more with his hands than with words. I wondered how he got the scars on his hands—random cuts varied in length and depth like grooves on bark—but I didn't know how to ask him. He had grime under his nails—worker's hands, I concluded—and even though they were cut so short, it looked as if he'd been chewing them to the bone. The index, middle finger and thumb of his right hand were nicotine stained. I wondered if I was heading in the same direction if I continued consuming cigarettes as if they were sweets.

I tried not to be obvious in my contemplation, but he must have noticed because he smiled awkwardly when I gazed at his face for too long. His black hair and side-burns were turning grey at the temples, and it kind of suited him. It made him look wise and self-assured, like someone who had been through every single life experience and had accepted the outcomes, no matter how unjust some might have been. I wished I could have looked equally at ease with my existence and not so fervently desperate to be someone other than myself.

I couldn't help glancing at the tattoo of the naked woman on his arm—I was capable of admiring her in full splendour. It was

94

finely traced in a blue so dark, it might as well have been in black. There was no colour pigmentation, but the drawing was incredibly detailed—the eyes, the mouth, the fingers—and about ten centimetres in length and five in width. How long had he been sitting in a chair in agony while the tattoo artist completed his work of art?

The tattooed woman was bare-breasted with a waist was so tiny, it defied the laws of biology. Her hair was dark and long, and her eyes large and sultry in a Marilyn Monroe kind-of-way. She was beautiful even if somewhat vulgar for my taste. What exactly did she mean to Michael? Was she the woman of his dreams? Nakedness in the form of unattainable perfection?

He tried to talk to me some more, but we just ended up getting frustrated with one another. He gave up on the conversation and grabbed his guitar resting against the edge of the table. He sat it on his right thigh and played a couple of major and minor chords in succession, but they came out all wrong, like an amateur singer who can't hold a tune. He stared at the guitar for a few seconds and frowned as if there were something terribly wrong with it—an incurable disease had eaten the musicality from the instrument and turned it into a worthless piece of wood. He turned the tuning keys and plucked the strings one at a time to let the sound of each note resonate like the ringing of bells at a Sunday morning mass. Within the four walls and the quietness of the kitchen, each note sounded loud and thick, even the high notes on the B and E strings. Knowing I was the culprit, I felt myself blushing, but he didn't notice—he was too preoccupied adjusting the tension of each string until he managed the correct pitch.

When he was done with the tuning, he opened a sheet music on the table and played *Time of your Life*. He could sing well—his voice smooth and warm like hot milk, words pouring from his mouth like a river running into the sea, harmonised perfectly with the strumming of the chords.

I wondered why he wasn't playing with a band at a restaurant or a wedding reception. If he'd been in France, he'd be offered a job immediately—not many French people sang in English convincingly, and those who did were only credible to those who couldn't tell the difference between singing in English and speaking in tongues.

My mother was hanging out the washing with John and

Melissa, who had been interrupted from their television viewing, much to their annoyance. I didn't have to help because none of it was my washing, and as much as my mother pointed out she was strict when it came to house duties, she was also fair. I'd only been in the house for one day, so obviously none of the laundry was mine.

Michael finished playing *Time of your Life* and rolled a cigarette as easily as I made a cup of coffee. He placed the cigarette between his lips, lit it up and made eye contact with me, daring me to fall into the same cardinal sin of substance abuse. I responded by glancing at his cigarette and then back at him, my eyes smiling. He understood without a syllable passing from my mouth to his ears. Smokers language—no need for words. He glanced across the kitchen window to see how my mother was progressing with the washing.

I did the same.

The basket of wet clothes was still half full. I could hear John's voice and my mother's. They were arguing, but it was in English, so I had no idea what their disagreement was about.

Michael turned his attention back to me and handed me the cigarette he had already begun to smoke. I took a long drag and it tasted like heaven, even if it was much milder than a Gitane. The flavour of tobacco leaves filled my mouth, my lungs, my nostrils, my brain and every cell in my body. I hadn't smoked a cigarette since the one in the toilet of the Boeing 747 on my way to Australia. The first nicotine rush hit my nervous system and injected me with a ray of sunshine.

Michael kept glancing back towards the kitchen window in fear of what my mother would say or do if she found out he was letting me smoke. But it wasn't like he was responsible for my vice. I'd been an unrepentant teenage smoker for a year now and proud of it—it felt good to be bad, even though I didn't start smoking for that reason.

He stared at my face while I smoked, almost as if he was considering taking *advantage* of my youth and naivety—but I didn't feel uncomfortable like someone of my age should have been. For years it had only been my father staring at me with the same intense look. In spite of my precocious awareness, grown-up men didn't frighten me.

Michael must have realised when I didn't cough that I was an old hand at smoking, and it made me feel kind of special. We were the only two sinners in the household and smoking together was our secret.

After the third drag, he tried to retrieve the cigarette from me, but I resisted. I took as many drags as possible. I was a junkie who hadn't injected her fix for a week and was making up for lost time. I feared not being able to smoke for a long time, so I made the most of this one.

Michael looked again across to the backyard, through the kitchen window, but this time I didn't bother joining him—I was too busy enjoying killing myself slowly with his cigarette.

Then the voices from outside got closer to the back entrance of the house.

Michael's eyes widened.

He said something I didn't understand, but his tone of voice told me he wanted me to stop smoking, or life was going to turn into a living hell for the both of us—especially for him.

But I resisted. What would happen if my mother walked in and saw me smoking? She'd know who I really was—not the sweet, little daughter of a priest she had conjured somewhere at the back of her mind.

Michael tried to snatch the cigarette from me, but I pulled my head back like someone avoiding getting slapped.

He rolled his eyes and retrieved his arm.

My mother's voice echoed from the laundry.

I kept the cigarette casually dangling between my lips.

Michael's cheekbones moved as he ground his teeth like an angry dog, and for a split second I thought he was going to jump the table and grab me by the throat. But I never showed fear.

He never had time to make a move.

My mother walked into the kitchen, her back to us while in conversation with John or Melissa. The bottom of her blue dress flapped against her legs from the wind entering the laundry through the back door.

Just as she was about to turn around and catch me in the legally-forbidden, juvenile act of filling my lungs with a cocktail of over 4000 different toxins wrapped in a paper foil half the length of a grey lead, I squashed what was left of the cigarette into the glass ashtray.

My mother turned around and instinctively her eyes met those of Michael.

Melissa's eyes met mine.

I blew the last of the smoke from my mouth.

Melissa glanced at the ashtray and back at me. She knew I knew she knew, but she didn't say a word—she just glared at me strangely.

I opened my eyes wide, begging her not to say a word. She paced across the length of the kitchen and stopped at the fridge. Casually, she removed a carafe of iced water and poured herself a glass. She gulped three quarters of the contents in three seconds.

Michael threw me a look, his eyes narrow with anger and his face drained of colour like someone who'd just been stabbed in the back with a thirty-centimetre blade. I knew he felt betrayed, but that was the whole point of my little game—even if I had nothing to prove. Sometimes the daring and the adrenalin rush was enough to justify the action.

My mother asked him something in English. He just brushed off her question with his right hand, the way parents often dismiss a child's request for an explanation to the unexplained.

Michael rolled himself another cigarette. He focused solidly on his task so as to avoid eye contact with everyone in the room.

My mother turned to me. 'If his smoking annoys you, I'll ask him to stop.'

CHAPTER NINE

Monday morning came around like an unpredictable icy storm in the middle of a warm summer afternoon. All night I had tossed and turned, anxious about the day that lay ahead and my biological clock's insubordinate insistence on continuing to function on European time.

When my mother knocked on the heavy wooden door of my room, I felt groggy. My head was buried in the thickness of my duck-down pillow and refused to lift itself and let me boldly face the challenges of the day.

My bedroom was plunged into darkness and made making me feel as if I'd been woken up in the middle of the night and not half an hour before sunrise.

All night I'd been incapable of distinguishing one hour from another, with only the ticking of my watch to remind me time was slowly drifting by. I longed for a good sleep and not having to face this new world abruptly vested upon me by the hands of fate. I ignored my mother's knocking—maybe if I ignored her, she would forget my existence and get on with her daily routine.

At my mother's second request, I struggled to push off the warm quilt wrapped comfortably around my body like a second skin. I am a caterpillar forced out of its chrysalis before undergoing full metamorphosis and emerging as a beautiful swallowtail butterfly, I lied to myself.

Light from the kitchen seeped under the door like melting butter and allowed me to place my naked soles firmly on the cold, wooden floor without tripping over my shoes or *Les Plaisirs et Les Jours*.

Once up, I pulled open the heavy, emerald drapes of my bedroom window aside to uncover a world blanketed in morning dew and illuminated by a pale, white sun hiding behind an ash grey sky. It was my second morning in my new home. I had yet to adjust to the scenery of an effervescent backyard with its broken, wooden fence, green bushes and a white, fishnet hammock suspended between two bent apple trees located at the far end of the property.

I yearned for some wine to help me get the day on the way, but I already knew there was none in the house. In the middle of the night I once again ransacked the kitchen in the hope Michael or my mother had hidden a bottle of Chardonnay or Riesling. All I found was beer stocked up in the lower compartment of the fridge in aluminium cans labelled *Foster's*.

Desperate, I grabbed a can, pulled the ring and swallowed a mouthful of the cold, fermented beverage as if it were lemonade. The bitterness forced me to empty the contents of the can into the sink. White froth grizzled like a frying egg on a cooking tray. A minute later the small amount of beer I drank made me sick like a rat that swallowed the poisonous, green pellets left purposely at the bottom of the cupboard.

I decided to toss the empty can over the fence of our backyard for fear of someone finding it in the rubbish bin the next day and pointing the finger at me. I was bare foot and wore only my yellow, flannel pyjamas. I crossed the yard, the cold, moist earth searching between my toes like insects scavenging the rotten carcass of an ill-fated animal. The moon was full and round—a Chinese lantern painting the yard in blue tones and shadows like in a scene from a horror movie. The cold of the night slipped through my skin like razor blades. I could hear traffic in the distance and something rattling in the bushes. In spite of dreading an encounter with a nocturnal creature, I managed to reach the wooden fence, toss the empty beer can into the next door property, and return to the back door without screaming in fright or tripping over any unforeseeable obstacles.

In the morning, while I finished pulling the drapes open across my bedroom window, I noticed crusted, dried mud on my feet as if I'd been finger-painting with my toes in grey and chestnut colour and forgot to clean-up afterwards.

For breakfast we ate boxed cereal with coconut bits and dried fruits laced with cold, full-cream milk poured from a carton container. I wasn't used to eating cereal for breakfast, but it tasted like sunshine and summer and perked me up a little and made me realise maybe the day would unfold more blissfully than I anticipated.

Everyone seemed happy and cheerful, like people getting ready for a big birthday party. John and Melissa were still in their pyjamas and my mother in her blue bathrobe. John's thick brown hair was unkempt and he sported bum fluff on his chin like an artist who didn't need to look neat to impress.

Melissa made me toast and spread it with a salty, black substance called Vegemite, which reminded me of petroleum erupting from the earth like I had seen on the cover of an old National Geographic magazine resting on the coffee table in the lounge room.

I sniffed the toast—it smelled of beef stock and salt. This was no marmalade or honey. Reluctantly, I took a bite since everyone was daring me to the challenge, as if my agreeing was an initiation into the Australian way of life.

I masticated on the Vegemite toast. When I nearly vomited as if I'd just swallowed a glass of bleach, they all laughed heartily. John was the loudest, his voice booming like a trombone.

I rushed to the toilet outside and emptied the chewed mixture of bread and black, pasty substance from my mouth with the help of my index finger, and brushed my teeth and gums in the process.

When I returned to finish my breakfast, John and Melissa had left the kitchen—they were getting dressed for school, my mother told me. They breakfast dishes were in the sink, floating in dishwater like sinking ships.

I poured myself a glass of one-hundred-per-cent Australian orange juice from a two-litre container to get rid of the taste of Vegemite. I drank it in one go. It tasted like sweets so I poured myself another glass.

'Where's Michael?' I asked my mother. She was busy shelving the plates and saucers from the previous night in the pantry. She wore a pair of jeans and a red, hand-knitted cardigan over a yellow tee-shirt. Her blonde-bleached hair was tied into a ponytail. Whenever she walked past me, I could smell jasmine shampoo and coconut soap. Her skin was stretched like parchment and almost translucent; her eyes sad, heavily weighted with secrets from the past.

'What?' she said. She placed the last plate in the middle shelf of the pantry.

'Where's Michael?'

'Gone to work.'

'Doing what?'

'He's a diesel mechanic.'

'Oh,' I said, as if her answer explained everything.

And then it occurred to me I did hear a car engine in the early hours of the morning, but at the time I was drifting in and out of sleep, and it sounded more like a cat purring. The purring blended in with the rustling of the trees in the backyard, the breathing of the wood all around me, the voices in my dreams, like angels in secret conversation, and the ticking of my watch.

I told my mother I felt sick and didn't know what was wrong with me. She said it was normal, and what I was suffering from was called jet lag. It would take me one to two weeks to get over it, and she had suffered from the same fate when she first came to Australia. I wanted to tell her there was something more to it, like I was a closet alcoholic, and if she didn't give me a glass of white wine soon I was going to die. If she had known what a desperate and self-destructive creature secretly inhabited the body of the innocent-looking teenager before her eyes, she might have never picked me up from the airport and invited me to share her life.

We walked the whole way to school because Michael had taken the blue Jeep Cherokee to work. It took us a good half hour to get there. John and Melissa seemed embarrassed to be walking alongside my mother—they didn't say so but kept five metres in front, as if my mother and I were covered in leeches and they were afraid of contamination. They whispered secretly to one another, conspiring against us.

The sky was covered in marshmallow clouds, soft, tender and sweet, and the sun shyly peaked between them as if it had done wrong and was afraid to show its face. It looked as if it might rain before we reached the school. Fortunately, my mother had the good sense to remember to take a large umbrella with her.

Every house we passed had a front yard, a fence and a letterbox, in all different shapes and colours, each one reflecting the personality of its occupants. Home owners were those who kept their yards in good condition, my mother said. Tenants didn't care as long as they had a roof and they didn't get evicted. Their front yards were not maintained and housed a variety of junk—tyres, mattresses, broken furniture, shoes, broken bikes. But everyone had a home, a family, a place where they belonged.

As we passed a dental clinic, I wondered if Melissa had told John about my smoking. She certainly had made no attempt in any shape or form to communicate with me about it, and I hadn't noticed Michael or her arguing over anything. I had to be friendly with her because as long as she kept her mouth shut about my smoking, she'd continue to have latent power over me.

'What's wrong with those two?' I asked my mother.

'They think it's shameful to be walked to school by a parent.'

I couldn't imagine being ashamed of walking to school with my father by my side—I would have traded in anything, even my new country, to have him walking beside me.

Uniformed kids appeared from every street corner, their dark blue high school bags hanging from one shoulder, sending their spines into dangerous curves. They reminded me of laboratory mice racing for the cheese at the end of the labyrinth. I was the only student without a uniform or a high school bag—a turkey in a gaggle of geese. I wore my white summer dress from France and one of Melissa's hand-knitted jumpers—a pastel pink creation with three yellow flowers stitched on the right breast pocket. Louise had been right about it being cold in winter in Australia— not as cold as in France, but cold enough not be walking around wearing a knee-cut, light-cotton dress, like a fool who couldn't tell one season from another.

My mother must have sensed my alienation.

'We'll get you a uniform soon,' she said.

When we reached the front of the school gate—a high metal fence with the school's blue-red-and-white logo and the letters DHS—I felt scared and excited all at once, my heart hammering through my chest like a giant clock. John and Melissa had abandoned us and vanished into the crowd of blue and grey jumpers, blending in with their friends, forsaking me into an unfamiliar world of strange faces and loud voices.

'How am I going to cope with English?' I asked my mother.

'They've got special classes for people like you.'

Special classes. I hadn't even begun school, and already I felt like an idiot, an outcast, someone who needed special attention because of my inability to communicate properly. How I wished I had bothered making more effort learning English while I had the chance. Maybe Louise had been right when she concluded the reason why my father had made me learn English was because he knew I would end up in Australia. Then why didn't he tell me? At least I wouldn't have wasted all that time being disheartened about learning a second language and maybe I would have made an effort. We waited on a wooden bench—which might as well have been made of granite as far as our buttocks and our backs were concerned—facing the principal's office. Once more, I had a sinking feeling of displacement, like everything around me was not real, and soon I would wake up from a dream or a nightmare. I longed for the comfort of the world I had left behind, no matter how distasteful it might have seemed at the time—the acrid taste of Gitanes on my tongue and at the back of my throat; the cheap wine I managed to obtain with little trouble; the company of strangers who had somehow taken on an embellished significance in my too-often nonsensical life.

My mother checked her watch every five minutes, even though there was a large clock hanging on the wall in front of us. I was trying to see what my father saw in her, but it was hard to imagine what she would have looked like fourteen years ago. I'd seen photos of my father when he was younger, and it always amazed me how time and gravity inflicted their tolls on people. My father had been handsome once, which explained to a certain extent why my mother had bothered with him, even though he'd been a priest and she'd been a free-spirited young woman. But the passing of years and ill health had been cruel to his looks, much more so than to men who had aged alongside him, and who did not suffer from the same detrimental fate.

We waited and waited for those in authority to allow us the privilege to exist for half an hour in their invaluable lives. The reception area was a museum of past and present principals and vice-principals—photographs adorning every wall, framed in expensive solid dark oak and embellished with gold lettering with the names of the subjects and the appropriate years of service. The whole area smelled of wax and shoe polish and felt as formal as the entrance of the Australian Embassy in Paris. The people who ran the school thought themselves important and made sure everyone understood this was the case.

'I hope we're not going to be here all day,' my mother said.

We'd been sitting there, eyes crossing every corner of the room for over half an hour, bored to the point of counting the nails on the bench facing us.

Since my father died, I'd waited for something to happen, for my luck to change, for God to vest upon me gratitude and good fortune. But as I sat there, next to a complete stranger whom I had to accept as my mother for better or worse, in a place as alien to me as a prison would have been to a first-timer, I realised the waiting wasn't over yet. Maybe waiting was all there was—people anxiously awaiting the next plateau of their lives, always hoping for a greater happiness.

When we finally got to see the principal, my neck was sore from sitting crooked on the wooden bench.

During the next six months I had to adapt to my new world like a migrating stork setting out on its thousand-kilometre journey from Alsace to sub-Saharan Africa. At times I didn't think my brain was going to cope with the culture shock and the difficulty of having to learn a new language. Half my school days were spent in English As A Second Language classes, which I enjoyed at the start because of all the attention I was receiving, but after a few weeks I grew tired of seeing the same faces continuously throughout the day.

I was the only French person in our ESL class. There were a lot of Greeks and Italians and some Arabs. There were Yugoslavian and some Vietnamese. The ESL teacher spoke French, which came in handy whenever I couldn't cope with my work.

Learning English was like having a limb cut off and waiting for it to re-grow. I grew exhausted of not being able to express freely what was on my mind; of people making me repeat everything I said three or four times; of only being able to convey simple thoughts; of other students talking to me as if I were a five-year old.

I found it odd students had to wear school uniforms, which gave them the appearance of serious, English boarding school pupils, and yet created mayhem in the classroom like packs of wolves. I remembered my school days in France where uniforms didn't exist, but discipline in the classroom and total respect for the teachers were the norms. It was hard to comprehend how teachers could teach while students chatted amongst themselves and barely paid attention to their studies. I waited in anticipation for one of the teachers to eventually lose his temper, but, much to my disappointment, none of them ever did. I would have liked to see some authority inflicted on those who had total disregard for their teachers, especially the music teacher, whose pain at being ignored could be read in the sagging sadness of his eyes.

Everyone at school thought it was really nice I was French, and they made a big deal out of it, but I didn't understand what all the fuss was about. I hated to be the one who didn't fit in when all I wanted was to be a drop in the ocean.

A group of boys kept eyeing me during recess and lunchtime and laughed like morons. One morning, before my maths, just outside our common room, a redhead with freckles approached me and asked something in English I didn't understand. Yet, somehow, he made me understand how every time someone asked me *that* question, I had to answer 'yes'. So he asked me the question again to see if I understood what I was supposed to say, and I answered, 'yes'.

All the boys laughed.

Home life became a routine of returning back from school, doing homework and watching television. I didn't watch television—only John and Melissa did and sometimes my mother when she was bored and had nothing else to do. She complained she didn't like television, but she still ended up watching either way, as if admitting she hated watching it made her a better person. I refused to watch it altogether, although had I bothered watching it even a little, it might have helped me with my English comprehension. But the thought of sitting on a couch for hours and staring at a cathode-ray tube shooting electrons at my brain didn't seem like a good way to be passing time. I would have rather occupied myself devising thirty-six ways of slicing my wrists.

Michael taught me how to play chess. We spent countless hours at the kitchen table hunched over our pieces like two monks at a monastery intensively preoccupied with our scribing tasks. He always won when we first started playing, but after a few weeks I managed a few checkmates, but I was never really sure if I won them out of merit, or if Michael let me win so I wouldn't feel inadequate and lose complete interest in the game.

'What is your name?'

'My name is Clotilde Benoît.'

We played on a hand-made, wooden board with matching pieces he bought at the Sunday market for three dollars. It was scented in tea tree oil and smelled like India.

I used to play checkers before Michael taught me how to play chess, and only when I played chess did I realise how dull checkers were.

I liked the way a chess game was devised—Kings, Queens, Bishops, Knights, Rooks and Pawns, sixteen pieces each, thirty-two all together, two colours, sixty-four squares to fight over, endless combinations and only one winner. It felt as if we were battling for some medieval empire of great importance, but the difference was chess involved careful strategic planning rather than mindless violence.

I liked the way my mind was completely engrossed in a game of chess, and nothing else mattered, not even who I was or what the future had in store for me. I liked making a move called castling—shifting my King and Rook, or Queen and Rook, simultaneously to assigned squares on the game board. It seemed to mess up Michael's strategy.

I liked the smell of Michael's cigarettes when we played chess, so much so, it became difficult to disassociate one from the other. I liked the way he frowned every time it was his turn to play; the warmth in his eyes when he studied me while I puzzled over my next move; the way the smoke from his cigarette half-concealed the features of his face; the broadness of his shoulders and the tone of his arms.

'Checkmate!'

'*Et Merde!*

'Wanna do another one?'

'Yes, *d'accord.*'

We tried to communicate with one another, and since I had learned a few basic English sentences at school, he helped me with them.

'What is your name?'

'My name is Clotilde Benoît.'

I played with the white pieces because they were white, and white was pure and innocent. The black ones were for Michael through process of elimination. Even though he played black, I never saw it as his colour of choice. I think he didn't really care what colour he played, and I probably wouldn't have either if I kept winning nine games out of ten. But he was a man and black seemed more appropriate.

I also liked playing white because I got to make the first move every time we began a new game. He'd been playing longer than I had, so I needed some sort of advantage.

'Where do you come from?'

'I come from France.'

Sometimes he got me into checkmate with five moves, which was really frustrating because no matter what I did, or how long I studied the game, he always managed to outwit me. I wondered why he became a mechanic when it was obvious to me he could have been anything in life. When he played chess or when he smoked, I could tell he was thinking some important thoughts, not like other people I'd known—not like my mother, John or Melissa. His concentrated frown reflected substance and depth in spite of his rugged appearance.

'How old are you?'

'I am thirteen years old.'

'Where do you live?'

'I live in Dandenong.'

'What school do you go to?'

'I go to Dandenong High School.'

'Checkmate.'

'*Et merde!*

'We say "shit" in English.'

'Shit!'

The absence of wine was a major drawback during the first month of my new existence. Still I handled the withdrawal better than I'd first expected and soon realised maybe my alcoholism was nothing more than wishful thinking—this way I had been able to blame my changing moods on substance abuse rather than my inability to adapt. After four weeks, the idea of drinking repulsed me, and I was proud I'd managed to turn into a normal person—if I didn't count cigarettes.

Cigarettes were far too easy to obtain, and unlike alcohol, I truly became nicotine addicted whether I chose to accept it or not.

Whenever the opportunity arose—usually in the middle of a chess game, when my mother, John and Melissa were busy frying their brains in front of the box for three or four hours in succession—Michael offered me the opportunity to practice my cigarette rolling, even though I had given him hell the first time he offered me the chance to smoke in the house. I became so good at rolling cigarettes, I ended up doing it for the both of us.

During a chess game Michael watched me lick the length of the paper with my moist tongue, and even though we kept our observations to ourselves, we knew there was something intimate about rolling a cigarette for another person. When I passed him his cigarette, the edges of the paper were still wet from my saliva, and I became acutely conscious of the essence of my gesture when he placed it between his lips. He must have felt something as well because after the first intake of nicotine he grinned and blushed from such pleasure, you'd think I'd just rolled him a joint.

The door in the lounge room was kept shut because the sound from the television was too loud for Michael and I to concentrate on our game of chess. We were sitting at the kitchen table, facing one another, cigarettes in hand, pondering on our next move while keeping our ears on red alert for the squeaking of the hinges from the lounge room door. Since the lounge room was right at the other end of the hallway, from the moment we'd hear the door being opened, there would be enough time for me to pass my cigarette to Michael or to crush it into the ashtray. We thought ourselves really clever, but I feared one day I would get caught like Judas with his right hand in a bag of coins.

For some unknown reason, I seemed to be doing more chores around the house than John or Melissa.

And then I noticed everyone played little games so they ended up doing as little as possible. Whoever showered last in the evening had to clean the bathroom, so John and Melissa made sure they always jumped in first—even when they knew I'd been last for two days in a row. We were supposed to take it in turns, but they purposely forgot. And with my little English, I couldn't even argue with them. When I complained to my mother in French, she just brushed me off and said they had been helping around the house long before I came into this family—so you have nothing to complain about.

John and Melissa were also conveniently not there on Saturday mornings—him working with Michael on the Jeep Cherokee and her attending a game of netball—so I was stuck helping my mother with the rest of the house cleaning. By the time we were finished, I was so exhausted, all I wanted to do was crawl back into bed and sleep for the rest of the day.

For the first time in my life, I was experiencing the bliss of a conventional upbringing.

My mother and I didn't get as intimate as I had hoped, like the way my father and I had been. She seemed to be purposely distant from me, even when we were alone in the kitchen, or cleaning the house on Saturday mornings, and no one was there to disturb the precious mother-daughter bonding. Our conversations remained contrived and were nothing more than a form of politeness rather than an exchange of meaningful ideas and opinions like those I used to have with my father. The distance between us felt so great at times, I wanted to scream at her—I wasn't just another person she met on the street, but her daughter, and since she had ignored my existence for a good part of my life, maybe it was time to open her eyes and let me inside her heart.

But when she was standing in front of me, a mug of coffee in her hand, her expression serene and in control, I couldn't help feeling selfish for wanting more from my mother after she had opened the doors of her home and welcomed me as one of her own. Sure, I was her daughter and I felt almost within my rights to claim the love I craved for, but inadvertently, she could have left me in France where I would have made no demands on her. Eventually, I convinced myself I was being ungrateful for all she had done for me, and all I needed was to learn to be patient.

But at night, alone in my bed, I cried myself to sleep, craving for the warmth of my father's heart and my mother's acceptance.

Whenever Michael was too busy fixing the Jeep, and I had nothing to do, I lay in a hammock attached to two trees at the end of the backyard. They were apple trees, but the apples they produced were small and filled with holes from worms and other creepy crawlers feeding on them. One day I bit into an apple I snatched from the tree and mistakenly decided it had yet to be turned into a worm haven. It tasted like wet chalk, so I spat out the bite and tossed the apple across the yard—when it came to culinary taste, worms had a long way to go.

Sometimes I just closed my eyes and fell asleep on the hammock because I was tired of everything. But I was also happy. It was the first time in my life I felt like I belonged to a 'complete' family. The only family I had previously known consisted of my father and myself. Although I only realised it now, our two-person family wasn't a happy one because my father was always sick, and I missed the mother I'd never seen. My father and I were like a dog walking on three legs and trying to make them work harder to compensate for the missing limb.

Alone in the backyard, I noticed the clouds above my head were filled like giant grey sponges. I read Proust in French even though I should have been studying my English readers. But what they gave us were primary school books, which dulled my intellectual curiosity. I was tired of reading about cats and dogs and kids and games. It was like I'd stepped back ten years into childhood, and I could sympathise with how other immigrants gave up because of boredom rather than their inability to grasp the language.

When I got tired of reading Proust, I just lay there and watched the sponges of clouds move very slowly, but fast enough for me to be able to notice the change. The dirt and the grass in the backyard smelled crisp and fresh like a new life. I thought a lot about my own life and the world around me, but came to no conclusion. I pondered over learning the guitar, and how I was soon going to ask Michael to teach me for no other reason than the desire to learn and to enjoy his company.

I closed my eyes and smelled his cigarettes on my fingertips and longed for a game of chess.

In early September the weather turned warmer and the days longer. People watched less television and spent more time outdoors, playing cricket in parks or just strolling the streets for something to do. Even Michael and I played chess on a small card table on the back porch, a table retrieved from behind the washing machine in the laundry for the whole of winter. From the patio we smelled the new season of apples at the far end of the backyard—sweet and tempting even if they were inedible.

My English had improved enough for me to be able to carry on a simple conversation without feeling like a complete fool, but I was still far from being fluent. I understood far more words than I could use to express myself. My ESL teacher told me it was normal for new immigrants to gain faster comprehension of a foreign language than the ability to speak it.

After supper, John and I walked the streets of Dandenong. He showed me all the shops and what was cool and what wasn't. He was getting sick of watching television in the evening, and since the weather was improving, he thought it better to spend time outdoors like the rest of the world.

The streets were filled with people, and the only places open were amusement parlours and take-away shops. Every shop was made of concrete slabs or brick veneer with large windows and lettering. It was a town with no real history, where nothing from the past could be read in its architecture—a town whose only claim to having roots was the hundred-year-old Town Hall—an unadorned grey construction whose clock had been stuck on one-twenty-three for the past eight years.

John bought us a family-size Aussie pizza with egg and bacon, and we played pinball at the amusement parlour not far from the train station.

I told him about the boys at school who kept asking me the same question, and I always answered yes, and they kept laughing at me.

'What exactly did they ask you?'

I tried to remember, but I wasn't sure. And then, without thinking, it came out of my mouth, as if someone was secretly whispering the words in my ear.

'Do you wanna fuck?' I said.

John laughed and told me what it meant. I felt redness on my face. I'd been made a fool of for months—the immigrant girl, the fresh-faced wog without a word of English.

CHAPTER TEN

His name was Trevor. He was the only boy who didn't laugh when others made fun of me. I didn't really notice him straight away because he was hiding behind his friends, and when his blue eyes met mine for the first time, he chose to look the other way. I thought he was shy, and it was nice since everybody else was loud and obnoxious. He wasn't much taller than me, and his hair was so black, it looked as if he'd coloured it with charcoal. I liked the way he walked around with his hands deep inside the pockets of his grey trousers, as if nothing in the world really mattered. His expression was of someone permanently lost in thoughts, too busy living in a fantasy world to deal with the reality of every day life. He made me think of myself a little, but I wasn't sure why. Maybe it was the way he seemed to be standing apart from the crowd even though he was in the middle of everyone.

A girl in my class, Tracy—not someone I would necessarily call a friend—told me he was older than me, and if I was interested in him, I should ask him out. I didn't have the courage. Firstly, he belonged with the enemy, and the last thing I felt like doing was joining his group. And secondly, just because I had developed a mild interest in him, it didn't mean he felt the same about me.

I choose to remain indifferent for the time being.

One day I was queuing up at the canteen to buy a roll with cheese and tomato. The sun was high in the cloudless sky and blinding anyone who stood beneath it for too long. Boys played recklessly amongst its burning rays, while girls chose to hide in the shadow of the portable classrooms, and gossip about everyone they knew.

I spent my lunchtimes and recesses reading boring books in order to improve my English. I had resolved not to remain handicapped by my language deficiency for the rest of my life, and the sooner I did something about it, the sooner I'd be able to shed off this inferiority complex which tied me to the tall mast of social ineptitude.

I noticed people wearing thick scarves and beanies of multiple colours even in hot weather—black and red, light blue and white, dark blue and white, yellow and black—and for a while, I thought it was a fashion trend. Someone in the ESL class told me The Grand Final was coming, and I had to choose which team I barracked for. The Grand Final was the end-of-season football game, and I had to pick a 'team' otherwise I was 'uncool'. I chose St Kilda and everyone laughed at me.

'You can't choose St Kilda,' John said when I got home. 'They're at the bottom of the ladder. Pick Hawthorn or North Melbourne.'

He explained The Grand Final was the big event of the Australian Football League, and the scarves were the colours of the teams, and everyone, no exception, had to barrack for a team.

'Footy is like a religion in this country,' John explained while we were putting the dishes away one evening after dinner. 'But instead of worshipping the gods on Sunday, fans worship them on Saturday afternoon. Trust me, you've got to barrack for Hawthorn or North Melbourne.'

'But I don't want to wear the colours everyone else is wearing. I like black and red.'

'St Kilda is a losing team. They only won a Grand Final in 1966 and never managed another since then. Don't go for the losers.'

I stuck with St Kilda.

My father had told me the meek would inherit the earth, and I believed him.

I spoke to Trevor for the first time in the canteen as I waited for my turn to be served behind a bunch of giggling high school girls who kept eyeing boys two rows to the right.

'Did he see you? Did he see you?'

'Oh, man, he's such a spunk!'

'I'm so in love.'

'I saw him first.'

'No, I saw him first.'

'He loves me, anyway.'

'Bitch'

I was wearing my red-and-black St Kilda football team scarf and beanie and looked inconspicuous in the middle of all the other students. My stomach rumbled from not having eaten anything since breakfast. The canteen smelled of pies and hot dogs and sweat from all the other kids queuing up for food as if the world was going to end. The air was cold and the earth moist from a downpour, which miraculously ended ten minutes before lunch.

Trevor approached me from behind and placed one hand gently on my shoulder blade. 'Good choice of team. You don't want to be lost amongst the herd.'

His voice was a runaway train. I felt his hot breath at the back of my cheek as if he'd just kissed me there.

I turned around, smiled and asked him what 'herd' meant. He said it was a large group of mammals living and feeding together. I understood he meant the other students who all wore the same football colours and hung around in groups. I was glad I'd chosen to wear the colours of the St Kilda Football Club.

From now on, Trevor and I ate lunch together. We attempted to communicate with one another, but it was difficult because my English was very rusty. I was glad he had been the one who'd initiated our friendship. I'd have hated to be in the position of looking as if I'd shown too much interest in him. If we ended up hating each other one day, at least I wouldn't have to live with the knowledge I'd made the mistake of making the first move. This way I could always claim he was the one who came and hassled me.

Trevor was the only person I hung around with at school. I made very few friends because no one fancied someone they couldn't communicate with—and most of those who did talked down to me as if my inability to express myself effectively was a sure indication my brain was fried.

But Trevor it was different. He was patient with me. Body language and gestures could express far more than people ever realised.

At times, when I truly couldn't understand what Trevor was talking about, he wrote his thoughts down on foolscap paper. If I still didn't get it, I checked one word at the time in my French-English/English-French dictionary. It was time-consuming, but we were not in a rush, and taking the time to bother bridging our cultural differences made our friendship stronger.

But mostly, we communicated simply by being in each other's presence. Often we would spend our entire time together barely saying a word. We sat on wooden benches outside the school buildings, or by the steps of a portable classroom, or against the gate of the football oval. We observed the world around us, not really interested in being involved.

Day after day, I noticed how gangs of boys and girls always consisted of the same people, and how they always gathered in the same locations, claiming their own territory as if they were scared of venturing anywhere else.

A particular group of girls sat by the steps of the library and talked throughout lunch. I wondered what they had to say to be talking so much. Trevor reckoned they were talking about the boys they wanted to ask out, but had no idea how to go about it. When I asked him how he knew, he said he just did because girls thought and talked about boys during the first two-to-three years of high school. It almost annoyed me how he was right, and how I, myself, had been wasting too much time thinking about him instead of my school work, my English reading and the world around me.

A group of boys chose a windowless, grey wall of one of the school buildings and played by throwing a tennis ball against it, in the same way squash players throw a little black rubber ball against a concrete wall. But instead of using rackets the boys used the palms of their hands.

Other boys, like Trevor's friends, played on the school oval, kicking anything around, pretending it was a football.

Within a month Trevor and I became almost an item. We were a couple, except we had not taken a chance at being intimate and we never talked about it. The thought of making a pass at Trevor had occurred to me, but that's all it remained—a thought. My heart was still bruised from David's betrayal, and to add to my confusion I wasn't really sure how I felt about Trevor. It was just nice to have someone around who cared, and if I made a move on him, I feared losing the friendship and being by myself again. Loneliness was not a world I wanted to return to.

On a Friday afternoon, in the last week of September, Trevor asked me if I wanted to come over to his place. We were standing by the school gate knowing the weekend would be long and boring without seeing each other. His parents were going to be away for the entire two days and stay over at a friend's holiday cottage at Philip Island. We'd have the whole three-bedroom house all for ourselves with no one in sight to bother us.

'I can't,' I said, 'my parents would never let me.'

I knew I would have been able to go and visit him if I chose to —maybe not staying overnight on Saturday, but certainly during the day—but I didn't want to make it too easy for him. He would get the wrong idea, the way David did back in France when I agreed to go up and visit his apartment. I dreaded finding myself in the same predicament again, when a moment's decision could mean ruining a friendship or giving myself away too easily.

On a Tuesday morning, at recess, in the first week of October, Trevor's friends saw us together. Trevor had slowly drifted away from the boys he'd been hanging around with, the same boys who had been making fun of me when I couldn't understand English properly. I remembered how the redhead—the one whose face was spotted with freckles—had instructed me to say 'yes' every time someone would asked me, 'Do you want a fuck?' He was the leader of the gang. He pointed in our direction and led his friends to participate in the mockery.

Trevor and I were sitting on one of the wood-and-metal school desks left outside because they were too good to throw out and too shabby to use in the classroom. Graffiti covered the desk in blue biro, black marker, carved in wood with the sharp end of a compass; devotions of love—Debbie 4 Christian 4 Ever—insults, penises, breasts, immature poetry, answers to tests, mathematical equations, cartoon characters, radio station names.

The sky was clear with little fluffy vanilla cushions in the horizon and a mild wind blew from the west.

The redhead, along with his friends, laughed loudly enough for Trevor and I to feel irritated and partly intimidated by their obnoxious behaviour. I wanted to smack the redhead in the mouth, but I knew better than to give them the satisfaction of seeing me reacting to their insults.

'Hey Trevo!' the redhead yelled, 'You're giving her some, eh?'

'You wait here,' Trevor said and walked to where the group was before I had time to hold him back.

117

I watched from the bench as Trevor stood in front of his friends and discussed one thing or another with the redhead. Within twenty seconds of Trevor being in the middle of the group, a scuffle broke out. The redhead and a blond kid jumped on Trevor when he tried to take a swing at the redhead. They pushed him to the floor, and the redhead sat on his chest, riding him like a horse. The other boys cheered them on like fans at a football game eagerly waiting for blood to spill. Arms and legs flew around like knives and swords. Trevor tried to free himself. The redhead and the blond kid kept him pinned to the asphalt like the Romans did with Jesus on the cross.

Panic-stricken, I jumped from the bench and rushed to where the boys were. I was Joan of Arc—too young to fight but willing to join the battle and save their honour.

The hungry crowd was so preoccupied cheering, no one noticed me coming their way. With full force I swung my schoolbag filled with books in an arc, like a samurai beheading his opponent, and struck the redhead on the left side of the face. His green marble eyes opened wide and he stumbled sideways, like a drunk who'd finished the last bottle, and let out a dog-beaten shriek. I took advantage of his moment of recovery to grab a handful of straw hair from the blond kid and yank him backwards until he hit the pavement like a bag of bones.

The crowd cheered in amazement

Trevor got on his feet, blood dripping from his nose.

The redhead looked up and realised what had just happened.

'You bitch, French fuckin' bitch!' he spat at me as if I were a witch who'd just cursed him with a deadly spell.

His group of spineless friends joined in.

'Yeah, you fuckin' French whore!'

'Go back home.'

'Wog.'

'Arsehole.'

'Snail.'

And then they retreated like scavengers who'd realised the prey were still alive and well. Trevor tried to stop the bleeding from his nose with the back of his hand. The defeated screamed abuse as they moved away from us, but I was no longer paying attention.

'Are you all right?' I asked Trevor.

I feared his nose might have broken during the fight. My right index finger traced the line of his jaw.

'I think so,' he said, 'it's just bleeding.'

We walked to a drinking fountain. I held on to his arm like a nurse helping the wounded in a military hospital. I retrieved a white, cotton handkerchief from my bag, folded it in half and drenched it in cold water. Trevor stood still, his eyes almost shut, while I gently wiped off the blood smudged on his upper lip and nose. Whenever I finger-brushed his face, I noticed how soft his skin was. My face was so close to his, I smelled vanilla, bubble-gum and blood.

'Hold the handkerchief under your nose for a minute,' I said.

He did as I told him and kept the bloodstained, white handkerchief at an angle to stop the bleeding. His chestnut hair was unkempt and spiked with perspiration, his cheeks painted red, and his breathing fast and irregular. I wanted to hug him, but because he held the handkerchief to his face, and other students were walking past and looked at us as if we were two monkeys in a cage, I held back.

When he opened his eyes again, he looked right into mine.

It was like getting hit square in the face.

I knew we'd made a connection.

'What have you done to your dress?' my mother yelled.

It was early Thursday morning and we were getting ready for school. I was waiting for her to finish packing my lunch. She knew something was going on because I began wearing the make-up I brought from France, and I'd shortened my school dress. It hung just below my underwear.

She said it in French, and John and Melissa had no idea what was going on, but at the tone of my mother's voice, they raced out of the kitchen and vanished down the hall. I knew they'd be waiting for me by the front porch because I wore a school uniform and looked the same as the other students, they no longer needed to be ashamed.

'You look like *une putain!*—a whore—She screamed, her crimson face so close to mine, I saw spit on the corner of her lips. 'Where the hell do you think you're going dressed this way?'

She ordered me to go to my room and change into my marine school trousers even though I was already late.

'Look at the weather!' I yelled back at her. 'It's going to be twenty-seven today. Everyone will be wearing a dress, and you're making me wear trousers. It's so stupid!'

'I don't care what everyone else will be wearing—no daughter of mine is going to school looking like a slut.'

'Ah, yeah, like you suddenly give a shit about me.'

'What did you just say?'

'Nothing.'

I went to my room and changed into trousers.

And then it became a habit. *What a bitch!* Everything I hated wearing, she forced me to wear. If I wore something I liked for a day, she said it smelled, and I had to put it in the wash by the afternoon. But when I hated an item of clothing, she forced me to wear it for a week. It felt as if she purposely challenged my need for independence and enjoyed seeing me getting upset over trivial disagreements.

When night came, alone in the darkness of my room, I told myself it might just be my imagination, my mother couldn't have been so sadistic to impose her power over me in regards to my dressing only because she relished in my suffering. But our clashes were too frequent and too bitter to be insignificant, no matter how much I tried to tell myself I was suffering from paranoia.

'It's a generation gap thing,' Trevor told me when we were having lunch together at school. 'Everyone argues with their parents.'

'Yeah, but I really think she hates me.'

And the more she confronted me, the more rebellious I became. I tucked my high school dress in my bag and changed into it in the school toilet before class began. I wasn't going to told who I should be, especially by someone who'd never cared about me for the first twelve years of my life.

I rolled up the bottom half of my jumper the way I had seen other girls do it so their waists seemed smaller and their breasts more protruding. I let my dark hair grow long and uneven. I pushed it up into a loose bun held together by a large pink plastic clip and let strands fall over my face. I wore thick dark mascara à la Brigitte Bardot and rouge on my cheeks. I plucked my eyebrows until there was only a pencil-thin line arched over each one of my eyes.

I stood in front of the mirror in the school toilet cubicle and smoked a cigarette I'd rolled myself the night before when everyone was asleep. I pouted my lips, put one hand on my hip and kissed the mirror from a distance. Saucy. Something was happening to me but I wasn't sure what. I stared at my reflection and admitted I did look kind of awkward in my bony frame. My big blue eyes were coloured with pain.

Two girls walked into the room, plain-Jane types with blue-and-white high-school dresses cut just above the knees and jumpers pulled down to their full length. They were about my age but too conservative for me to have noticed them in the past. They were teachers' pets—nice girls with pressed uniforms and hair parted in the middle and no make-up whatsoever.

I tried to ignore them and pretended to be in the middle of fixing up my hair. I pulled strands over my face with wet fingers as if using gel, and I became a French starlet I'd seen in a magazine laying on the coffee table back home.

The girls' eyes threw darts at my reflection in the mirror, and I felt a pain at the back of my neck like someone pinching me with overgrown fingernails. I dared to return their stare—if they had something to say, they could just say it, and I wouldn't lose sleep over it.

Pink-cheeked, they looked away like thieves ashamed of their own existence after getting caught with a hand in the bag.

I was changing and I liked it.

Other people noticed the change so I knew it wasn't an illusion. Boys at school whistled when I walked past them in the courtyard. The male teachers were more patient and dedicated to my learning. John and Michael glanced at me with a glow in their eyes, which spelled excitement and danger all at once.

In the evening, after dinner, John insisted on having our daily walk. I obliged because it was better than sitting in front of the television or listening to my mother lecturing me on the realities of life, and how I was turning bad and how something awful was going to happen to me if I continued to walk *this* path. I wanted to tell her I liked the path I was walking on, and everybody else did too, and she was the only one who resented what I was becoming. But even with my newly-found confidence, she was more a woman than I was, and the game I played at school didn't gel with her the way it did with everybody else. She too had been a woman-child once and knew my power was a double-edged sword. Still, I wanted to tell her I'd found the power, and I liked it and I was keeping it. She shouldn't have left me behind when I was a baby because now it was too late for her to try to gain back control of my life.

But I didn't dare confront her—not yet anyway. I was afraid of the effect she had on me when we argued, how she could make me feel so small, how I wanted to run down the street and throw myself under a bus. She didn't even realise when she told me I looked like a slut, she might as well as sliced me in half like an orange. She was my mother, yet she had no idea how every insidious comment she made about me—no matter how indifferent I might have seemed at the time—was a bullet through the heart.

And it wasn't just the way she passed judgement on my clothes that cut through the core of my self-worth, but also the bitterness in her eyes when we disagreed over trivial matters. I was a rodent invading her household, and she had yet to figure out how to dispose of me.

I could have argued endlessly, but instead I choose to lock myself in my room with Michael's acoustic guitar and skinned my fingers on the F Major chord the way I had slit my wrists when I couldn't take it any more

John took me to a game parlour a couple of streets away from our George Street home, one hundred meters from the train station, past a fish-and-chips shop and a taxi rank where the drivers were half asleep or reading thick, paperback airport novels. Inside the parlour music poured from a CD jukebox like at a nightclub, and pinball machines and arcade electronic games beeped and rang as if the world was coming to an end. The place smelled of rancid sweat, cigarette smoke and wet dog. The carpet was food-stained beyond redemption, and the ceiling coloured nicotine.

A man in his early twenties—unkempt blond hair, a gold sleeper in his left ear and a nose too big for his face—was supposedly monitoring the customers from behind a counter, where he was also responsible for providing change and selling soft drinks and salty packaged food. He was too busy flicking through a skin magazine with a large-breasted woman on the cover to bother paying attention to the in-and-out traffic.

There were advertising posters plastered all over the wall behind the counter—Four'n'Twenty pies, Coca Cola, Big M flavoured milk. The people in the advertisements were young and beautiful, full of life, and played outdoors along great Australian beaches, cruising in a four-wheel drive, or surfing like gods of the ocean. The message was loud and clear—if we smoked cigarettes and consumed enough junk food, we too could find beauty, freedom and happiness.

I wore a cropped, white tee-shirt and a short, pink skirt I picked up for sale at Westco, where the clothes had the designer look but the quality was unbelievably nauseating. My hair ran freely over my shoulders. My smile was painted in bright cherry lipstick. I looked like one of the Big M girls with strawberry flavoured milk running down their breasts as if they were incapable of drinking without dribbling. All the boys kept staring at me and wanted to eat me alive, right here, right now. I felt like the homecoming queen. Girls gave me nasty looks as if I were a serious threat to their womanhood.

'Why don't you date someone?' I asked John.

He slammed into a pinball machine with a picture of Keanu Reeves in *The Matrix* on the front panel. He wore jeans and a flame-blue flannel shirt with the sleeves ripped off, his biceps bulging like bread rolls. The sleeveless shirt looked good on him in a bohemian kind-of-way, and if I hadn't been his sister, I would have considered going out with him.

'Haven't found anyone I like,' he said and added another five thousand points to his score. The machine went into a spasm of bleeping lights and ringing bells.

'You're good looking—you shouldn't have any problem finding someone. Three girls in my class asked me about you. One of them is really cute and her parents are rich. I can talk to her if you want.'

'I don't want a girlfriend—I've got to look after my little sister.'

'I can look after myself.'

'I like being with you.'

'Baby-sitting?'

'Yeah, so what? I like baby-sitting.'

We both giggled and he lost his fifth ball to the game.

One night John and I got home a little later after nine. Darkness surrounded us like trees in a forest. The sky was dotted with stars.

A moon the size of a tyre shone brightly enough for us to observe in blue and grey shades each other's face.

We stood near the patio like a couple who'd just returned from a late-night party and were trying to get inside the house without waking up the kids. We'd just spent the last three hours in the streets of Dandenong and at the amusement parlour, where John beat his record on the Keanu Reeves pinball machine for the third day in a row. We had talked about school, home, parents, music, stupid jobs, relationships, everything and nothing, and enjoyed each other's company while eating pizza, drinking Coke and sharing cigarettes.

My back to the house, I fished into my black, vinyl handbag for the keys to the front door, sorting through lipstick, eye liner, touch up, pens, receipts and empty packets of gum.

The front yard was creepy—bushes and trees, branches reaching out like witches' arthritic fingers along the narrow brick pathway to the front porch. The night smelled like death, moisture and dirt.

It was relatively warm for late September, and we could have gone straight to the back of the house and sat all night on the hammock in the backyard and continued to discuss the trials and tribulations of life.

John was standing close to me, his breath on my cheek like the softness of a pillow. We were both scared my mother would tell us off for coming home so late, but John told me not to worry because she wasn't his real mother.

I said, 'You're not the one being harassed everyday on how you dress, on your make-up, on your homework—not as you are doing any—or how you waste too much time playing guitar or playing chess with Michael. You're a boy, it's easy for you.'

'She just yells a bit, no big deal.'

'She's my real mother, and I don't like getting into arguments with her.'

'I'll tell her I was the one who held you back.'

'Jeez, why do I suddenly feel reassured?'

His cheap, citric aftershave whisked past me like a summer breeze. Up-close, his skin was snowflake flawless, especially at night, where shadows ironed out faults and the mind was less critical. It felt so strange and yet so natural to be so close to someone whom I didn't need to fear or be jealous of.

He turned around and smelled my hair a little too long for it to be a casual motion.

And then he tilted his head forward and kissed me, his lips crushing against mine like the pressing of palms. I held his kiss the way a lost child holds on to a stranger's hand. He tasted like pizza and ice cream. Martine had warned me about boys. They are like cigarettes, she said, they're bad for you, but you'll never stop wanting them. Now I finally understood what she meant. John was only thing that mattered. I had learned nothing from the way David broke my heart in France a year ago—and I didn't want to learn.

I accidentally dropped my keys on the patio. They crashed like broken glass.

John moved away from me and kneeled down in the dark.

'Shit, where are they?' he said.

I went down with him, my hands reaching out into the emptiness below me like someone reaching for a wall in a room with the light turned off. Our hands swept the dry planks of the patio—as I feared being punctured by splitters of cracked, rotting wood—and then we heard the metallic sound of the keys.

'Got them,' he said and rose to his feet.

When we got inside the house, my mother was reading in bed, Melissa was watching television, and Michael was smoking on the back porch. No one seemed concerned we got home late.

We whispered and stole kisses in the darkness of the hallway.

Alone in bed, I couldn't stop thinking about John—the taste of his kiss in my mouth, the bulging of his arms, his flame-blue flannel shirt, the sweet smell of his cheap aftershave still on my hands and face. Knowing he was sleeping under the same roof as me made my plight even more unbearable. He was my brother, and I knew what we did was wrong. But he wasn't really my brother—we were not blood-related, and he might as well have been the boy next door. So, how could it have been wrong?

I stayed awake for an eternity and stared at the white ceiling above my bed. Wind shuffled leaves in the backyard like kittens lost under the house. The smell of John's aftershave lingered on the pillow he had swapped before going to bed. I fought the desire of wanting him so badly, but it was like trying to breathe under water. God was watching, and he would send me to hell for my impious act—a lost soul amongst those who had let themselves be hugged into the open arms of temptation.

It was Trevor I liked—I tried to convince myself—even if John was sweet, classically good-looking, and my best friend outside of school. But we were caught in an irresolvable turmoil. There'd be no point in carrying on and pretending our moment of delusional passion was any more than a lapse of reasoning. I would have to lie and tell him his kisses were the result of our confused relationship.

But to date Trevor had never made a pass at me, even though I'd been secretly waiting for him to seduce me. John and I had taken an apple bite from in the Garden of Eden, and I decided it was time to make a move on Trevor—John would clearly understand last light's *incident* meant nothing to me.

I smiled in the darkness and felt pleased with myself—I had everything under masterly control—I was a woman now and I had power.

At one in the morning I finally closed my eyes and fell asleep.

The taste of John lingered in my throat like the sweetness of wine from the bottom of a barrel.

One day after school, Michael taught me how to play *You Were Meant for Me* on the acoustic guitar, but I couldn't sing it properly because of my accent. He said I should persist because one day my accent would fade away, and by then I would know how to play the guitar and sing the way it sounded on the recording.

I tried, but my voice was weak like that of a dog that had lost its bark. My French accent was too strong and forced me to be self-conscious, which in turn restrained my ability to sing in tune. Michael said my singing sounded cute, but I didn't think so—I would have rather sang properly than what he perceived as cute. Had Jewel recorded *You Were Meant for Me* the way I sang it, she'd still be living in a van with her mother on jam sandwiches and dreams.

We were sitting on the back porch with its decaying planks and peeling paint. The sky was a cloudless blue and the air bathed in the smell of recently cut grass and crushed apples. I wore my high school uniform, and he wore his greasy denim work overalls. My mother was inside cooking. Melissa was out with her boyfriend. John was busy re-nailing and re-painting the front fence, which was falling apart after at least fifty years of negligence. My mother had ordered John to fix it after he missed out on cleaning the shower for two weeks in a row.

'Do you love my mother?' I asked Michael.

I looked down the neck of the guitar and practised an A Major to B7 transition.

He stared at me for fifteen seconds as if I'd asked him the square root of some six-figure number. You'd think after living with my mother for five years, he'd have a stock answer.

'Love is never the reason why people are together,' he said.

I knew he was going to say before he said it.

'You sound like my father.'

'Well, then, I guess he must have been right.'

The fingertips of my left hand were marked red by the steel strings of the guitar. I was getting a blister on my index finger, and soon I wouldn't be able to play at all. If I persisted long enough, Michael said, my fingertips would toughen up like the skin on a crocodile's back, and then I'd be able to slide my fingers up and down the neck of the guitar as effortlessly as Jimi Hendrix did before he choked on his own vomit decades ago. I asked him who Jimi Hendrix was, and he looked at me as if I'd just landed from the moon.

'Forget it,' I said. 'Do you believe there's such a thing as love?'

He smiled awkwardly as if I'd asked him for a million dollars. 'It's a myth. People think they love another person, but it's the idea of someone loving them they are really attracted to. People are selfish in nature. They can't really love someone whole-heartedly other than themselves—and that in itself is an impossible task.'

'Love is not kind. Love is a traitor.'

'Yeah, well, I suppose it's one way to put it.'

Trevor and I were sitting at the edge of the school football oval, our backs pressed against the galvanised fence like two drunks who could no longer stand up and didn't care either way. We were watching Trevor's old friends having fun by kicking an empty carton of chocolate-flavoured milk around the yard like people watch sport on television with the safety of detachment.

It was a fine spring day with a hint of summer with orange streaks painting the horizon like a Turner painting. Black-and-white Magpies crossed the length of the football oval and tried to peck some of the kids on the head but retreated at the last moment when they realised the size of their prey.

We were side-by-side, me resting slightly more against him than him against me, my bony arm sunk into the softness of his shoulder. I could feel his lungs contracting and relaxing with every breath he took. It would have been obvious to anyone the way we behaved towards one another indicated more than friendship. I certainly felt like there was strong emotional connection between us, but Trevor seemed aloof to our intimacy—he would probably be the last one to know, much to his surprise at the revelation from his friends and acquaintances. His indifference made me even more determined to proceed with my insidious plan. I decided to control the rage inside me by doing what I felt was right and refusing to let the devil play with my emotions. He had destroyed my father's heart, and he wasn't going to destroy mine.

Without warning, I tilted my head and rested it against the grey softness of Trevor's sleeve. Like a sick child, I pretended to be taken by a spell of tiredness. I felt Trevor twitch a little and sensed his eyes on me, but I closed mine so he wouldn't suspect anything. As soon as my eyes were shut, much to my surprise, I thought about John—I knew he was somewhere in the school yard thinking about me. When I saw his face in my mind's eye, I jolted from my pretend drowsiness and forced myself to remain in the present time.

'You okay?' Trevor asked. He looked straight into my eyes and smiled.

I smiled back. 'I'm okay.'

Before he had time to say another word, I pushed my head forward and kissed him on the mouth the way John had kissed me. His lips were soft and warm like the healing rays of the sun over our heads.

From the way his eyes came to life—round and livid with speckles of green and yellow—I knew he'd been taken by surprise. Still, he offered little resistance—not that I had expected him to.

For the past few weeks, I'd worked hard on making myself irresistible—I wore more make-up than usual, pink socks instead of the regulated white ones, cheap jewellery and plastic hair clips, everything designed to highlight my femininity. I wanted to look the cutest I possibly could so he would find himself tempted like someone who'd been given a bag of full of money with no strings attached.

When our lips parted, he titled his head back a little and said, 'What happened?'

'What do you think?'

He frowned.

I kissed him again, this time with more passion.

He loosened up completely and kissed me back with urgency, like someone who hadn't drank a drop of water for thirty days straight.

And all of a sudden, an object came landing on our heads and bounced back against the fence and into the grass. Surprised, we both looked up as if a cloud fell from the sky. We spotted an empty carton of chocolate flavoured milk by the side of the school fence.

Only ten meters from us, the boys who were previously playing with the milk carton burst into laugher like characters in a morning cartoon.

'Hey, lover boy, you wanna share her around?'

'So that's what they call a French kiss?'

'Is it true she tastes like French vanilla?'

'Can we toss her around for a game?'

Trevor jumped to his feet.

I grabbed him by the sleeve. 'Don't worry about it.'

Arseholes!' He screamed at them, but his anger made the boys laugh even louder. I knew they wanted us to react to their childish behaviour, to acknowledge their existence as if they were important enough in our lives. I could see it as clearly as I could see Trevor's redness in his face and his lips flaring up like a rabbit caught in a trap. We didn't have to put up with their condemnation, but sometimes the only solution was to walk away.

I stood up. 'Come on, let's go. They're not worth it.'

Trevor hesitated, but I grabbed the sleeve of his shirt and pulled him towards me.

'Let's get out of here,' I said.

He hesitated for a few seconds, and finally let me drag him away towards the school library.

The sun glittered between the trees and straight into our eyes as we walked alongside the galvanised fence in the opposite direction of the boys who continued to shoot bullets of abuse from a distance.

'I'm going to get them,' Trevor said. Bitterness infested his voice like a mouthful of ants. His jaw trembled from the grinding of teeth and reminded me of myself when I was upset or angry and wanted to kill someone.

We'd walked less than a metre when the empty carton of chocolate flavoured milk landed at the back of Trevor's head and forced him to jolt two steps forwards.

Loud laughter erupted behind our backs like Chinese firecracker.

Trevor turned around, his face reddening worse than before.

I pulled him hard towards me. 'Don't worry about it, they're idiots. Let's go.'

But he managed to loosen himself from my grip and kicked the milk carton towards the group of boys as if it were a football. It landed right at their feet.

'Leave us alone!' he screamed.

The redhead yelled back, 'Come on, you chicken shit, show us what you've got. Or you gonna get your *French whore* to defend you again?'

Something within snapped like a rubber band stretched beyond its elasticity.

Before Trevor had time to realise what was happening, I paced towards the redhead. 'What did you call me?'

He mimicked my accent, '*What did you call me?* You're a French whore. Why don't you go back to your own country?'

I slapped him on the face as hard as I possibly could. The way the red-head's eyes rolled to the top of his eyelids reminded me of a lighting effect on the *Matrix* pinball machine John played at the amusement parlour.

'Ah, shit,' the redhead cried and held on to the side of his face as if I'd hit him with a cricket bat. When he pulled his hand back, the five fingers of my right hand were etched on his cheek like engraving on copper. The palm of my hand hurt.

The rest of the group stepped three metres back and formed half an arc around us.

Trevor was now by my side, ready to pounce on anyone who dared lunge at me. 'Come on,' he said, 'I'll take you all on.'

The redhead stepped backwards and joined his friends.

'Fuck you, Trevor,' he said, 'and fuck that French bitch of yours —you're going to pay, you god-damn fuckin' arsehole. The two of youse.'

'Let's go,' Trevor said and pulled me by the sleeve of my school dress.

We moved away from the group as they cursed promises of revenge.

And then Trevor grabbed me by the shoulders, turned me around and kissed me passionately while giving the finger to the redhead.

Eat this, arsehole.

I was sitting at the principal's office, the redhead on my left with his mother, and my mother on my right, like four prisoners on death row.

The red-head's name was Tony Horne—I'd found out when the principal's secretary contacted my mother the previous day. I had 'behaved in an unacceptable manner' by using physical violence towards one of my fellow students. I was a violent and dangerous person who resorted to hitting people when I could have simply expressed myself with words, and the principal wanted to see my mother as soon as possible with the victim's parent so I could personally apologise to Tony and his mother.

The principal, Mr Turner—a middle-aged man, wore cropped salt-and-pepper hair, a grey jacket, a yellow, striped tie—looked more like a bank manager than someone who worked at a high school. His cheeks were permanently flushed, the way they usually are with people who drink too much. I knew about his vice because I'd seen street beggars in Strasbourg suffering from the same happy-looking complexion.

'You can't go around hitting people,' he said and jackhammered his silver pen on the top of his timber desk—tap, tap, tap—like a green woodpecker boring its strong chisel-like bill into a tree in search of worms or insects. His eyes were round and polished like glass beads, and I couldn't read them the way I did when I wanted to know what was going on in someone's mind.

I turned to the left to contemplate my adversaries. The redness of my fingers' impression on Tony's cheek had turned bluish-purple and made me proud of what I had done. The fact his mother noticed the blemish that same night and reported it to the school authority was even more hilarious. No matter what the outcomes of this meeting would be, I had marked my territory— no apology would ever take away my dignity.

Tony was staring down at his black leather school shoes. He was not the lout I had encountered previously in the school yard, but a picture-perfect portrait of an innocent little boy who had been abused and betrayed by how some voracious bitch. Still, he must have felt ashamed how this dramatic turn of events had come to the attention of the principal. Wasn't he man enough to handle his own problems? Soon, everyone at school would know he had been ratting on me, clearly a worse act than being caught wagging or smoking. And to add to his disgrace, a girl hitting him would make him a walking joke.

His mother, who bore the same flame-colour hair as him, never took her eyes off the principal's face. She was thin-lipped with freckles covering her face and had sticks for legs. I could smell her rancid body odour from where I was sitting, a vinegar-like stench whisking from her perspiring armpits.

'He called her a whore, for God's sake,' my mother said, her voice strong and commanding.

'I understand,' Mr Turner said, 'but all she had to do was come to my office and report it. We can't have students beating each other up every time they disagree about something. This is not the first time it's happened.' He turned to me. 'Apparently you attacked Tony and another boy two weeks ago. I don't know what it's like in France, but in Australia, this is not the way we deal with problems.'

I refused to get involved. No matter what I said, no one was going to listen to me. I was the bad apple filled with worms, and they might as well have tossed me in the backyard of my mother's home with the other rotten apples. School worked on a system of guilty until proven innocent, and I didn't have the ability or the confidence to defend myself.

When the principal asked me if I understood the seriousness of the situation, I nodded so I wouldn't have to hear more of his reprimand. Pass the sentence and get it over with.

'If this happens again,' he said, 'I'm going to have to expel you from this school. Do you understand?'

I nodded again, but they could all go to hell as far as I was concerned. I had this urge to punch the redhead in the nose in front of everyone to show them I didn't care about their stupid rules, and if they didn't like it, they could always send me back to France.

And then the principal mentioned something about make-up and how my school dress was cut way too short, and pink socks were not in regulation with the school uniform code of conduct, but I wasn't really paying attention any more—I thought about smoking a cigarette instead. An adult would have done the same under pressure—slide a cigarette between her lips and suck on it obsessively, regardless of what people around her thought. But to everyone's eye I was a child, and a child had as much right as a lamb waiting for the blade.

My mother threw me a look that said *I told you so.*

When we left the principal's office, she said, 'I'm transferring you to another school next year. You've only been here four months, and already you're causing havoc.'

'You can't, I was only defending myself.'

'By beating someone up?'

'He started it.'

'Did he hit you?'

'No, but he started it. I've got friends now, you can't force me to change schools.'

'I can do whatever I want. You're thirteen and I'm your mother. I don't know how your father brought you up, but your behaviour is bordering on delinquency.'

Michael was waiting for us by the school gate, his backside pressed against the passenger door of the Jeep, his eyes squinting from the burning rays of the sun. It was good to see his friendly, familiar face. Maybe he and I could disappear and escape this world of lunatics, runaway into the outback and live amongst the Aborigines—him the strong father figured I longed for—and no one would tell us what to do.

I wanted to run over and hug him and ask him to take me away from this nightmare. But as I approached the car, he threw me a sour-milk look, and I realised I was once more on my own.

I understood how Jesus must have felt when they nailed him to the cross.

CHAPTER ELEVEN

October came and went like a speeding train, destination unknown. I was still at school, and the temperature already soared to thirty degrees plus during the day and made it difficult to concentrate in class or bother with homework by the time I got home.

Early in the morning, while still in bed, I could tell it was going to be a scorcher of a day. The air was maple syrup thick and smelled of eucalyptus from the trees lining up our street. Breathing was sticking one's head into a baker's oven. My fingers turned into thick sponges filled with too much blood, and by the time I showered and put on my school uniform, the red alcohol of the koala-shaped thermometer attached to the fridge had climbed to twenty-five degrees.

I saw Redhead Tony twice by the metal lockers in B-block. He was all by himself after being rejected from his pack for being such a wimp. When his eyes crossed mine, he drew a shy-boy smile and looked embarrassed. Other kids had been teasing him, calling him 'snitch' when he used to be called 'red'. When someone yelled 'snitch', he didn't respond, but you could tell he knew the nickname was meant for him because all of a sudden the colour of his face matched that of his hair. I kind of felt sorry for him because he had once been very popular, and now he was a loner—I'd been there, and I knew how loneliness sometimes could tear you worse than a grenade in hand.

One morning, during the second period, I was enjoying a cigarette after excusing myself from my ESL class under the pretext I had to go to the toilet for *that* reason—girl's advantage.

I was behind the school hall, convinced no one would find me since everyone was in class—students and teachers alike.

The sun was bright in the sky and aching hot, so I stood under the shade of a persimmon tree, not far from the grey back wall of the school hall. No one ever walked past there because there was simply no need to. I felt safe and burden-free, smoking my cigarette like someone getting paid by the hour, my back against the bark of the tree and my left leg pushed up at a right angle. I observed the magpies circle the yard and plunge towards the grass with daring kamikaze precision, only to swing into an arc at the last second and ascend back. I sucked on my cigarette enthusiastically and wished I were a bird.

Halfway through my cigarette, Tony suddenly appeared at the corner of the building like a killer in a dark alley, a metal rubbish bin in one hand and an awkward grin painted on his face. When I first saw him, I panicked and feared he'd wanted to give me a good beating since we were alone. I remained where I was, like the tree I had backed against. Full of bully confidence, he dropped the bin on the hot asphalt and walked casually to the shade of the persimmon tree where I was still smoking my cigarette. He must have been on yard duty for the rest of the afternoon—the reason why he was carrying a rubbish bin around with him like someone takes a dog for a walk.

I felt a fist-size knot down the base of my stomach when he reached the under-foliage of the tree. He was sweating from working under the sun, pearls of perspiration covering his face, and I reassured myself he needed the rest much more than I did. Still, another voice at the back of my mind told me if all he wanted to do was rest, then there were other shadowy spots around the school yard

He'd lost weight since the day at the principal's office, and one didn't have to be a genius to figure out the stress of being an outcast had been burning, which had in the past turned into puppy fat—welcome to my world.

I waited for an avalanche of insults to hit me like stones from a mob.

He said, 'I'm sorry about the way things have turned out.'

I stared at him for a few seconds and took a drag from my cigarette to kill the fear from my mind. There was sincerity in the green pasture of his eyes took me by surprise.

'So am I,' I said.

I offered him one of my cigarettes.

He smoked it slowly, and we didn't speak another word.

I broke up with Trevor because all we ended up doing was arguing about how he wished we'd remained friends, and how I should have never made a pass at him. I granted him his wish one day without any explanation. I just disappeared at lunchtime into the library to secretly read my books in one of the study cubicles, or lost myself in the school grounds, or walked the streets like a homeless person trying to find a home in a world that had no time for those who looked for mermaids at the bottom of the ocean.

Whenever I saw Trevor at school, with or without his friends, I took off in the opposite direction and hid amongst other students or paced as fast as I possibly could without turning back. He said we should remain friends if we ever decided to break it off, but I couldn't understand how I could remain friends with someone who I'd previously kissed in front of everyone, and now I suddenly had to act distantly polite. It was easier to make a clean cut, to forget about the past altogether and to move on. School would be over soon, and my mother had already received confirmation from Noble Park High School that I would be able to start the following February after the summer holidays. Breaking off with Trevor hadn't been very difficult. I was stronger than I had ever been with David. My heart was still intact—not made from sugar and spice, but copper and lead.

In one week, I eased off on the make-up—no more cherry-red lipstick, rouge for my cheeks, teased hair and extremely plucked eyebrows. I became tired of being the chick boys drooled over and girls wanted to punch from sheer jealously—I was a trouble magnet, and everyone had told me so. I wanted to crawl and curl up into a corner like a cancerous dog waiting for his last breath and hoped no one would notice me.

I stored all my make-up in the backpack I took from France with me and tossed it on top of the wardrobe of my room like a bad curse. In spite of my preceding desire to belong to this world, I didn't want to be pretty any more—I didn't want boys to fall in love with me, or look at me as if I was something they could devour with their eyes. I wanted to be a passenger on a train watching the hazy landscape shift before my eyes.

After school, I sat in my room and practised *Who Will Save Your Soul* on Michael's acoustic guitar, and it made me want to return to my father's tombstone and lie next to him for eternity.

One afternoon on my way back from school, I received a letter in a pink envelope with little hand-drawn stars in red ink on the front and the back, and a blue *par avion* sticker on the top left corner. It smelled like talcum powder. The sender's name was Martine. I had no idea how she got my address, but I could only assume it was Louise who gave it to her. If it was, then I wondered why Louise had never bothered writing to me. She had promised she would, but promises were like the weatherman selling you golden days of endless sunshine in the middle of a downpour. She was probably too busy babysitting another homeless kid who was slowly but surely being sucked into a vacuum of illusion and despair.

Martine was no longer with her dark-haired boyfriend. He did, however, leave her a legacy to remember him by—a three-month pregnancy and nowhere to go. She toyed with the idea of moving back to Strasbourg because the social services in Alsace were more efficient than in the South of France, and the few people she knew in Strasbourg could initiate her into motherhood with understanding and friendship.

She wrote how she wished I was still around, and even though I was much younger than her and lived halfway around the world, she considered me her best friend. And not just best friend, but the best friend she ever had, even if she never realised it at the time. And she missed me a lot. And was it possible for her to come to Australia? And was there anything I could do to get her there?

When I finished reading the letter, I cried, not because I missed her as much as she missed me, but because I knew there was nothing I could do to alleviate her misery. I also cried because she seemed so intelligent back when I first met her, and she used to shower me with all her wisdom, and now getting pregnant at the age of fifteen seemed like a silly thing to get herself into. Was this the price to pay for wanting to be loved so badly?

The letter remained answered for two whole months.

John and I were playing pinball machine at the amusement parlour —lights flashing and bells ringing like emergency vehicles, cigarette smoke bathing the whole room in a creamy yellow haze. He bought me a packet of menthols through his friend Chris who was old enough to buy anything he wanted. Chris wore blond sandy hair down to his shoulders, tight denim shorts, white singlets and labourer's boots. He called everyone cobber or mate. He always ate a Four'n'Twenty pie or a Chiko Roll and drank a coffee-flavoured Big M milk when we arrived at the amusement parlour some time after supper. His carefree attitude made me even more desperate to grow-up and be able to do whatever I wanted without being overly concerned about someone else's opinion.

John pulled a cigarette from his own pack and said, 'If mum finds out you've got cigarettes, it's got nothing to do with me.' He looked good in his v-neck blue shirt and green Husky trousers.

'As if I'm going to rat on you,' I said.

'I'm just saying.'

I ended up smoking the packet in two days in the confinement the toilet attached to the back porch or at night lying on the hammock in the backyard, or whenever I went out with John. My mother never caught me in the act, and if she had, I wouldn't have been overly concerned because I knew she wouldn't have be able to be everywhere I was, and nothing could force me to stop smoking unless I chose to quit myself.

John had gone out of his way to make me happy many times because he knew I was sad. He walked me to school every day, with or without Melissa, and began to spend some of his lunchtimes with me in spite of having friends he'd been neglecting. He randomly bought me Mars bars and icy-poles I never asked for. He'd heard from my mother I would be moving out of my current school by the end of this year and begin Year 8 at a new school the following year. He felt sorry for me, he said, and wanted me to remain in the same school as him.

'It doesn't matter,' I said, 'I don't have friends at school any more, so it's not like I'm going to miss anyone.'

'What about Trevor?'

'It's over.'

'What happened?'

'Nothing really, it's just over.'

I didn't want to hang around anyone but John. I felt comfortable with him, like a sister is supposed to feel with her big brother.

Maybe I was being naive and only saw what I wanted to see, and one day fate would slap me in the face like a bullet in the brain.

I began writing in my diary again in the privacy of my room, but I wrote in French to keep it consistent with the original entries I'd made with my Mont Blanc fountain pen. Every time I opened the diary, I brought it up to my face, closed my eyes and took a deep breath. I smelled my father's home, his piped tobacco and *eau de vie*. I wrote my thoughts and feelings in detail as if doing homework, and someone would grade my efforts. When I finished the writing, I held the diary close to my heart and cried.

A week later, on an unbelievably hot night, John and I were coming back from our nightly walk, laughing at his jokes as we often did, lemonade icy-poles melting all over our fingers, sweet and sticky but deliciously cold like hugs in winter.

'What do you call a woman who gets her period?' he asked.

'Don't know.'

'Self-saucing.'

Daylight stretched until 10 p.m., so no one really cared where we'd been as long as it wasn't dark, and we were together.

'What do you call a blonde with her hair dyed black?'

'Don't know.'

'Artificial intelligence.'

We shared one of my menthol cigarettes and sat on the back porch because the inside of the house was like a furnace, and you couldn't breathe without bathing in your own perspiration.

No one was home, and we weren't sure where they'd gone to, but we guessed they might have decided to walk along the shore to dip their toes in the cool of the seawater to relieve themselves from the unrepentant heat.

The temperature was in the low thirties, even at that time of the night, so I wore little else but my cotton, white summer dress from France. When I stood in front of the mirror in the bathroom at home, I could see the lines of my underwear through it. The boys at the amusement parlour noticed too because every time I turned around to check the crowd, someone's eyes were cast down to my buttocks, and when my eyes met his, he either blushed or threw me a daring look as if I was suddenly going to drop everything and come down on him. I didn't wear the dress to show off or get unwarranted attention—those days were over. It just happened to be the only dress I could stand when the heat softened the asphalt like butter out of the fridge.

John took a long drag from the cigarette, shortening it by a third, and passed it on to me. I watched him blow the smoke from his mouth, slow and pensive, like a private eye from a black-and-white fifties American cop television series who had too much on his mind and not enough time to solve his cases. Perspiration masked his tanned face against the light from the patio bulb like oil from a can.

I took a drag, and he casually placed his right hand on my left knee, the way he often did when he began a new conversation.

'I've got something to tell you,' he said.

The sadness in his eyes spelled out his revelation would be serious, and the tightening of his fingers on my leg confirmed it.

'What?'

'I don't know how you're going to take it.'

'John, just say it.'

'I'm in love with you, and I don't know how to handle being your friend or your brother or whatever any more.'

I sucked on my cigarette, re-positioned myself against the hardness of the planks and looked at the stars above. It was a beautiful night in spite of the heat. The gods in heaven were laughing at us and wondered what kind of fools we were to be playing with hearts and minds as if they were cards in a poker game.

John waited patiently for a reply, but I remained still on the floor like a turtle on its back. Sweat ran between my shoulder blades and through my dress and stained the untreated, rotting planks of the patio.

'That's all you've got to say?' he asked.

I felt the weight of his stare on my face like an iron mask. The thickness of the silence was too much to bear.

'Well,' I said coolly, 'you'll just have to get over it.'

I was waiting for him to jump me and cover me in kisses while I'd protest just for the sake of it.

But John changed the script unexpectedly.

He jumped to his feet before my eyes had time to meet his, and he went inside the house and slammed the fly screen like a car backfiring in the peacefulness of the night.

My eyes searched through the velvet darkness of the sky and

tried to find Venus.

That night I couldn't sleep between the heat and John's confession of love. My thoughts were filled with the times we'd spent together, and whether he really loved me, or if he was just drowning in disillusioned infatuation.

And then I thought about how Martine had loved this guy, and he had loved her, then she got pregnant, and he ran away.

I went outside and lay on the white, fishnet hammock under the apple tree, the earth smelling dry and hot like midday pavement in the streets. Still, in the darkness and at the far end of the backyard, the temperature was much cooler than inside the house. Maybe I would spend the rest of the night there, lonesome but feeling oddly self-sufficient.

I smoked a cigarette, the orange tip glowing in the darkness of the night like cats' eyes. I wanted to be loved by someone who truly cared, but I feared men and pregnancy.

I looked up at the clear sky above and wondered if each soul had a star to it. Which one was my star? Maybe I was the only starless soul cursed to travel the world endlessly by herself.

I lit another cigarette, and suddenly a shadow appeared beside me and almost made me jump out of my skin.

'Where did you get the smokes?' the shadow said.

I didn't look at him but I heard Michael's tension in his voice —an over strung violin about to snap.

'Bought them.'

'You're too young to buy cigarettes. John bought them for you, didn't he?'

I knew there would be no point lying, and frankly I didn't care what he thought. He was a partner in crime—he let me smoke when my mother wasn't around, so did it really matter where I got my cigarettes?

I shrugged. 'His friend did.'

'What's going on between the two of you?'

His questioning took me by surprise. I had no idea he'd noticed any connection between John and me because he was never there when we hung out together.

'What do you mean?' I tried not to show my surprise by taking another drag from my cigarette.

'He's my son, and I don't want you hurting him, you understand?'

He was addressing me the way adults spoke to children— respect your elders, period. It distressed me more than he could possibly have realised.

My free hand gripped tightly the mesh of the hammock. 'I'm not hurting John. I don't know what you're talking about.' I took another drag from my cigarette.

'Look, Clotilde,' he said, 'I know where you're coming from, and I know where you're going. I've seen girls like you all my life. You walk into a place, you take over, you think you own everything. Well, it doesn't work that way, not around here, anyway—and the sooner you understand, the easier things are going to be between us.'

I wanted to jump off the hammock and run back to my room. I didn't like what he was saying, or the way he was saying it. Maybe there was too much truth in his words.

'John and I are just friends,' I said. 'We're brother and sister.'

'Yeah, you're not your mother's daughter for nothing—her blood runs in your veins, don't you ever forget.'

His words and accusative finger hit me hard like a blow to the chest.

And then he left just as he came, a shadow in the night, a ghost whispering into the foliage of the apple tree.

I traced a winding, blue vein on my wrist with my index finger and wondered what type of venom was mixed with my blood.

It was too hot to eat cooked food, so I told my mother I would make a salad for dinner. One hour later, we were sitting at the kitchen table, feasting on spiced potato and chickpea salad, which tasted of olive oil, sour cream and finely grated lemon rind. I tore the recipe from an old issue of *Woman's Weekly* and had to ask my mother to translate the ingredients in French for me.

Eyes crossed the table, from Michael to me, from me to my mother then to John, from John to Michael, from my mother to Michael. Melissa was the only one left out—she seemed lost in her own thoughts, most likely thinking about her beau. She spent little time at home, and it was almost as if she were invisible, but no one really seemed to care.

Silence hung in the air like a full moon on a Friday the thirteenth.

'What the hell is going on?' my mother finally said, her nostrils flaring slightly.

No one volunteered.

John and Michael played with the salad the way painters play with oils and brushes.

Melissa looked up as if someone had said a four-letter word.

I rose from my chair.

'*Demandes-lui*' I told my mother, indicating Michael.

'Ask him what?'

I didn't wait for the result—I raced to the back porch, the devil on the run. Voices in the house were getting louder like screams for people being tortured. I paced to the safety of the hammock and rocked myself between my only true friend—the apple trees. The air was thick and syrupy, the grass yellow and uncut. I felt as if I'd been hit at the back of the head. I didn't care. I didn't want to care. Not now—not ever.

Three minutes later John appeared, a strained smile on his face like a salesperson trying to convince you the dress two sizes too small will fit you like a body glove.

'What did he say to you?' he asked as soon as he approached the hammock. He stood there, his knees melted into one. He was wearing jeans and a white, cotton tee.

'Nothing.'

'Come on, you can tell me.'

I locked my eyes with his. 'He's your father, why don't you ask him?'

He held my stare for a few seconds and sat next to me on the hammock. The apple trees bent, and I thought they were going to snap under both our weights. The smell of his aftershave drifted past me like sunshine on a cloudy day.

I cast my eyes towards the house to check if we were being observed.

'I don't care what he thinks,' John said. 'This is between you and me. He should mind his own business.' He paused for a few seconds, his hand dug deep in the pockets of his jeans. 'Come on, let's get out of this place. It's fucking depressing.'

I followed him to the gate.

143

We went to the amusement parlour—coloured lights, bells ringing, cigarette smoke and people shouting like Christmas day. We were such regulars, everyone said hello to us. I wondered if they knew we were brother and sister. Maybe they thought we were a couple. I kind of liked the idea, so I stood close to John when he played his pinball machine with Keanu Reeves on the glass panel.

'So what did he tell you?' John asked as he pushed another silver ball the size of a marble into the game. His white tee-shirt stuck to his back like skin on bones.

I told him the truth. He scored another five thousand points.

He didn't seem surprised and kept his eyes on the game. 'Don't worry about it, he's big on talk, but he doesn't do anything. That's my father, all right.'

'Yeah, well, I'm not going to stand around to find out. I don't like it when he gets mad.'

He didn't reply but concentrated on his game instead. He beat the side controls of the machine like someone punches a wall. Orange, red, yellow, green, blue lights flashing. Keanu Reeves beats Hugo Weaving. Keanu is a beam of light, two near-naked women by his side groping at his legs as if he were God and they were mere mortals.

John beat the highest score while his older friend Chris kept eyeing me from a distance, his stare hostile like silver bullets— more rape than desire.

When we returned home, John kissed me on the front porch—two young bodies hot and sticky from the heat of the day. I let myself go. His arms were around my neck—strong like a vice—forced my lips to crush against his. When I pull back, his face felt so familiar, it was as if I was looking into a mirror and staring at the reflection of my own nakedness.

'What are people going to think?' I whispered.

'I love you, Clotilde, and I don't give a shit what everyone else thinks.' He kissed me again.

He was fifteen, I was thirteen, and the whole world could go to hell.

He was right about that.

CHAPTER TWELVE

In the early hours of the morning, when it was still dark outside and everyone was asleep, John pretended to be going to the bathroom, but instead he sneaked into my room and climbed into bed. We stayed together until the first rays of light filtered through the green curtains and bathed our tangled bodies in a strange glow like paint on canvas. Sometimes he would fall asleep, his head resting against my chest like a little boy—hair unkempt, mouth open, eyelids moving like ripples on water. His skin was silky and warm and reminded me of freshly ironed sheets my mother carefully stored on the middle shelf of the laundry closet.

When he woke up, he kissed my eyebrows, cheeks, nose, mouth without stopping, like a puppy starved of affection.

And then he left the room.

For the next hour or so, before it was time to get up and get ready for school, I remained awake, my head on the side of the pillow where he'd been resting his. I closed my eyes and filled my lungs with his masculine sweat and cheap aftershave. I daydreamed he was still holding me in his arms and protecting me from everything in this world I had grown to hate. His fingers traced the length of my arms and gently rubbed the back of my neck. He toyed with my hair, his warm breath blowing the side of my face like waves dancing on the shore.

My mother's steady knock on the door jolted me back to reality.

School finished in mid-December, and we moved from George Street to a house in Noble Park, just alongside the railway track, a five-minute walk to Yarraman Station. Michael and my mother had managed to save enough money to put a deposit on the three-bedroom brick veneer home with a large backyard and a two-room bungalow attached to a double-garage with a mechanic's work pit —all in the middle of heavenly suburbia.

Since the house only had three bedrooms, I had to share my room with Melissa. During the whole time I'd been living with her in Dandenong, she'd been a ghost in my life, vanishing at supper time and most weekends, but now she spent most of her time in the new house.

One evening, Melissa and I were in our room, me lying on my bed and reading my Proust novel in French, her arranging her make-up and jewellery in little brown cardboard boxes she'd bought at Camberwell Market two Sundays prior. The temperature had been in the mid-thirties for the last few days, and I could smell the jasmine from a neighbour's garden three houses down from ours.

We slept on a bunk bed Michael had built from pine—he stole the design from an Ikea catalogue my mother left lying year-round on the coffee table in the lounge room. I slept at the top, and she slept at the bottom because she was scared if she rolled too close to the edge of the bed, she would fall over and shatter her bones like glass on pavement. I preferred sleeping at the top, so it didn't bother me she chose to sleep underneath. One Saturday night when she stayed at a friend's place, I tried to sleep in her bed, but it felt claustrophobic, like being locked up in a coffin after they had accidentally certified you dead and thrown away the keys. I wondered if my father was dead or if someone had made a mistake.

I wore nothing but blue underwear and a skimpy, pink top with a yellow flower stitched on the front. It showed off my belly button and my lower back. My skin glistened with perspiration like someone covered in tanning lotion. It tasted salty on my upper lip and at the corners of my mouth.

My mind was only half focused on the novel. The other half observed Melissa sitting on a wooden stool in front of the vanity mirror, a silver brush in her hand. I'd never noticed before, but her nose was so straight, it seemed to form a right-angle triangle. Freckles adorned her complexion, and her blonde hair was down to her back, right to the line of her white panties. She was only a year older than John, but sixteen years old seemed so far away and so enviable when you're younger. She was a woman and I was precocious thirteen-year-old who didn't want to wait. Her breasts

146

were rounded and pointy at the ends and her legs smooth and polished like gems. I could see what boys admired in her—she seemed to be blessed with purity, like clouds turning into rain after a merciless heat wave. She said she would find herself at home some day in the country or by the seaside, and suburban life was just a state of adjustment she was enduring for a couple of more years.

She saw me studying her in the vanity mirror.

'How come you don't wear make-up any more?' she asked.

'It's too hot,' I lied.

'You've given up on him, haven't you?'

'I can't wear it at school—the principal said it doesn't comply with the school regulations.'

'That's because you don't know how to put it on properly.' She turned around and faced me. 'Come down, I'll show you.'

She wore her make-up in a way, it looked as if she wasn't wearing any. The first time I had seen her on that Sunday morning in July, the day after I arrived in Australia, she looked as plain as she did now—not plain to the point of being common, but plain in a way that made you stop and look.

'Make-up is supposed to enhance your natural beauty,' she said. 'It should never be used as camouflage. If you apply it properly, the teachers at school won't even notice you're wearing it.'

I climbed down from the bunk.

She passed me a moist, white face towel. 'Here, wipe the sweat off your face.'

I did what she told me, and she made me sit on another wooden stool she kept next to the vanity mirror. I'd never been so close to her before. Her skin smelled like strawberries and vanilla yoghurt.

With a soft, yellow, round sponge, she applied foundation the colour of a natural tan to my face.

'You've got to go easy on the base,' she said. 'Some girls put so much on, it looks as if they've touched up with car paint.'

I wanted to laugh at her comment but refrained because she was still applying the foundation. In my mind's eyes, I saw a girl walking around with her skin as polished as the paintwork on Michael's Jeep, and then cracking under the sun like dry earth after a seven-year drought.

She outlined my lips with a long, salmon-colour pencil and

painted the inside a fairy-floss pink. I was a doll being touched up for a garage sale.

'Men don't like women with too much make-up,' she went on, 'the less, the better. I remember when you had to look like a rainbow just to attract the opposite sex. Today is a case of less is more—man go for the natural look.'

I felt myself blushing, heat at the back of my neck like a hot iron too close to the skin.

'What wrong?' she said. 'You never think about boys?'

'Of course,' I answered sheepishly.

'So what's the name of the boy you're giving a hard time?'

'We've split.'

'Because of John?'

I saw my eyes getting bigger in the mirror. 'What do you mean?'

Her eyes met mine and she smiled. 'I'm not stupid, Clotilde, everyone knows there's something special going on between the two of you. You're like one person who's been spilt in half.'

No wonder Michael felt he'd had to give me a little talk the day John told me he loved me.

'It's not what you think,' I said.

'It doesn't matter what I think.' Gently, she layered mascara on my eyelashes with a small black brush. 'It doesn't matter what anybody thinks. If you love each other, it's all that matters.'

Didn't it bother her that it was her brother I was lusting after?

'What about you?' I asked.

'What about me?'

'Do you still see him?'

'It's not working out. Love doesn't always work out, you know.'

'I know.'

She finished applying the mascara and fixed my hair with the silver brush and hairspray from a black aerosol can the length of my arm. When she was done, I smelled as if someone had forgotten to turn off the gas.

'What do you know about love, anyway? she asked.

'Love is not kind. Love is a traitor'.

She nodded approvingly. 'You're very smart for your age,' she said.

I didn't feel smart. Had I been smart, my school report would

148

have been filled with straight As, and I wouldn't be wasting my time chasing foolish dreams of the heart.

Melissa and I were shopping for clothes at a boutique where everything looked awfully expensive and the sales girls talked and acted as if they had the best jobs in the world. Melissa said someone ought to remind them it didn't matter how glamorous the boutique looked, at the end of the day they were just salesgirls in a retail shop and not supermodels.

The whole decor was plastic—other than the mirrors attached to the walls and the metallic clothes racks—red chairs, green counter top, blue drapes, pink lights, yellow price tags, orange clothes hangers. It even smelled of plastic.

The air conditioning hummed from the back of the shop like a lawnmower on an early Sunday morning annoying everyone within a two-hundred-metre radius. Given the thirty-three degree temperature outside, I could have spent the whole day in the middle of this multicoloured, plastic, contemporary museum— even if it meant putting up with a hazardous amount of snobbery from the sales assistants.

Melissa held up a burgundy-colour dress cut at the thighs with a five-centimetre spilt on both sides and a gold zipper at the back. I had seen girls wearing the same type of dress in a variety of other colours and I liked them.

Melissa said, 'When you pick a dress, make sure it's sexy, but it shouldn't look tarty.'

'What do you mean?'

'Well, something sexy has to give the impression it's you who's sexy, not the dress. If the dress seems like an obvious attempt at exposing yourself, then you'll end up looking like a slut. Guys don't like sluts. They don't respect them. You'll end up being used, and you'll never know whether they want you for just one thing.'

'But being wanted is nice either way,' I said.

She stretched the dress carefully across my waist to see if it would fit.

'Yes, but it's nicer to be wanted by someone who loves you than by someone who just wants to take advantage of you.'

'Advantage of what?'

She threw me a look—the kind of look mothers gives their

children when they don't understand why they shouldn't be playing with matches.

'You're not serious?' she said.

'It just seems to me, if anything, I'm the one who would be taking advantage of them.'

'Yeah, well, don't fool yourself.' She checked the hand-written price tag and hung the dress back on the rack. Sometimes you think you're the user, but the truth is you're being led and used without even knowing it. Older people have a way of making you do what they want while you believe you're still in control.'

I snatched the dress from the metal rack. 'What's wrong with this one?' I asked.

'You look cheap in it.'

I wasn't expensive, so what difference did it make?

John and I were on our way back from the shops next to the railway crossing, the sun burning mercilessly on every inch of our exposed skin. He wore a white singlet, blue shorts and a pair of black thongs. I wore a new yellow dress with double-stitched pockets Melissa had bought me—this one looks sexy on you, she'd told me when she paid cash for it at the sales counter.

The sky was a deep, heart-wrenching blue, and the air dry and hot and smelled like crates of fruits and vegetables from the Dandenong Market. It was Saturday afternoon, and, in spite of the good weather, most people were home glued to their television sets like zombies, watching Pakistan vs. Australia in a five-day test cricket match.

The soothing percussion of metal on metal from a train in the distance filled the air like a swarm of bees dancing in sunlight.

John carried a one-litre carton of milk in a grey plastic bag. I chain-smoked menthol cigarettes as fast as I could because once we would reach home, it would be virtually impossible for me to find a place to indulge my addiction.

The day before I'd noticed my fingers were nicotine stained. I tried to scrub the yellowness from my index and middle finger with the hard-bristled brush Michael used to clean the grease off his hands after he worked on the Jeep. I drew blood but the stain remained on my skin like a cheap tattoo done in a backyard shop where the person who did the tattooing looked like a character from a b-grade horror film.

'Do you really love me?' I asked John and tried to form rings with the smoke the way I had seen more experienced smokers do. I liked the way the little hallows above my head made me look like a fallen angel.

His eyes met mine. 'Of course I do. What kind of a question is this?'

'But how do I really know?'

'Because I'm telling you.'

'Yes, but how do I really know you're not taking *advantage* of me? Like, how do I know you're not just with me to please yourself, and you don't really care about me as a person?'

He stopped and stared at me hard.

'What?' I asked.

'How could you ever think I'm taking advantage of you?'

'I don't know, I'm just asking.'

He stopped walking and I stood with him. Waves of annoyance filled the blueness of his eyes like water fills a glass. He dropped the plastic bag with the milk carton on the grey pavement and placed his hands on his hips. He looked strange, like someone's father who about to give you the beating of your life.

'Have you been talking to Michael again?'

'No.'

'Well, this doesn't sound like the kind of thing you would come up with. Someone's been feeding you lies.'

'I was just wondering.'

He just stared at me for the next few seconds. His eyes were glassy, and I couldn't tell whether he was going to hit me or burst into tears.

He tilted his head to the right. 'How could you ever doubt my feelings for you?'

'I never said I doubted. I just wondered why.'

His hands shook and his left foot tapped nervously on the ground. 'You know, you don't have to try to find a reason behind everything. I just love you—there's no hidden agenda here.'

'Okay, okay,' I said, 'I believe you, don't get all worked up— and I'm just trying to figure out things for myself.'

I tossed my unfinished cigarette by the kerbside and pressed my lips against his.

My eyes bathed in the yellow rays of the sun and the

watercolour blueness of a cloudless sky.

I turned one of the two rooms in the brick veneer bungalow attached to the double garage into my own sanctuary. The room at the back had two white French windows, red carpet, yellow painted walls and mismatched wallpaper on the doors, but it was one metre longer than the front room. I choose it as my home away from home, a place where I could be myself without having to worry senselessly about how others perceived me or question endlessly the meaning of my existence in a world.

Michael and my mother furnished the back room with an old, green couch and a student desk made of cheap, gloss varnished plywood with protruding rusty nails on the sides and pen graffiti carved into the surface. The whole place smelled of mildew and dead moths like an attic, which hadn't seen sunlight in a hundred years—but I didn't care because it was *my* room.

I attached to the walls posters of Britney, Grinspoon, Avril Lavigne and Eminem I pulled out from *Smash Hits*, even though I knew little about what was happening in the world of music and television. These people looked so confident and in-your-face, I wanted to be like them.

In a small pine bookcase—Michael hammered it together on a Sunday afternoon when he'd finished working on the Jeep and there was nothing else for him to do—I arranged my small collection of school books, ESL learners and Proust novels I'd managed to bring from France. Two vanilla-scented, thirty-centimetre, yellow candles stood on the top shelf between framed photos of my father, Martine and Louise. It had only been six months since I left France, but my recollections of days-gone-by felt as if they belonged to someone else.

Melissa measured and sewed curtains for the windows—fluoro orange speckled with white dots like a ladybug whose colours had passed the expiry date. She'd bought the material at the Dandenong Spotlight store for twenty-nine cents per metre, a bargain according the sales lady at the counter. The brightness of the orange curtains and the yellow walls made the room happy and lively—my own private world in shades of amber, just what I needed to cheer me up.

During the two weeks before Christmas, I spent most of my time in the room, lying on the green couch and listening to classical music on the ABC. No one else at home liked classical music, and I wasn't sure if I really liked it myself, but I knew I didn't hate it, and it was a good change from pop music, which kept coming at me from everywhere—at home, at school, at the supermarket, in the car, in the streets.

When the temperature reached the low thirties outside, my room stayed relatively cool because of overhanging branches partly concealed the French windows. It didn't get hot until late afternoon when the sun hammered down on the two windowpanes like hail during a freak storm and forced me to retreat to the backyard under the shade of a black olive tree.

Alone in my room, I found the peace and happiness I longed for—hours on end where no one battered me with their philosophy of how the world was or how it should have been; of how people behaved badly; and if I wanted to become a good girl, all I had to do was obey whoever was filling my head with indispensable advice, which would save my soul from eternal damnation.

John hooked up a summer job working at Michael's garage—some kind of unofficial apprenticeship, which got him more excited than if he'd found a bag filled with fifty-dollar notes. He didn't seem to mind working in the middle of summer because the place was fitted with air conditioning and he was getting paid $7.50 an hour. We didn't get to see each other during the day, which was just as well because as much as I longed for us to be one, I also hungered for privacy the way some older people long to die.

In the mornings, I borrowed Michael's guitar and practiced my chord sequences from a yellow laminated chord chart I bought with pocket money my mother gave me from my father's trust account. I played until my fingers became numb and my skin red raw from pressing the steel strings against the fretboard. The tips of my fingers burnt like I had grown nails there and someone had pulled them with a pair of pliers.

In the afternoons, I read out loud from my English readers in the hope of improving my pronunciation but gave up in frustration when the words came more French than English. Anger spoiled my mood like sour milk, and the English readers flew across the room and crashed with a flat thump against the wooden door leading to the other room. In retaliation, I re-read my French Proust novels. I lay comfortably on the old, smelly green couch, the white pillow from my bedroom propped up behind my head, summer sweat trickling behind my neck, my belly and all over my legs until I could no longer bear it and had to retreat to the backyard under the shade of the olive tree and the cool umbrella of a garden sprinkler.

In the evening, I wrote a new entry in my leather-bound diary and tried to capture the essence of every single day so later in life I would remember every detail of what the world had been like when I was too young to be a woman and too old to be a child. I removed my father's black-and-white picture from the top of my bookshelf, pulled it from its blue plastic frame and stored it between the front cover and the first page of my diary. I stared at the photo for a little while before I began a new entry and read the sadness in his eyes and told him he was still in my heart even though he was no longer in my life.

One early morning after breakfast, Michael and John had left for work, and my mother and Melissa were in the kitchen arguing about how Melissa took her family for granted; how she carried on as if the family home was a hotel she could waltz in and out of as she pleased; how she was never there for supper, and if this family was falling apart, Melissa was partly to blame.

Melissa's defence was her age. At sixteen, she insisted, she didn't have to obey every rule, especially when those rules were designed to facilitate my mother's life and had little to do with keeping a family together.

'Don't use that tone with me,' my mother shouted. 'You don't respect anyone, that's what you problem is.'

'Respect is earned, mum. How can I respect you when you treat me like shit?'

They both constructed compelling arguments, but I took no part in the debate for fear of becoming the recipient of their undiluted anger. I ate my cereals drowned in too much brown sugar and full-cream milk and drank my cold, one-hundred-percent orange juice. My eyes cast down to the red-and-white chequered table cloth, I assumed the role of a deaf person as if the elevated, angry voices around me were nothing more than a gentle wind playing with the leaves of a majestic maple tree in the backyard.

154

The bright morning sun cut across the room through the white drapes of the only window in the kitchen and landed in the middle of the table, catching a thousand specks of dust glittering like damselflies under a full moon.

I thought about John who was working all day and wouldn't be back until at least three in the afternoon, black grime under his nails and hair smelling of engine oil and grease. He tended to stay up late at night watching television—re-runs of old American films or television series—and on the weekends you couldn't get him out of bed before ten. Since we'd moved to Noble Park, and I shared my room with Melissa, he no longer sneaked in and out of my bed before dawn. I missed his nocturnal company, but not having him disturbing my sleep meant waking up refreshed every morning.

I tuned out of Melissa and my mother's argument, which had now escalated to almost a fistfight.

'You're not even my mother anyway, so where do you get off telling me what to do?'

'Come here, you little bitch! I'm going to teach you some bloody respect.'

Outside the heat continued to hammer down like rocks falling from the sky. In the early hours of the morning, I feared the worst of the high temperature was yet to come. It was almost hard to exist on those days when the world seemed to be made of a thousand suns. Every surface was hot to the touch, and the only places providing a bearable environment were under a cold shower or in a room fitted with air conditioning, a luxury only a few people could afford—and those who did had to pay the price of the colossal power bill arriving at the end of summer, like someone paying the price of a painful sunburn at the end of a long day under the sun.

Tired of listening to my mother and Melissa squabbling over trivialities, I showered and changed into my new, yellow, summer dress I'd washed and put out to dry the night before. I sat on Melissa's wooden stool in front of her vanity mirror and applied my make-up the way she had diligently taught me—a light layer of natural-looking foundation, salmon-colour pencil for the contour of my lips, fairy-floss pink lipstick to match, and black mascara for my eye lashes. It took me a good half hour to get it done the way she showed me, but by the time I finished, I was bright and happy, a butterfly dancing in the heart of a tropical forest. I styled my hair with her silver brush but didn't bother with the hairspray.

I borrowed Michael's guitar, like I did every morning, and retired to my room in the bungalow to practice my chord sequences.

Much to my pleasure and everyone else's surprise, I had become a competent guitar player in just over six months. I knew my major, minor and seventh chords without looking at the fret board. I was capable of playing any of Jewel's songs from her first album *Piece of You* and two of my favourite songs from Lene Marlin, *Sitting Down Here* and *Where I'm Headed*. My singing, on the other hand, wasn't up to scratch, but I was gaining confidence and had developed an attitude of impassiveness when performing in front of people. I placed my faith in what Michael had told me when I first began playing—in the long run, my singing would improve as long as I practised it alongside my guitar playing.

I was playing *You Were Meant for Me* along Jewel's original version pouring from a portable blue CD player Michael bought me from the Sunday market. I was practising the opening riff— Cadd9 G6 C Em—when John entered the room without warning. I saw him from the corner of my eye but was too absorbed in my music to acknowledge his presence. He approached me from behind and kissed me at the back of the neck—an odour of mechanic's workshop whisked around me—his lips coarse and dry from the heat. I noticed he was still wearing his oil-stained, blue overalls, and immediately sensed Michael couldn't be too far away. Fearing the worst, I jumped from my seat, and tossed my grey plectrum on the desk amongst the sheet music.

'Not here,' I said. 'Are you crazy? What if someone walks in on us?'

He kissed me again, this time on the right cheek, and forced me to sit back on my chair. He shifted his face down to the side my mouth, his moist tongue tickling my skin.

'Who's gonna walk in on us?' he said. 'Mum and Melissa are in the house tearing each other's hair out, and Michael stayed behind at work.'

He was right of course, but there was constant fear at the back of my mind drilling into my skull and reminding me our relationship was a sin of the greatest magnitude. God would avenge himself one day and forsake us to the burning flames of hell for eternity.

'How did you get here?' I asked.

'Caught the train.'

He kissed me again, this time on the mouth, his lips parting, his tongue searching for mine.

He grabbed my hand. 'Let's sit on the couch.'

Carefully, I placed the guitar against the edge of the desk—the fretboard facing down to ensure the guitar wouldn't slide and crash to the floor. The curtains and the sun coming through the French windows filled the room in a magical orange glow.

I gave up any resistance, got up from my chair and I jumped on the couch with John. We kissed passionately like I'd read in books. He tickled my ribs and my underarms and forced me to lose self-control.

I laughed hysterically, and he must have thought it was a green light to do as he pleased. He rubbed my small breasts through the thin material of my yellow dress—like he had done once when we were alone in the old house and he used to creep into my room in the middle of the night—but as soon as his dirty hands reached my white panties, I pushed him away gently.

'Don't,' I said, 'please, don't even try.'

'Ah, come on, we're just having fun.'

Quickly he pulled at the elastic of my panties and slid one hand between my legs as smoothly as someone changing gears.

I pushed him back, harder this time, sending him off the couch, his right shoulder hitting the red carpet with a muffled sound.

'That's it,' I said and pulled my yellow dress down to cover my white panties, 'you can leave now.'

I stood up from the couch at the same as time as he jumped to his feet. He rubbed his right shoulder with his left hand as if he'd just been in a boxing ring with a fierce opponent and was suffering from dislocated his shoulder.

'What?' he said. 'What's wrong with you?'

I paced to the front door and turned around to face him. 'I just don't want to, okay? Why can't you understand?'

'I thought you loved me?'

'Of course I love you, but it doesn't mean I want to get pregnant.'

He laughed.

'It's not funny,' I said.

He moved close to me, held my little, fleshy, white hands in his long, grease-strained ones. 'You can't get pregnant unless you want to.' He let go of my hands and removed a little white square from the right pocket of his workman overalls. 'And I've got protection, anyway, so there's not going to be an accident.'

'I'm only thirteen and a half, John, I'm not ready, okay?' Annoyed, I paused, thought about David and added, 'What is it with you guys?'

'You're not ready for what? Who are you going to lose your virginity to? A complete stranger at the back of a car when you're so pissed you won't even know what's going on? You should be grateful I'd give myself to you this way.'

I stood in the middle of the red carpet like someone stands in the middle of an empty room, his voice an echo bouncing from one wall to the other, in and out of my mind, like a mantra from within my head. He sounded so convincing, like a parent or a teacher who knew what was good for me and was justly and selflessly sacrificing himself for my unconsumed but feverish carnality.

I wanted him, but not in the way he wanted me. I craved the love, the security, the feeling of being needed for the person I was —the knowledge there was someone who longed intensively for my companionship.

And, yet, he was right—in a covert and lewd way, I did want to make love to him too, but I pictured the moment as something special, not copulating shamelessly like animals in the back room of some bungalow in the middle of suburbia in thirty degree heat with the risk of having my mother walk in on us.

'That's not fair,' I said. 'If you love me like you claim to do, you should trust me—give me a little time to think about it.'

'Sure,' he said, his sinner's eyes cast to the floor, 'but don't make me wait forever.'

And then he slammed the door and left the room without another word.

I was alone in the confinement of my sun-blessed, summer room as if he'd never been there and I had imagined the whole incident.

Gently, I sat back on the couch and bathed in an orange glow of light—big warm tears like pearls rolling down my face and then down my dress.

I played with the elastic of my panties—exactly where he had touched me—and imagined my small, round fingers to be his long, bony ones.

CHAPTER THIRTEEN

Christmas came and went uneventfully like a storm sweeping from the ocean, engulfing the city and the coast, as if something rather special was going to change our lives, but in the end it was just a passing phase. People returned to their monotonous and often-meaningless daily lives, working at jobs they didn't like so they could buy things they didn't need. The only ones who seemed to be enjoying the celebration were children. They were showered with a thousand-and-one gifts on Christmas morning, and carried out the spirit of Christmas for a few more weeks, engrossed in novelties given to them by a mysterious man with a long, white beard.

My mother bought me a uniform for the new school I would be attending in February. She said it was expensive—*un prix exorbitant*—so she couldn't afford to buy me any other gift this Christmas, but maybe next year when finances wouldn't be so strained. But it felt as if she bought me nothing either way because she would have had to buy me the school uniform—Christmas or no Christmas. I felt betrayed. I had been awake half the night wondering what sentimental present she had chosen for her one-and-only daughter, especially when she'd never ended up giving me anything for my thirteenth birthday.

The jumper was buffalo grass green, and the shirt grapefruit yellow. The colours clashed like gold and plastic, but I lied and politely told her I liked the present and offered her a bear hug, which she took reluctantly. I must have been cursed with one hundred years of karma to be stuck with a mother who couldn't show any genuine form of affection.

Michael bought me a half-size acoustic guitar fitted with new D'Addario steel strings and a steel-reinforced neck. He pointed

160

out to the truss rod inserted along the inside of the neck of the guitar was a sign of good craftsmanship, and that in the long run the guitar would keep its shape and not bend under the tension of the strings. He bought it second-hand at the Sunday market for a good price, but he wouldn't disclose its value, because it was a Christmas present after all, he said, and people should never reveal the cost of presents.

I was so overwhelmed by the guitar, I wanted to embrace him—more genuinely than my mother—and cover his face with kisses. As I held the guitar in my hands, I wanted to cry but held back my tears like an overflowing dam ready to burst. My mother was watching my reaction—hawk-eyed and fish-lipped—so I swallowed my enthusiasm like a shot of whisky and said 'thank you' instead. I didn't want her to think I liked Michael's present better than hers even though it must have been obvious.

'What is she going to do with that?' she said and threw Michael a sidelong gleam of motherly mockery.

John had squandered all his hard-earned holiday money on new a BMX bike with fat, red rubber wheels and a black frame, so he gave me a gold locket in the shape of a heart he'd shoplifted three days before Christmas from Myer—the undeniable proof of his devoted love for me.

I wanted to slaughter him when he admitted he nearly got caught steeling the 9ct pendant and chain. He made a run for it when a security guard intercepted him outside the department store and ordered him to empty the contents of his pocket.

John didn't bestow me with the locket on Christmas morning because he feared my mother and Michael's reaction; they would have rightfully realised the heart-shaped, gold locket was much more than an innocent brother-to-sister gift, especially Michael who had scorned me for tampering with his son's emotions as if John were a stringed puppet and I the devil in a yellow dress.

After the festive season, it was more heat and more endless weeks of keeping oneself busy until the new school term begun.

My mother, Michael, John, Melissa and I spent evenings walking Frankston beach with thousands of other people who could no longer bare being indoors, sweating profusely and absorbing liquids by the gallon, like Antarctic bears mysteriously drifting to the west coast of South Africa.

I had never experienced days where the red alcohol from the thermometer attached to the fridge rose to thirty-eight degrees and remained there throughout the night. Melburnians complained endlessly wherever I went, and the hotter it got, the more numerous and contagious their whining—it wasn't just the unbearable temperature, but also the ever-increasing price of petrol, the way young people no longer respected their elders, and the influx of foreigners taking jobs from *real* Australians.

Older people, who knew their limitations, spent time at the cinemas or shopping centres where air conditioning was ample and as free as salt in the ocean. The foolish ones, who thought themselves invincible, were overcome by heat strokes and rushed to hospital and kept under critical care until the heat wave outside dissolved like cream in coffee.

I wrote a letter to Martine two weeks before school began, partly because of boredom, and partly because I had been putting it off for two months now and my response was somewhat overdue.

With the physical distance and time between us, it felt as if we had little left in common. In my mind I had always pictured her as a symbolic tower of strength to model myself upon—my first true mentor after my father. But now she'd got herself pregnant and seemed to have lost control over her future, and I no longer knew how to relate to her. The roles were reversed. Suddenly, I was the mentor, advising her on how to take charge of her destiny, assuring her in the end, no matter how idealistic it might have sounded, God had his reasons for leading us onto the path we walked. *One day it will all make sense*—I repeated the words my father had drilled into me during those difficult times when doomsday seemed the day after tomorrow. But I didn't really believe anything I wrote—I just felt it my duty to comfort her. Maybe my father had felt the same way towards me.

I drew flowers on the envelope with pink, blue and green markers, and stuck little silver stars at each corner. I drew a smiling face of a sun on the back flap. I tried hard to make the letter happy and hoped it would bring some joy into her life, and she would be able to pass the joy on to her newborn. I had read somewhere how a mother's reaction to her surrounding environment was passed on to her child, which meant if Martine gave birth to her baby while

162

fearing the world around, the baby would grow up fearful of the world too. I was uncertain as to how this rule related to people like me who never had a chance to be brought up by their own mothers. Maybe my father's inability to breathe the air freely meant, in some strange way, I too was unable to inhale life fully.

I left the letter next to my bed on the side-table, and stared at it every night before I went to sleep. Was I doing the right thing by answering Martine's letter? It took me a week to resign myself to posting it. The silver stars I had stuck on the envelope made it look like a Christmas present, perhaps the only Christmas present she would be receiving—love sealed in an envelope from someone whom she would most likely never see again.

The evening I sent the letter, I dreamed of Martine hooked up to a heart monitor, her stomach swollen like a balloon, her skin talc-powder pale like my father's just before he passed away.

On the second Sunday in February, freshly out of bed and showered, Michael toyed around with the Jeep like he did every weekend. After observing him for a few weeks after Christmas, I began to believe there was nothing wrong with the car, and whenever he buried his head underneath the bonnet, or fixed things for hours, which didn't need fixing, he was simply killing time or indulging in a passion none of us truly understood.

John, Melissa and my mother had gone to the Dandenong Trash & Treasure Market for want of something better to do other than sitting around and watching paint peel off the wall. They would return with arms full of junk—a Picasso print, a copper candle holder (like the one my mother's friend used to have on top of the fireplace), a set of Funk & Wagnall Encyclopaedia (1969 edition, G and I missing), a blue navy cap, old black-and-white postcards from Paris, a Marlon Brando style leather jacket with stitches undone—which would end up collecting dust until someone decided to get rid of it all with the weekly garbage collection.

Michael and I hadn't indulged in a game chess for a while, not since he'd chastened me for infecting John's mind with the poisonous concoction running through my veins—a direct infusion of my mother's vile and corrupted mind, according to him. There had been a painful distance between us like two dogs competing for the same couch. I preferred it when we were close companions and conspired together over cigarettes or learned a new chord progression on the guitar. I felt as if I'd lost an important connection in my life, the closest I've had to a father since my father had died.

I got bored practising the same chords and lyrics from a song I made up, locked up by myself in my red-carpeted summer garden, my buttocks hurting from being compressed on the white-painted, wooden chair, my eyes desensitised from the brightness of the sun beaconing through the orange curtains. It was time engage in a conversation with Michael, to bury the hatchet, to smoke the peace pipe.

I left my guitar and sheet music behind, straightened my yellow dress, and entered the first room of the bungalow used as a general storage room—unopened cardboard boxes filled with clothes we would never wear and junk we would never use from our move from Dandenong were stacked up to the ceiling and taking most of the wall space. I pushed open the glass-paned window connecting the bungalow to the garage.

Michael was inside the mechanic's pit, toying with the brakes, the Jeep jacked up above him like a massive bull. From the doorway, all I could see was his tanned hands and forearms with his sleeves rolled up half way and a glimpse of his denim overalls.

I approached the car cautiously, afraid my sudden appearance might cause him to bump his head with the undercarriage of the Jeep.

A small radio with poor reception at the back of the garage was whispering a tune at such low volume, I wondered why he bothered with it in the first place.

The pit was made of four concrete walls with a rusty metallic staircase attached to one end—whoever worked on cars could get in and out with ease. The walls and the floor area were covered in black, greasy stains. From the inside of the pit, a whiff of oil and mildew spread around the double garage—an odour Michael would carry with his perspiration throughout the day.

I walked up to him and kneeled down the side of the car. 'Do you want a coffee?'

He stopped what he was doing and looked up. He seemed surprised to see me there. 'Are you talking to me?'

'Well, yeah, there's no one else around.'

'Sure.' He continued what he was doing.

I raced to the kitchen and in three minutes I was back with two instant coffees in ceramic mugs.

Outside it was warm, and I should have served him a cold drink, but weather permitting or not, coffee was an indulgence we both couldn't miss.

'There's your coffee.' I kneeled down next to the brake pad he was fixing.

He looked up from the pit and locked his eyes with mine. 'How come you didn't go to the market?'

'Don't like it, there's only rubbish there.'

'I agree.'

I pushed the coffee mug towards him. 'It's going to get cold if you don't drink it.'

'It's okay, I'm taking a break, anyway.'

He climbed out of the pit, his arm bulging with hard muscles and protruding veins. I observed the tattoo of the naked woman on his forearm move as if she were alive, her jutting breasts larger than I'd remembered, round and full and more provoking than any I had seen in real life.

Every time I noticed Michael's tattoo, I wondered what my mother thought about it. Did he have it done before or after he met her? Maybe she hated it but never discussed it because there was nothing she could really do now short of amputating him. I liked it myself, but I wasn't sure why. I know I should have found it offensive. I read somewhere pictures of naked females degraded women and conditioned men to treat them like sex objects. Didn't women treat men like sex objects? I couldn't quite comprehend what the gender wars were about or maybe I didn't want to know.

We sat against the cool brick-veneer wall of the garage and faced the passenger side of the Jeep, like a father and daughter would have if we were members of a conventional family. I was truly happy for just a moment, blissful like a lost child in winter who had finally found her way home, imagining Michael to indeed be my father—not step-father, which could never be the same, irrespective of any rose-tinted lenses one chooses to wear. This was *our* house, and we were sitting in *our* garage, drinking *our* coffee and looking at *our* car. But as I smelled his manly, bitter-sweet odour, I painfully realised my world was a borrowed world, one of make-believe and wishful thinking.

We drank our coffee in silence like a couple going through a divorce who had nothing left to say to one another after twenty years of quibbling.

The car looked like an out-patient who had to remain on crutches for a while—old and new brake parts and empty boxes laying around the floor—waiting for Michael to perform surgery and replace body parts that didn't need replacing. I wondered what it would be like to have my own car and be able to drive wherever I pleased.

Michael said, 'Hey, it sounded good from here.'

'What?'

'The song you were playing before.'

'Something I wrote.'

I didn't want to tell him John wrote the lyrics, otherwise he would have started all over again about the type of girl I was, and how he'd dealt with women like me all his life. Did he truly believe I was one of *those* women?

I emptied my mug of coffee while Michael explained how he was relining his brake pads because the car wasn't braking as well as it should, and if he didn't bother with it, we would all end up wrapped around a tree one of these days, mashed up against the engine block and the steering wheel, an absolute delight for the State Emergency Services officers who'd have to scrape off what was left of us and estimate the number of people who were in the car by identifying the remaining body parts.

By the time he got into the technical aspects of relining the brake pads with the metal drums, I'd lost complete interest. I held no fascination for cars and anything associated with them, other than the freedom they could provide, and, of course, sometimes, the driver or the caretaker, who happened to both be Michael in this case. He looked good underneath a car, in his denim-blue overalls, his cigarette surgically attached to the right corner of his mouth, his eyes squinting from the smoke, a three-day stubble, and an exaggerated frown every time he faced a technical challenge which left him bewildered.

I nodded and pretended to be interested in his encyclopaedic knowledge of the Jeep Cherokee. Naively, I stared at him in a way other men would have justly interpreted my action as a come-on. But Michael was used to my provocative stares. He'd done the same to me from the day we laid eyes on each other. It was just a game we were playing, and we both knew the rules. We just never talked about them. At thirteen I was a child, and he was a man—fully mature, aware of his charm and his rugged good looks, irresistible masculine power he had over some women, including my mother and, to a lesser degree, myself. Awareness stopped us from pushing the boundaries of decency, of risking opening wide the doors of decadence, like wilful sinners who had no moral limitations and who reacted ferociously to every impulse.

I continued to stare at him like a child fascinated by the seven colours of a rainbow. He noticed my gaze but remained mute for the next fifteen seconds or so, his blue eyes piercing my virgin soul like a full-metal bullet through my inapt heart.

And then he smiled.

Something inside me weakened because his smile wasn't like any smile he had ever showed me before. It must have been the sweet smile he saved for my mother, or other women he secretly seduced. I'd never noticed in the past, but there was a lot of John in him—the way his lips curled up at the corner of his mouth like tiny hooks, the soft bread-roll chin, the daring hypnotic stare, the pendulum-like rhythm in his voice. I could see John there in a few years with his own tattoo, stubble, weathered skin and work-hardened hands.

He drank the rest of his coffee in one go and placed the empty mug on the stained concrete floor. I was still sipping mine. It was too hot, and I had already burnt the surface of my tongue to finely-grained sand paper. The coffee tasted like pulped cardboard, but low-grade brew was still better than nothing.

'Want a cigarette?' he asked.

I hadn't smoked a roll-your-own for a while, and honestly, I had ardently hoped he was going to offer me one. I did come for a peace pipe, but since neither of us smoked the pipe, peace cigarettes had to do.

'Sure,' I said.

He removed the tanned leather pouch of tobacco from the breast pocket of his denim overalls and delicately undid the black lace, as if he were playing a wind instrument. He glanced in my direction and saw me observing him prepare the ingredients for the too-commonly-neglected art of cigarette making. Only those who took the time to roll cigarettes could truly appreciate the hypnotic effect of watching another smoker roll his own.

'You do it,' he said, 'I like to watch you rolling them.'

167

It sounded like he'd just asked me to undress for him and perform a sinful act he'd be able to savour all by himself in the privacy of *his* garage.

He passed me the pouch and two blades of white paper.

I messed up the first cigarette. I was out of practice.

'Hold on,' he said.

He took the messed-up cigarette, finger-brushed my hands in the process, removed the tobacco from the inside and used it to roll up a new cigarette. His fingers were greasy from working on the brake pads, yet none of the grime seemed to be adhering to the whiteness of the paper.

When he slid his tongue along the length of the cigarette paper, my face was so close to his, I felt the warmth of his breath on my cheek. I could smell sweat, nicotine, grease and alcohol. I could almost smell the ink of his tattoo.

He finished rolling one cigarette and turned to face me.

'There you are,' he said and offered the cigarette between his right thumb and index finger, his words almost entering my mouth.

I thought he was going to kiss me. I closed my eyes and waited for his lips to crush against mine, for his strong masculinity to take *advantage* of my innocence and naivety. I wondered what he tasted like. It was immoral, I knew, but I wouldn't tell anyone—it would be our secret, my lover's and mine, our own little privy act of indecency. I waited, his mouth so close to mine I could feel his heartbeat. I took in the air he breathed out. It tasted acrid and strong, like a glass of burgundy.

I waited.

Nothing happened.

'Are you okay?' he said.

I opened my eyes.

He was just staring at me, his eyes those of a worried parent.

I took the cigarette he offered and lied, 'It's hot in here; I'm not feeling too well. Why don't we go and smoke outside?'

'Sure.'

We stood up from the concrete floor, and I led the way, my head filled with confusion and self-loathing. The tension in the air followed me like a poisonous fume. Had I been misreading everything that had been going on? Was I so feverishly in need of love I imagined impossible scenarios in order to appease my unquenchable thirst for belonging?

And then, just before I reached the glass-paned door leading to the bungalow, I felt his right hand on my hip digging into the softness of my flesh. His fingers were claws.

Then his left one.

I was compliant and scared, but at the same time relieved I had been right all along—the thunder between us hadn't been a sole product of my feverish imagination.

He pressed the softness of his belly against the small of my back and the yellowness of my dress.

'You're a bad girl, you know,' he whispered into the side of my neck and kissed me there, his lips thick and moist like a sponge. 'If your mother knew what you've been up to, she'd send you back to France on the double.'

I turned around to face him and said, 'You wanted this from the very beginning, admit it.'

'Not true.'

'Yes, it is, you told me I had the same blood as my mother running through my veins. It's the reason you were angry with me when I got too close to John—you're jealous.'

I'd never seen Michael blush before, but he did, even through the layers of tan skin and stubble—redness so deep, it looked as if he'd just got sunburned. His blue eyes sunk inside his head so quickly, it reminded me of a cat rounding its back in self-defence.

He took one step back. 'You're too smart for your own good.'

I smiled but he walked away as if I'd just dug a twelve-inch blade in his heart.

There was a full moon outside my window, round and blue like a bad omen, a premonition of the wrath of God. It cast large shadows from the persimmon tree in the backyard, and any movement sent the shadows spinning around the four walls of my bedroom and shifted the room on its axe. It scared me. I was walking on quicksand. Will I too suffer an eternal winter?

I reflected back on the morning and wondered how the day had gone so wrong. Maybe coming into this family had been a mistake. I hadn't returned to the garage after Michael left me alone in the backyard. I hadn't found the courage to face him because I no longer knew what he was thinking, and whether I had crossed a line that should have never been crossed.

He didn't come to dinner that night.

When John went to fetch him, he stayed in the garage and said he hadn't finished with the car. No one questioned his motive. I kept to myself throughout the rest of the evening and feared the bomb was going to explode any minute. Had I lost my mind by challenging him the way I had? Was he going to tell my mother? Maybe he would tell her seduced him—even though I tried hard to convince myself he was the one who seduced me—and she would send me away with all my belongings in a single bag and a future coloured shades of grey.

I hugged my pillow as if it were a person who could understand my anguish. I almost wished Michael had told mother about the incident so I wouldn't have to stay awake all night clutching at the fear of the unknown.

Let the dice roll and seal our fate.

In the early hours of the morning, when darkness is still king of the world and emotions are skinned raw, nausea wrapped me in its blanket like a newborn. I seriously felt like ending it all right there, right now. I pictured myself walking to the kitchen, grabbing the largest carving knife I could get my hands on, walking down to my bungalow summer garden, cutting myself lengthwise at the wrist and bleeding to death—crimson blood blending in with the red carpet. By full daylight I would be gone, and there'd be no need to face another day of confusion and dread.

But the first ray of sunlight replaced the full moon, and the largest carving knife in the kitchen drawer hadn't moved an inch.

I turned the taps of the shower anticlockwise and let the water run for a little while. My reflection in the mirror above the hand sink looked like that of someone five years older. My eyes were puffy, red and underlined with dark pockets—little bags stitched there overnight by the ghost of Dr Herrmann. My dark hair was straw-like and knotted. It would need extra conditioning. I turned around and grabbed the silver towel holder with both hands.

I never made it to the shower.

Darkness swallowed me whole.

CHAPTER FOURTEEN

My father's bony fingers gently caress my face.

Clouds merge with stars and planets in a tremendous Milky Way—everything around is as bright like the burning rays of the sun; white light scorches the pupils so intensely, my father's face is almost invisible.

Roses all around me—red, yellow, blue, mauve, green, white, grey, orange, brown, purple, silver, gold. The air smells of strawberries, butter and nutmeg.

Music plays in the background, then all around us, a single chord held for four bars at a time, stately notes played in contrast, strings introduced in groups of four notes rising in tone and pace and followed by wind instruments.

The city of Strasbourg is white—virgin snow covering the rooftops of the medieval vernacular buildings, like it periodically has for hundreds of years during the winter months.

'Winter is man's punishment for losing his faith, for not believing in eternal life, for thinking himself ruler of the world and his destiny. And when all goes wrong, he will blame it on God Almighty, never on himself.'

The Christmas tree is still up in the corner of the living room, and the presents have been left unopened. My father's eyes are glassy, almost translucent, but his face radiates with energy. He is smoking his pipe, his *eau de vie* by the side of his armchair. There is no traffic outside when I look from the window—not a single soul. The world has ended and everyone has gone to hell.

There is sand all around us and a sun so hot I can almost hear my skin sizzle. My mother is laughing. John keeps telling me he loves me and now would not be a good time to leave. Melissa says she warned me about wearing dresses that make me look like a

171

slut. My father says someone will take *advantage* of me.

I am at the plastic boutique, surrounded by thousands of dresses. The shop assistant asks me if I want some help, and I say no—I will whistle if I need her. A dog barks in the distance.

Michael grabs me from behind, each hand squeezing too hard at my hips, drawing blood and staining my yellow dress. I smell motor grease, cigarette and alcohol. I smell ink from his tattoo. The woman on the tattoo is moving. I look down the side of my arm and see the tattoo of the naked woman Michael has inked on his forearm—mine has bigger breasts. Her face is my mother's face.

I am at school and people are laughing because my dress is too short. And then I notice I'm not wearing underwear. And then I walk the school yard without clothes, but nobody seems bothered by my nakedness. I am waiting for someone to ask me why I'm not wearing my uniform, but even the teachers speak to me normally as if there is nothing wrong with me prancing around in the nude.

I walk naked in the snow but don't feel the cold. The sun is hot and the snow bright white, like bed sheets soaked in bleach.

I close my eyes.

Michael kisses me on the mouth.

His kiss tastes like John's.

I open my eyes.

And it's my father staring back at me.

When I woke up, there was a nurse next to my bed, all dressed in white like the snow in my dream. She had red hair and green eyes and smiled like a television host. I was feverish and trembling, a lamb on its way to the slaughterhouse. She passed one soft hand over my perspiring forehead and brushed back my hair with motherly touch.

'You're going to be all right,' she said in a cotton-wool voice, like someone telling you you're going to live even though you've just impacted with a ten-ton truck.

'What happened?' I asked and noticed the clear, plastic IV attached to my bony, white arm and the grey curtain pulled halfway around my bed and held by a metal frame. 'Where's my mother?'

'You're going to be all right,' she repeated. 'Don't you worry about anything.'

How could I not worry? I had no idea where I was. It smelled like a hospital room—clean sheets, commercial detergent, chemicals, medication, plastic—but there were no other patients.

I tried hard to remember—pain piercing my skull like nine-inch nails hammered down to their full length.

The bathroom back home.

It's all I remembered.

I closed my eyes and passed in and out of consciousness for an indeterminable amount of time.

My father dressed in a tweed jacket is standing above my bed, his pipe in his right hand, his expression painted white like the snow-filled clouds of my birth town. His eyes are round and alarmed. The pressure in my head is worse than before. A vice tightens my skull, crashes it, and cuts like a knife into the soft layers of my spongy brain.

I reach out with my right hand to touch my father's face, but the more I reach, the further back he recedes—a ghost vanishing into the blazing sun.

Whispered voices woke me up from a deep, drowsy sleep at the bottom of the ocean. I swam to the shore and ran down the beach, fine pebbles of sand warm between my toes and the soles of my feet, a phantom shipwreck with three broken masts behind me, the sky red and angry.

'She's lost a lot of blood.'

'Is she going to be all right?'

'The doctor is not sure if she'll make it through.'

'Why?'

'Don't know.'

'Did she say anything to you?'

'No.'

I opened my eyes, heavy like lead, and tried to make some sense of the world around me. Everything was too bright, as if someone aimed a pen-torch right into my cornea. It was too warm in the room, a reservation in my own private hell. It smelled like a backyard in bloom.

'She's awake.'

I recognised my mother's high-pitched voice transcending from the top right corner of the bed, almost lost amongst other sombre whispers.

The plastic IV still attached to my arm feeds some clear liquid into my vein. Something was tightly wrapped around my head, and when I touched it with the tip of my fingers, it felt soft and velvety —a bandage. I didn't understand how I got to a hospital and why I was there in first place. I had no recollection of having harmed myself. I knew I had thought about it with absurd intensity, but I'd never proceeded with slicing my wrists. Maybe someone else hurt me. Maybe Michael. He feared I was going to rat on him to my mother about how he kissed me, so he tried to kill me.

'*Où suis-je?*'

'You're in hospital, Clotilde,' my mother said matter-of-factly. 'You fell over and hurt yourself.' She was now standing by my side and blocking the view from the only window in the room. I noticed red and yellow carnations in a green vase on the side-table —the odour I took in when I woke up. There was a card with splashes of blues and green next to it.

'With what?' I asked.

'With what what?'

'With what did I hurt myself?'

'You fell against the hand sink in the bathroom and then crashed against the tiled floor.'

I tried to remember but my memory was like a handful of clay in a bucket of mud. I'd woken up and went to the bathroom and ran myself a shower. Did I return to the kitchen to grab a large and sharp carving knife? Did I slit my wrists?

'Where did you find me?' I asked.

'In the bathroom, I told you.'

I remembered my room in the bungalow, the orange drapes, the blood dripping on the red carpet. It was a dream, wasn't it? I'd never cut my wrists. It didn't really happen.

My mother's explanation was a blank page I had to fill.

'Tell me more,' I said.

'Michael found you in the morning when he got up to go to work,' she said. 'He's very distressed. He's blaming himself.'

'He didn't do anything.'

'He said the two of you had an argument. What were you

174

arguing about?'

I held my silence for a few seconds like someone holding her breath under water. Uncertain, I looked into her eyes. No compassion—just intense curiosity with a dash of fear.

'What did he say?' I finally asked.

'He wouldn't tell me. He didn't want to tell me.'

More silence.

'Did he touch you?' my mother said. She caressed my arm.

'No,' I said without hesitation. He'd never touched me. All he did was kiss me at the back of the neck—it was not abuse. My father used to hug me and kiss me on the forehead and the cheeks. It was just affection.

'Are you sure?' my mother asked, 'you can tell me if he did.'

'He didn't, *okay*?'

We were both surprised by my anger.

'*D'accord*,' she said, 'you don't have to exhaust yourself now, but if you need to talk, you know I'm here.'

There was someone else in the room. He looked like a doctor or a nurse, or some medical person of one kind or another. He wore a long white overcoat, the kind we were forced to wear during science pracs at school, and rimless glasses and grey hair.

'Who's he?' I asked.

'A psychiatrist. He's going to ask you a few questions later. He'll want to know if everything is okay.'

'Like in my head?'

'He wants to know if there's any serious damage. You've fractured you're skull—the fall has caused a diffused brain injury.'

I nodded, but I was done with the questioning. I wanted to go home and away from this room. All this whiteness around me, the smell of medication, the IV, the heart monitor, the flowers and the card on the side-table, the cleanness of the place, the lack of personal items—everything reminded me of my father's death bed.

I didn't want to die—not here, not this way.

The psychiatrist wanted to have me transferred from the Royal Children's Hospital to a private clinic in Richmond straight after my convalescence, where I would be put under close examination and led through a series of tests and programs to evaluate my mental ability and general coordination.

I refused. I just wanted to go home as soon as I felt better.

I suffered nausea, headaches, dizziness and amnesia. The doctor said I was lucky. Most people with diffuse brain injuries ended up in a coma, sometimes for weeks. I was out for only four days. They put me on a ventilator. They did a second CT scan to check for haemorrhage and skull fracture, just to be safe. I swallowed a cocktail of medication, Astrix 100 during the day to combat the pain, Carbital at nighttime to help me sleep. I couldn't eat solids, so they fed me IV fluids for the first three days. I began eating soft foods on day four—canned fruits, mashed potatoes, boiled vegetables, yoghurt.

Sometimes I phased in and out of consciousness. I had no idea where or who I was. It was just this moment in time, in a white room, all by myself. Here. Now. The smell of hospital disinfectant, clean sheets, medication. The taste of my saliva. The bruising on my skinny arm from the needle attached to the IV. It was small world, and it kept getting smaller, like the light of a locomotive travelling in reverse down a long, dark tunnel.

John came to visit every day. It gave me a sense of orientation and stability; otherwise I would have gone completely insane.

The first time he saw me, he cried, his blue eyes red raw with tears the size of five-cent coins. He couldn't even pronounce his words properly, chocking on them like a mouthful of pins. When everyone was out of the room, he sat on the edge of my bed and kissed me on the mouth, his lips chilly hot with passion and hunger. He tasted like outdoors and freedom.

Whenever he left, in spite of the ghastly state I was in, my mood took on an optimistic outlook. No boy had ever cried for me before. I felt his pain in my heart like fingers squeezing the large ventricle. I would have liked to care for someone the way he cared for me, but I didn't know if I were capable of it.

At night I found it hard to sleep, even with my intake of sedatives. Maybe I should have spent more time with my father when he was dying. Maybe my absence was what killed him in the end. Maybe he never received the love he needed to fight his unrelenting sickness.

But I was young and afraid, and no one explained to me how important love is in someone's life—even in older people's who somehow managed to convince the world they were doing fine without it.

Michael came to see me with my mother but she wouldn't leave him alone with me, her eyes filled with austere suspicion. She stood at the corner of the room, seated on a white, metal-framed chair, while he sat on an unvarnished, wooden chair next to my bed. His eyes were swollen and grey from lack of sleep—remorse eating away at the core of his consciousness like battery acid poured over unscarred tissue. His hands were gripped together like a vice, and at times he seemed to want to beat something or someone—a boxer in the ring waiting for the authoritative sound of the start-up bell.

'I'm sorry,' he kept repeating like a pendulum, but I wasn't sure what he was sorry about. I hadn't figured what went wrong, and who was the real culprit of my convalescence. It was an accident. It wasn't like someone hit me over the head with a blunt object. It could have been worse—I could have died or turned into a teenager with the mental capacity of a cucumber.

'It's not your fault,' I said. 'I didn't sleep well. I should have stayed in bed and told everyone I was sick.'

He didn't cry, but I could tell he wanted to. He held back his tears because he was a man from a generation when crying was only allowed for women and children.

Whenever they departed in the evening, I stared at the whiteness of the heavenly ceiling from where angels would suddenly fall and rescue me. As soon as I felt better, the doctors would put a metal plate at the back of my head. My skull was badly shattered at one point, and it would never mend by itself.

Metal-head.

I could already hear the other children at school having fun at my expense. I would become a freak. A thirteen-year old Frankenstein.

When I returned home, my head was shaved, smooth and hairless as a pinball. The doctors couldn't fit the metal plate at the back of my skull with the amount of hair I had. They said they had to shave a square big enough to cut through the skin, but I told them to go ahead and shave the lot. I couldn't see how I was going to walk around with a shaved square at the back of my head—better off looking like Frankenstein than a fruitcake.

In the bathroom at home, I held a portable mirror against the mirror attached to the wall to scrutinise the scar left behind from the operation. The black stitches were still there, protruding like whiskers, and would remain for the next two weeks. The scar was about ten centimetres long, the thickness of a second skin and pink like a pair of lips. I was too stunned to cry. I just stared at it and touched it with the tip of my fingers. It felt weird, like it didn't belong to me.

Throughout the day, I suffered headaches bordering on migraines, forcing me to take a ton of prescription painkillers, which ended up making me lethargic.

I spent a lot of time in my room, lying in bed, thinking about what had happened. If I hadn't flirted with Michael, he wouldn't have kissed me, and I'd still have a head full of dark hair and a fully functional brain. The doctors had yet to determine the extent of the damage—would I still be capable of adding up simple sums and following logical instructions? Every time I tried to concentrate or read, it felt as if the plate at the back of my head was going to push into my skull and turn my brain into mush.

And yet, in spite of all the difficulties I faced, I was looking forward to life, to going back to school with my baldness and new-found ugliness. I wanted to challenge the world to mess with me.

I stared at the mirror for a long time and read the features of my face—my eyes, the scar and its stitches at the back of my head. *Who is this girl looking back at me?*

The doctors had done a good job with the metal plate. I couldn't even see it through my skin. They must have moulded it in the form of my skull. Once my hair would grow long enough, no one would ever notice.

The scars would only be on the inside.

CHAPTER FIFTEEN

I went shopping with my mother for a hat because she insisted there was no way I was going to go to my new school looking like *that*. Outside it was too hot, the sun flame-throwing its deadly rays on every passer-by.

Everyone in the streets and the shops kept staring at me—children and elderly people more blatantly than people my mother's age. With my recently shaved head, they probably assumed I had some malignant tumour and had to get radium treatment.

We passed a group of boys my age.

'Oh, yuck!' one of them said behind my back.

I swallowed his words like poison ivy.

We bought two hats, one blue beanie and a straw hat with a red band around it. I liked the beanie better—it was cotton soft and made me look cool—but my mother liked the straw hat. When I wore the straw hat, I looked like a girl who studied at an expensive, private school, where every one wore uniforms pressed and starched as if their parents had purchased them the previous day.

My mother wanted me to wear the straw hat at school, but I refused. I wanted to wear the beanie. She gave in. She didn't bother arguing with me any more. Being scarred had its advantages.

The teachers didn't care which hat I wore. They said it was up to me. They addressed me as if I were five year old. I was getting more attention from them than I could handle. *Are you all right? If you need to take a break at any time, you don't have to ask, just leave the room quietly. Is there anything else you need?* They never questioned why I didn't do my homework. If I declined to participate in any form of class activity, it was all right too.

I should have caved my head in a long time ago.

As soon as I began to attend Noble Park High School, I had to see a school counsellor, even though I told the school principal and my mother I didn't feel the need to. There was nothing wrong with me, but everyone insisted how talking to a professional about how I felt about my accident was good for me. They all knew what was good for me. After you have an accident, everyone always seems to care. Prior to an accident, no one gives a shit. I could understand why some people spent their lives imagining illnesses, going from hospital to hospital, chronically complaining about one ailment or another.

The counsellor, Mr Carrington, was a tall, skinny man with hair the colour of winter wheat and a ponytail held together by a common elastic band. His nose was long and pointy, and his chin ran into his neck like a Volkswagen Beetle. I guessed him to be in his early thirties, but he could have easily been five years on either wayside of the scale. His chocolate brown eyes sank into his cranium, making it difficult to assess whether his interest in people was genuine or just part of a job he did to pay the mortgage and keep the family together. He looked like a hippy from the seventies who smoked pot for breakfast.

His office was the size of a large pantry and cramped with files and books on youth psychology and psychoanalysis— *Understanding Adolescence; Theory and Problems of Adolescent Development; Manual of Child Psychology; The Psychology of Sexual Emotions; Dynamics of Adolescent Adjustment.*

I felt like a freak of nature.

Mr Carrington never said anything of value. All he did was ask me how I was adjusting to my new school—as if it was the real reason why I was forced to see him—and what was on my mind (a rust-proof metal plate, didn't he know?). Even I could have done his job without having had to struggle at university for four years

'What have you got to tell me this week?' he asked at the beginning of our second meeting. He held his hands together, palm against palm, fingers pointing to his lips, as if he were praying to save my unredeemable, flawed personality.

'Nothing,' I said.

I was sitting in an injection-moulded, plastic orange chair, the type that always ends up giving you a sore butt at the end of a class.

Mr Carrington, on the other hand, reclined comfortably in a leather-bound executive chair, his feet propped up on the desk, his peace symbol tee-shirt reeking of marijuana. So much for the making the patient feel at home.

'Well,' he said, 'you know I have to write up a report about the outcomes of these sessions, and so far you've been very unwilling to cooperate.'

I shifted uncomfortably on my chair, aware he was trying to mind-rape me. 'I've got nothing to tell you.'

'You've got nothing to tell me, or you don't want to tell me?'

'What the difference? All you care about is whether I've said enough for you to write up your report.'

'it's not true, Clotilde, I do care.'

'Yeah, right. You're getting paid to do this—how could you possibly care?'

He locked his eyes with mine unconvincingly, the way politicians do on television the night before people have to rush to the polls. 'I do care, you'll just have to trust me.'

'Well, I don't care—and it's my choice.'

'You're not making it easy.'

'Give me one of your joints, maybe I'll start talking then.'

'Are you making friends at your new school?'

'Actually, give me two. I've got a headache you wouldn't believe, so if you give me two, I can take one home.'

'You're being unreasonable.'

I leaned forward and spoke louder. 'Am I now? Tell me then, in your report, do you write you smoke marijuana at the introduction or at the conclusion of our sessions?'

After four weekly sessions, much to my contentment and to his relief, I was no longer required to see Mr Carrington—courtesy of an official complaint to the school principal by Mr Carrington about my unwillingness to help myself and my need to exert my nastiness on those who were only trying to rescue me from an inescapable life of delinquency.

There was this one girl at my new school, Veronica, who sat with me in Geography and Maths. She had a round, chubby face, red cheeks, blue eyes, and blonde hair cut just below her neck. She was from Yugoslavia, and she kept telling me about all these problems back home, and about all these people dying, some of them members of her extended family.

I'd read something in the newspapers about political violence, but I wasn't much into politics and world issues. I only half listened because she was kind enough to bother sitting next to me. I could read in her eyes the pain and the distress the war in her birth town was causing her. When she went home after school, her parents talked constantly about the war, as if nothing else in life mattered. They couldn't see how they were poisoning their daughter's youth with their bitterness, fear and resentment. Veronica pointed out how she had nightmares about people dying, and she never got enough sleep as a result. I didn't know what to tell her. I had only experienced the death of my father, and, like her, I wanted people to comfort me. She was hanging on to the wrong person—there was no room in my heart for someone new.

Melbourne weather was as predictable as a drunk lashing out without warning, cursed with tempestuous behaviour and lacerated with bouts of violence. Summer ended as abruptly as it had arrived, and we were greeted by the new season with sudden downpours at all times of the day.

Sometimes, when doing homework in the bungalow all by myself, I liked to listen to the rain play percussion on the tin roof. At other times, I did nothing at all—I just sat at my desk and looked out the window, the orange curtains pulled open, and observed fat silver needles crash against the glass like insects deprived of any sense of direction. I loved the metallic and wholesome odour of the rain, and the way it washed away the sins and miseries of the world whilst breathing life into God's creatures.

When I got tired of being inside the bungalow, and the beating of the rain on the roof was too melodic to resist, I purposely stood under the rain—cold drops exploded on my bare arms and my face like tears falling from the sky.

My mother and Michael were in the house concocting roast chicken and baked potatoes for dinner. Melissa was playing volleyball for her school team and wouldn't be home until later in the evening. No one questioned the real motive why she went out, even though it was obvious to everyone volleyball had never been her favourite pastime. My mother was far too busy worrying about my recovery—my injury might have temporarily opened her eyes to the fact I was her daughter—to bother with Melissa who was, after all, old enough to look after herself. The irony was how Melissa had tried to tell my mother many times before how at the age of sixteen she was more a woman than a child. And it took me bursting my head open to get my mother to finally agree and let Melissa do as she pleased.

John read the lyrics of a new song I wrote. We were alone in the bungalow. He cried openly like a little boy, rivers streaming down his face and soaking the top of his white tee-shirt like the rain that would come pouring down again later in the evening. Since my accident and his visits to the hospital, his crying had become as regular as the need to eat. Crying is therapeutic, but when someone cries every time they look at you, you get this sense of bewilderment there is something so awfully wrong with you, but you're the only one who can't see it.

'What's the matter?' I asked.

He didn't answer straight away.

'I didn't mean to make you cry,' I said.

'It's not that,' he said. 'The lyrics are nice, I like them. You're really good at this, I mean, given English is not even your first language, it's quite amazing. I can't wait to hear the finished song.'

'So why are you crying?'

'I don't know, I just… I don't know where to start.'

I placed one hand firmly on the softness of his blue jeans to let him know he could trust me, no matter how difficult he believed his problem to be. He had been there for me when I was in hospital, every day after school, even when he looked as if he hadn't slept a single hour the previous night. I had seen him dozing off on the wooden chair next to the hospital bed, his neck twisted, his eyes raw from crying and sleeplessness. Many times I begged him to go home and explained how he didn't have to come and see me every day—I said I understood how stressful it was to visit a sick person on a regular basis in hospital because I had endured the same fate when my father was convalescing.

I rubbed the palm of my hand against his thigh, his flesh warm like freshly baked bread. 'Tell me what's bothering you?'

'We need to talk.'

'About what?'

'About us.'

I pulled my hand back from his thigh, the jaws of fear biting mercilessly.

'What do you want to talk about?' I asked.

'I think we should slow down a bit.' He stared down at the red carpet.

My eyes dug into his face like two sharp knives aiming to kill. Since I came back from hospital, we had been more distant than ever. Michael and he treated me almost with contempt, as if I had purposely knocked my head against the sink and the bathroom floor in order to make them suffer. Or maybe it was me who was being paranoid.

'What's wrong?' I asked. 'Don't love me any more? Is that what's bothering you?' Anger crept into my tone more than I would have thought possible.

'Of course, I do,' he said and still looked down to the floor. 'It's just—'

'It's just that I'm too ugly for you, and you're too embarrassed to be seen with me.' I turned around and pointed at the scar at the back of my head. 'Is that what's bothering you?'

Why did he come to the hospital crying every day when I was sick? And why didn't he tell me sooner what was on his mind instead of playing lovesick games for the past few weeks?

I jumped from the couch, acid running through every single one of my veins and pumping in my head like blood on a hot day. How could he do this to me, *and* at a time like this?

He grabbed me by the arm, his fingers digging into the softness of my skin like rusted nails. 'It's not what you think.'

'Don't touch me,' I snapped and pulled my arm back.

'Okay, you've changed. And it's all wrong, we shouldn't be doing this. You were right the first time, brother and sister, you know, I just couldn't see it.'

Très convenable!

I looked across to the backyard though the windowpane. Past the red maple, the fence was falling apart, and if Michael waited any longer to fix it, it would end up falling into the neighbour's yard and joining the two rusty cars sitting on slabs of bricks, growing weeds from the inside. It seemed as if everything good was decaying, and everything bad was taking over.

John took two steps back and said, 'I can go now if you'd prefer to stay by yourself.'

'Go on then, piss off!' I tore the heart-shaped gold locket from around my neck and threw it at him. It landed at his feet like a handful of mud. 'You're just a common thief, anyway.'

He hesitated in picking it up and tried to catch my eye to no avail. Finally he left it where it was and aimed for the door.

When I was alone in the room, I doubled over on the couch and cried like the day my father died.

My hair was beginning to grow back, and I looked like a skinhead. If I'd had tattoos and an earring through my nose, I could have passed as one of the genuine items. I was one hundred percent done with looking pretty and feminine and trying to please the male population. John and I hadn't spoken for a month, and I had no intention of doing so.

I no longer wore my blue beanie at the new school and became a little more popular as a result. The other kids at school thought my cropped hair, jeans and flannel shirt looked 'really cool', and I was asked to join different groups of people at lunchtime.

Anger suited me better than beauty.

I was washing my hands in the girls' toilet near the assembly hall—hot water steaming the mirror, the room reeking of urine—when Veronica appeared unexpectedly. She didn't say a word, but walked up right behind me. She inspected the healing of my scar. She has been playing this little routine since I'd returned to school, my unofficial voluntary nurse on day duty.

Over the past few weeks, she had put on some weight and reminded me of little round doughnuts sitting behind the glass counter at our local bakery. I, on the other hand, had left all my puppy fat at the hospital and all my clothes were suddenly hanging from my bony frame. Veronica's face was flushed, a healthy looking glow in spite of the sleepless nights she still suffered from her war-torn nightmares.

'Does it hurt?' she asked.

'No.'

I finished washing my hands with warm, soapy water and

turned the taps off. Our reflections were looking back at us in the mirror above the hand sink. We couldn't have looked more different, me with my five o'clock shadow covering my scalp, and her looking like Heidi from a three-grader's picture book.

'Can I touch it?' she asked.

'Sure.'

Gently, she placed one finger over the scar and ran it along the full length as if it were a line on a roadmap.

'It's healing,' she said. 'In a few months, you probably won't even see it.'

I didn't answer.

She went on, 'Does it bother you to have a scar?'

'Not really.'

'I wish I had one.'

'Why?'

'Because people seem to love you more when you're scarred.'

My mother was in her room, reading a fat Bryce Courtenay paperback novel the size of a dictionary, two pillows propped up behind her head, the blinds half shut, letting in only enough light for her to be able to decipher the words on the pages. The room smelled of lavender and facial cream, and the musky odour couples leave behind.

I stood still in my torn jeans and blue flannel shirt, unannounced and uninvited, my right shoulder pushed against the wooden door frame

All the furniture in the room was black like friends at a mourning—two side-tables, a large chest of drawers, a metal-framed vanity mirror with matching table, a pivoting full length mirror—even the full-length drapes adorning the windows hadn't escaped the hands of darkness.

My mother didn't notice me at first, too absorbed in her reading, a convent girl at her prayer. She looked much younger than my father, but my father's ageing was easily explained by his ill health. Her long, blonde hair draped both sides of her face like sheets of velvet, and her face was painted with serenity and the abolition of sins from past lives. Yet there were too many questions, which remained unanswered, too many mysteries hidden behind her quiescent face.

Unlike my father, my mother didn't adhere to a particularly strong philosophy of existence, neither religion-based, nor Proust-inflicted. In her eyes, the endless questioning of one's temperament might have been nothing more than an additional and pointless burden to carry on the already all-to-cumbersome walk of life.

Even though I had been with my new family for nearly a year, I had yet to drill my mother about the nature of her relationship with my father. Perhaps I felt like I didn't know her well enough to dare question the decision she made more than a decade ago. No one could blame her really, not if my father's version of the story was an accurate one. He had refused to leave his priesthood to marry her, and in all fairness, no woman in her right mind would have bothered staying with him.

What I had not yet come to terms with was how my mother could have left me behind with a Catholic priest who was forced to pretend I was an orphan when in reality he was my father. Why hadn't she bothered taking me with her to Australia, especially when she had just given birth to me, and the crucial mother-to-child bond of our relationship had yet to be formed?

My mother had intended a long time ago, if my father died, I would come back and live with her. Undoubtedly, she must have realised how all the years we'd been separated would have taken some toll on the relationship we had yet to have. She must have known the day we would come together we would meet as total strangers, unaware of each other's predispositions and habits.

'Why did you leave me?' I asked in French.

She propped her head up from behind her paperback and glanced in my direction the way people do when someone knocks at the door.

'*Ah, c'est toi!*' she said, 'I didn't see you there.'

Of course it was *moi*—who else was going to question her in French?

She hadn't answered my question, but I knew she'd heard it.

There was a nervousness in her face so obvious, her eyelids flickered like butterflies' wings on a warm summer day. Surely, she must have anticipated one day I would come up and ask her *the question*. Perhaps she thought it'd happen after we'd both been sharing secrets about our pasts, when neither of us felt threatened or embarrassed by the other person's inquisitive behaviour. But right at this very moment, she had to re-adjust her thinking and

187

tap into the storage tank of her mind, where she had conveniently filed away the perfect answer for this unforeseen but inevitable encounter between mother and daughter.

'Why did you leave me?' I repeated, the way parents question children when they don't want to wait for an answer.

'*Pardon?*'

I could see her mind racing at a hundred kilometres an hour. She pretended to be concentrating on the pages of her book, but her eyes flickered way too fast for her to be doing any reading.

'You heard me,' I said. The tone of my voice was firm and determined.

I moved inside the bedroom.

She slowly closed the paperback novel and placed it by the side-table. She purposely avoided any form of eye contact, like an accused in a courtroom eluding answering the question put forth by the prosecutor.

With exaggerated mannerism, she stepped from the bed, the right foot down first and then the left—like walking on eggs—bent over, straightened up the black quilt, turned around and pulled open the drapes, daylight entering the room in the same way the first ray of the sun must have entered Alibaba's cave after thousand years of darkness.

I was still waiting for an answer, my fingers locked nervously together at the front of my body.

She took her time and straightened her mauve pullover.

She said, 'It's not straight-foward. I can't answer your question with a simple "yes" or "no". If you want answers, we'll have to have a proper discussion.'

'Well, let's have a proper discussion then.'

'I don't think so, Clotilde, I'm not in the mood.'

'You're not in the mood? I wasn't in the mood when Papa died, and I had to deal with it.'

'it's not fair—I'm not the one who killed him.'

'Nothing is fair.'

She walked passed me, like a person walks past a beggar in the street and looks the other way to avoid the embarrassment of refusing to help, and aimed for the door.

'Now is not a good time,' she said, 'we'll talk later.'

And then she walked out on me like she had done thirteen years ago.

CHAPTER SIXTEEN

One rainy afternoon, I came home early from school, my blue flannel shirt soaking wet like a bath towel, which had been used to dry off a dog left outside during a storm.

I knew my mother had an appointment at the dentist for a molar cavity, which had caused her to lose too much sleep at night. Michael wouldn't be home until four o'clock. John and Melissa were still at school, and they usually got home at around the same time as Michael. I skipped my afternoon classes of Maths and ESL without telling anyone—little Miss Renegade, juvenile delinquent of the highest order. I knew the roll would be taken during afternoon classes, and eventually, before the week would end, the form coordinator would be asking me why I had been skipping school. I had plenty of time to fabricate a little white lie to cover my tracks.

As soon as I got inside the house, I called out for my mother, but as enthusiastically anticipated, no one replied. Relieved, I headed straight for the bathroom and dried my short, spiky hair with a clean, orange hand towel scented with rosemary and jasmine shampoo. I never took an umbrella to school, not because I had anything against umbrellas like some other kids did, but because they were too cumbersome to carry around throughout the day. And anyone who did bother bringing umbrellas ended up losing them or having them stolen by other students.

My face was flushed from the cold rain and the thrill of what I was about to do. I looked as if I'd run ten times around the block without taking a break. I justified my insidious plan on my own simplified reasoning—if people refused to provide answers to my unconventional past, I had every right to seek them out by any possible means.

Grey clouds hovered above Melbourne and its adjoining suburbs like a plague that would eradicate every sinner from the surface of the earth. The scantiness of sunlight made the bathroom dull in spite of its white wall tiles and hand basin. I tried to read my face in the mirror, but plainness was all I could see. Boys and girls at school told me I was pretty, but I didn't see it as such—no generous lips, no excessively long eyelashes, no gem-like irises. Plainness was as much my middle name as white was the colour of snow.

I touched the scar at the back of my head with the fingertips of my right hand. It was still there, hidden under a mass of new hair, like a sin from the past waiting to be unveiled—a small, stitched-up mouth with thin lips and no voice.

I finished drying my hair, spiked it up with a little gel and went straight to my mother's bedroom.

The bedroom smelled of the tantalising, musky sweetness I noticed the other day—the essence of Michael, my mother and something else, which I didn't want to hypothesise too much on. Stillness hung in the air as if the whole world had come to a stop right at that very place, a forbidden sanctuary where those who entered did so at their own peril. Maybe it was the reason why my mother's bedroom felt as if it didn't really belong to the rest of the house.

I stood in front of the bed and tried to picture my mother and Michael making love, but it didn't feel right. During the past year I observed no signs of affection between them, or any indication they were attracted to one another. Maybe eternal love was a myth, and little girls had been fed lies from an early age only to wake up one day and realise love was a lie itself. Had my father been right after all?

I searched the drawer by her side table. Carefully, I emptied the contents and placed each item on the floor in a layout, which would make it easy for me to return everything where I'd found it —marine blue and black underwear; gold earrings with white pearls; a blue plastic pen; two paperback novels, *Coma* and *Papillon*, both in English; a purple hair brush with a wide head; a packet of twenty tampons with two missing; three gold rings almost identical; a blank notebook with the first few pages torn out; and black stockings scented in lavender fabric softener.

I wasn't sure what I was exactly looking for, but reading Proust had taught me how adults always held on to dark secrets, lingered on unfulfilled and unresolved emotions, continuously jabbed at open wounds infested with pain in the foolish hope they would heal with the passing of time.

Maybe my mother concealed a diary somewhere where she kept her memories fresh and alive, ready to be poured over by anyone who lacked decency and personal integrity, the way I did on that particular grey afternoon.

I went to the kitchen, grabbed a red plastic chair with steel legs and returned to the bedroom.

I placed the chair in front of my mother's opened bedroom wardrobe. It suddenly occurred to me I shouldn't be doing this, but my nosiness was more zealous than my self-consciousness.

Unwillingly, I messed up the top shelf above the clothes rack, sending two of my mother's jumpers—a sky blue and an egg shell —silently falling to the polished floor boards below like clouds made of cotton wool.

The inside of the wardrobe stank of mothballs so badly I had to turn my head around and catch my breath, as if someone had sprayed insect repellent in my face. Somewhat taken by surprise, I nearly fell off my chair in the process of messing up my mother's belongings.

I regained my composure and stretched to the full length of my body on the chair. I peered to the back of the top shelf, my chin resting awkwardly against the wooden edge. In my mind's eye, I saw myself fall over and crack my skull open once more—if I died because of my snooping around, at least there wouldn't be any retribution.

There was a pink cardboard box with hand-painted daisies at the far end of the shelf, carefully hidden behind a pile of summer shirts and dresses.

I pushed myself up half way onto the shelf, my feet dangling freely in the air, taking another chance at fracturing my skull. Stubbornly, I placed both hands on each side of the box and pulled it entirely off the shelf and brought it down to the polished floor. I sat cross-legged in front of the box—the muscles of my stomach cramped as if someone was about to hit me in the belly. Finally, I took a deep breath and lifted the lid off the box.

A silver—or white gold—ring with a deep-set garnet; a twenty-two-carat gold crucifix attached to a fine matching chain; several pairs of earrings, all gold, and all encrusted with different sizes of white pearls; a French passport—*Républic Française; Passeport.*

I flicked through the passport—a photo of my mother years ago. Her birth date read *16 dec 1970. Date de déliverance/*Date of issue read *15 mai 1988.* She was only eighteen years old on the picture. She didn't look much different from today, except she was rounder in the cheeks. Her hair was the same bottle blonde. She looked more Scandinavian than French. My father had told me she'd been unusually beautiful. I could see Melissa on the passport photograph, even though she wasn't my mother's daughter—plain, but heavenly like the hills and the forest, and luminous like the white sun in the middle of a dark night.

Then I did a quick mental calculation. I was born in 1976. My mother conceived me when she was sixteen. My father was born in June 1952. He would have been thirty-four when my mother gave me birth—the same age as Michael. They would have made love when she was fifteen and he was thirty-three.

I stood still and re-calculated all those dates in my head. Had I made a mistake somewhere? Something was not right about those dates. How could my mother have been only sixteen years old and my father thirty-four? He would have been old enough when he fathered me to have been her father. How did she get to leave France at such a young age? If she was French, why was her name Rhonda and not a name more French sounding, like Sophie or Monique? And why did my father never mention she was half his age?

Was this the reason why my father had concealed from me every picture of my mother? How could he have explained my mother had been a child when she gave me birth?

I returned all of my mother's mementoes back in the blue box, my mind filled with confusion like decaying autumn leaves on a grey-stoned pavement.

CHAPTER SEVENTEEN

Karin asked me what my brother was like. Was he single and was he looking? We were sitting next to each other in art class wearing white coats—stained in ultramarine, dark green, yellow ochre, cadmium pale red—to protect our clothes from paints, engrossed in colouring whatever we could lay our hands on. We looked liked little rainbows behind our desks.

Outside the rain was drumming rhythmically against the large windowpanes of the classroom, the sky pencil grey like the end of days.

The room smelled like a bowl of oranges from the citrus turpentine and the cheap acrylic paint.

I was re-copying the cover of a science-fiction book someone tossed in the school yard—a vulture-like animal devouring a horse still alive and standing on its four legs. Other girls in the class painted mundane subjects—portraits of people, landscapes, still lives, the person next to them, the teacher. I wanted to be daring, to give Mrs Morgan, our art teacher, a little shock treatment, to defy convention for the sake of it rather than to express myself with brush strokes and pencil lines.

Karin kept herself busy with a still life of nebulous flowers in a blue vase she copied from the depth of her imagination. She was lucky to have imagination. All I could do was observe and reproduce the world around me through the coloured lenses of my past.

I met Karin with two of her friends, Stacey and Trish, two weeks prior. They always hung around together in the school yard and in the classrooms. Even though I'd swore I'd never join a group, I'd somehow fallen into their gang after they caught me smoking at the back of the gym one lunchtime and decided I was

194

cool enough to be seen with.

Karin became my best friend because she was smart, and I found myself captivated by people who used their brains. She was also attractive and bubbly, and made me laugh. Her hair was tied into a pony tail and she wore purple lipstick and a pink and a yellow plastic bracelet Whenever we spoke, she held her face so close to mine, I could smell perfume—a basket of fruits and candy in an aerosol can she bought at the local supermarket. I liked the way her green eyes always seemed to smile, how they were filled with joy and exhilaration for life, like those of a puppy who'd stepped into the outside world for the first time. I wished I could be just like her—still excited about life.

She was also really popular and daring with boys, but didn't go out with any of them. The boys in our class were too young and too immature to bother with, she said, and if she was going to inconvenience herself with the burden of a relationship, it would have to be someone who was older than her—a man, not a boy.

I stopped sitting next to Veronica in class even though I knew she desperately wanted to sit next to me. It wasn't as if I hated her, but I needed diversity, and I wanted to be with people who were fun rather than people who felt sorry for themselves. I had been dwelling on my own misery for too long, and I felt an urgent need to embrace life a little more.

As soon as Veronica and I had entered the classroom, I had rushed and sat next to Karin as if we were attached by the umbilical chord. Veronica seemed confused, her eyes frantically searching the classroom for me as if I were her long-lost sister. When she spotted me with Karin, she went and sat by herself at a large table perpendicular to a window overlooking the school yard I felt ashamed and stupid, but I knew it was the right thing to do. I didn't want to be a hypocrite and sit there and listen to her war stories when the fact was I'd lost complete interest—I had tried to make my message loud and clear in the past, but I might as well have been communicating with a tree. A few months down the track, it would have been much harder to disassociate myself from her, and the pain of rupture might have caused the both of us more distress. Letting go of Veronica right now was easy—my whole life was about letting go of people. I was an expert. If I ever made it to thirty, I'd be awarded an honorary doctorate in fractured relationships.

The small silver radio at the back of the room was blasting hits after hits on KISS FM through a trebly, ten-watt, single speaker, which shook like a battery-operated, laughing doll. Britney were getting excited over a man with no name. Stacey and Trish lip-synced to the song every time the chorus came on and made facial expressions as if they meant every word they pretended to be singing. They could have been pop stars themselves with their braided hair, pastel-colour hair clips and plastic jewellery.

Mrs Morgan—over thirty and underfed—didn't care whether we chatted or listened to music as long as we did our work and cleaned up our mess fifteen minutes before the class ended.

'So what is he like?' Karin asked me casually and proceeded to clean her No. 2 brush in citrus turpentine, wiped it on a clean white rag that left traces of yellow ochre in the process.

'Like a brother,' I said. 'What do you want me to tell you?'

I knew she wasn't going to stop discussing John, even though she must have realised from the bluntness in my tone I was annoyed at discussing him.

I withheld the truth from her even though we were good friends. Karin would never have understood why I flirted with my own brother, even though I'd told her he wasn't my brother in the sense of blood relation. And even if I had told her the truth, and she had somehow understood, I would also have had to explain why John and I had split up—an incident I was trying to deal with in the same way I had to deal with the death of my father.

Karin dipped her brush in ultramarine paint. 'What does he do when he gets home?'

'You know, what everyone else does—watches television.'

I painted the ribs of the horse blood red, slicing into its flesh with the tip of my brush as if it were a knife. The vulture was pulling at the muscle on horse's back, stretching it like mozzarella cheese on pizza. The horse's marble eyes were wide open, naked with pain.

'He's really good looking, you know?' Karin said.

My eyes met hers. 'Why are you telling me this?'

'Because I've seen you two hanging around together.' She paused and added, 'more than once.'

'Of course, we're brother and sister.'

'A friend of mine was at the amusement parlour where you hang

196

around, and she swears you were more than just friends—I'm not gonna say it, but you know what I'm talking about.'

I tried to recall all the times I was with John at the amusement parlour—virtually every day of the week for months. There might have been times when I got too close to him, when people might have rightfully confused us for a couple, especially since we didn't look one bit like siblings.

'He was just showing me around,' I said and felt myself blushing.

'You can tell the way you talk to each other, you know—'

'You can tell what?'

She turned around and faced me. 'The body thing you do. When you talk to him, you touch him all the time, like on the arm, or the shoulder. And I bet you don't even realise you're doing it.'

I had no answer—how could I blatantly refute the truth when she was looking at me? I unlocked my eyes from hers and dipped my brush in red and then added too much blood to the ribs of the horse. I held the canvas at an angle and let the blood drip alongside its limbs.

'It's okay,' she said. 'I won't tell anyone.' She paused for a few seconds. 'You don't mind if I borrow him from you?'

I opened my mouth, but no words came out.

Karin and John began going out together only one week after she asked me if she could borrow him. I had told her it had nothing to do with me, and if she wanted him so badly, all she had to do was ask him. But now the two of them were together—it was like walking with poisoned arrows in my back.

We still sat together in class, but her relationship with John affected our friendship. She spent most of her free time with him, and it distressed me more than I'd admitted to her or even myself. I had become accustomed to having her around, like one gets used to the sun in summertime. The one time I'd managed a healthy friendship with someone my own age, God had betrayed me once more and had shattered my illusion of being a person worthy of love. Karin's interest in John made me ponder on her motivation in wanting to be my friend in the first place. I hadn't figured out if I was jealous of John or Karin or both. I should have adhered to my own stupid philosophy—don't get too attached to anyone because in the end people always leave you.

At night I found it hard to sleep, and in the early hours of the morning, I yearned for John so badly, I was almost willing to go to him and beg him to take me back.

If it was my body he wanted, he could have it.

I turned fourteen in July, right in the middle of an Australian winter.

It hadn't rained for four days, but the sky was covered in dull-grey clouds and the air was frostbite cold. I had falsely believed the sun always shone in Australia, no thanks to the glossy brochures from travel agencies I had collected in France. Why had my mother decided to remain in Victoria when other states, like Queensland and Western Australia, bathed in sunshine throughout the year?

Karin was nice to me for the whole morning. She brought me a red box of fine chocolate made in Switzerland, which would have set her back a bit in pocket money. We scoffed it down during our mathematics class like two starving orphans in the streets of Bangladesh, while the teacher was busy writing on the blackboard. Before the lesson was over, my stomach was aching as if I'd swallowed a handful of broken glass.

Karin also gave me a birthday card with a teddy bear on the front and red and pink hearts all around it.

It read:

My Dearest Clotilde,

I think you're a really cool friend and I like your French accent, I wish I had one just like youse. I know we haven't known each other long but I really like you and your the best friend I've ever had and I wish you a really good and really cool birthday. Happy 14 and I hope we stay friends forever and ever and ever...

love always and forever,
Karin
xoxoxoxoxo

I read the card three times from start to finish and was moved to tears, my heart melting like candle wax—but I held back from fear of looking too foolish.

It was so cold, even in the classroom, the chill penetrating every layer of skin and flesh down to our bones, so we kept our jumpers on. I stopped wearing my school dress a month ago. I didn't like the green school trousers and hated the way it dug into my crotch, but because of the cold and everyone else wearing theirs, I followed the crowd for a change.

My hair had gained a reasonable length, and the scar at the back of my head was now fully hidden. Still, I felt as if I was only putting on an image, the real me was the person hidden behind the scar, the girl with a bruised heart and shattered ego, who forced herself to believe she was worth something in a merciless world.

Or maybe it was me who stopped caring.

Someone in the front row asked why the gas heater wasn't turned on. It was broken, Mr Green, our mathematics teacher, told us and explained how he was really annoyed at working under these conditions, this was third-world standard and unless we complained, it would soon become the norm. He said something about the Communists, and how their fate had been sealed because they chose to never complain about anything. He said later in life we should never let people choose for us, we would be capable of doing anything we wanted, and as long as we believed in our right to claim our existence as our own, we would always be free. The whole class stared at him as if he'd had his front lobe surgically removed

'Let's have lunch together,' Karin said ten minutes before the bell went off.

'What about John?' I asked.

'Bugger him. He can wait until tomorrow.'

Trish, Stacey, Karin and I had lunch at the back of the school, hidden behind bushes and trees, like thieves who purposely resided in places no one would bother to search. No boys pestered us there because the place was virtually invisible from the main school yard The trees acted as shelters against the cold wind. The earth was still damp from recent rain, and the smell of bark and dirt filled our lungs like the warm and comforting aroma of a coffee shop.

I'd just finished a small packet of cheese-flavoured Twisties— my fingers saffron from the colouring of the snack food—when Karin stepped in front of me.

'Close your eyes,' she said. 'I've got a surprise for you.'

'What is it?'

'Not telling. It's for your birthday. Close your eyes.'

She wasn't holding anything in her hands, and there was no budge under her green school jumper. I glanced towards Trish and Stacey, but they didn't have anything either. They just stood there, acting as innocently as if they were part of the greenery, two angels who had never committed a sin throughout their entire existence.

'Where is it?' I asked.

'What?'

'The present.'

Karin hesitated for a few seconds. 'In my bag.'

'You're not going to hurt me?' I hated practical jokes where the only people who were laughing were those who were not on the receiving end.

She smiled broadly. 'As if, come on, it's your birthday present.'

'You already gave me a box of chocolates.'

'It was just for starters. And promise you won't open your eyes until I tell you to.'

Trish and Stacey were next to her giggling like a couple of bell birds. I didn't like the way the whole situation was unfolding— there was kinetic tension in the air, as if a giant elastic band was about to snap—but Karin was right, it was my birthday, and she'd asked me nicely, so I had no choice but to oblige.

'Stand against the tree,' Karin said.

I stepped back, my spine pressed against the trunk of a large eucalyptus tree, its presence reassuring in the fear of the unknown. 'Is it heavy?' I asked.

'Yes, it's heavy. Now close your eyes.'

I did what she told me, my hands flat against the coarse bark of the tree. No matter what was about to happen, I would keep my balance. I held on to it as I would have held on to my father had he still been alive—the same way people held on to the past for fear of the future.

'Don't open your eyes until I tell you to,' Karin added.

'Okay, okay, just hurry up, I'm getting nervous.'

The suspense made me want to run to the bathroom. I was waiting for her to say something else, but she didn't. I listened but I couldn't hear the zipper from her school bag. I knew they were up to something mischievous, and I would end up regretting going along with Karin. But I told myself she was my friend, she was a beautiful person, and she would never do anything to hurt me. If what she had in mind was a badly placed joke, I would force myself to see the funny side of it. I didn't want to lose Karin any more than I already had.

I waited for about fifteen seconds and squeezed the bark of the tree with my fingers as if would make a difference to what was about to come. Anxiety was eating me raw, and I waited restlessly hoping for whatever Karin had in mind to be over and done with.

I heard giggling and someone whispered, 'Come on, are you going to do it or what?'

And then, without warning, I smelled Karin's fruit and candy deodorant close to my face and the pressure of her lips against mine.

I opened my eyes like a door kicked in.

Karin was forcing her tongue inside my mouth as if she was trying to eat me from the inside. It lasted about three seconds, and I pushed her back.

'What are you doing?' I screamed.

'Happy birthday,' she said. 'I've never French kissed a French person before, and I wanted to know what it was like.'

Trish and Stacey were laughing their heads off, holding on to their stomachs as if they suffered from period cramps, tears in their eyes, the colour of their skin radiating like people who'd been sitting around a camp fire for too long.

I was too shocked to laugh with them. I could still taste Karin on my tongue—sour cream and honey.

Hastily, I wiped my mouth with the back of my sleeve and threw her a dismayed look as if she'd just hacked off my nose with a rusted blade.

'What's the matter?' Karin said. 'You didn't like it?'

I was too stunned to answer. It wasn't as if I had never thought about what it would be like to kiss another girl before—I came close to it with Martine when we got drunk and end up spending the night in my bed, but it never happened.

'You want to try again?' she asked.

'No, thank you.'

'What's the matter? Scared I'm going to bite you?'

'Piss off.'

Stacey said, 'I'll have a go.'

Karin moved close to Stacey and kissed her on the mouth like I had seen it done in films between the hero and the heroine, smooth and passionate, savouring the experience like a slice of mud cake toppled with fresh cream.

'See,' Karin said, 'it wasn't bad. And at least it's safe. We know we love each other. It's not like with boys when you always wonder what's at the back of their minds.' She stepped in front of me. 'Let's try again. But this time don't push me back.' She was still smiling and trying to make me see the light side of the whole incident.

I didn't agree or disagree. By now, I was curious and decided to be submissive. She pressed her lips against mine and we kissed the way I had done it with John. It tasted the same as with boys, but it felt strange. She smelled good, like peaches and vanilla. We kissed for a full thirty seconds while Stacey and Trish giggled behind our backs. I closed my eyes and let myself fall deep inside an emotional and sensual vacuum, where a kiss meant more than lips and tongues touching, where souls were grafted together like vines from different regions to produce the lightest, softest and fruitiest wine.

And suddenly, silence.

Karin's arms were resting on my shoulders when I opened my eyes, the taste of her kiss still in my mouth, leaving me with a thirst for more. I could see hints of ginger and grey in the crystalline green of her irises and felt myself being hypnotised by the overwhelming presence of another person's sensuality. We pulled our faces apart, and when I noticed the frown on her face, I thought she was going to announce I was a hopeless kisser, and ask me who had taught me to kiss so awkwardly?

But she was looking over my shoulder and slightly to my right. Before I turned around, I felt a strange presence lurking behind me.

Karin's eyes met mine again and ordered me to look behind my back. Slowly I turned around.

John was standing there, his jaw slack, his shoulders rounded like a wounded animal.

I tried to say something but embarrassment sliced my tongue.

He dropped his school bag to the ground.

'What the fuck are you doing?'

John must have said something to someone, because before the week ended, rumours were spreading around the school faster than a bout of mad cow disease about Karin and me kissing because we were lesbians. No one told me directly to my face, but people were acting peculiar around us—even the students whom I had been friendly with in the past treated us as if we *were* the contagious disease, as if talking to us meant a fate worse than death.

Veronica kept her distance in class, this time avoiding sitting next to me at all costs, and when our eyes met, she blushed as red as a traffic light and turned away. Who knows what people would be saying about her if she tried to be my friend again. *Is it true you and Clotilde make love on the weekend?*

But in the end, I tried hard not to care—it just showed how shallow everyone was with their preconceived ideas of what was normal or abnormal. I liked boys, there was no doubt in my mind, but it didn't mean I would go around gay bashing if I saw two boys kissing. What did it really matter that Karin kissed me?

Boys gossiped amongst themselves in the corridors, and every time Karin and I walked past them, they threw us long, lusty stares like kids mouth-watering in the confectionery alley of a supermarket.

'Can we watch?'

'How do you guys actually do it?'

'Do you use a dildo?'

'Dykes.'

Of course, the whole incident also meant John and Karin were no longer seeing each other, not in a boyfriend and girlfriend type of way. John and I never talked about the incident. I felt sorry for him, but in a way, I was satisfied fate had punished him for having dumped me so mercilessly. Now he knew how difficult it was when he couldn't have the person he wanted. My experiment with Karin had undoubtedly challenged his manhood when he deduced Karin preferred to kiss me rather than him. I delighted at the thought of his anguish as fervently as a hunter gathering his traps filled with prey.

Karin and I were sitting at a table at the school canteen and eating salt and vinegar chips in a buttered roll and drinking strawberry-flavoured milk. Karin reckoned the attention we were getting was hilarious.

'I love it,' she said. 'It's like instant fame.'

'I can think of other ways of getting famous.'

'I mean, don't you think it's fun. Everywhere we go, everybody knows us. Maybe we should try for a band or something. You know, like, check it out, it's the band with the two dykes.'

I gulped half my carton of milk in one go. 'I'm not a lesbian, Karin, okay?'

'Neither am I, but hell, it would be fun.' She paused, frowned and added, 'And what are you getting so worked up over?'

At home, I spent most of my time in the solitary confinement of the bungalow—a quarantined bitch in her cage. I wanted to avoid John as much as possible because I wouldn't have known what to tell him. But when you live with people, you can only avoid them for so long. Eventually you have be prepared for the day when an encounter is going to become inevitable and two wills come crashing head on like a bus and a ten-ton truck.

The day of reckoning occurred one Saturday morning when I returned from the bungalow after having got up early to practice my guitar playing. I was still the early bird in the family home, no matter how I late I went to bed the previous night. By 4.00 a.m. my biological clock rang unrelentingly. I was in need of a hot cup of coffee to warm myself up. Rain hadn't stopped beating against the windowpane of my bedroom throughout the night, like fingers tapping impatiently on a tabletop, and, as a result, I'd anticipated a grey and chilly morning. The inside of the bungalow was as cold as the crisper compartment at the bottom of the fridge.

I crossed the backyard—the grass too long and too wet—and wiped my muddy feet on the floor matt in the laundry, leaving chocolate-brown streaks and two small water puddles in the process. The chill of early morning penetrated every single one of my bones.

I ventured into the kitchen through the laundry door leading to the inside of the house and longed ardently for the warmth and comfort of my bed in spite of having got up early through my own foolish determination.

And there he was, right in front of me, Michaelangelo's David cleverly concealed in the flesh of a human being, spreading butter on toast on the yellow kitchen bench, still dressed in his grey, oversized pyjamas, his hair ruffled from sleep, barefoot on the kitchen tiles, a solemn expression on his face.

John and I locked eyes for a few seconds, dazzled like kangaroos in headlights, unable to say a word. I guess he too must have known we would eventually end up catching up with one another.

Like me, he'd been unprepared for the encounter, and his defences were down. It took us a few seconds of reflection to crank up the gears of our psychological nerves and build up invisible walls of defence before the inevitable war of words.

As soon as I gathered my thoughts—electricity almost buzzing in my ears, the lightning before the storm—I tried to walk past him. He took one step back and blocked my way like an officer in charge at a crime scene.

'You're not going to try to avoid me for the rest of your life, are you?' he said angrily.

But I wasn't scared of him. 'Move.'

'Why should I? It's my home as much as yours. And what the fuck were you doing with Karin? Did you talk her into this?'

I threw darts so sharp with my eyes, he must have felt the imaginary pricks coming through the back of his head. 'Keep your voice down. Someone's going to walk in on us.'

'I talk as loud as I fuckin' want to.'

'Yeah, and you swear as much as you want to as well. I know, you don't have to be told what to do. You're big enough, tall enough, man enough to do it your way. You make me sick.'

He pulled his face right up to mine, shiny spit at the corners of his mouth, sleep in his eyes. 'I bet you did it to piss me off. You just thought by taking Karin away from me, you were going to punish me.'

'You're so wrong.'

'Oh, am I now? Well, excuse me, but whatever it was Karin and you were up to when I got to the back of the school did look like two girls giving each other a smuckaroo.'

'I'm not saying we didn't. But it wasn't something we did against you. God, you think you're so important, our whole lives and everything we do revolves around you.'

It stopped him like a knife in the gut.

I pushed him aside with the palm of my right hand. 'Now, let me go, will you?'

He grabbed me by the arm. 'You still love me, don't you?'

'I don't care about you, John,' I lied. His grip tightened around my arm as if it were my neck, and he'd purposely wanted to choke me. I pulled my arm back, hard. 'Now let me go and mind your own business.'

He moved to the side—ladies first—and I headed straight for my room, the tightness of his grip still lingering in the tender muscle of my right arm.

I slammed the door—a gun shot in the house—and threw myself on the bed like a rag doll.

Unyielding tears washed the tiredness and anger I'd build up inside.

It had been raining endlessly for days, tears falling from the sky like in a world coming to an end. I had been awake most of the night, the way Joan of Arc would have been the day before they burnt her at the stake. I wanted to be burned at the stake too, my grey ashes scattered around the French countryside in Alsace, Bas-Rhin, the province of my birth.

La douce France.

I wanted to be able to express myself freely, not like someone who was chewing on a tube of toothpaste every time she tried to say a word. I thought about the Arabs in France, and how badly they were treated, and how they too had problems speaking the language without mispronouncing every second word. I felt like one of them—unwanted and ashamed. Maybe we were better off in our country of birth, no matter how harsh the conditions of living, where we don't have to try so hard to belong.

By 4.00 a.m., when the ringing of my biological clock kicked in, I didn't bother going to the bungalow because of the rain and the cold, and also because I didn't have the energy to do anything. I just lay in bed and stared at the ceiling, wrapped in the warmth of my sheets and thought about all these new people who had abruptly entered my life a year ago.

Melissa had gone to an eighteenth-birthday party the day before and stayed over at her friend's house. The room felt empty without her, even though at such a ghostly hour she'd be asleep. The sound of another person breathing in the middle of the night reassuringly reminds you you're not alone in this world—and I missed her as a result.

I thought about my mother and how she gave birth to me when she was only sixteen and my father was thirty-four. What had really happened between them? Had their lovemaking been legal? I wanted to ask her, but I didn't know how to approach the subject —I had rummaged through her personal belongings, and there would be no rational explanation if she found out.

Someone opened the door of my bedroom without knocking.

I nearly fell out of bed—a sentinel woken up in the middle of her shift—but managed to gain balance at the last second by grabbing the frame of the bed.

It was John in his pyjamas.

'What do you want?' I said.

'Shhhhh,' he said, his right index barring his lips.

He shut the door, and I propped myself up on the bed.

'What?' I said. 'I didn't ask you to come here.'

He stepped forth, climbed to the top bunk and sat on the edge of the bed without being invited. 'I don't want us to be enemies,' he said.

'Well, whose fault is it?'

'See what I mean? What's the point of arguing about everything? It's like we can't even be friends any more.'

I shifted the blue pillow behind my back. 'All right, but you didn't really give me a chance. What did you expect? We haven't talked for weeks.'

'I'm sorry, I guess I was jealous.'

'Jealous of what? You're the one who dumped me!'

'I was surprised, I never realised you were into this girl thing.'

'For God's sake, John, it's not what you think. You didn't even want to listen to me.'

He gazed at my face for a few seconds and pulled the bottom of his pyjamas above his belly button. 'Okay, then, tell me.'

I explained to him everything that had happened before he saw Karin and me kissing. I explained how I had nothing to do with it, well, not the first time she tried to kiss me anyway. And then, the second time, I was just curious and wanted to know what it felt like, no hidden agenda.

'So, you didn't feel anything for her?' he asked.

'She's my friend, you idiot. We were just experimenting, like you know, it didn't mean anything. It was just for fun. And now you went and told everyone, and they all think we're sleeping together. How do you think it makes me feel? I can't even walk down the school corridors without someone calling me a dyke.'

He cast his eyes down. 'I'm sorry, I didn't mean to. I was just so angry. I told Ron, and he must have told someone else, and you know what it's like at school, everybody talks.'

'Well, thanks a lot, anyway. What am I supposed to do now? How am I going to get people to stop picking on me?'

We stayed quiet for a little while, and then, without warning, he took my hand. 'We can try again, if you want,' he said, his voice was jam on warm toast. 'I can talk to Ron, see if we can reverse the rumour.'

I hadn't even met his so-called friend Ron. I didn't even know he had a friend called Ron.

'I don't know if it's a good idea,' I said, 'us living together with the same parents. I don't know if it's ever going to work—maybe we're rushing into things a little too fast.'

'I still want you, you know.'

'Yeah, well, I don't know if I want you.'

He twisted his lips—the hurt of rejection.

Now he knew.

'Can I kiss you?' he asked.

'Why?'

'To just experiment, you know, like you and Karin. You don't have to love me. It's been a while and I want to remember what it feels like.'

I stared at him for a few seconds and tried to assess if he was tricking me into something I would end up regretting. I wanted to kiss him more than he could have ever thought possible, but giving in so easily would make me look weak. I had to hold him back a little, make him beg for a little longer. I was a woman, I had control, I could play this game for as long as I desired.

His eyes were begging like those of a puppy.

In the blueness of the moon, his lips were strawberries and cream. I wished I could have looked as good as he did in the morning.

'All right then, one kiss only,' I finally said. 'But it doesn't mean anything.'

'Sure, just one kiss, and it doesn't mean a thing.'
When his lips crashed against mine, I knew I was doomed.

CHAPTER EIGHTEEN

My mother and I were putting the washing on the line in spite of the menacing grey clouds hovering above our heads. The wind was bitter cold, and I wondered why my mother hadn't bothered taking the washing to the coin laundry at the end of our street. For a couple of dollars, our entire wash-load would have been warm and dry and ready-to-wear. I put the question to her in French while we carefully unfolded a wet, pink, queen-size sheet and placing it on the umbrella-shaped clothes rack with some difficulty. We only spoke French when there was only the two of us.

'Because using a tumble-drier makes the clothes smell,' she said matter-of-factly, and this was the end of the conversation as far as she was concerned.

I didn't want to tell her I liked the smell of clothes when they come from the coin laundrette, like hot bread from the bakery, and how at least there was no chance of them being showered with bird droppings.

Michael's Jeep was roaring in the garage, a wild beast in need of taming. He'd just changed the alternator, which had given up on him a while back without his knowledge. One flat battery. He replaced it, and the new battery went flat within a week. He knew then it had to be the alternator.

My mother and I stretched the sheet across the line, the muscles in my shoulders hurting.

'Yes, but at least everything will be dry in an hour,' I insisted. 'And hanging the clothes outside doesn't mean they're going be dry by tomorrow morning.'

'All right, just put the pegs on the sheet and stop being a pest.'

I hadn't even realised I was being a pest. My point made perfect sense, and now I was certain she would not take up my advice, only because it wasn't her who suggested it. I knew I shouldn't have been worked up over hanging up the washing, but her tone of voice had upset me.

I should have shut up instead of letting all my anger out like an over-boiling kettle steaming at the spout.

'You know,' I said, 'if you're not happy having me around, you shouldn't have arranged for me to come to Australia.'

'Don't be silly.'

'No, really, what's the point? Since I've been here, you're the only person in this family who treats me as if I'm part of the furniture. *D'accord*, we went shopping for a hat the other month, but we hardly talked. We never do anything together, it's like I'm not even your daughter. I haven't seen you in twelve years, and I don't feel any closer to you than the day I was born.'

I swallowed my saliva. Maybe I'd pressed too far, I wasn't sure. I'd never argued angrily with my father before, and I'd never managed a serious talk with my mother, so I had no idea about what was considered to be a reasonable way to debate a point with my parents. But in spite of my awareness, frustration was pushing me forward, and all the self-reasoning in the world couldn't have held me back. I wanted to draw blood, and I wanted it now. The need for answers clouded my sense of judgement like a bum who had too much to drink.

My mother reached down to the floor and grabbed a handful of plastic pegs. She placed a blue one to the right of the sheet, a red one to the left, and two yellow ones in the centre, approximately fifty centimetres apart. She didn't answer me straight away. I could tell from the expression on her face—squinting eyes and pencil-drawn pursed lips—she was puzzling over an appropriate answer. I waited for her to shout at me, to tell me what an ungrateful child I was after she'd taken me into her home and treated me the same as everyone else. I almost wanted her to insult me so I'd be able to argue some more about how I couldn't feel any love between us, and how I couldn't understand why, after all those years of separation, it felt as if we were not really mother and child.

'What do you want from me, Clotilde? You've got a roof under your head, you're fed every day, you're getting an education—what do you want from me?'

My irritation burst the seams of reasoning. 'I want to know why you left me behind after you gave birth to me at the age of *sixteen*;

211

I want to know why you didn't take me with you; I want to know why you never tried to contact me for the first twelve years of my life; and I want to know why you're treating me like a stranger after making me come all the way from France.'

She looked at me like an angry man who wants to destroy the pretty face of a girl who has rejected him.

'I'm doing the best I can,' she said, 'given the circumstances.'

'And what circumstances are those? Because Papa didn't want to marry you? Is that how you justify leaving me behind? Is that it? What about me? *What about me?*'

'You're too young and you wouldn't understand.'

I let go of the sheet, circled the washing basket and planted myself at her feet.

'I'm not *too* young, and you know it,' I said. 'What about you? You were pregnant with me when you were fifteen and Papa was thirty-three. Are you going to tell me what happened? I'm your daughter, *nom de Dieu!*

She spat her words back at me. 'I don't have to explain myself, *d'accord?* I didn't have to bring you to this country in the first place, so don't make me regret it.'

'I've got the right to answers—I didn't ask to be born.'

'And I didn't ask for you either,' she said firmly.

My world came suddenly undone—my mother just had pulled the pin from the grenade I've held in my hand all those years.

'What did you say?' I asked

'Nothing.'

'You said *I didn't ask for you either?*'

We locked eyes with one another for an intense ten seconds, like two dogs waiting for the other to bite.

'Don't worry about it, Clotilde, just let this one go.'

'No way. What was it? You couldn't wait to give yourself away but knew nothing about the birds and the bees? Did you throw yourself at him? Were you a whore?'

She slapped me so hard, I thought the metal plate at the back of my head was going to come out through my eardrum. I nearly lost balance and caught myself just in time against the clothes rack with my right hand.

'Don't you ever talk to me that way,' she said bitterly. 'I couldn't have loved you more if I tried.'

The side of my face was sandpaper. I rubbed it with the palm of my hand, tears streaming down my face.

'What did I do?' I whispered between sobs. 'What did I do that was so horrible for you to abandon me at birth?'

She kicked the laundry basket, sending all the wet clothes flying on the grass—my school jumper, her blue dress, John's denims, white tennis socks, boys and girls' knickers, all spread like cards against the greenness of the lawn.

She stormed off, her blonde hair trailing behind like a flame.

'You didn't do anything, Clotilde, it was your father. He raped me, all right—you want to know, well, now you know.'

She left me alone in the backyard, hanging on to the clothes line as if it were the mast of a sinking ship. Images of my father—the man who had been the only one I unconditionally loved until the day he died, after he died, throughout my life—flashed like slides from a projector running at high speed.

I closed my eyes and saw his face, the honesty in his eyes, the permanent frown etched on his face like a scar from a battle. Now I knew where the poison flowing through his veins and heart came from. Now I knew why he had an unshakeable and desperate need to not let go of the past. Now I knew why he believed winter was man's punishment from God for his sins, and why he could have never married my mother. It had nothing to do with his faith in God or his love for her. God never took his breath on that hospital bed half a world away—he choked on his own disgrace.

Something inside me shattered like a plate slipping from a pair of hands and smashing against stone.

I watched my mother disappear inside the house and slam the fly screen behind her—the same way people resort to violence when they are unable to deal with frustration. The fly screen bounced back against the wooden door frame and smashed into the wall of the house before stopping halfway open—the thunder before the storm.

Tears kept running down my face, into my neck and down my chest. My head was pulled back, eyes towards the heavens looking for an answer I knew I would never get. The grey clouds spiralled like a hurricane above my head, and I smelled rain in the distance. I tossed my head forward and looked at the mess of clothes on the grass. Big drops fell from the sky like tears from angels crying at how the devil had fooled us all.

213

I was so stunned, I didn't even see Michael approach me. He was in his blue overalls—his hands covered in grease from working on the car, his expression the same as when he came to visit me at the hospital after my four-day coma.

'Are you all right?' he said, his face so close to mine, I smelled his tobacco breath.

I looked up to him. 'Why didn't you tell me? You knew all along, didn't you? Why didn't you say something?'

He looked back at me, his jaw slack and his eyes filled with wetness. I'd never seen Michael cry before, and I never thought he'd be capable of it. But tears were streaming down his face as the rain turned into a downpour.

I came crashing into his arms and beat him on the chest with both my fists, but he held me tight until I no longer had the energy to fight. Silver sheets of rain covered our clothes and bodies until we wore soaked to the marrow.

'Why does everyone always leave me behind?' I asked.

'No one leaves you behind—not on purpose,' he said. 'It's just the way things are. No one can really explain.'

'Does it ever get better?'

'It gets better as we grow older—or maybe you just get used to it, I don't know.' He held me in his steel-strong and protective arms, the familiar smell of garage oil, the only comfort I knew at that moment.

I was tired of swinging desperately from one person to another in search of the love my father took with him to the grave. Alienation was a killer, and I didn't know how to fight back.

'I'm sorry,' Michael said.

Rainwater dripped from his chin and straight into my eyes.

CHAPTER NINETEEN

I refused to go to school or eat anything. I was the child of a rape, the product of someone's cardinal sin—of a man who preached the love of God and talked about harmony between people on Sunday mornings, and then committed the worse of treacheries.

Every time my mother looked into my eyes, she would have seen the eyes of my father—the bastard who had stolen her innocence, the man who had destroyed her childhood, the traitor whom I had looked up to for so many years, believing every word that came pouring from his mouth like a fountain of truth and wisdom.

I hadn't been conceived from love, but from lust—maybe I deserved all the bad things happening to me.

It was night time and I felt dizzy from not eating. I'd been almost starving myself for a week, not from deliberate choice but because the thought of eating made me nauseous—like the thought of someone loving me. I spent all my time in my bedroom and refused to see or talk to anyone. Morbid thoughts crossed my mind—the tempting fate of suicide and the freedom attached to it; pools of crimson blood and shaving blades; women being raped and beaten and yelled at; and fear of all men.

Love is not kind. Love is a traitor.

He should know—he wrote the book.

In the early hours of the morning—when my stomach rambled like a kettledrum, and I felt so sickened, I pictured myself fainting —I sneaked into the kitchen and ate breakfast cereal straight from the box. The sugar kept me level-headed for a little while like a shot of whisky calms the nerves

Alone in the coldness of the kitchen, sitting in the dark, my back pressed against wooden bench, the world seemed like a strange place to be in. The ticking of the clock counted the seconds, and I wondered if I was the only person in the world who desperately wanted to go home but had no home to go to.

At the kitchen table, I rolled myself a cigarette from Michael's stash and smoked it without fear of getting caught.

Another night Michael and my mother were screaming at each other from the kitchen, angry voices like people shouting on television—I was waiting for a gun to go off like in one of those shows where the husband goes crazy and decides to wipe out the whole family. Done. No one's going to nag me any more

I couldn't understand everything they were saying—shouting is always hard to understand from another room—but I heard my name mentioned a few times. Somebody threw something across the room, and it smashed against something else. There was more profanity coming out of their mouths than oxygen entering their lungs.

It felt good they were fighting over me because I felt so insignificant over the last few days, I might as well have evaporated into thin air. I wondered if they ever loved one another, or if their marriage was one of convenience. Maybe love was only a need like hunger, a desire we could never permanently appease. Maybe love was an endless well where foolish people like me constantly drank from but never quenched their thirst.

Or maybe love was a mother who willingly sacrificed herself to give birth to a child she never chose to conceive.

One week later on Monday, I got up at 5.00 a.m., amazingly alert for someone who'd managed very little sleep throughout the night. M senses were raw. Even the light coming through the bedroom window was a hand on my face.

When I stepped into the darkness of the hallway, everyone was still asleep, but I knew by 6.00 a.m. Michael would be up and getting ready to go to work. I didn't want to see him or anyone else. I made my way to the bathroom.

The air was chilled, so I showered at length, washed my hair twice with rosemary and jasmine shampoo, and rinsed it under water so hot, it reddened the skin on my chest like a rash.

When I stepped in front of the bathroom mirror, I noticed how blood-drained my complexion was in spite of the hot shower I'd just taken. For a brief moment, I considered putting on some make-up before leaving the house, but changed my mind when I realised how little time I had in front of me.

When I returned to the bedroom, Melissa was still asleep like a cat curled up in front of a gas heater, so I was careful not to wake her up.

I could have worn any clothes I wanted—my mother wouldn't be here to disapprove this time—but at the last minute I decided to dress in my school uniform. It would end up looking less conspicuous if someone got up before I left the house. I hadn't been to school for nearly a week in spite of my mother's protest, so it felt kind of strange wearing my green school trousers—like slipping into someone else's skin.

I filled my school bag with a pair of jeans, my blue and yellow dresses, a hand-knitted jumper from France, a bomber jacket, and a pair of desert boots. I took the blue beanie because of the cold but I left the straw hat behind. I threw in a deodorant spray, a toothbrush, some toothpaste and the bottle of rosemary and jasmine shampoo. Now they could brand me a thief as well as illegitimate.

From my bedroom drawer, I removed the diary my father bought me three Christmases ago. I flicked through the pages and glanced at the black, handwritten words layered pages after pages with my Mont Blanc fountain pen. My index finger traced the world map on the cover, soft and warm like fresh dough. I had travelled exactly halfway around the globe to come to this country.

I closed the diary and held it to my chest, the leather smelling like a new pair of shoes. After thirty seconds of hesitation, I placed the diary between my jeans and my hand-knitted jumper and zipped the bag up.

I hitch-hiked along the left footpath of the Princes Highway, my schoolbag strapped over one shoulder and cutting into my flesh from the weight of my belongings, forcing my spine into a dangerous curve.

All the houses looked the same—brick veneer or weatherboard, classic design, three or four bedrooms, with a fence in the front and a metal gate and a number to help visitors locate family and friends.

You could tell the rented homes from the mortgaged ones—long grass, flowerless strips, faded window frames; used tyres and engine blocks on display for the world to see; crates of milk filled with a year's worth of newspapers; shoes gathered on the porch like soldiers waiting for an inspection; children's toys left laying in the yard and the driveway for anyone to take.

Mortgaged homes were cherished like new cars, washed and renovated at the first sign of degradation. Gardens were laboured over on the weekends, particular attention given to the edges and the flowerbeds. Front doors and window frames were freshly painted, and their colours matched the aluminium guttering. These were homes designed to give you a sense of belonging and security. They frightened me the most because they reminded me of something I'd never have.

The sky was overcast—white and grey pastiches of clouds with yellow streaks of light breaking from the east—but it didn't look as if it was going to rain. I hadn't bothered taking an umbrella with me since the weather is the last thing on one's mind when running away from home. I wasn't particularly cold—my mind was numb and indifferent to the outside element, unlike when I woke up earlier on and felt acutely alert. My thoughts were too pre-occupied with anxiety and despair to bother about trivialities like the weather

Cars drove past but not a single one stopped. I'd heard about the risk of hitch-hiking, but I didn't care. It would have been bliss if someone abducted me, strangled me and disposed of my body somewhere in outback, hundred of kilometres from any form of civilisation. I would be so badly decomposed by the time a man and his dog would find me, it would take a whole week of painstaking forensic analysis to identify my body.

Everyone I knew would feel terribly guilty.

And I'd be happy at last.

I sat next to a telephone booth, opposite the taxi rank and removed my shoes. My feet hurt, especially at the back, just above where the hard edges of my shoes met my ankles. Blood visible through my white socks. I removed the socks and threw them on the stained, grey concrete, along with my school shoes. Both the back of my ankles were abraded, skin peeling off like wallpaper. I removed my desert boots from my school bag and changed into them. I'd been walking all day, and it hadn't occurred to me to change into more comfortable shoes. I'd been too preoccupied with my own pain to think about anything rational.

Strangers were walked past and glanced like people do at the display of shop windows. Men had lust in their eyes, women pity. Nobody asked me what I was doing or if I was all right. Faces were everywhere, numerous and nameless like blank sheets of paper. Who cares about that girl in a high school uniform and bloody socks sitting next to a telephone booth. I could have thrown myself in front of the first yellow taxi pulling off the rank, and still no one would have cared. I was just another lost soul, an opportunity for the tabloids the next day.

I sat on the cold stone steps of the City Baths and feared the night ahead. I was tired from walking all day, and if I managed to stay awake for another half hour, it would have been a miracle. I was a little hungry, but I could sustain since I'd become accustomed to eating almost nothing for the past week. My body managed with air and sunlight—a plant abandoned in someone's backyard.

From my school bag, I removed a new packet of cigarettes and a red, disposable lighter I stole from John's side-table drawer in his bedroom the night before. I removed the gold foil from the box, pulled a cigarette out and lit it in the cup of my hand. I smoked my cigarette slowly like someone much more experienced. It tasted like freedom.

People walked in and out of the City Baths—wet hair and eyes chlorinated and bloodshot like junkies—most of them ignoring me as if I were part of the stone decor of the building. I fancied them assuming I was waiting for my parents to give me a lift after I'd been practising my breaststrokes for the national junior championship. Wishful thinking—I had no parents, no home to go to. For the first time in my life, I had this sinking sensation I truly was an orphan. It didn't matter if my mother was still alive —she might as well have been dead like my father.

I finished my cigarette and crushed the butt under my desert boots. The orange glow sparkled vividly in the darkness of the night like miniature fireworks fading into the cold stone of the stairs. The desert boots were much more comfortable than my school shoes, and already I felt the pain dissipate like the fear of the unknown.

The air was getting really cold, so I put on my bomber jacket and my blue beanie and ended up looking like an Eskimo who landed in the wrong country.

I pulled my diary from the school bag and wrote down my thought for the day—*The world sux*. My mastery of slang had improved dramatically in one year, mostly from hearing other kids at school talking and trying to communicate with them.

I closed my eyes and drifted out of consciousness until I finally fell asleep like a drunk who knew her resting place was not amongst those who lay at night in the warmth of a bed made with clean sheets smelling like lavender from a plastic bottle.

I dreamed of school and John and his fingers between my legs searching between the elastic of my panties. I dreamed of Rhonda and my father. I was naked in the middle of Flinders Street Station but no one seemed to care. I tried to cover myself to no avail, so I pretended nothing was wrong. People didn't stare or look, as if it were perfectly normal for me to be walking around without any garments. The weird thing was I was conscious I was dreaming, and I had had a similar dream a while back, but in the other dream I was at school.

And then a stranger's hand woke me up so vigorously, I thought the world had come to an end.

Linda was twenty-seven years old and had left home at the age of sixteen because her father was an alcoholic, and he used to beat his wife and his children whenever he pleased, which happened to be on a daily basis. She lived alone on the third floor of a small apartment in Carlton, and said she never wanted to be involved in any serious relationships with men again after she had collected more than her reasonable share of broken hearts.

'They're all the same,' she said. We were sitting next to each other in a green and yellow tram, which rattled and hummed like an asthmatic. 'They'll tell you about love, and how much they need you, and then they go and sleep with someone else. I've had it, you know. Sometimes you wonder why we even bother. Maybe I would have been better off being a lesbian.'

I wanted to tell her love and sex were two different things, but what did I know anyway?

Half an hour later, we were sitting on white chairs at the kitchen table, drinking coffee and smoking cigarettes like two friends who'd finished another hard day at work and needed to unwind. She woke me up on the steps of the City Baths when she saw a guy snatch my school bag. He ran off, and we followed him up to the RMIT building on Queensberry Street, but we lost him by the time he reached Lygon Street and vanished in the night amongst a crowd of restaurant goers.

We looked for the bag for a little while around Argyle Square, hoping the snatcher might have dumped it somewhere when he realised its contents were of no value to him. But to my despair, we didn't find the bag. I lost my toiletries and all my clothes. When Linda woke me up, I was still clutching the diary as if it were my last meal.

The kitchen was small and painted a white so pure, it reminded me of winter in Strasbourg. It was warm and smelled of baked cookies and almonds, but there was no food visible other than a small straw basket on top of the fridge filled with bananas, apples and pears. Yellow curtains adorned the windows. It was like a doll's house, perfect to the last detail with cork plate mats and salt-and-pepper shakers. I could easily imagine myself living there. Having a little place of my own, where I could come and go as I pleased, not having to answer to anyone, leaving a mess around if I felt too lazy to pick up after myself. There would be no television but ashtrays in every room and long, lazy Sunday mornings where I would strum my guitar in bed and write songs to express the pain inside. My life would have depth and meaning—God would have miraculously decided I was a worthwhile person after all.

Linda was beautiful, but not in the way I was used to. Her skin was flawless and white like fine china. Her face radiated innocence and sensuality all at once—big, pearly eyes with dark long lashes, a button-sized nose, churning creamy lips, cropped blonde hair. She could have been a boy who looked too much like a girl.

But below the neck, Linda could have never been a boy because she had a chest twice as big as mine, the type I once longed for when men began to notice me. She wore a white, see-through blouse with little yellow and red flowers stitched all around. I was afraid she might notice how mesmerised I was by her presence. I wanted to tell her I wanted to be just like her when I grew up, but I'd only met her less than two hours ago, and if I shared my conviction, I would have undoubtedly come across as stupid or ignorant or both.

Her voice was deep and sultry for someone who looked so innocuous, and it made her even more unusually attractive. I was a little girl standing face-to-face with a princess. Her manner was casual and effortless, as if she was perfectly comfortable with who she was. And you could tell by the way she smoked her cigarette, she didn't smoke it for the sake of impressing anyone—she held it casually like an extension of her hand, the way some people held a cup of coffee all day long, as if they were at risk of a sudden caffeine withdrawal seizure.

'I read this thing,' she said, 'how you can tell a person by the way they look after their room, you know, like when everything is a total mess, it means your life is a total mess.'

'Really?' I tried to act more surprised and interested than I was. Adults put on this act all the time, as if even the most trivial bit of information was something fascinating. If you listen hard enough to people, they believe you really care about them.

'Having control of your life is important, it's power,' she went on, 'and it's the reason I like everything to be in order around here.'

I nodded but couldn't offer any comments. She had lived through more than I had. All I knew was no matter how clean my room was, my life always turned out to be a mess.

We smoked and stared at one another for a full minute and tried to read our faces like the pages of a book.

'Did you runaway?' Linda finally asked.

'Sort of.'

'Well, either you did or you didn't.'

'I did.'

She took a giant drag. 'And how old are you?'

'Seventeen.'

'Liar.'

'Sixteen.'

She stared at me suspiciously. 'Your parents are going to be looking for you, you know?'

I told her I didn't have any parents, my father was dead and my mother didn't want me because my father raped her, how I came to exist. I told my life story in five minutes, the way people do it on talk-back radio when they know they're going to get cut off if they bore the host and the listeners with mundane details.

She listened without interrupting, and it felt for the first time someone was really listening, and according to my theory, this meant she wanted me to know she cared about me, even if deep down she didn't.

When I finished, she stood up. 'You better go and have a hot shower before you catch something. We'll get you some new clothes tomorrow.'

I stayed under the shower for half an hour and closed my eyes. The hot water caressed my scalp, and I felt the plate inside my skull getting warmer than the rest of my head.

It had been a long day, and I felt as if I were living in a dream and soon I would wake up, and I'll be in my room at my mother's place, and everything would be back to normal. But when I opened my eyes, I was still under the shower, surrounded by peach-colour tiles with little flower motifs. My new world was as real as the steam surrounding me.

I washed with lavender soap and apple extract shampoo.

While I wasted her water, Linda popped her head into the bathroom and told me she had to go to work. I tried to ask her what she did for a living, but she had already left.

Half an hour later, I was fast asleep on the blue sofa she had garnished with a clean white sheet and a large brown quilt that smelled of lemon-scented washing powder.

I slept for twelve hours straight.

The lounge room looked different in the daylight. Now I could clearly see a flat-screen television in one corner of the room, a silver-finished hi-fi system with hundreds of CDs lined up next to it, a bone-colour coffee table with a bong next to a small blue-green glazed plate with what looked like dried-up tobacco, and a glass cabinet with an assortment of plates and bric-a-brac.

It was warm in the apartment, maybe even too warm for my taste. I needed to get up before I threw up all over myself.

I shed the sheet and quilt and lurched forward, supporting myself with my left elbow, and looked towards the entrance of the lounge room where I felt a presence lurking like a black cat searching for scraps in a dark alley.

Linda appeared, bags under her eyes as if she'd been awake all night—she must have been doing the graveyard shift somewhere.

She was dressed in a black cocktail dress and stilettos and wore a white pearl necklace, as if she'd just come back from a party for the rich and famous.

'Morning, honey,' she said. 'Did you sleep well?'

'Like an angel.'

'Good, then we can get your room ready.'

The phone only rang twice before it was picked up.

'Hello?'

It was Michael's voice, tense like a spring.

'Hi, it's me,' I said.

'Where are you?' Panic.

'I'm fine, I'm staying at a friend's place.'

There was a pause, then: 'Why don't you come back home? Everyone's been making themselves sick wondering where you've gone to.'

'I'm not coming back, Michael. I just rang to say I'm okay, so don't worry or call the police. I haven't been kidnapped or anything. I've got someone looking after me, and she's real nice. She said I could stay at her place for a while.'

'The police are already looking for you. Tell me where you are, and I'll come and pick you up right away.'

'No, Michael, it's over. Rhonda doesn't want me in her house. I'm not coming back, I don't want to argue with you, okay?'

There was another pause, and I heard him saying something to someone else on his end.

'Look, Michael,' I said loudly into the receiver, 'I've got to go now.'

'Clotilde, just wait—'

I hung up on him and bawled my eyes out.

CHAPTER TWENTY

While Linda was still asleep, I searched through her apartment, not because I was looking for anything in particular, but because one could read a lot about a person by inspecting her surroundings. Linda herself had already told me you could tell a person's state of mind by the tidiness of their room.

In the lounge room, where I'd spent the night, there was a glass cabinet filled with collector's plates; a hand-painted, blue ceramic vase; a photo of a young man, who could have been a boyfriend or a relative; a series of ashtrays from Western Australia, Queensland and New South Wales; two black candle holders without candles, and two empty silver picture frames with the price tags still attached.

There, almost concealed behind one of the plates, with a print of a view of the Sydney harbour and the Opera House in the background, was a pink, plastic tube the length of my stainless steel ruler from school and the width of my wrist. It took me half a minute to figure out I was looking at an enormous penis. I felt heat on my face for I had never seen one so large in my life. At school we had observed penises in textbooks as part of our science class when we studied human reproduction, but nothing came close to the size of what was erected in front of my eyes. And the fact I had never seen a penis in real life frightened me even more. I knew about sexual intercourse, and I knew a penis was supposed to enter a vagina for pregnancy to occur, but I couldn't conjure how in the world something so big could enter the tiny entry of a woman's sex. Maybe what I had before me was an up-scale model of the real organ for study purpose. Maybe Linda was a sexual educator of some sort, and she needed to use this large model so students at the far end of the classroom would be able to see the construction of the male sexual organ.

I scrutinised the giant plastic penis as if it was a venomous snake or a giant spider. It had a vein running down its side, and if it had been real, it would have looked downright revolting. Why in the world would anyone want to insert such an odd-looking thing inside them?

My mind mesmerised by the size of the enormous penis, I pondered on the weirdness of human nature—men and women everywhere around the world, from presidents and kings to movie and pop stars, from teachers and parents to the nice husband and wife serving me at the local milk bar, all on their hands and knees at various stages throughout their lives, involved in the insertion of enormous penises inside vaginas. The whole concept seemed totally absurd in my young eyes, and I wondered whether God had been popping ecstasy tablets when he came up with the blue print for reproduction.

I slid open the smoked glass partition of the cabinet and grabbed the penis as if it were a toy. It was rigid and rubbery like a bicycle handle. What the hell was it for? I held it firmly in my small hands, turned it around, followed the skin-colour vein with the tip of my index finger. Was this really what an erect penis looked like? I had heard and read about the term 'penis envy', but as I held Linda's penis in my hand, I could not imagine why in the world I would envy owning such an ugly and repulsive thing.

There was a rectangular latch half the size of a matchbox at the base, underneath the length of the penis. I undid it and removed the lid. The silver heads of two AA batteries stared back at me. I closed the latch and turned the plastic penis around. I found a switch the same colour as the penis near the circular base. I flicked the switch and the artificial penis came to life, shaking as if it were in the middle of an epileptic fit. It scared the living hell out of me and slipped from my hands and landed head first on the beige carpet. It continued to vibrate and crawled on the floor like a small animal looking to escape its predator.

I could feel more heat on my face at the thought of Linda walking in the room and asking me why I was toying with her penis.

Down on my hands and knees now—like someone looking for a missing contact lens—I managed to grab the penis and switched it off.

I placed it back in the glass cabinet, my hands shaking and perspiration running down the small of my back. Tens of questions were running through my mind, but the answers I conjured up for myself were too scary to dwell on.

I didn't want to know, and I wasn't going to ask.

I had been at Linda's for a week and made myself quite at home. I missed John and Michael, but there was too much to do to let myself be depressed. There was a second bedroom at the end of the hallway—perpendicular to the bathroom—used for storage. We bought a steel-framed, single bunk from Ikea in Moorabbin and turned the spare room into my bedroom.

Linda took the opportunity to get rid of the boxes of junk she had kept in the spare room. I wanted to go through the boxes before she gave them away, just in case I found something I could use, but Linda insisted we didn't have time, and if she didn't find any use for whatever was in the boxes, how the hell did I expect to find anything of value myself. I didn't want to argue with her. My mind was filled with the excitement of living a life I had only dreamed about a week ago.

The room was a little bare, but it wouldn't remain so for too long. I would attach colourful pictures on the walls, prints of joyful works of art, like paintings of Van Gogh and Turner, sunflowers and sunsets adorning every surface of my room. I decided since I had had the courage to change my life, I might as well go forth and feel positive about the world around me because I had read somewhere if you believe in a dream long enough, eventually it will come true.

Linda said we would go back to Ikea the following week to buy a study desk for my room. I told her I wasn't too keen on going back to school just yet, and she said I might change my mind in the near future.

At my age, I was legally required to attend secondary college under the supervision of my parents or guardians, but since Linda wasn't my legal guardian, she felt no obligation to obey the rules.

Her resolution filled my agenda to the letter. My school days were over, and I was going to get myself a job.

On Saturday night, I told Linda I had a job interview.

'What is it?'

'Not saying.'

We were in the lounge room, her smoking her bong and me my cigarettes. The yellow drapes were closed and the heater was turned on high like in a sauna, the two of us bathing in smoke and perspiration. We were both dressed down to our underwear and white tee-shirts, blue pillows supporting our backs. Linda had put on Madonna's *Ray of Light* CD, electronic loops screaming from two speakers at each end of the room.

'Well, you're going to have to tell me what the job is eventually,' she said, her mouth sagging and her eyes half shut.

'Oh, you'll know, don't you worry.'

She seemed intrigued, but not concerned. She took another deep drag from her bong, the whole apparatus bubbling like water on the boil, and closed her eyes. Whatever she was smoking filled the apartment with an acrid smell, but it seemed to give her greater satisfaction than cigarettes.

'You should try this shit,' she said, her voice mellow like a scoop of chocolate ice-cream melting inside her mouth.

'What is it?'

'Marijuana.'

I nodded and she showed me how to smoke it. I took a drag, but didn't feel anything at first. It took a full minute to hit me. My brain was floating in a tank of champagne, bubbles bursting everywhere around me.

'How is it going?' Linda asked.

'Wow,' I said, 'I think I'm going to throw up.'

'Then it's working.'

The modelling agency I had an interview with was in a brick-veneer suburban home with a trimmed front yard, roses lined up against a white picket fence, a garden gnome with a blue vest and a pointy red hat—a perfect picture just like in one of those happy-family American sitcoms. The only indication the Georgian house was a modelling agency was a small gold plate near the doorbell which read 'Media Models Inc.'

The sky was the same grey as the pavement and the air bone chilling.

I wore a red velvet dress I stole from Linda's wardrobe while she was out working for the night. The dress was slightly oversized, but it was still better than wearing the yellow tracksuit outfit Linda bought me on my second day at her place. She said we would get me more clothes by the end of the week, but she'd been so busy, we hadn't had time to do any shopping. I put a whole lot of her other clothes in a white, plastic bag.

I had used Linda's make-up since mine had been stolen along with all my clothes. Painstakingly, I blow-dried my hair, which had gained a few centimetres since I came out of hospital, and with the help of some extra-strength gel, I spiked the tips to give my strands more texture, the way I had seen it been done in fashion magazines.

I tried hard to convince myself I looked seventeen years old, although my face was too round, and my body could have done with a few more kilos. I worried a little people at the modelling agency might be able to see through my disguise as clearly as through a sheet of glass.

I rang the doorbell once and waited. The woman on the phone told me to come at 10.00 a.m. I checked my watch. It was 9.52 a.m. Linda said I should never be late for a job interview, and if I could get there ten minutes earlier, than it was even better.

The door opened and a sickly-looking woman appeared before me. She was in her early fifties, her lips bright red and too much rouge on her cheeks. Her attire had been out of fashion for half a century—an aqua, Jacqueline-Kennedy jacket and matching skirt—and her bleached hair was piled up to twice the height of her face. She tried hard to conceal her age, and in spite of using a copious amount of make-up, deep-set lines were clearly visible under her eyes, forehead and neck, like the prominent veins, freckles and bumps on her bony hands.

'Clotilde?' she asked, forcing a friendly smile. Her irises had lost their colours, and I couldn't tell whether they had once been blue or green. They were hidden behind a veil of years foregone, their pigmentation washed away by the passing of time like natural light on an oil painting.

'Yes,' I said.

'Well, come in, we've been expecting you. My name is Kathryn.'

Her voice was surprisingly girlish for her age, and when she spoke to me on the phone the Friday before, I had imagined her to be in her twenties.

I followed her into a badly-lit hallway and into what was

229

supposed to be the reception area, but looked more like a photographic museum. Colour and black-and-white framed photographs adorned every wall from floor to ceiling like pieces from a jigsaw puzzle. It smelled of dust and perspiration, like a prison cell with no natural light.

'Have you modelled before?' She pushed a green, padded chair in front of me. 'Please, take a seat,' she added before I had time to reply. I wondered if this was going to be one of those one-way conversations, where someone asked you all the questions and provided you with all the answers before you even got a chance to swallow your saliva.

I sat on the pillow-soft chair and looked at all the photographs around me. The models were absolutely gorgeous—genuine smiles, designer haircuts, beautifully applied make-up, expensive designer clothes. Every face was a flower in bloom. How did I even begin to believe I would be capable of modelling? I wanted to run out of the room and scream how I had made a mistake I was only fourteen, not seventeen, I shouldn't have come here in the first place. I wanted to tell the truth with all my heart, but my knees were welded together, and my mouth filled with cotton wool

Kathryn locked her eyes with mine. 'Are you all right, dear?'

'Yes, yes, I'm fine.'

She smiled again—crooked, yellow teeth—a smile which told me she knew I was lying, but everything was going to be all right, and all I had to do was follow her instructions, play the game, join the dots, and see what picture would emerge.

I took a deep breath. 'No, I haven't modelled.'

'Well, it's really not a problem. We can teach you everything you need to know.' She looked at me suspiciously. 'How old did you say you were?'

'Seventeen.'

'Jeez, you do look young for your age.'

'People always tell me so.'

She sat on a black, leather-bound executive chair behind a giant mahogany desk with a green banker's lamp. 'All right then, let me tell you how this works. Do you know what test shots are?'

I said no with my head, my hands nervously grasping at my knees.

'Basically, we're going to get the photographer to take a roll of

230

film to see how you look in pictures. From this, we'll put together a folio of the best shots and then we'll present them to magazines and television channels.'

I nodded.

'Did you bring a change of clothes with you?'

'Yes.' I lifted the white, plastic bag beside me. It contained two other dresses—a blue one and a silver one—and a two-piece, pink bikini. I had no idea why I'd packed the bikini, knowing I'd be incapable of gathering enough courage to put it on. Maybe this modelling business wouldn't be so easy after all.

'Good,' she said. 'Well, if you just wait here, I'll get George to take some test shots.'

She left the room and let me panic by myself.

I looked more closely at the photographs around me. There was a series of old black and white shots, and I could have sworn the woman in them was Kathryn, except with the passing of time, I couldn't be absolutely certain.

Within thirty seconds, Kathryn walked back in the room.

'Just follow me,' she said. 'George is ready. And bring your bag with you, dear.'

I followed her back into the darkness of the hallway, the floorboards polished and slippery, and to another room at the back of the house.

George the photographer was hiding behind his 35mm camera mounted on a tripod and playing with the zoom lens. The rest of the room was filled with boxes, silver cases and a variety of photographic equipment, including a photo-flood light, a quartz light with barn doors and several tripods.

Like in the reception area, framed photographs of models were scattered around the four walls. A large window down one end of the room let natural light in.

'Here she is,' Kathryn announced.

I remained hidden behind her, too shy to make a forward appearance.

George stepped from behind the camera. He wore his hair long in a ponytail, and his bushy beard reminded me of a stock man His denim blue shirt was open to the third button, revealing chest hair and a gold chain, and his flares were too tight at the hips. You could tell he thought he was a real lady's man, someone who didn't

231

need to try to get the girls' attention. I had seen boys like him at school, smooth like the swing of a professional tennis player, constantly passing one hand over their hair and pretending to be indifferent to the presence of girls.

'How are you, love?' he said with a clipped English accent.

'Good.'

I wasn't. My stomach was churning itself into a knot.

'I'll leave you to it,' Kathryn said and left the room.

Come back, I screamed inside.

George checked me out as if I were a piece of furniture on discount he was considering taking home with him. I felt his eyes, deep blue like the flame of my lighter, penetrating every inch of my flesh.

'You done this kind of thing before?' he asked while loading a film into the camera. Click, snap, click, snap.

'No.'

'Okay, okay, darling, no problem. We're only going to take a few test shots.' He spoke fast as if he were paid by the word.

He pulled a high, wooden chair in front of a white curtain and next to a silver, umbrella-shaped reflector.

'You sit there and look happy.'

I did as he told me.

'Just stare at the lens of the camera and pretend you're looking at someone you know, and you're really glad to see him. Just relax, you know, act natural and everything will be okay. Trust me.'

Click, click, click, click.

The flash burned my eyes.

I tried to do what he told me, but I was so nervous, my smile must have looked as natural as if someone was holding a knife under my chin and ordered me to think happy thoughts.

'You need to relax a little more, darling. Don't think of the camera; pretend I'm not here. Think of yourself looking into a mirror, you know when there's no one around, and you're pretending to be seducing your boyfriend. It's a bit like acting. You ever done acting at school? You know, like in a school-play, kind-of-thing? You should, it will help you with your modelling career.'

Click, click, click, click.

More bright lights.

No matter what he said, I just couldn't make it happen. I felt like he was asking me to undress in front of him. I knew what men did to women. I couldn't trust him, not without someone else around.

He stepped out from behind the camera.

'Darling,' he said, 'you're looking really tense, you need to loosen up. This is not hard, believe me, I take hundreds of shots a week, and the less you think about what you're doing, the easier it gets.'

'I'm trying.'

'Just be yourself.'

He stepped behind me and placed both hands on my shoulders. 'Relax, your muscles are so tense.'

He rubbed my shoulders a little too hard, a baker working his dough. His fingers were large and strong, and, as he continued to massage up and down, and I thought he was going to break my collarbone.

'I'm okay now,' I said. 'I think I can do this now.'

'It's okay, darling, I know what I'm doing.'

I bet you do! The next thing you know, his hand will be right down the back of my dress and he'll tell me it's to help me relax.

'Really, I'm fine,' I said. 'And you're hurting me.'

'Right then, if you want a drink to loosen you up, I've got some stuff right here in the fridge.' He pointed to a small, white bar fridge sitting in the opposite corner of the room. 'I keep films and chemicals in there, but it's also good to keep other stuff. Maybe you'd like a glass of wine or something?'

'No, no, I think I'll be okay now.' If he had given me a glass, the way I felt, I would have drunk the whole bottle.

He stepped back behind the camera and without warning began shooting.

Click, click, click, click.

The flash light forced me to close my eyes—a thousand suns burning my face.

'You need to keep your eyes open, darling,' he said, 'I can't get a good shot if you keep closing your eyes. We're wasting film.'

'I'm trying.'

Click, click, click.

He shot a few more times, but I couldn't keep my eyes open.

They stung as if someone was squeezing lemon juice into them. Hot tears rolled down my cheeks.

'Look,' he said, 'let's see if we can do this without the flash. Go and stand next to the window while I change to a 400 film.'

He undid the latch at the back of the camera, pulled the old film out and placed a new one in. He did it so fast, it almost seemed like a magic trick.

I moved to the front of the window overlooking the greenery in the front yard. I turned towards the camera.

'Just lean against the window's edge,' he said.

He turned the tripod around and aimed the lens towards me.

'Now,' he went on, 'just relax and pretend I'm not here.'

Easier said than done.

Click, click, click, click.

He finished one film and loaded a new one.

'You're doing well,' he said, 'just look around the room now.'

My eyes scanned the walls of modelling photographs while he continued shooting as if he were discharging an M-16 at the enemy.

'This is good, this is good,' he said. 'Did you bring any change of clothes with you?'

'Yes, in the bag.'

'Good, okay, you stay here.' He walked to the bag, unzipped it and went through its contents. He pulled out the pink, two-piece bikini and said, 'Hey, wow, good thinking. Now you go and put it on for me.'

He walked to the window and handed me the bikini. I looked around for a place to change, but the only door was the one leading into the hallway.

'Where?' I asked.

'Eh?'

'Where do I get changed?'

'Ah, well, you can change behind the reflector.' He smiled broadly and did a thing with his eyebrows I didn't like.

'You don't have a bathroom or something?' I asked.

'Sure, but it'll be faster this way. Just go behind the reflector. Don't worry, I work with girls all the time. You're safe with me.'

I did what he told me. Behind the reflector, I pulled down my dress and change into the bikini. I kept on my white panties and bra. I came out with my hands in front of my body.

'What have you done?' he asked, his hands spread as if I'd just smashed the lens of his camera.

'What?'

'You've kept your undergarments on—get them off. How am I supposed to make you look good if you wear clothes under the bikini? Come on, missy, you're wasting my time.'

'I'm sorry.'

I returned behind the reflector and stripped naked. I thought he was going to appear any second and ask me how I was doing. I'd never changed into a bikini so fast in my life.

When I finished dressing, I still felt totally naked. I stepped out from behind the reflector.

'You look great,' he said. 'Now, go and stand by the window and try to look sexy.'

I stood awkwardly against the window's edge and tried my best to relax. And then he raped me with his camera.

Click, click, click, click.

CHAPTER TWENTY-ONE

Linda and I had just finished a dinner of Mediterranean pasta with small calamaris, ripped Romano tomatoes, olive oil, parsley and freshly ground pepper. It smelled like Italy.

It hadn't taken me long to figure out Linda wasn't much of a cook, so within a month of being at my new home I took over the kitchen. When my father was ill, I did most of the cooking at home, and now I was used to coming up with simple dishes, which took a little time to concoct but tasted good just the same.

Much to my contentment, Linda seemed glad I'd taken on the responsibility of cooking, although she never admitted to it as such. But the delighted look on her face when I told her dinner was ready showed her appreciation. She gorged down her meal in less than ten minutes without a whisper, like someone who's been feeding from garbage dumps for a month.

I had no idea what Linda ate for dinner before I came into her life, but the cupboards were bare and the fridge empty as if giant rodents had raided the place. I told her if she wanted me to dish up a new meal every night, she would have to fill the kitchen with basic food essentials—salt, sugar, flour, rice, pasta and vegetables. She ended up giving me the money and told me to do the shopping.

Since I was living rent-free and not contributing financially to anything in the household, I was happy to do the cooking and take care of most of the cleaning while Linda was sleeping during the day.

After dinner, I dried the dishes and put them away. Linda had washed them only because she'd insisted it wasn't fair I did all the chores in the house.

'Yes, but you work, and I don't,' I said.

'It doesn't matter. I'm not letting you stay here because I need a slave.'

She vanished from the kitchen for a couple of minutes—she wanted to show me something, she said. I could hear her move objects in the lounge room, where she spent time watching television or flicking through women's magazines. And then I heard a familiar buzzing noise setting off an alarm in my head.

When Linda returned to the kitchen, I nearly dropped a white dinner plate on the tiled floor. She was holding the plastic penis and swinging it in the air as if it were a baton and she were the conductor of a symphony orchestra.

'Have you been playing with my dildo?' she asked. She smiled broadly as if I'd won a million dollars.

I felt my face reddening.

'No,' I lied.

'You have, I know.'

'No, I didn't.'

She stepped forward and placed her free hand on my left shoulder. 'Now, I know you have because it was turned the other way. The head usually faces towards the television. And I know I haven't been using it, and there's no one else in this house, so?'

'I didn't know what it was, I was just curious. I didn't mean to...' I placed the plate I held in my hands on the bench for fear of dropping it.

'It's okay,' she said. 'It's not going to eat you.' She removed her hand from my shoulder and flicked the switch underneath the dildo and it began to vibrate like an electric toothbrush. 'Isn't it cute?'

I'd found nothing cute about it the first time I saw it, and a re-run didn't persuade me otherwise. I wanted to run to the lounge room and hide under the couch.

'Have you used it?' she asked.

I had no idea what she was talking about. What was I supposed to do with it? Wasn't it just a decoration or a toy of some sort?

'You don't know how to use it?' she added—mockery and tenderness in her eyes all at once.

I shook my head.

She stared at me for a few seconds. 'You do know what a dildo is, don't you?'

I looked at her blankly. If the penis had been a gun, I would have grabbed it from her hand and shot myself.

She pondered on what to do next. Then she tendered me the penis like a coffee spoon. 'Here, hold it, see how it feels.'

I didn't want to hold it, but she didn't ask me—it was an order. I wanted to tell her I knew how it felt—like a hard piece of rubber —the stupid thing jumped out of my hands the last time I held it.

But I said nothing.

I took it in my hand as if it were a thirty-centimetre turd and said, 'What do I do with it?'

'What you would normally do with a penis.'

I stared, waiting for the rest.

'Oh, my God,' she said, 'I didn't know. You're still a virgin, aren't you?'

My lack of penis envy had betrayed me.

She laughed, her head tossed back and all her gleaming, perfect white teeth showing, but I didn't see the funny side of the incident. If she'd been in my shoes, she might have knocked me dead with the penis.

'I was just dusting the photographs,' I said, 'I must have shifted the dildo by accident, I didn't use it, I swear. I didn't know how to use it in the first place.'

'Hey, what you do in your own time is your problem. Just make sure you clean it when you're done—I've never shared my dildo before.'

And then she left the kitchen.

Now would have been the perfect time to leap from the third floor of the building and crash head first into the pavement.

The telephone rang while Linda was asleep. I picked it up from the kitchen while running through the employment classifieds of the newspaper, my index finger blackened from the print. I was desperate to find myself a job and make some real money. I had yet to hear from the modelling agency, and I hadn't built up the nerve to ring them to find out what was happening with my shots.

Linda was eyeing me every day while I went through the newspaper, but she didn't inquire about my progress. I knew she was waiting for me to claim defeat and go back to school. But it wasn't going to happen. I would find a job, and I'd show her and the rest of the world I was capable of being self-sufficient.

'Is Linda there?' an authoritative male voice at the end of the line asked.

I sipped from my hot cup of coffee and said, 'She's asleep.'

'Can I speak to her?'

'She's asleep.'

'Well, can you wake her up?'

'I don't think so.' I twisted the telephone chord in my hand and kept my eyes on the classifieds, not really concerned about who this man was or what he wanted. Since Linda had been working all night, I wasn't going to be the one to barge into her room and tell her to get up. If it was urgent, he could always call the police or the ambulance.

'And who are you?' he said.

'Clotilde.'

'Okay, Clo-whatever-your-name-is, go and wake up your mother up.' His tone of voice had changed. He pronounced each word carefully, like someone leisurely dealing cards from a deck one at the time.

'She's not my mother.'

He snapped, 'Just go and wake her up, you little shit!'

I hung up on him and went on reading the classifieds.

When the phone rang again, I pulled the plug from the wall.

I got a call from Kathryn from Media Models Inc. a week after the shots were taken. My job hunting since modelling at the agency had led me to a dead end. Still, I was persistently pouring over the newspaper employment classifieds like a detective trying to solve a homicide—every day without exception I checked every single ad —the boxed ones, the line ones, even the ones printed between the news items in the business section of the newspaper.

Outside it was pouring, rain beating heavily against the kitchen window like fingers at a keyboard, the sky the colour of dishwater. I had the newspaper spread all over the kitchen table, little silver scissors by my side, and a mountain of ads I'd clipped.

I tossed my half smoked cigarette in the ashtray when Kathryn announced herself on the phone.

'The pictures are great,' she said—her voice akin to two-year old—'I think we can do something for you. Why don't you come in tomorrow? If you have time, of course.'

Oh, I had plenty of time, all the time in the world in fact. I tried to look for work, but I was either too young, too woman, too small, too pretty, too foreign, or didn't have enough experience. I even began watching daytime television—*The Young and the Restless, The Bold and the Beautiful, Days of our Lives*. If it was my time she was after, I certainly had a superfluous amount—I even began drinking again.

'Tomorrow is fine,' I said slowly as if checking my busy schedule in a diary. 'What time?'

'Whenever, I'll be in all day.'

When I hung up, I threw the newspaper and all the jobs I clipped in the kitchen tidy and poured myself a glass of Chardonnay to celebrate.

The moment I walked through the door of the agency, Kathryn was all smiles, like the first time she met me a week prior. I wiped my feet on the doormat, leaving a shoe print of mud and rainwater, and entered the darkened hallway. It was 'dear this' and 'dear that', and it felt as if I'd already landed a multi-million-dollar contract with a cosmetic conglomerate.

She made me sit opposite her mahogany desk on the green chair like the last time and said, 'George took three rolls in all, and we got at least six good quality pictures. We want to use all of them for your folio.'

I nodded but didn't want to show too much excitement—it would look unprofessional.

The expression on her face—eyebrows in an arch and eyes hungry like those of a person starving—told me she was waiting for some kind of verbal response.

I said nothing.

'Well,' she said, 'here are the shots.'

She opened a cream-colour manilla folder and passed five glossy, colour prints of myself in Linda's red dress and pink bikini. I never suspected how skinny I would look in the pictures—bones and ribs sticking out like matches lying on a tabletop. I flicked through the prints one at the time while Kathryn never lifted her eyes off me. The pictures did not compare with those of the models mounted on the walls in the room—I looked like a ferret caught in a trap. I wanted to cry but held back my tears. What had

I really expected?

'So,' she said, 'what do you think?'

I looked at her and then back at the prints. I wanted to tell her the photos were horrible, but instead I said, 'I don't know, you're the expert.'

'Well, I'm telling you, they're really good. I think we can put together a good folio for you. Now, you have great potential, I mean, look at the way you smile at the camera—I think we can work out a special deal.'

What the hell was she talking about? They were going to pay me already? Maybe there was nothing to this type of work after all. Trust your instinct.

'One hundred media cards,' she said, 'with one photo at the front, five in the back, all your measurements, plus the folio properly packaged together for only $295. It's $200 less than our normal price, but I've spoken to George, and he agrees you have great potential. We think you're going to make it. Just get your guardian to sign the release form. Take your time. You've got fourteen days to pay, and you're on your way. I've spoken to a client about you, and he's already interested.'

She pushed her hand forward and shook mine as if we'd just signed a lifetime contract. 'Welcome aboard,' she said with such assertiveness I was left speechless. 'We're going to make you a star.'

Saturday morning, we were having breakfast on the balcony—peach and apple toasted muesli with coconut and banana bread—overlooking the inbound traffic of those who were brave enough to get up early on the weekend. The day was unusually blue and sunny for winter, much to everyone's surprise, especially since it had been raining continuously for nearly two weeks.

Linda chose coffee with cream over orange juice, even though she'd be going to bed soon and wore her working clothes—grey flannel jacket with a white cotton shirt and charcoal pinstripes pants—from the night before. She still hadn't told me what she did for a living, and I gathered it meant she didn't want me to know. Maybe she was a host of some sort-at-a-night-time television show, and she was famous, and I was the only who didn't know.

When I told Linda about the modelling scam, she said I should have mentioned it to her from day one.

'I wanted to make it a surprise,' I said and dipped a fresh croissant in my smoking bowl of white coffee. 'I wanted to show you how I could take care of myself.'

'Yes, well, I could have steered you in the right direction if you'd bothered telling me. Half of these modelling agencies make their money from inciting naive, young people like you.'

She took a multi-vitamin and washed it down with her coffee.

'It's not like we got done,' I said.

'Sure, except these people are expecting me to fork out the bill for the three films and development they've spent on you.'

'I can pay as soon as I get a real job.'

'Don't you dare—they're not going to see a cent out of my or your pocket. If they want to go to court, we'll go to court.'

I liked Linda's attitude. She was streetwise and assertive— exactly the character traits I needed to get myself a real job and fight a world filled with louts and thieves.

The second job I went for was one advertised for masseuses. I rang the number out of curiosity because the ad also mentioned you could earn a lot of money and no experience was necessary.

'We will train you,' the woman said at the end of the line, 'there's lots of work available.'

When I arrived at the place, a two storey terrace in Richmond, girls in cocktail dresses were lined up in a room, each with a number pinned to their chest. They were heavily made up, like models from the covers of fashion magazines. The whole place smelled of Chanel and Estée Lauder perfumes. I knew then something was definitely wrong. Initially, I thought I might have taken the address incorrectly over the phone, and I was standing in the waiting room for a film audition. My English was far from perfect, and when people spelled out street names too fast, I found it hard to follow them. I always seemed to be confusing the vowels 'e', 'i' and 'a', mainly because in French the 'i' is pronounced the same way as the English 'e'. And I could never tell the difference between the English 'a' and 'i'.

A strikingly beautiful woman in her mid-twenties came up to me, an inviting smile, like Kathryn from Media Models Inc. She wore black moss stretch-wool trousers and ciré jacket—she looked more like a banker than someone who worked for a massage parlour. We introduced one another, and she confirmed I was indeed in the right place, and she was the person I spoke with on the phone.

'What's going on here?' I asked.

'Well, this isn't really a massage parlour—it's a handshake parlour.'

I had no idea what she was talking about. She must have realised by the slackness in my jaw.

'It's really easy,' she said. 'All you have to do is give them hand jobs. You can make a lot of money. Some of our best performers make up to a $1000 a week. Of course, I couldn't tell you the details over the phone. You never know who's going to be answering the ad.'

At night I told Linda the story of the handshake parlour. I explained how I didn't know exactly what a hand job was, but I knew it was something sexual, and when she explained it to me, I felt even more sickened than I did in the afternoon.

We were eating goat's cheese and basil scrambled eggs with grilled tomatoes, a recipe I pulled out from an old issue of a *Women's Weekly* I found on the coffee table in the lounge room.

'Well, what did you expect?' Linda said, 'they were going to pay you one thousand dollars a week to massage people's backs? They have professionals doing that kind of job, not young girls walking off the streets. Of course it was going to be a job of a sexual nature.'

'I don't know what to do,' I said. 'I really want to make money.'

'You should just go back to school. You're seventeen, so you've only got one year to go, anyway.'

'I'm not seventeen,' I said.

'I know. Why do you think I took you home with me?'

I stared at her blankly.

'Because if I didn't, somebody else would have, and then God only knows how you would have ended up.'

I scooped up some of my scrambled egg with French bread and wondered how long she had known about my age. I stared at her for half a minute, but she went on eating. Why did she really care about me? Why didn't she just return me to my parents? What concern was it to her if someone took me home and took *advantage* of me?

'Where do you go at night?' I asked.

'If I told you, you wouldn't want to live with me.'

'Of course I would, it wouldn't change a thing. Plus it's not as if I've got anywhere else to go.'

She puzzled over my reply. 'You're right.' She paused, sipped from her glass of water and continued, 'I thought you would have guessed by now.'

'You're not a prostitute, are you? I mean, this man who called the other day and wanted to talk to you while you were sleeping, he wasn't a customer or something?'

'You're very close, but no, Clotilde, I'm not a prostitute—I just run the business.'

'Uh?'

'I own an escort agency with a friend of mine. I just sit at the desk, collect the money and make sure everything runs smoothly.'

I finished my scrambled eggs, not surprised one way or the other. 'And it's the reason you can afford to have me around?'

'Let's just say yes, I make plenty of money, so there's really no need for you to get a job. Plus I enjoy the company without the complications. You needed someone in your life, and so did I. I see the worst of men on a daily basis, so I'm not interested in a relationship.'

'Will you throw me out when you are sick of me?'

'I won't throw you out until you decide to leave,' she said and placed her hand over mine to confirm the sincerity of her words.

I was moved to tears but smiled instead. 'Most people can't stand having me around for too long.'

I finally decided to go back to school because I was sick of turning up for interviews promoting jobs just one step away from prostitution. I'd never thought of selling my body for a living, no matter how much money they were willing to pay me. I did ask Linda if I could go with her to visit the escort agency one night, just to see what it was like. I'd never seen or talked to prostitutes before, and I thought it'd be interesting.

Linda said I was too young, and it would be illegal for her to have me inside the establishment. I insisted to no avail. She also said sometimes they get idiots visiting the brothel, and then she showed me a bruise on her shoulder to prove it. I told her to get a gun for protection, and she said if she did, there wouldn't be many clients left alive.

On a Tuesday night Linda stepped into my room just when I was about to go to sleep and she was about to go to work. She usually came into my room every night to say goodbye. I think she might have been a little worried about leaving me by myself, even though it wasn't the first time, and we both knew I wouldn't leave the house, and nothing could possibly happen to me.

My bedroom looked more lived in now because I had really settled down—clothes thrown at random on the floor, prints of Turner and Van Gogh on the walls, a boom box by the window, make-up and cheap jewellery on the dressing table, overdue library books piled up on the side of my bed, CDs spread like dominoes It took a little effort for Linda to make her way to the bed. She sat on the edge and passed one hand through my hair.

'You be good now,' she said. She looked nice in her white pearl necklace and black, flocked Georgette dress. I wished I could look this good when I put on her clothes, but I was bone and skin. Linda's body was filled with womanhood—assertiveness and self-awareness of its enigmatic power towards men. She could have been a prostitute if she wanted to, and she would have made a lot of money. Men would have been drawn to her like moths to a light bulb, caught in a web of artificial seduction, only to be led off on the sixtieth minute of the hour, or whenever they ran out of money.

I scrutinised her face in the dim, amber light of my bedside table. 'Doesn't it bother you to be collecting money from women who sell their bodies?'

'It's a job, they chose to do it.'

'Yes, but it's prostitution. Don't you think there's something wrong with prostitution?'

She shifted uncomfortably on the bed and said, 'Everybody is prostituting themselves. If you're working all day in an office, it's one form of prostitution. If you work as a checkout chick, it's another form of prostitution. When you're giving your time for the purpose of making money, you're really selling your body.'

'Okay, but what about my school teachers? Are they prostitutes because they teach us?'

'The mind is part of the body. They're being paid to use their

245

minds, therefore they're selling their bodies. Yes, it's one form of prostitution.'

The next morning when I went to school, I couldn't help seeing all my teachers as nothing more than common whores. By the end of the day, however, I wasn't fully convinced of Linda's assessment of the working person. It seemed to me she had devised her own theory to justify she was working in an industry most people regarded immorally salacious.

When I got home in the afternoon and she was up from her day sleep, I could have told her what I'd figured out during the day, but she was spreading butter and honey on freshly made toasts for us to enjoy over coffee and cream, and I decided it wasn't worth the trouble. Who was I to judge what other people did for a living? Maybe one day I would find myself in a position of extreme hardship, and only then would I be able to assess whether life really offered us many choices.

In July, during Melbourne's wettest season, I turned fifteen. I went to an all-girl school, and it was just as well because in the past I found myself too easily distracted by boys. I thought I was going to miss John much more than I actually did. I didn't mingle too much with the other girls, mainly because they all knew each other, and I was the newcomer. It wasn't a new experience for me, and I kind of enjoyed it, seeing how people lived in different parts of the world, and how I could just come and fit in.

I was a quiet student who applied herself diligently to her work. I'd had enough of rebelling, so I decided to make the most of my new life. I excelled in most subjects, in spite of my limitations with the English language.

For my birthday, Linda took me shopping for new clothes. We shopped at Myer and David Jones in the City. She bought me a grey nylon shift dress, a wool sweater with sheer yoke, a knitted dress with belt, two silk shirts—white and a black—a yellow, padded cotton shirt, and matching wool jacket and trousers. I got a free makeover at the Clinic counter, and Linda ended up buying me an entire make-up kit, including foundation, eye shadow, lipstick and blusher. I'd never been so spoiled in my life.

When we took the tram back home—the rain glazing every surface like frost—I wondered how my mother, John and Michael were coping with my absence.

246

'Do you think they miss me?' I asked Linda as the tram travelled north along Sydney Road, its iron wheels singing a balmy melody.

'Of course they miss you, even if you think they don't like you, they'd still miss you. Don't you miss them?'

'A little I guess, but I like it here, and I like living with you.'

She smiled and squeezed my hand.

CHAPTER TWENTY-TWO

This girl, Trish, and I were smoking dope in the girls' toilet of C-block. I stole the stash from Linda when she'd gone to work at night. Everybody thought it was really cool I could afford to have dope. Most girls didn't have the money, and those who worked on the weekends didn't make enough to splash it all on weed. I sold some home-made joints at a small price for those who were desperate enough. Michael's lessons on rolling-your-own-cigarettes came in handy. Because Linda worked at night, I rolled up the cigarettes between 10 p.m. and midnight. I carried them in empty packets of cigarettes.

Linda never noticed her stash diminishing—or she chose to turn a blind eye because she knew I couldn't afford to buy my own. She, herself, was smoking the stuff and obviously believed using marijuana on a regular basis was harmless. Of course, she had no idea I was selling part of her supply to kids at school, otherwise she would have put a stop to it immediately.

I don't know why I began smoking dope. It all started on when Linda made me try it for the first time, and even though I hated it —the smell, the acrid taste, the way it made me feel as if I was sinking inside the couch, my legs going wobbly, losing myself into a timeless wavelength—I got hooked to its addictive nature. And smoking it from a bong really made the whole experience much more intensive and overwhelmingly psychedelic.

Seeing Linda smoking it night after night, and smelling it all over the place, like incense in an Indian temple, and then offering me a drag, well, before I realised, I chose to be a user. I never thought there was anything wrong with what I was doing. Everybody I knew was smoking dope, and no one got thrown in jail for it. And in the past, alcohol screwed me up much more than dope ever did, and yet boozing was considered pretty normal and perfectly legal.

But here we were, on a very bright September morning, my world about to fall apart for the five hundredth time. The sky was unusually crisp like in a Spanish postcard, no clouds in sight and no indication a huge thunder was just around the corner. It was almost like being in a scene from Alice In Wonderland, especially when you're in the middle of filling yourself up with dope.

Trish was resting against the white, wooden facade of the first cubicle, her brown hair falling over her blue eyes in a careless fashion, the way it often did when people inhibited themselves with artificial substances.

We wore our red school dresses because we preferred dresses to trousers, not just because they were comfortable to wear, but dresses made us feel more like women, and at the age of fifteen, we wanted to become women more than anything else in the world—and for once it had nothing to do with wanting to attract boys into our emotional web.

I was smoking my home-made joint in quick, short bursts as if taking my time would cause the cigarette to dissolve in my hand. We were between a maths and geography class, and soon someone would notice our absence.

Inhaling the joint felt as good as if I'd just gulped two glasses of white wine in less than thirty seconds. My brain was simmering in marijuana nectar of the finest quality at no cost to me whatsoever. Trish had to pay me three dollars for the privilege of smoking her own. She nicked the money from her mother's money box, a huge pig made of ceramic and pink glazing. Her mother collected fifty cents coins, and by the time the ceramic pig was one third to one half full, it was impossible to tell what was going in and out.

I was standing face-to-face with Trish, and from the cocker spaniel look on her face, I knew she too was getting high. She smiled, and her eyes rolled as if someone was performing some enjoyable yet indecent sexual act on her.

I had tried to be good, and even made a resolution—if I kept on the straight and narrow for the next few years, I might even make it to university and become whatever I'd want to. But life got boring, and I needed some excitement. Homework could only keep my interest for so long, and in an all-girl school, you're bound to get up to some mischief.

249

Trish saw them first.

She dropped her joint to the concrete floor and crushed it ferociously with her black school shoe as if it was a redback. But too late. Even if we did manage to get rid of the joints in time, the place stank so badly of dope, a blind person would have guessed what had just been going on.

'All right, the party is over,' a male voice said behind my back.

There were two of them, dressed in pale blue uniforms with Victoria Police identification badges stitched-up on the sleeves. Their tags read 'Constable Stewart' and 'Constable Anderson'.

Constable Stewart was the older one, probably in his late forties, and wore his grey hair cropped like an army recruit. Constable Anderson looked in his mid-twenties, and his eyes expressed surprise at what he had just uncovered with his partner.

'You girls have quite a little scheme going around here,' Stewart said, his hands on his hips, the way mothers do it when a room needs to be cleaned up. 'All right, let's go. You're both under arrest.'

We got dragged to a white police panel van parked just outside the cubicle. I couldn't even walk a straight line, so the young constable helped me by holding on to my arm and leading the way. His hands were soft, like someone who'd never worked a day in his life.

The school principal was there, in his yellow tie and grey suit, waiting for us, and so was Mr Aspinwall, the security guard, dressed in his police-imitation uniform. I bet Aspinwall thought himself a big hero for catching two schoolgirls smoking dope. He would undoubtedly recite his legendary tale at family gatherings and camp-fires for years to come.

Trish was in tears, snot running from her nose as if she had a cold, but I kept a stern face. I was still stoned from the joint and had to refrain from bursting into laugher.

When we got in the back of the van—which smelled of alcohol and urine—and they locked the door, Trish lost her composure completely.

'My parents are going to kill me!' Trish screamed. 'What the fuck am I going to do?'

I was thinking about how Linda was going to get really angry with me for taking some of her stash to school. And then I laughed quietly to myself. For some unexplainable reason, getting caught smoking dope in the toilet seemed like the most hilarious incident. Linda had told me the marijuana was top grade, and she'd been right.

We stayed in the van for a few minutes while outside the cops discussed our foreseeable future with the principal. We could see them through the mesh window at the back of the van.

And then the principal's face contorted and he made a hand gesture as if to say, 'take them away.'

The cops got in the front of the van. Constable Stewart turned around and saw Trish in tears.

'There's no point crying now,' he said, 'what's done's done. We'll notify your parents, you'll get a warning if it's your first time, and it'll be the end of it.'

I felt partly relieved. In my mind I had already pictured the next ten years of my life in a prison cell, sharing a room with a full-on junkie who was hooked on heroin or crack, or something far more hazardous than marijuana could ever be.

Trish was still crying, the flow of tears streaming down her face and creating a large wet patch at the front of her school dress. Her little, round cheeks and her nostrils were strawberry red. She was such a crybaby. I couldn't believe I'd got caught smoking a joint with someone who'd crumble under pressure so easily.

Still, I couldn't help feeling compassionate towards her. I rubbed her forearm gently, her skin soft like wool, and said, 'It's going to be all right. Look at it on the bright side—we'll probably get suspended from school for a couple of weeks.'

She turned to me, red eyes filled with venom. 'If you didn't bring fuckin' dope to school, we wouldn't be in this mess!'

They kept us at the police station for two hours. We were taken in separate rooms with a chair and table and a round clock, which seemed to be running backwards. The room smelled like dust and carpet. Constable Stewart advised me I didn't have to answer any questions until my parents arrived, but if I wanted to talk, I could talk.

My back was sore from sitting crookedly in the police van, and the top of my cranium hurt from having hit my head on the roof when I stood up to get out of the vehicle. The dope was starting to wear off, and I could now see more clearly the seriousness of the situation I'd gotten myself into.

Trish's parents came on the double, and she was gone before I even had time to talk to her. I wanted to tell her how sorry I was, and I never meant for her to get into trouble.

Of course, straight away, everyone figured out I was the bad apple filled with worms. Trish had always been a good kid, and if she didn't hang around with the likes of me, the thought of smoking dope would never have occurred to her—heaven forbid.

The white door of my room was open, and I could hear all the commotion going on in the other interrogation room, some kid who got caught breaking into a unit.

Constable Stewart came in, his walk smooth and efficient like a cat on night prowl, sat opposite me at the table and opened a manilla folder with no more than two sheets of paper.

The walls of the room were painted grey without a single poster in sight. There was nothing in the room but a yellow Formica table and four green, padded chairs. A small electric heater was humming, even thought it wasn't really cold. My arms were folded over my chest, and my head hung loosely, eyes cast to the tabletop.

'All right,' Stewart said, 'you haven't told us the whole story.'

I looked at him expectantly, passing one hand through my hair and feeling the metal plate at the back of my skull.

His sleepy, brown eyes met mine as a warning he'd be able to read through me if I told one single lie. His chin almost ran into his neck—the consumption of too many calories and a lack of physical exercise.

'You're the girl who vanished from home a few months back,' he said. 'Your name came up in the missing person's list. How come you haven't gone back to your parents? There's a note here which says you rang them up and told them you weren't coming back.'

I didn't reply. I was trying to peer over his file. There was a colour, school photo portrait of me in my blue Dandenong High School uniform. I don't know how I managed to look so happy on the photo when at the time all I wanted to do was step in front of a bus.

Stewart tapped his blue biro on the tabletop and made me even more conscious of the weight of the silence around us.

He continued to stare at me and finally said, 'Look, you don't have to talk to me, but you will have to talk eventually. You can wait until your parents get here, or we can do this now and save you the embarrassment.'

'Don't send me back,' I said sheepishly.

'Well, it's not my decision. Who are you staying with? I need a name, an address and a telephone number.'

I could have chosen not to tell them, but I knew they'd be able to get the information from my school enrolment. We should have lied when we filled the forms, but Linda didn't want to get in trouble with the police, especially being in the escort business.

By now, I really didn't care any more. Everything good in my life had always been taken away from me. I'd been cursed from the day I took my first gulp of air. I wanted to hang on to Linda and the new life I had gotten used to in the past four months. But the curse was here again, hovering like a dark, menacing cloud, the way it did when my father died, when my mother told me I was a child of rape, and now again when my life had almost been perfect.

I told him everything. The booze, the drugs, the cigarettes, where I lived, where I came from, and what Linda did for a living.

'And does she make you work at the brothel?' Stewart asked.

'Of course not, what do you think?'

'Well, I don't think this is necessarily an of-course-not type of situation, given you get the marijuana from her. Do you understand you can be charged for distribution of a narcotic?'

I threw him a blank stare.

'Do you know what this means?'

I said no with my head, even though I understood, but I could tell by the eager look on his face he wanted to enlighten me with his knowledge.

'It means you could end up in a juvenile detention centre—trust me, it's not a place you'd want to call home.'

For the next half hour, we discussed the minute details of my life, beginning with the death of my father and ending with my undeniable marijuana habit. He listened attentively like a counsellor at school, but unlike a counsellor, he seemed to really be paying attention.

When I had finished my tale, Stewart's expression softened. The stern look of the serious cop who caught me smoking in the school toilet had vanished. He reminded me of Michael, the way his eyes used to study me with such sympathy and understanding, the way my father used to look at me when we spent time together, reading Proust or listening to the radio.

Stewart told me he had a daughter my age, and he knew how difficult things could be when you're a teenager. Adults were teenagers once, didn't I know, and it hadn't been easy for them either. If I'd stop treating adults like the enemy, maybe I wouldn't find life so difficult. It was all a matter of adaptation, of fitting into the system, of making the most of what I was given instead of wishing for a better world.

'Look,' he said, 'I understand what you're going through, and I know the world is not a perfect place, but you can't go around selling dope because you've had a tough childhood. It's not a way out, believe me.'

'I'm sorry.' I genuinely was, but probably more for myself than for what I had done.

'One day, you'll live in the real world,' he said, 'and you won't be able to solve all your problems by running away and smoking joints.'

Oh, well, now I knew what my problem was. I'd be living too long in a world not 'real' enough. Like school wasn't the 'real world', and home wasn't the 'real world' either, and all the years behind me were not part of the 'real world' either. Where had I been for the past fifteen years?

Constable Steward stared at me for what seemed to be an eternity, his eyes drilling into my mind as if they were fingers. I wanted to beg him to let me go, if he did I would never touch another joint for the rest of my life. I wanted to say I wasn't really a bad person, just a little confused at times, and if he wanted I would see a counsellor and sort everything out in my head.

'I think we can work something out,' he finally said. 'Maybe we can make a deal, and it's only because I like you, so don't think I'm saying what you did is all right. I'm giving you a second chance here.'

I was really not in the position to tell him what to do with his deal, so I accepted to his offer.

'This is what we'll do,' he went on, 'I won't press charges on the personal use of marijuana or distribution of a narcotic to your school friends if you go back to your mother and stay there. And it means not running away one week later, otherwise I'll charge you with every count of possession and trafficking under the book.'

Wow, what a deal. Did he actually expect me to jump over the table and give him a hug? Take your pick. Do you want to go to prison, or do you want to go to prison?

'And if you ever get caught smoking or distributing dope again, same deal. I want you to keep your nose clean for the next five years. You've been officially cautioned here, so don't take this lightly. Have we got a deal here?'

'Sure,' I said, knowing his deal was not up for negotiation. What was I going to say?

'Good,' he said, 'let's get this paperwork on the way, and you'll be home in no time.'

I wanted to jump the table, grab his gun, stick it between my lips and blow my brains out.

CHAPTER TWENTY-THREE

No one spoke a word during the whole way home. Michael was driving and Rhonda was staring out the passenger window like someone's pet on a day trip They hadn't changed in four months —other than looking a little older, most likely from lack of sleep over my vanishing. She still smelled of facial cream and he of cigarettes and grease.

I was hoping they would at least say something, even if it was just to tell me off for running away so I'd knew where I stood. Silent treatment was the cruellest form of punishment because I had no idea where I stood. It was like being in one of those horror films, where you don't know why you are locked in a room all by yourself, and all you could do is wait and see what tortures your capturers have got in store for you. It was easier to get bludgeoned on the spot like a baby seal and feel the pain for only a split second rather than eternity like someone slowly dying of cancer.

Outside, the sky was as clear as when the constables pulled us out of the school and threw us into the police car—a very bright September morning when fallen angels drop from the sky and change your life forever.

Michael took the day off work to pick me up with Rhonda. Apparently John wanted to come as well, but Rhonda refused, insisting he should be going to school rather than being distracted by my juvenile behaviour. They told me all everything within five minutes of seeing me, big hugs, we missed you, do you know how much we've been worried, and all that jazz, and then blank—I was the enemy, the traitor, the unworthy child who's made their lives hell for the past four months.

Forty minutes later, we pulled into the driveway. The buffalo grass had been recently cut and the house looked smaller than I had remembered. It reminded me of those Lego constructions I used to make with my father when children still played with toys rather than computer games—but houses made of Lego bricks never had rotting patios and parents who didn't talk to you. It was weird coming back here, like so many things had changed in my life in such a short time, but this little suburban world had remained the same.

'What's going to happen to Linda?' I finally said. I was tired of listening to my own thoughts bouncing from one side of my brain to the other like a baby's rattle.

'She'll be charged with kidnapping and supplying dope to a minor,' Rhonda said tartly, 'and a stream of other related charges —serves the bitch right.'

'She was nice to me.'

'She should have contacted the police when she knew you ran away from home—you're fourteen, for Christ's sake.'

'Fifteen.'

'Fifteen, whatever.'

Yes, I could see how it was going to be back to these 'whatever' situations, where nothing I said or did would matter—maybe even less now than before I ran away and let them haggle over the most absurd banalities.

I was a thorn in my mother's side, the ugly child she never asked to have but now had to endure since my father was dead.

It was mid-November and the school year was nearly over. The heat had replaced cool spring days characterised by bouts of unpredictable showers. We wore our summer school uniforms—a one-piece, cotton dress for girls with little white socks in brown leather sandals. Boys were allowed to remove their ties once the temperature reached thirty degrees Celsius, but many never bothered wearing them at all. I'd been in Australia for nearly two years, but I had yet to get used to the hammering summers. which turns everyone into a facetious moron.

It hadn't been an easy two months. I had gone back to a daily routine of attending school and returning home every afternoon, fearing another one of my mother's lectures on morality and responsibility to society and other people. But with a goal at the end of it all, I realised I could put up with just about anything. John had a sedulous plan, which would set me free once and for all. He hadn't told me what the plan consisted of, and he said the less I knew about it now, the better it was.

I kept to myself at school. Word had gone around, and all the students and teachers knew I had run away. Those who didn't know me personally would have heard something through the grapevine. I had caught the disease, and nobody wanted to be infected. The hell with the lot of them. In the four months I'd been away, I'd learned not to care what people thought. I'd seen another world out there, a world different from the daily suburban life everyone else had to deal with in this pitiable town.

I was forced to see the school counsellor, dear Mr Carrington, who said I had a case of borderline personality disorder.

Mr Carrington still wore his hair in a ponytail and was clinically detached in a way which made it clear he was only doing his job. He said I couldn't accept who I was, my life and the people around me, and this was the reason why I was rebelling. If I continued to walk the path I had laid down for myself, I would undoubtedly become psychotic in the near future. I thought counsellors were supposed to make you feel better—the bastard was trying to destroy the little self-confidence I had left. Why couldn't he just shoot me in the head and get it over and done with?

'Maybe it's because no one gives a shit,' I said.

'Well, yes, there is some truth in what you're saying,' he said. 'Your development history shows evidence of severe rejection in childhood and the absence of conditions for forming secure personal relationships. Of course, your behaviour could also be triggered by some genetic influences—one can never really tell. If you continue to behave delinquently, be aware it might affect your social well being permanently.'

'You're saying I'm crazy.'

'No, I'm not.'

'Yes, you are, you're saying I'm crazy. You're an arsehole, you know?'

He swallowed and wrote something in his notebook.

Six months ago, I might have bothered taking it even further, but now I was completely disinterested in the adult world. They lived to criticise and control one another, and loved to patronise people younger than themselves. I had wanted badly to grow up into a mature woman for so long now, but now I wasn't sure any more I didn't want to be part of this on-going war between the adult world and teenagers, especially if I had to take on the role of an overbearing adult. It was almost as if we were creatures from another planet, and as if our will for independence was a threat to the existing world of grown-ups. What was it which scared them so much? Did we remind them of who they once were, and it was too much to bear?

Michael had resumed giving me guitar lessons in the bungalow. We were sitting on high wooden chairs he'd painted white during the four months I vanished. Maybe deep down he believed I would come back and the reason why he painted the chairs.

The room felt smaller than I remembered. There were cobwebs in the corners of the ceiling, and the air smelled of mushrooms left in a dark corner of a pantry for too long. The orange curtains were faded from too much sun and the dust. The music partitions I had left on the table were still there, untouched for the entire time I had been away. Dust and dead insects had settled on the window frame and reminded me death was just another part of life.

'You should have taken the guitar with you,' Michael said. His eyes were deep and sad, almost deluded. 'It was a gift.'

'I wanted to, but it was too big. Next time, I promise.'

I thought he was going to say something about me having hinted about running away again, but he didn't.

He taught me how to play the arpeggio for Stairway to Heaven, a song I would eventually learn to hate because everyone who ever learned the guitar seemed to think they absolutely had to have this tune in their repertoire.

I hadn't played the guitar for a while, but I'd forgotten nothing. In fact the break from practising only made me a better player. It was invigorating to let my fingers run along the fretboard and pluck the strings as if nothing else in the world mattered. Playing music was a wonderful escape from the dread of every day survival.

'Something you need to know,' Michael said, 'but don't tell your mother.'

My fingers froze on the fretboard. 'What?'

'No charges have been laid against Linda—Rhonda only told you so you wouldn't go back and visit her.'

I had spent sleepless nights picturing Linda in a three-by-five cell for the next ten years all because of my reckless behaviour. I stared at him speechless.

I wanted to hug him to show how much I appreciated him telling me the truth. But I hadn't forgotten the way he grabbed me from behind on that particular morning, his warm kiss at the back of my neck while I was dressed in my yellow dress. I still hadn't figured out if his affection could have meant anything more than just paternal love. In a way, I wished it had meant much more to him. I wished I'd been a threat to Rhonda and her relationship with him, she'd have been deprived of the love I'd craved for, the love she never had the courage to give me—and she'd be so thirsty for acceptance, she would no longer have the strength to fill her lungs with the breath of life.

The morning I left home for the second time, the sky was different shades of amber, like a painting done by numbers, yellows, reds and oranges slicing into one another like a perfectly layered cake. You could already tell it was going to be a scorcher of a day, people melting on the side walk, too burnt out to carry on with their daily routines.

John helped me pack my bags. I didn't take much because I didn't have much. Most of my new clothes had been left behind at Linda's. I had asked upon my first week of returning home if I could get them back, but my mother said she wanted me never to have anything to do with *that* woman again. She was a whore, and I should have known better than to hang around whores. I tried to explain how Linda wasn't a prostitute, just a businessperson, and even if she'd been a prostitute, she was a nice person, and other people out there were far worse than prostitutes.

For weeks my mother and I had on-going arguments about me having run away, and how selfish and irresponsible I was for my age.

One Sunday in October after a lunch of cold chicken and salad, Rhonda wiped the tabletop and I dried the dishes. She told me how at my age she was already working full time and helped her parents to bring up her brothers and sisters. We spoke in French because there was no one else in the kitchen. Michael was in the garage and John in the backyard. Melissa wouldn't be back until the following day.

'This generation has no idea of how to be responsible,' she said. 'All you think about is yourself and what's in it for you. We were never like so selfish—we had a deep sense of responsibility to our family. I would have never ran away at your age.'

I couldn't stand it any more. 'And I suppose leaving me at birth without a mother was a real responsible thing to do?'

Like a swing from a machete, she slapped me so hard on the side of the face, I felt the metal plate shift at the back of my head. She said, 'You have no idea what you're saying, no idea whatsoever.'

And then she rushed out of the kitchen, and I was left holding the side of my left cheek like someone holds a handkerchief to a blood nose.

'You're going to take those jeans with you?' John asked.

He had showered, and his shoulder-length hair was combed back and blow-dried. He wore 501's and a black tee-shirt with a Led Zeppelin imprint. He wasn't even into Led Zeppelin, but he thought the tee-shirt looked cool because it had a picture of a man with wings reaching out to the sky. He said it was 'mythological', but I had no idea what the word meant, and from the look on his face, after I asked him, he too was clueless. Led Zeppelin might as well have been from another planet since the band appealed to generations born nearly three decades ago.

'I've already packed a pair of jeans in the bag,' I said, 'I don't need another pair.' I thought it easier just to buy whatever I needed as I went along than burden myself with too many clothes, especially when I had no idea where I was heading.

I said, 'Where are we going? Are you going to tell me or what?'

'Nope. The deal is I get you out of here, and you trust me.'

'What if your plan doesn't work?'

'It's a sure thing.'

I wanted to believe but it was difficult. Whenever something seemed like a sure thing, I ended up finding out there was no such thing as certainty. Whatever dreams you held on to ended up slipping between your fingers and were gone forever. People were just like those moths searching for the light, thinking it is happiness only to end up burning themselves and having to take a few steps back. I had been back and forth so many times, moving blindly into the darkness seemed to be the only plausible resolution to life's search for a happy existence.

We left home quietly like burglars who had ransacked a house while the occupants were asleep.

We walked to Yarraman station, me with my bag and John carrying my guitar. The air was thick and warm like maple syrup and smelled of vanilla ice cream. I filled my lungs with the new season, the flowers and trees blossoming into the front yard of every house we walked past. There was hope in spring, as if God was giving us a chance to start all over again—even if we were not a little wiser.

The 7.23 came at 7.25. We got in the train, which was already crammed with people at such an early hour of the morning. Everyone looked as if the end of the world was near, and I suppose if I'd been in their shoes, I'd believe the same thing. People smelled like bathrooms and toilets and seemed incredibly disorientated. There was graffiti on the door and some seats were cut, yellow foam pushing out like somebody's intestines after the stitches had come undone.

I sat by the window. A businessman was sitting opposite me, but he might as well be in bed at home. He looked in his late thirties and wore a grey suit with a red tie. His rubber face was pressing against the windowpane, and his eyes were closed. I wanted to give him a jumper from my bag to use as a pillow. Looking at the way the side of his face pushed against the glass, by the time he'd wake up, he would undoubtedly have a migraine for the rest of the day. How could people work so hard and forget to sleep?

The engine roared and the carriages moved, but it felt as if it was the world outside which had just shifted on its axis.

I looked past the businessman and across the window. Hundreds of houses flew by me like splashes of colour on a canvas. I pondered on how in each of these houses, there was a family, and in each family there were people, and each person was looking for her own slice of happiness, the way seagulls hung on to the long, last ray of light at the end the day.

And then I cried in silence, not wanting John to see me.

CHAPTER TWENTY-FOUR

Linda was waiting for us at Richmond Station. We hugged as if we hadn't seen each other for years. In two months she hadn't changed much other than looking a little tired, her eyes heavy and worried. She wore a white cotton dress down to her ankles and her blonde hair was spiked up with gel. I'd almost forgotten how beautiful she looked. For a few seconds, I fantasised she was my mother. Oh, God, how I wished she could have been my mother— life would have been much simpler. Someone who loved me for who I was, who could accept my qualities as well as my faults, who didn't ask me to change the way I did things or the way I thought, who could guide me gently and wisely without having to resort to verbal abuse or harshness.

Leaving my mother behind seemed like the best solution—I could have stayed with her, and I could have finished high school, maybe even go on to university and eventually turned into a robotic moron who works eight hours a day, five days a week for the next forty-or-so years of my life. Since my father died I'd been searching for stability and reassurance, and now I wasn't sure what I wanted after all.

Linda moved her smiling face away from me and said, 'I missed you in spite of all the shit you've made me go through.'

'I'm sorry.'

'Hey, you didn't know. Blame it on your youth, it's what everyone else would have done.'

I couldn't believe she still liked me in spite of my betrayal. I had failed her when she'd been the only person who'd been decent to me. How could I ever repay her generosity?

And then it occurred to me I had no idea why Linda was meeting me at the train station.

We drove to Linda's apartment in Carlton in a new, black Mercedes Benz.

'When did you get the car?' I asked and passed one hand over the smooth, plastic dashboard. I'd never been inside a new car since Louise's Peugeot in France, and I had to admit I was impressed. It smelled like new plastic.

'Sold the business,' Linda said, one hand on the steering wheel, the other on the gear stick. 'The cops gave me a hard time after they picked you up at school. They kept saying I wasn't a person of good character, and they would have my license revoked, and they would close my business down. I didn't want to wait until the hammer fell on my head, so I sold it within weeks of them raiding the place to search for drugs. Of course, they found nothing, so I was free to do what I want with the business. But I knew it would have been only a matter of time before they made my life hell.'

'How are you going to make a living?'

She turned to me and smiled. 'Don't you worry; I've made enough money in the last few years to last us a lifetime. It was all part of the bigger picture. I would have kept the business for another couple of years, just for the sake of it, but then I realised it would have been greed. I don't need more money, I've got another idea.'

Half an hour later, we were sitting at Linda's kitchen table over cold drinks. A lot of questions remained to be answered. What was I doing back at Linda's apartment? What did she want from me? Would I have to go back to the same school and be put to shame? Would they force me to see more counsellors and shrinks?

'I don't understand how I'm going to be able to stay here?' I said.

'It's all arranged,' John said, even though I'd been addressing Linda.

'Your mother has agreed to let you go,' Linda said. 'You can live with me until you're eighteen, and then you go where you please. She pays me a monthly allowance from the money your father left for you to help with expenses. In spite of everything, she still wants you to be happy. And she knows you're not happy living with her.'

'She's not happy living with me.'

'True, I guess.'

'Will I have to go to school?'

'No immediately, but we'll have to start thinking about it soon.'

I didn't want to go to school. Kids were mean and nasty to one another, and I had seen enough mean and nasty things to last me a lifetime. Maybe I'd be able to talk Linda into hiring a private tutor, and then I'd never have to leave the apartment, and I'd never get myself into trouble again.

John stayed with Linda and me for the night. We bought Kentucky for dinner because Linda's fridge was empty. Since I'd left her, she'd gone back to her old habits and hadn't bothered cooking. The chicken tasted good but I felt bloated and sick after I finished like a kid who swallowed a whole bag of lollies. I wasn't used to eating deep fried food in such quantities and washing it down with half a litre of soft drink. If I was going to stay with Linda, there would have to be a serious change of diet in the household. Of course I knew Linda wasn't going to complain because she liked good food like the rest of the world, but she just couldn't be bothered cooking.

After dinner, John didn't want to go back home just yet, and apparently Rhonda had agreed he could stay the night if he wanted to. It kind of took me by surprise because I'd never thought my mother would actually give in to something. But it showed how little I knew about people, and the most predictable characteristic about them was how they were unpredictable.

I'd been so used to Linda going to work at night, when she announced she was retiring to bed, I nearly fell off my chair. It took me a few seconds to recall she'd sold her business. There would be no more night shifts, no more staying at home by myself and being woken up by her in the early hours of the morning.

'You two have a good night,' she said and left the kitchen before John or I had time to reply.

After she disappeared from sight, John threw me a deep, intense look as if Linda had given him the green light to go ahead and do as he pleased.

I stared back at him, but when our gaze became too intense, I looked up and said, 'We better get your bed ready. You must be tired after such a long day of running around.'

I was lying in bed awake, thinking about life and how John was sleeping on the couch in the lounge room when I wanted him to be here with me. I was fifteen after all.

By one a.m., when the world was fast asleep and nothing seemed to matter, when wrong and right were only divided by a fine line drawn by the strong arm of morality, I sneaked into the lounge room dressed with nothing but an oversized yellow tee-shirt. Even though it was dark, I could sense John was awake. His breathing was deep as if he was actually asleep, and I wondered whether he purposely pretended to be. The room smelled musky, like his bedroom at home, masculinity oozing out of his body and entering every porous and textile surface around him. I took his smell into my lungs, making him a part of me without asking for his authorisation.

I stopped next to the couch, which had been turned into his bed for the night in the same way it had been my bed the first night I'd stayed at Linda's place. His presence was electric.

I kneeled down and placed my face close to his.

'Do you want to come to my room?' I whispered.

There were a few seconds of silence. Movement in his eyelids told me I'd been right about him being awake.

'Sure,' he said. 'I can't sleep either.'

Without further prompting, he pulled the quilt from the top of his body and stepped from the couch, brushing my arm in the process.

Quietly we sneaked back into my room. He was following me like a shadow, his warm breath exhaling onto the nape of my neck.

'You go in first,' I said and pulled the sheets from my bed. The moonlight outside made the room bright enough for us to see the outlines of the furniture. He was shirtless, and, bathing in shadows, he looked more muscular and defined than in the daytime.

He slipped into my single bunk.

I jumped in straight after him and pulled the white sheets on top of our bodies. We both turned to the side, facing one another so closely, our warm lips were almost touching.

'Are you going to come and visit me now and then?' I asked.

'Of course, I can come and see you every weekend if you want.'

'What's Rhonda going to say?'

'I don't give a shit what Rhonda's going to say.'

I didn't reply. I liked the way he was assertive, the way he knew

266

what he wanted and didn't care how anyone else was going to react. I wanted to learn the ability to focus on the one thing important to me without being perturbed by what people around me thought all the time. I wanted to find peace of mind and stability within myself so I wouldn't have to waste so must time and energy trying to establish where I fitted in this world.

John kissed me on the mouth and I kissed him back, and then his hands began searching under my tee-shirt. His fingers were smooth and long and made me shiver all over. I wondered if he thought my breasts were too small because I knew guys liked large breasts on a girl, and I wasn't one of those girls.

John slipped one hand between my legs. I was going to protest, but I held back. I thought about whether I truly loved him or not, and concluded it didn't matter one way or the other—maybe it wasn't love I needed after all.

John didn't come back to see me every weekend like he had promised. For two weekends in a row he did, but afterwards, he told me he was too busy with his school work. I knew I lived too far away from him, and he was probably tired of making the trip from Dandenong to Carlton every weekend. Of course he was never going to be admit it, and I didn't expect him to. He'd got what he wanted in the end, he'd made love to me, and he'd probably realised, like I did, it was time to move on.

I expected myself to be crushed by his abandonment, but I wasn't. The day after we made love, something in me changed. I walked around the city by myself, no longer mystified by my surroundings, like the world had suddenly become a less menacing place. The sun was high in the sky, and even the grey buildings looked magnificent—sculptures drawn by the hands of men.

'You're a woman now,' Linda told me that night. We were sitting in the lounge room, her flicking through magazines and me reading a novel in English. I wasn't reading French books any more.

'What do you mean?'

'Oh, I know, I've seen you beaming like a lamppost for the past few weeks.'

I felt myself blushing. 'Well, surely it doesn't mean anything.'

'Sure it does. You just won't admit it took someone else to set your free.'

I didn't want to believe her because if she was right, it meant I would always be at the mercy of someone else for my own happiness.

I took a cigarette and lit it. 'Do you think that's all there is to it?'

'Who really knows?'

I sucked obsessively on my cigarette and did a facial expression adults often did when they didn't have an answer.

At night, I was alone in my room, sitting on my brown quilt, my father's diary open. I wrote in today's entry. I wrote something about Linda, and Martine. I wrote about Michael and my mother. I wrote about all those people at school who had been my friends, and all those whose lives I had somehow touched with my existence and who had touched mine in exchange. Everything had to go. The end was only when we stopped caring for life, or when life stopped caring for ourselves. There was no God. There had never been, and my father had always known. He just never bothered to tell me.

When I finished the last sentence, I placed my fountain pen by the side table and tore every single page from the diary, shredded pieces like snow falling in the winter landscape of my hometown. I said goodbye to the faceless presence of my father, and afterward I straightened my school uniform and rested it over the back of the wooden chair next to my desk for the following day.

www.ingramcontent.com/pod-product-compliance
Lightning Source LLC
Chambersburg PA
CBHW022002010726
47494CB00003B/854